CRIMSON DAWN

THE DEMONIC CONVERGENCE
BOOK 2

SUE ALLERTON

Other works

The Demonic Convergence
Until My Last Breath
Crimson Dawn

Coming Soon:

THE DEMONIC CONVERGENCE - BOOK 3 – THE DARKEST HOUR

THE FORGOTTEN CHRONICLES - BOOK 1 – THE CRUCIBLE

THE SONG OF RUIN – BOOK 1 – CROWN OF BLOOD

THE THIEF JOURNALS – BOOK 1 – CURSES AND BLADES

A TALE OF THE SEAS – BOOK 1 – SIRENS CALL

For everyone who found comfort in the pages of books.

1

Niah

She leapt to her feet gracefully, a curse escaping her clenched teeth as Fin chuckled, prowling around her like a lion analysing his prey. Niah rolled her eyes.

"Show off," Dea called from the sidelines, sitting on the grass cross-legged. Niah lowered to a crouch, feeling the familiar leather grip of the training sword beneath her touch. Fin lunged. With a smirk and a mere flick of her fingers, she hoisted him into the air.

"Now who's showing off," he grinned. Niah set him lightly on his feet, "that's also cheating."

A month had passed since the birth of Thamere. During that time, she had learnt how to use her power as an advantage in battle efficiently. Cassia had put her to work helping with the construction of the town. The job was hard at first, and she had done more damage than building, but the more she did, the better her control became. The spell weavers had been piecing together buildings throughout the island. At the centre of the town was a large round building known as the Chambers. It was used for council meetings and was the home of the Elders. The underground rooms had been built first, seeing as vampires couldn't survive in the sunlight. Surrounding the Chambers were essentials, weapon forges, an infirmary, a food hall, training rooms, an extensive library, and halls for spell weavers and casters to study and store their books and ingredients. The buildings were all made of stone with slate rooves and single-pane windows.

On the second ring were the Council leaders' houses, the barracks for the warriors behind them.

Thamere was far from finished. They had dug out wells for water, farms lay in the more remote parts of the small island in between the main town and the forests where the fey and lycanthropes had made their home.

They were training on the grounds just beyond the town. Many of the hybrids preferred to train outside, though there was still a large training hall. In addition, they had begun training with the other species, lycanthropes and fey, as well as vampires at night.

Of course, they still had to go back to the human world. In the Chambers was a room specifically for portalling. There was a constant portal powered by the orb used to create Thamere. The room was lit by torches, at the far end was a large golden archway with intricate detailing, the orb embedded at the top. The portal shimmered like water, the colour of moss. To the right of the portal stood a large shelf with small glass orbs lining it, they were used to get back to Thamere, as well as anywhere else in the world. As the days passed, they received more and more reports of demonic activity.

Fin and Merida had kept the secret of her locket that had been a tracker. They felt like it would raise suspicions in those who already thought she was involved with the Shadows,

Benjamin for example. The dagger she had had with her since she was young was tested as well, luckily, it didn't have a tracker in it.

In return, they had kept Merida's secret. She was ill, though she wouldn't tell Niah exactly what was wrong. Fin knew, but it was not his secret to tell, and she wouldn't ask him either.

It appeared everyone felt more at ease in Thamere. There was no longer a need to hide. The fey were at peace here, they had been hunted for their wings or teeth in the human world, not by humans of course, by other races, specifically spell weavers of the rogue Lunar Coven. Lycanthropes helped each other, helped the werewolves during their monthly transformation. Even they found it easier because it meant they didn't have to live in fear of hurting humans. There had been a few incidences during the last full moon where some hybrids were curious what it was like to witness a werewolf transform and ended up a bit mangled. They lived, and healed quickly, though their egos took a lot longer to heal. The werewolves showed no remorse, if you go hunting for trouble, you deserved what you got. Even the odd rogue had requested to join the Alliance, they were welcomed, providing they could pass the test.

Morena White, the Great Sorceress of the spell weavers and casters, had enchanted a stone - the truth stone - which could read the holders intentions. If they meant well, the stone would burn white, if they meant harm, they would burn. In reality, the stone would burn their hand a bit. Morena was very dramatic about her spells.

Since the battle with the Shadows, they had not seen anything of them. More than likely because they weren't able to find Thamere. Though they had been taking extra measures when travelling back to the human world, keeping the orb to hand in case they needed to escape quickly. There hadn't been a single attack, even as groups went back to the human world for supplies or demon attacks. Niah couldn't help but think the demon attacks were more to do with the Shadows than the disappearance of the Furies from the human world.

"That was a nice trick," a familiar voice called, Niah looked up to see Nick, Rae, and Adora strolling toward them. Niah straightened, sheathing her training sword. Dea looked dreamily up at Nick, he was Fin's height, though not as muscled, thinner, his face slightly more defined in the cheeks. His pale green eyes stood out against the bronze of his skin. Niah couldn't deny he was good looking. Rae was a short girl with choppy, sandy hair that hung to her shoulders, her nose was sharp, and she had thin lips which seemed mostly turned down in a frown. Adora was thin, luminous dark skin with matching eyes that seemed to bore into your soul. Her hair was dyed honey with hints of caramel running through it, curled around her head like a halo. She had three scars that wrapped around her upper left arm where she had been scratched, unlike Nick and Rae, she was a werewolf and had been turned. Niah was enjoying training with other species, they had different skills, strengths, and weaknesses.

"I don't think you could beat me without using tricks," Adora grinned devilishly, Niah chuckled. Lycanthropes and werewolves it seemed, were very confident in their abilities. Fin gestured with his head, smiling as he went to sit next to Dea. Niah unstrapped her belt from around her waist holding her sword and tossed it aside.

"Shall we see?" Niah purred, Adora let out a laugh, her eyes sparkling. Nick and Rae sat next to Dea and Fin to watch. The gentle breeze shifted her ponytail as she took a crouch. Adora sauntered around her in a circle, swaying her hips as she walked. Niah laughed slightly and straightened her spine as she closed her eyes, listening for Adora's footfalls. The wolf lunged, her foot landed and Niah stepped to the side, twisting her shoulders to avoid the other girl's fist. Adora grunted as she righted herself. Niah moved again and Adora's foot sailed past her head.

"And I called you a show-off," she heard Dea mutter from the side. Niah smiled to herself, and she dodged another punch. She raised her leg and landed a blow to Adora's chest. The wolf flew backwards, landing in a heap on the ground. Niah opened her eyes to see Adora scramble to her feet, her teeth bared in a snarl. Her eyes ablaze with amber. Werewolves had a short fuse and were easy to piss off. Looking at Adora now, she was furious. She sprinted toward Niah on all fours like the wolf she was, she was fast. Niah dodged her quickly by leaping into the air. By the time she had landed, Adora had already turned, catching Niah by the waist and throwing her to the ground. Niah grabbed the girl in a headlock, Adora thrashed to get free, clawing and kicking frantically. Niah let her go, jumping to her feet quickly. Adora crouched in front of her, a low growl rumbling through her chest. She lunged again, catching Niah across the stomach with her nails, tearing the fabric of her shirt. Niah had landed a swift punch to her jaw, sending the other girl spiralling to the ground. Adora was lying on her back, breathing hard. She shook her head.

"I'm so out of practice," she panted, Niah offered a hand out to her, she took it and climbed to her feet.

"Try not to lose your temper," Niah suggested, she heard a laugh from the side and turned to glare at Fin.

"Says you," he scoffed, she rolled her eyes.

"I do not lose my temper than often,"

He got to his feet, a grin across his face, "Oh really? You broke my favourite training staff yesterday."

"Well, you shouldn't be poking me with it while I'm trying to sleep," she retorted, snatching up her belt. She preferred having swords strapped across her back, but was told she should train with them in all ways.

In the weeks it had been since that first night in Thamere, when Fin had told her he would only be with her; there had been nothing but passion. In the way she thought passion should be anyway, the way it was described in books. Even though they hadn't gone *that* far, they shared so many kisses her lips had been swollen. Fleeting kisses, soft kisses, hungry kisses, and lying in the grass under the stars kisses. He assured her he wouldn't pressure her into anything, not that she ever thought he would. Though before anything else, he was still her Commander. She spoke to him with respect during official meetings, lowering her eyes slightly, no matter how much he hated it.

He snaked an arm around her waist, pulling her close, and she looked up at him through her lashes, his eyes danced mischievously, making her cheeks burn, she wasn't used to such physical contact, let alone in public.

"Okay, I'm out," Nick said, smacking the ground as he got to his feet, "I don't need to see this freaky hybrid sex."

"You sure? It's a good show," Fin called after him, Nick waved a hand over his shoulder but carried on walking without a glance back.

"He has a point," Dea quipped as she too got to her feet.

"I should get going anyway, I'm needed at the Chambers." Fin said, gazing down at Niah, "I need to speak to you later though." he murmured with a guarded tone that suddenly matched his expression. She gave him a quizzical look, but he kissed her on the forehead before quickly striding away, leaving her wondering what was wrong. She pushed the thought away, turning to Dea. Rae and Adora had followed Nick back toward the town.

"What was that about?" Dea asked. Niah shrugged, shaking her head slightly.

"I guess I'll find out later."

"You know Benjamin's still preaching that you should be sent to the Shadows as a 'peace offering'," Dea scoffed as they started back toward the barracks. Niah gazed up at the light layer of clouds rolling across the sky.

"Yeah, I know. It appears he's not the only one," she frowned. Benjamin was the former leader of the English facility. Niah had saved him by offering to exchange herself for him as a ploy to hold Karliah hostage. He hadn't forgotten what they had asked for in exchange for him, and held onto that; along with the knowledge that Niah had spent her life with the Shadows. He was convinced that's how they always knew where to find them. Of course, he wasn't wrong.

They gave her a locket when she was young which allowed them to track her. She managed to figure this out before going to Thamere, not that she thought they could find them there anyway. The island was cloaked, the barriers were so strong that not even Morena could bring them down from the outside. Unless you were brought here, you'd never find it. The cloak also acted as a repellent, any ships going by would simply go around it.

Niah and Dea headed into the kitchen of their barracks. Despite the buildings being big on the outside, they were much larger on the inside, easily able to hold over a hundred people. Everything on the inside was wood. It reminded her of a rustic log cabin she had seen in pictures, with beams high up and wooden pillars throughout. There was a large stone fireplace downstairs in a room filled with bookshelves, comfy seats, tables, and a chessboard. Fin wasn't happy about the lack of TV, there was no electricity, though running water and heating had been installed – which seemed mainly for the other species rather than hybrids, since their bodies adjusted to temperature -, Morena had said they were working on electricity, but they could do without for now. Toward the back of the downstairs was a kitchen, stone floors with a huge beech wood table. An island that held a stove, cupboards full of food and multiple iceboxes – of which the ice never melted - holding meat and other perishables.

Dea had been teaching Niah how to cook, or trying to. So far, she had successfully cooked an egg without setting the whole thing on fire. Dea was sitting on the countertop with her legs dangling over the edge as Niah poured herself a glass of water.

"We should get ready, we have patrol soon," she said before taking a swig of water.

"Oh yeah, where are we going this time?" Dea asked, examining her nails closely.

Niah shrugged, "Somewhere called Dubai."

"I do love Dubai, a shame we're only going for a patrol," Dea sighed wistfully, "something's bugging you," Niah looked up to find Dea gazing at her thoughtfully.

"What makes you say that?"

Dea grinned, flicking up a finely groomed brow, "You have your Gren face on."

"Gren face?" Niah turned to lean against the counter with her arms crossed.

"Yeah, you know, all brooding and serious," Dea said, making an exaggerated frown.

"I do not have Gren face."

"There, you just did it again, What is it?" Dea pressed, Niah sighed. She knew once Dea caught wind of something, she wasn't letting it go.

"Don't you think it's strange that we haven't seen or heard anything of the Shadows since we came here?"

"I guess so," Dea shrugged, "take it as a good thing."

"I don't think it is though," Niah frowned, Dea sighed loudly, hopping down from the counter.

"Speak to Merida about it, try not to worry though. Everything has changed," she said before sauntering out of the kitchen, leaving Niah alone.

Dea was right, everything *had* changed. Though Niah wasn't sure if it was entirely a good thing. Everyone seemed happy enough, the new way of life was extremely popular and there hadn't been any attacks, apart from the increase in demonic activity. It couldn't be a coincidence.

A knot had formed in her stomach, it seemed that the happier she felt, the tighter the knot grew. She hadn't said anything to anyone about it, she didn't know how. They should all be happy, so why did she feel like there was a shadow looming over her?

She sighed and went to her room. It was slightly bigger than the one at the Perth facility. Wooden floors with a decorative rug, the wood was all the same tan colour. A set of drawers, a large desk, her weapons cupboard with the trunk at the bottom. A double, four-poster bed against the back wall with nightstands on either side and a small bathroom leading off to the right.

Fin had spent many nights in her room, and she in his. Not every night, he was still a Commander and needed to deal with various matters at any given time. And sometimes she just wanted to be alone, which of course, Fin understood and would let her be, always with a smile and an open invitation to his room if she changed her mind.

The spell weavers had done an amazing job erecting all the buildings and furnishing them. Though it still didn't feel like home. The facility had been too modern, too open, and airy, the compound had been too cold and claustrophobic. But Thamere? She didn't understand what it was, but there was darkness hanging over them, that apparently only she could feel.

She pulled on a pair of thick, tough blue jeans with her knee-length flat boots that laced up the front of her shins. A black t-shirt, and her thick, black leather jacket. They couldn't wear their armour while patrolling the human world, it couldn't be cloaked. They had to make do with magically infused normal-looking clothes. It did the job; they were tougher than normal clothes and could withstand most demon attacks but was still weaker than their armour. She strapped her swords across her back, her dagger with the green jewel in the hilt at her hip.

Fin

The meeting was in full swing. Most people had taken to the new structure relatively well, in hindsight, not much had changed. The Oracle Conclave were still the highest form of authority, the former leaders of the facilities were now Council members, and the once advisers were Commanders.

The council room in the Chambers was round, at the far end was a raised platform where the Elders sat, their symbols hanging on banners above each of them. The sword with angel wings and demon horns, the fey wings, the eye of the nocturnal, the staff with the orb, and the wolf howling at the moon.

A large U-shaped table dominated the room in which the council members sat around with their names printed on brass plaques in front of them. The council members all wore white robes with grey lining, the Overseer wore black, and the Ambassador wore Grey.

The council not only comprised of former facility leaders but also the former leaders of the other guilds. The Cross for spell weavers and casters, the Order of Nocturnal for the vampires, the Guild of Bones for the lycanthropes and werewolves, the Iron Union of the fey, and the Furies for the hybrids. All of which made up the Fury Alliance.

The Oracle Conclave made up of the Elders, Morena White of the spell weavers, Lord Keir of the vampires, Lyra of the lycanthropes, and Shade Rainrock of the fey. As well as Amarah and Ragnar.

Surrounding the initial half circle where the Council members sat, was another table following the same shape where the Commanders sat. Fin still couldn't quite grasp that he was now a Commander, he had been an advisor to Merida for decades, but this felt like a huge weight on his shoulders, a weight he relished.

He glanced at Merida in her pristine white robes, her hands clasped in front of her on the desk. She looked more like herself, her skin full of colour, her eyes and hair vibrant; no longer gaunt and pale. Though the distant look in her eyes still lingered from time to time. Her eyes were narrowed into slits, glaring at Benjamin as he spouted his usual nonsense of Niah being sent to the Shadows.

"Counsellor Benjamin, we have been over this more times than I care to count. Why must you persist?" Merida demanded with a clipped tone.

He slid his icy gaze toward her, "Because, Counsellor Merida, it seems all too suspicious, don't you think? She was born into their ranks, trained by them, she came to us and suddenly the Shadows knew where our facilities were, where our bunker was, something that has remained secret for decades. Not to mention they wanted her back during the battle at the Compound." Low murmurs rippled through the room, Fin watched Merida's jaw tighten, her fingers flexing in front of her.

"The battle where you were taken hostage, you mean? The battle where you were saved, by Niah, I might add, who agreed to go so she may take one of them hostage," Merida snapped; Benjamin flushed bright red as he glowered at her, pressing his lips into a thin line.

"How do we know she was going to do that? How do we know she wasn't going to join them?" he demanded.

"Because there are over seventy warriors who saw her hold a knife to Karliah's throat. And when it came down to it, she chose to come with us; she could have easily gone with them." Fin spoke loudly, his tone icy. Benjamin shot him a silencing glare, but Fin held his gaze, refusing to back down as he tilted his chin upward in a challenge.

"She could have been instructed," Merida was already shaking her head.

"She held the truth stone like everyone else. If she had such intentions, she would have been burned," she growled.

"She tampered with it," he argued desperately, why was he so hellbent on this? A loud bang echoed through the room. Everyone's eyes snapped up, Ragnar sat forward with his fist on the table, his eyes furious.

"That is enough," he thundered, "the girl has proven her intentions. Her past is unfortunate, but her past does not make her who she is. I will not sit here and listen to one hybrid trying to turn on another. We are united, or do you feel differently, Counsellor Benjamin?" he was silent for a long moment, to his credit, he didn't shrink under the iciness of Ragnar's tone, or his glare.

"No, Lord Ambassador." he ground out through gritted teeth.

"Very well. Now, we have our annual celebration coming up. Since we are an Alliance, I believe it only fitting that all species get involved this year," Amarah spoke softly, her voice carrying through the room musically.

The Day of New Life Celebration was the only holiday hybrids celebrated. It started centuries ago when hybrids were liberated. Demons birthed them, and it was demons who realised what they were and wanted to harness their power. Hybrids were used as weapons against angels. They were essentially slaves, kept in cages; only coming out when they were required to fight.

One hybrid managed to escape, Nayli. She gathered as many hybrids as she could throughout the world, with the army she had amassed, she attacked the demons holding the hybrids, and they all escaped; never to be captured again. From then it had always been a day of celebration for them. They had remembered it as the day where everything changed, they held a huge feast with fires and flowers, music and dancing.

"We would be honoured," Lord Keir spoke. The Council room had no windows so that vampires could attend meetings, there was a door beside the main doors that led to the vampire quarters underground.

"The celebration is in a week. We will begin preparations," Ragnar said, "if there are no other matters, I believe we can end there." he gazed out over the crowd; no one objected. Everyone rose to their feet as the Guardians stood to attention. The Oracle Conclave made their way from their platform, and out the door before everyone else started to move.

Fin turned as someone tapped his shoulder, Gren stood behind him, his green eyes wary and his lips set in a thin line. With the death of Helena of the English facility, a new Commander was elected in her place. Since the majority of Benjamin's warriors were killed, Grenville had been put forward by Merida because he led half the battle at the compound. The vote had carried, much to Benjamin's distaste, and Gren was promoted to Commander.

"He has it in for her," Gren muttered as they filed out of the room.

Fin Grimaced, "I think he has it in for all of us."

"We should be careful," Gren said in a low voice, despite now being alone, they were still inside the Chambers, and anyone could be listening.

"I think we need to do more than that," Fin murmured, Gren arched a brow, Fin shook his head, he didn't want to say anything more in a public place. Neither said another word as they stepped out into the warm sunshine of Thamere.

"The others are going on patrol, are you going?" Gren asked as he gazed at the weapons forge on the other side of the square.

"No, I have things to do. Misha and Velig are going with them," He would much rather be going on patrol with Niah and the others, but he had to check in with Merida. If he was going to tell Niah, he had to at least give her a heads up. There would no doubt be fireworks.

Velig was a very colourful spell weaver, often wearing bright pants with a contrasting blazer. His silver hair curled around his ears, with varying streaks of colour running through it; the colour changed daily depending on his mood. Misha had been at the Perth facility with them, a hybrid with fey blood. A pattern of pink and green scales stretched across her shoulders, her pointed ears just about covered by her choppy hairstyle.

The group strode up the steps to the Chambers. Niah gave him a dazzling smile, one he couldn't stop himself returning, the thought of what he had to tell her had his chest tightening. He draped an arm around her shoulders when she stopped beside him, wearing blue jeans, her leather boots that laced up the front of her shins, and a leather jacket. Her hair bound in a single braid dangling down her spine.

"Should we be expecting trouble?" Sai grinned, bouncing on the balls of his feet, throwing playful punches at Gren, but never hitting him; just to be annoying.

"You should always expect trouble," Gren rolled his eyes, taking a step away from Sai who looked like a child being scolded.

"You're no fun now you're a Commander," he sulked, Gren gave him a withering look, a small smile on his lips.

"We better go," Misha quipped. The others started walking away, he kissed Niah on the temple, she smiled at him before carrying on up the steps. He caught her hand and she turned to him with a raised brow.

"Be careful," he murmured, her brow furrowed slightly for a second before she grinned.

"I always am." she leaned down to brush her lips against his. Even after weeks of kissing, the touch still sent sparks through him. He savoured the kiss, not knowing how much longer he would get to enjoy them after he told her. Still, he smiled when she pulled away and watched her bound up the steps to catch up with the others, something tugged at his heart as she disappeared out of sight.

2
Niah

The Chambers were light and airy inside. The floors made of marble, wooden decorative pillars lined the way, archways on the outside of the corridor led out to the rest of the town. The further inside the building you ventured, the more decorative it became. The walls were lined with vines and flowers, which also dangled from the ceiling in glorious ropes threaded with silver ribbons. Tapestries and paintings hung on the walls, and busts stood proudly. She had never seen anything like it, not even on the occasions they had gone patrolling in the human world.

They made their way through the maze of corridors, Sai and Velig muttering to each other as Niah walked with Misha and Dea. She remembered Misha from the facility, she had nearly landed on top of Niah after falling from a beam. The half-blooded fey wore the same as the others, jeans with sturdy boots, and a hoodie under a leather jacket, her daggers at her hips, and a bow and arrows strapped across her back.

The weapons which weren't made of *Ruclite*, like Misha's bow, were able to be cloaked, so they didn't have to bother covering them up. Dea wore her long leather trench coat with boots that had a small chunky heel.

Velig was an…interesting character. He was like Dea, in the way he was happy and boisterous, only a thousand times worse. He always wore bright colours, today he wore moss green trousers, violet formal shoes, and a long scarlet jacket over a black ruffled shirt. Niah had commented how he looked eccentric, he quickly told her he liked to consider himself as flamboyant, at the same time as a streak of powder pink appeared in his hair as he swept it back from his face.

They arrived at the portal room. Velig picked up an orb, despite being a spell weaver, he couldn't portal back to Thamere, no one could, the barriers were too strong for them to do so and the only way in or out was through the portal room. Hence the need for the orbs. The portal was monitored, Guardians stood on either side of it, throughout the room, and outside the door. To the side of the shelves holding the orbs, was a large pedestal holding open a book; a needle next to it.

Niah pricked her finger, and pressed it to the page, leaving behind a black print. She watched it for a moment and waited as the blood faded, melting into the page. The others did the same, the Guardian standing next to the book gave them a single nod; permission to enter. She stepped through the shimmering, almost water-like surface of the portal. She didn't think there would ever be a time when she wasn't captivated by the beauty of so many colours whooshing past her. Another step and a wall of humid heat smacked her in the face, though the discomfort quickly faded as her body regulated itself to the heat.

They found themselves at the back of a narrow side street. Gathering themselves, they walked until they were just outside the mall, next to the fountain at the base of the Burge Khalifa.

Velig leaned on the metal railing, and quickly jumped back with a yelp, waving his hands, "Son of a_ that's *hot*."

The sun was bright, too bright. Velig noticed her squinting and held out a pair of aviator sunglasses he'd pulled from his jacket pocket. She popped them on, grateful for the shield from the scorching sun. She gazed at the people walking around. They mostly wore expensive-looking clothes, the women wore heels mainly, the men either wearing suits, or shirts and jeans. Some wearing shorts, they looked a tad more touristy though. And some wearing burkas or other traditional clothing. In the background, car engines rumbled, birds squawked above, and people chatted quietly.

"Where do we even start?" Niah murmured, not to anyone in particular.

Dea's eyes were fixed on the mall behind them, "Can we go look in the mall?"

"You think demons are into Prada?" Sai mused, Misha giggled slightly. Niah raised her brows at the fey girl, it wasn't often Misha laughed, let alone *giggled*.

"I'm not opposed to looking in the mall," Velig beamed, Dea looked hopeful and clapped her hands together, bouncing on the balls of her feet.

"We're here on patrol, we should stick to secluded areas," Misha said firmly, that girlish giggle a distant memory. She was a lot more focused than many hybrids Niah had met, she liked it; it meant she got to focus on the task at hand without actually having to say anything and potentially upset Dea.

They walked for hours, checking alleys and underground areas. Up until a few weeks ago, it was rare demons came out during the day, it still happened; it was just more common for them to come out at night. Lately, they were having more and more reports of activity during the day. And no one could figure out why.

After hours of walking, night fell over the city. If there was a demon lurking somewhere, they'd likely come out now the sun had gone down. They were checking alleys and empty side streets when something moved in the distance, Niah glanced over her shoulder and gave a quick nod. The others scattered to the sides, hiding in the shadows of doorways.

If demons thought there was just one, they would be more likely to attack, depending on the species and number of them. She drew her swords from across her back, creeping along the ground, searching the darkness for any signs of movement. The pale moonlight glinted off a puddle, it wasn't the usual rotten scent of demons that stuffed itself up her nose, but iron lingering in the air. Blood, human blood. A shiver crawled up her spine, her heart racing as she peered around the edge of a dumpster where the puddle trickled from.

A human woman with jet black hair cut shoulder length. She wore a grey pant suit, her eyes open wide and staring. Her mouth formed an O, her expression was frozen. Her blazer was covered in thick blood, almost black in the darkness, Niah moved the fabric aside to see her chest was hanging open, her ribs splayed out, and her heart missing. Niah's stomach churned as she reached and closed the woman's eyes gently, she had never seen a dead human before. There was something eery and strange about it, something wrong. Whether it was how she had been killed, or the fact that there wasn't a single trace of demons anywhere on the woman or in the area, she didn't know.

"Guys," she said quietly, they were beside her before she took her next breath, staring down at the woman on the ground. Sai knelt next to her, looking deeper into the gaping wound.

"This isn't demonic, at least not a demon killing I've ever seen before," he murmured, Velig tapped him on the shoulder, his fingers pulsing with a crimson light. Sai stepped out of the way and Velig waved his hand over the body, his eyes closed as he chanted something in a language Niah didn't understand. He had long fingers decorated with multiple large rings, the precious jewels in them flickered and danced as sparks shot from his hands.

"There *is* a demonic essence here, but that doesn't mean it was a demon," he said, his fingers dimming into the darkness. Dea stepped forward with her camera ready and started snapping pictures of the body. They weren't able to take human bodies through portals, their flesh would disintegrate, but they needed to know who and what could have done such a thing. Perhaps it was another human, but that didn't explain why there was a demonic essence on the body.

A heavy foot fell behind them, they turned to see a figure dressed all in black. They wore a long coat with a hood shadowing their face. Before any of them could move, the figure turned and darted. Niah glanced at Sai, who nodded.

"You guys stay here, we'll come back," he shouted over his shoulder as they hurtled through the alley after the figure. Whoever it was, they were fast. The figure leapt up on top of a small restaurant. Sai followed while Niah took a different route onto the rooftops, leaping from building to building easily. The figure came to a tall glass building and started scaling it, Niah and Sai followed, finding minuscule gaps between the panes of glass and the steel structure. The building was under construction, and a wall of glass hadn't been put in place on the upper floors, making it easy for them to get inside the building on an empty floor.

The figure stood in the middle of the room, a spear in hand. Niah lowered herself into a crouch. The whistle of a blade slicing through the air had her whirling, swords raised as the incoming blow clanged against them. Another dark figure in a hood. Sai lunged for the person in front, while Niah went low, sweeping the legs from under the second. They landed with a grunt, male.

He scrambled to his feet, holding a long sword, and slashed for her, but she was faster and dodged it. She went low, tried to sweep his feet again, this time he jumped over her leg. Her hand found a pile of sawdust on the ground, and she flung it upwards into his face. He spluttered, clutching at his face as she took a blade across the front of his thigh, he went down on one knee as she got to her feet, standing behind him with her blade kissing his throat.

"That's enough!" she shouted, the figure and Sai froze and turned to her. The figure dropped their spear and kicked it across the floor without hesitation. The figure Niah was holding dropped his sword. She yanked his hood down as Sai took hold of the other figure and shoved them to their knees in front of their companion before pulling their hood off. A woman.

They looked alike. Both with dark hair with a slight blue tint in the moonlight, he had dark green eyes, almost black. The girl's eyes were different, one eye was a pale green, the other icy blue. Both with a bright silver ring around the iris. Hybrids.

"Who are you?" Niah demanded, the two looked at each other, neither answered. Niah jerked the blade at the man's throat, causing blood to well on the metal. The girl gasped.

"Don't, Ember!" she screeched. Niah furrowed her brow, she didn't know that name.

"Tell us who you are," Sai growled, the man Niah was holding sighed.

"My name is Cole, that's Nyx," he said stiffly, the girls' eyes hardened, though she was staring at Niah with a familiar gaze, as if she remembered her from somewhere.

"What are you doing here?" Niah asked firmly.

"I'm not telling you anything." she spat viciously, Niah smirked.

"You will," she murmured. She took a set of *Ruclite* cuffs from the small bag attached to the back of her belt, cuffing the man, Cole. Sai did the same with Nyx. She steered Cole toward the edge of the building where there was no wall of glass.

"We can't jump with our hands bound," Cole protested.

"I'll catch you," Niah smiled sweetly, and pushed him off the ledge, following after him. They all landed on their feet. Niah grabbed hold of his jacket, marching him back to the others. Dea and Misha both stiffened when they saw Niah and Sai approaching with two hybrids in cuffs. She had to admit that there was almost a wrongness to it. They set them down on their knees, standing either side of them so it would be harder for them to escape.

"Why were you here?" Sai asked, gesturing to the body behind the dumpster.

"We were investigating that," the girl sneered, they all glanced at each other. Niah pressed her lips into a firm line, they weren't resisting like she thought they would.

"Who are you with?" Misha demanded.

"Who do you think we're with?" the girl, Nyx, said teasingly. Her eyes flicked to Niah, there was something there, as if she knew her, but Niah didn't remember seeing either of these two before.

"Did you kill this woman?" Velig asked, the girl glared at him for a moment.

"If we killed her, why would we come back to investigate?" she snapped, Velig paled as he flinched. Cole sighed heavily.

She glanced down to find him already looking at her, with that same look in his dark eyes. She looked away quickly.

"We're not *with* anyone. We're on our own," he said, Nyx glared at him.

"You're not with the Shadows?" Niah asked, Cole stiffened all over, Nyx looked away. Niah moved Cole's hair from the back of his neck. There was a faint grey mark in the shape of a solid circle, a controlling mark.

She sucked in a sharp breath, "You *were* with the Shadows though. This mark is faded, how?" no answer, "Look, you can tell us now or we can get the truth out of you another way."

"Do what you must. But we weren't the only ones with the Shadows, were we?" the girl sneered. Niah stiffened as Nyx's eyes danced wickedly. She could feel the eyes of her comrades burning into her as her hands curled into fists at her sides, biting down on the urge to demand what these two knew about her. Why they looked at her with memories in their eyes.

"Alright then. Velig, would you mind going ahead and explaining the situation? Come back for us as soon as you can," Sai said, Velig nodded and used the orb to open the portal, he and Dea stepped through. Moments later, Velig reappeared, his head sticking out through the surface.

"Bring them," he said, Niah and Sai hauled them to their feet, marching them through the portal.

On the other side, they were greeted by Guardians aiming their spears at them. Behind them stood Morena White, Amarah, and Ragnar.

"Young ones, why have you brought these two here?" Amarah asked, her eyes raking over the two captives.

"Apologies, Lady Overseer. We were patrolling and came across a human body with her heart missing, these two were at the scene; they have faded Shadow marks on their necks. We hoped they might be able to give us some information on the Shadows," Sai explained, Amarah regarded him thoughtfully.

"Very well. Bring them to the Council Chamber, we will question them there," she answered softly, she floated from the room with Ragnar and Morena behind her, Guardians trailed behind as others surrounded the two in cuffs. The girl was glaring, Cole was stiff. Inside the Council Chamber were more Guardians, Nyx and Cole were shoved to kneel on the ground once more, Morena waved her hand and chains fixed them in place as she stepped toward them. Nyx fought against the chains, swearing at everyone in the room. Cole remained still.

"Please, whatever you're going to do, do to me, not my sister." he pleaded, Morena gazed at him, a small smile on her face. Niah was staring at the two, sister? Perhaps it was just because they were so close, just as she thought of Sai and Gren as her brothers, and Dea her sister.

"As you wish," Morena grinned. She pressed her hand to Cole's forehead, her palm glowing. She closed her eyes. An image appeared in the air, a projection large enough to fill the room.

The image took form. A small cell with a boy inside, barely ten years old. He had black hair with a slightly blue hue to it that hung over his forehead and across his dark eyes. He desperately reached through the bars, trying to reach the cell next to him, his fingers scraping the ground. The next cell held a girl, the same age with the same dark hair. She was lying on the ground, either asleep or unconscious. The boy was crying, fat tears rolling down his cheeks.

He wore little more than rags. The room was white, the floors, walls and ceilings all made of the same white tile. Rows of white florescent lights lined the ceilings. They weren't the only cells in the room, each with a small child lying within. Images of injections flashed before the screen, though they were distorted and unclear. The images flashed through like that for what must have been years as the children aged to adulthood.

They stood in a long line, holding their hands behind their backs, heads low. The image showed a woman walking down the row, the only thing that was seen of her was her pale legs and high heeled shoes. They were forced to fight each other, beating each other to bloody pulps, sometimes even death. Another injection, the boy screamed, and so did the girl next to him. Their marks no longer making them obedient. No longer controlling them. A blurry image of someone dropping something outside his cell, a set of keys. The person was nothing but a blur, only a flash of dark eyes ringed in silver. They escaped, killing guards with their bare hands as they went, releasing as many prisoners as they could along the way.

The marks had faded, releasing them from the hold the Shadows had on them. They were in the outside world. Niah could feel the confusion and fear that the two of them had felt. They were running for years, decades by the looks of things. They found another group of hybrids, learnt what they were, trained for a while before branching off on their own. The images took them to that very night in Dubai, they found the woman and examined her before leaving to get supplies, the woman left, leaving Cole on that empty floor, and the next minute, she returned with Niah and Sai in tow.

✦ —✦ ⇐◈⇒ ✦— ✦

Cole flopped to the ground. The girl screamed, fighting against the chains to get to him.

"He's okay, just sleeping," Morena said reassuringly.

Just then, the doors burst open, and Benjamin strode into the room, red-faced and furious. He scanned the room with a snarl, his gaze sliding over Nyx and Cole before settling on Niah. He marched toward her, she didn't so much as flinch.

"Benjamin," Ragnar warned, Benjamin didn't seem to hear him. "Benjamin!" he didn't stop. He threw a punch, Niah barely had enough time to dodge, surprised by the speed of the attack.

"Restrain him!" Amarah shouted, the Guardians leapt forward, surrounding Benjamin, their shields raised, and spears aimed at him.

"Get away from me!" Benjamin spat, Niah glowered at him through her lashes. Fin and Merida burst into the room, taking in the scene with wide eyes.

"Counsellor Benjamin! Explain yourself!" Amarah yelled, her voice like death. Benjamin paled, realising he had ignored both the Ambassador and the Overseer.

"Can't you see? This is her doing, this is what she wants, she is bringing in those who are connected to the Shadows! She will take over!" he bellowed desperately, spit flying.

"Who's this prick?" Nyx grumbled, Niah couldn't help but smirk. Benjamin glowered at the girl on the ground.

"Don't speak to me, you filth." he snapped, Niah stood in front of him and folded her arms across her chest.

"If you had arrived only moments ago, you would have seen the truth of the situation," Niah Crooned, perfectly calm. His lips twisted into a snarl, a low growl rumbling through his chest. He swung his fist at her, but she was ready this time and grabbed hold of him. With a quick flick of her wrist, an audible crack echoed through the room as the bone broke. He cried out, but tried to punch her with his other hand, she smacked it away easily and drove her forehead into his nose. Another loud crack. Black blood poured down his lips and between his fingers as he clutched at his face when Niah released him, watching with silent satisfaction.

"I like her," Nyx muttered from where she knelt. Niah glanced at her before turning to the Overseer and bowing her head with her hands clasped behind her back.

"My apologies."

"*You* have nothing to apologise for. Get him out of my sight." Amarah snapped, some of the Guardians quickly escorted him from the room as he yelled and swore.

"This is, however, very disturbing. Girl, what is your name?" Amarah asked, looking at Nyx with piercing golden eyes.

Nyx pressed her lips into a firm line, and sighed in defeat, "Nyx, that's Cole."

"Nyx, after the Greek Goddess of the Night," Amarah murmured, more to herself than to anyone else. "You were both captives of the Shadows?"

Nyx gave her an icy glare, "You could say that, more like experiments." Niah closed her eyes and stifled a shudder, she hated to think what kind of experiments they were subject to. After all, she was an experiment herself.

"I see, the marks on your neck, they no longer work?" Amarah questioned.

"I guess not, they faded after an injection, I guess their experiment failed. They kept us obedient, they could torture us with them and kill us if they felt like it. Considering we're still alive, I guess they no longer have that power." Nyx explained, a bitter edge to her voice. Cole murmured, she tried to go to him, but the chains held her in place, rattling as she jerked against them with a snarl.

"There's no need for those," Amarah sighed, Morena waved her hand and the chains evaporated. The Guardians stepped forward, taking off the cuffs binding their wrists. Nyx crawled across the floor to her brother, pulling him into her lap gently and stroking his thick hair.

Morena climbed the platform to the Elders, they murmured amongst themselves for a moment. Fin and Merida crossed the room to Niah and the others. Fin placed a hand on her cheek, tilting her head from side to side, checking for injuries. She clasped his hands between hers to lower them, offering him a smile, his eyes remained worried, angry even. She rolled her eyes and gently nudged him in the ribs with her elbow. She wasn't used to people worrying about her.

"They will stay in the Chambers under guard, in the morning, they will hold the truth stone," Ragnar announced.

"You're holding us captive?" Nyx snapped.

"Child, your companion cannot travel, you both need food and rest. Come tomorrow, you will make your choice." Amarah replied gently, yet with a firm edge to her voice that silenced the girl before her. One of the Guardians lifted Cole into his arms, Nyx followed closely behind as they left the room.

"I'm going with them," Niah muttered to Fin, he opened his mouth to protest, but she had already followed after them.

Nyx glanced over her shoulder at her, "That was a good shot." She sounded like it pained her to give a compliment. Niah couldn't stop the smirk tugging at her lips. "What that arse was saying, about you wanting to bring those from the Shadows, what did he mean?" she asked, her voice low and wary. Should she tell her? Would it make her more understanding to know there were others like her? Probably not. It certainly didn't comfort Niah to know how many suffered and were still suffering at the hands of the Shadows. But if they knew something, *anything,* then it would be worth the risk.

Niah sighed, "I was raised by the Shadows," Nyx gave nothing away, only waited for her to continue, "I had a mark too, though they never controlled me with it, never hurt me. It suppressed my strength. A sealing mark." Nyx was quiet as they reached a windowless room with two beds inside, the Guardian lay Cole gently down on one of them and left to stand in the hall.

"And yet you're here, who are these people?" Nyx asked, standing by her brothers' side with her arms folded over her chest.

"We're the Fury Alliance. We fight against the Shadows, against demons. You could join us if you wish. If not, I suppose that's for the Elders to decide," Niah shrugged, Nyx looked as if she were going to say something but closed her mouth. Niah frowned.

"Cole called you his sister." Niah murmured.

Nyx cocked her head to the side, "Yeah? We're siblings, twins, to be exact." Niah had never heard of hybrid twins, but supposed it would be just like any other birth.

"You called me Ember, why?" she asked, Nyx gazed at her for a moment before answering.

"You just look like someone I knew, but she was prettier, so I guess I have the wrong person," she said firmly before slamming the door closed. Niah stared at the closed door. There was something else, Nyx had looked away during that explanation. Niah wasn't the best at reading people, but she thought Nyx was lying. And why wouldn't she? She was in a strange place where they had just rummaged through her brothers' memories and rendered him unconscious. She sighed, knowing she wasn't going to get any answers by standing in the corridor.

Fin

He knocked on the door to Merida's house. She opened it, offering him a warm smile as she stepped aside to allow him in. Her house was the same as the other Counsellors, a large stone fireplace, wooden pillars and beams, decorative rugs throughout, and comfy seats. He sat on a grey fabric sofa in front of the gently crackling fire and chewed on his lip, suddenly unsure of how to bring up what he'd come to say.

"What is it?" she asked, sitting in an armchair, and crossing one leg over the other as she leaned back, watching him warily.

He raked a hand through his hair, "I think we should tell her," she sucked in a sharp breath.

"Why?"

He shrugged, "She deserves to know," he knew why Merida didn't want to tell her. He wasn't exactly looking forward to it. She exhaled slowly.

Merida exhaled slowly, "What do you plan to tell her?"

"Everything."

"No."

Fin bristled, "She needs to know, Merida. Everyone does." She was silent for a long moment, gazing into the crackling flames.

"Not yet."

Fin rose to his feet and knelt in front of her, taking her hand in his, "You can't keep it from them forever." Merida took a deep, trembling breath.

"I know. But with everything else going on right now_"

"We'll work through it, together. But they *need* to know." He said firmly, but not without kindness. She held his gaze and pressed her palm to his cheek.

"You and I both know there's no way out of this." She breathed, the breath catching in her throat as her eyes welled slightly.

"If you told the others, then maybe we could find a way." He countered.

She shook her head, "No one has ever succeeded, there's no reason why this time would be different." For that, he had no argument. "As for Niah," she went on, "I have no answers for her, I don't know how it's possible."

Merida had told him everything only a matter of weeks ago, the night before the attack on the facility when they had all fled to the bunker. He understood her reasons for not telling Niah then, but she had the right to know.

"Then wouldn't it be easier to tell her so we can work it out?" he suggested softly.

Merida sighed, "It may mean she'll lose all trust in us."

"Then that's our fault for not telling her sooner." He said. Her eyes hardened slightly, but she pressed her lips together, her hand falling from his face.

"Fine, we will tell her tomorrow."

"I think it best if I do this on my own."

"Why's that?" she asked, her brow scrunching slightly.

"She'll be angry, I doubt you would want to fight with her," he said guardedly. Merida gave him an incredulous stare.

She murmured, "Fine, but keep anything about me to yourself."

"Including what you are to her?" another moment of silence fell.

"Tell her what I am to her, but that's all, if she wants more information, tell her to come and see me."

"Are you sure? What if you argue and you_"

"I am not a child to be coddled, Fin." Her voice was sharp, and he found himself dipping his chin. "I'm sorry," she whispered, pulling his chin so he would look at her. She hated using that commanding voice as much as he did.

"Don't be, I understand." He said, a smile curving his lips.

A loud bang at the door interrupted them. Gren burst into the house before Merida had a chance to say, 'come in', panting hard. They both stood abruptly, Gren wouldn't look like that unless it was serious.

"The squad came back with two prisoners, it sounds serious," he said quickly, Merida and Fin exchanged a glance before they all bolted out the house toward the Chambers. Benjamin was already running up the steps before they were close. Fin cursed under his breath, how had he found out so quick? They reached the top of the stairs when Talon emerged from the Chambers, looking over his shoulder at Benjamin.

"What's going on?" he asked.

Fin didn't slow down, "No idea yet."

He watched her leave. The room fell silent. Gren was in the Chambers when he saw Niah and the others and hurried to get Fin and Merida. Benjamin got wind of it before they had and beaten them there. He saw the look on Niah's face as Benjamin bellowed at her, saw her jaw set and the look of satisfaction as she broke his wrist and nose. He couldn't deny the satisfaction of watching the Counsellor clutching at his bloodied face. That satisfaction quickly faded once he saw the pain on Niah's features as Nyx said they were experiments. The same pain that had haunted her eyes for days after she killed Logan. He wanted to go to her, but he knew her well enough to know she didn't want to be babied. Especially in front of everyone else.

"This is rather troublesome," Amarah sighed, pinching her narrow nose between her thumb and forefinger.

Sai stepped forward and bowed his head slightly, "If you believe we acted foolishly, Lady Overseer, then I will accept the consequences."

"There's no need for that. Tell me, the images from Cole's mind showed a murdered woman, What can you tell me about it?" she asked.

"Her heart was ripped out, ribs tore open. Velig confirmed there was demonic essence there, though that doesn't mean it was caused by a demon," Sai explained, his hands clasped behind his back.

Amarah clicked her tongue, "I see. I will investigate this personally. You are all dismissed."

He left the room with the others, feeling as if all energy had drained from his body. Niah was sitting on the steps outside the Chambers. He held out his hand to her, she took it with a faint smile and rose to her feet, dark circles lined her eyes. He felt wavering all of a sudden, not wanting to pile on more pressure, more stress. But he had to tell her.

They walked hand in hand through the streets. Only flaming torches lined the way, lighting the town in a warm glow. They arrived at the training grounds and sat in the thick grass. Niah's swords discarded on the grass beside them. His heart wouldn't stop thundering, maybe in a few minutes, it wouldn't feel quite so daunting.

"You like her," he stated, she gave him a quizzical glance and rolled her eyes, though something darker lurked beneath the surface. He wanted to ask, wanted to know so badly what it was she was thinking. She would tell him in her own time. If she forgave him for what he was about to tell her.

"She's tough," she answered, he sat with his legs on either side of her hips as she leaned into him, her back pressing against his chest.

"As are you."

"Something's on your mind," she observed, his breath hitched in his throat, he distracted himself by playing with a lock of her raven hair. *The same could be said of you.*

"You asked me and Merida if there was anything else you should know," he murmured. She stilled, and hummed slightly, letting him know that she remembered vividly.

"Merida was there when you were a baby, she wasn't there for the birth. But she was there afterwards, she was there when you were taken." He said gently.

"I already know that," she whispered, her voice trembling slightly.

He took a steadying breath, "What you don't know, is that it was three hundred years ago."

"That's impossible." she breathed, tension thick in her voice.

"Merida thought so too. She is your Guardian, appointed by your mother, she has a connection to you. She thought you were dead. Until centuries later when she felt your spark reignite." He explained.

He remembered the night when Merida had burst into his room without knocking, he thought something terrible had happened. Her eyes were so wide and full of tears, and yet, she was smiling. Merida never told him why the girl was so important, not until the night before the attack on the facility. She only ever said that there was a hybrid in need of help, and it became an obsession for Merida to find Niah.

It broke his heart watching her get her hopes up time and time again when they thought they had found a trace of her, and time and time again, she would break down whenever the leads came back empty.

"Why didn't she tell me this?" Niah growled through gritted teeth, her body trembling against him.

"She thought you would want more answers," he said in a weak voice, knowing full well it sounded like an excuse. She jumped to her feet, her hands balled into fists. Slowly, he did the same. He said nothing, it would be better not to press too hard.

With her back to him, she hissed, "Why do you all protect me as if I am weak?"

"It wasn't that...she didn't know how it was possible, she wanted to find out how you were alive before she told you, to give you answers," he told her, his voice steady, soothing even.

She whirled on him with flaming blue eyes, "So why now? Why tell me now?"

He remembered the first time he saw her eyes like that, they were as beautiful now as they were then, even if they were full of pain and anger. There was something different, a silver ring around her pupil as well as her iris, they pulsed ever so slightly, and then it was gone in a blink.

The wind picked up, blowing the loose strands of her hair around her face. His chest ached. They should have told her from the beginning, he didn't know if she would hate him after this; he dreaded the very thought of it. Yet he would rather she hated him and know the truth than keep it from her to keep her in blissful ignorance.

He wanted to go to her, to wrap his arms around her, it took every ounce of willpower to stay put. Her Canines snapped down, long and sharp. It was a reaction from hybrids when they were royally pissed. There was a time when hybrids hunted animals with their bare hands, the lengthened teeth made it easier. Though they had a nasty tendency to come out when one was angry, or even turned on.

"We're no closer to figuring it out, no closer to answers. I thought it best you know. I thought if anyone would want to figure it out the most, you would want to." he said gently, her expression didn't change. Her hands relaxing and clenching into fists at her sides.

"I'm sorry, Niah," he murmured, her eyes were cold. Closed off, as if a thick door had slammed down, shutting him out. She had put a wall up between them, and he didn't blame her. He probably would have done the same thing. His understanding did nothing to ease the tightening in his chest. He may very well lose her after this.

"How am I supposed to trust you? Either of you," she spat, those sharp teeth glinting in the moonlight.

"That's up to you. But I promise you, there is nothing else we're keeping from you. You probably won't believe me, but that's it," he told her firmly yet gently. Her eyes dimmed to their usual onyx as she stood, emotionless. It was as if all feeling had abandoned her.

"By all means, perform a memory projection on me if you don't believe me." he offered. Niah searched his eyes, no doubt looking to see if he was joking. He wasn't. If it meant she would believe him, he would let her see every single memory in his mind.

"I can't do that spell." She said tightly.

"Then ask Cassia or Velig, if you need proof that I'm telling you the truth, then so be it." he held her gaze until she looked away.

"Leave me alone," she said, her voice empty. Those three words tore at his chest. Not just the words themselves, but the emptiness of her voice. Those eyes usually so full of love and longing when she looked at him, now hollow and cold.

"Niah I_"

"I want to be alone, Fin," she said again, the same monotone sound. His heart sank. She had closed herself off. No matter what he said, it would fall on deaf ears. He could almost feel her pain. She had been lied to her whole life and had finally found a place where she trusted people, only to have them keep important information from her.

He took a step toward her, her eyes darkened in response. He froze. He wanted her to know how sorry he was, though he couldn't find the right words.

He strode across the grass toward her, placing his hands on her upper arms. She was tense all over, though no more so than before he had touched her. At the least she didn't pull away.

"There's nothing I could say that will make any of this any better," he murmured, "we wanted to find out how any of this is possible before we told you, we wanted to give you answers. We should have told you, I'm so sorry we kept it from you. I understand if you hate me, but don't hate Merida; she's your Guardian." she wasn't looking at him, her eyes were distant.

"I said I want to be alone."

His hands fell away from her arms. He'd expected this, hell, he deserved it. But the reality of it hollowed out his chest.

"I think you should speak to Merida, she can explain better than I can." She refused to look at him. He sighed, "Come to me if you need to." again, she said nothing. Regardless, he'd always give her the option to go to him, even if he knew she wouldn't.

He started to walk away, but paused, "I'm sorry." Was all he said before leaving her standing alone in the darkness, wondering whether she would ever return to him.

He knew he deserved it if she didn't.

3

Niah

She watched him walk away, and exhaustion washed over her. The day had been long and draining. She was hoping to crawl into bed and fall into a deep, dreamless sleep. It didn't seem like that would happen now her nerves felt as though they were live wires. She sighed heavily. He didn't look back over his shoulder, she was almost thankful. She lowered herself into the thick grass and lay back, gazing at the stars above. They shone brightly, the moon in its half form bathing the world in a pale glow.

How could she possibly be three hundred years old? It didn't make sense. Her head had frozen, screaming at her that he was lying. How could such a thing even be real? She hoped he was playing a trick, though the pain in his eyes showed her he was telling the truth. She saw how much it pained him to tell her, saw him brace himself as if she would attack him. She had thought about it, if she was being honest with herself. Rage had taken over, and in that moment, it didn't matter that he was the person she cared for beyond comprehension. In all honesty, it had scared her. That she was ready to harm him. She receded into herself, almost lost herself to the anger in her veins.

What good would it have done? It wouldn't have achieved anything. Putting her walls up wouldn't achieve anything. She wasn't that same lost little girl anymore who needed those walls.

If she were to find the answers, she would need help. Picking fights with Fin isn't exactly what she wanted to do, she cared for him and didn't want to hurt him.

Despite being disappointed and angry at the news, what exactly did it change about her? She didn't feel any different. She knew she had to find out why and how it was possible. Her mind drifted to Nyx and Cole, how they looked at her, how Nyx had called her 'Ember'. She had never heard that name before, yet it niggled in the back of her mind.

Her head began to throb dully, her thoughts becoming cloudy. None of it made sense, and she wasn't going to find answers by staring at the stars. No matter how much they calmed her. All those billions upon billions of stars in the universe, and she was lucky enough to be gazing up at them. She wondered how many of them had already died, withered away into the void. She suddenly felt small. Her problems were tiny in the grand scheme of things. She hadn't dealt with seeing her former head mistress, not really, just shoved everything out of her mind, refusing to think about it. Ignoring her problems and pretending like they didn't leave some mark on her soul would only make them worse.

There was a hole inside her. Some deep, consuming abyss. It had been healing, growing smaller with each passing day. Yet, as soon as Thamere was created, the abyss stopped shrinking. She was no longer able to piece back together the broken pieces of herself, her trust, her mind, and body. She wouldn't be free of that abyss, always threatening, always reaching to drag her down into the darkness. How much would she have to give before she found out the truth? Would she pay any price? She had found something in the Furies. For the first time, she had friends. She had a Guardian, whatever that meant. She had a job; she was a warrior. For the first time, *she* was trusted. She should be thrilled. She should feel like the luckiest girl in the world, and in many ways, she was.

She was grateful for what she had, but her need to know, her hunger for the truth wouldn't fade. All those years spent in the library looking for answers, it wasn't in her nature to give up. Though she knew all too well that everything came at a price, and when the time came, would she be willing to give it all up? To pay the price just to know the answers to her deepest questions? The questions etched into her very soul, which she refused to even think. She shook the thoughts from her mind, whatever she had to do, she would find a way to do it without losing what she had found.

She got to her feet and started back toward the town.

The door opened slowly, and Merida stood on the other side. Her eyes widened as she saw Niah, and she stepped aside to let her through. Merida sighed, closing the door, and gestured for Niah to sit. The house was warm, filled with the flickering orange light from the fire. Niah sat on the sofa next to Merida, her legs tucked underneath her.

"Fin told you." not a question, her expression unreadable.

"Why didn't *you* tell me?" Niah asked, her voice sharper than intended.

"I didn't know how, I was scared. I thought you would lose trust in us," she said, "in me." she gazed at her with wide eyes, her voice pained as she said the last words.

"I have." Niah shrugged, "In all honesty. I gave you a chance at the bunker to tell me if there was anything else."

Merida sighed, "I know, all I can do is apologise, I am sorry, so sorry that I didn't tell you."

"I get it, you're both sorry," Niah quipped, "what I need from you now is two things."

"Anything."

"The first, swear you will never keep anything from me or lie to me again_"

"I swear I won't, ever."

"Second, I need you to help me find answers. Tell me anything you can, you're my Guardian, what does that mean exactly?" Niah asked, Merida smiled briefly.

"It's very rare. It usually happens when other species mixed with demon blood mates with an angel to create hybrid half breeds with other species. Of course, that doesn't mean a demon can't name someone a Guardian of their child. The parent would name someone a Guardian to protect the child and raise them. Your mother named me yours. It's a spell binding ritual, she is a spell weaver and was able to perform the spell herself. It means I can feel whether you're alive or not, I can feel when you're in danger.

When your mother was taken, I could feel you were still alive. A few days later, I couldn't feel you, it was as if a piece of my heart had died. I resigned myself to the fact that you were dead and that was that, until centuries later when that part of my heart reignited, and I knew you were alive. I never stopped searching for you," Merida's breath hitched in her throat, her ocean blue eyes filling with tears. Niah was silent. She had never heard of such a spell, not that it surprised her, there was still so much of the world she didn't know. She couldn't expect them to tell her everything.

"So, we're magically linked?"

Merida nodded, "Though I believe I feel the connection more than you do."

Niah was silent for a long time. She remembered the way she felt so comfortable around Merida when they first met, the way she had wanted to be honest with her. Niah trusted her. She hadn't understood why she trusted the woman so quickly, but she supposed she now knew why. The others she had come to trust so easily simply because she had never had friends. She'd never had those bonds before and that small part of her that craved closeness and affection had latched onto those bonds.

She didn't regret her friendships with them. But it was hard not to feel foolish for trusting so easily.

"The others don't know." Merida said, as if reading those very thoughts. She said she could *feel* Niah through whatever magical bond they shared. Did that also mean she could feel Niah's emotions?

"Fin knew."

Merida sighed, "I only told him recently. I needed help figuring out how you were over three hundred years old, and not remember any of it other than the last eighteen years."

"And?" she asked, "Did you come up with any theories?"

"I have one. We know the Shadows have different marks for different things, you mentioned before that there was a mark to prevent ones aging." Niah nodded, "It's possible that they could have marked you when you were an infant to keep you as a babe for as long as they did. The mark may have also had an effect on our bond which is why I couldn't feel you, and when it was removed, the bond was once again connected."

Niah folded her arms across her chest, "I don't understand why they would do that though, why keep me an infant for three hundred years?"

Merida shrugged, "I suppose you could have been the first hybrid they had. We know Cole and Nyx were experiments, I suppose it wouldn't be a reach to assume they were conducting those experiments for whatever it was they were planning for you."

Niah's head began to throb. She pinched the bridge of her nose, willing the headache to fade away. It didn't.

"Nyx knew me," Niah muttered, remembering the way the two had looked at her, the name Nyx had called her.

Merida blinked, "How?" Niah huffed a humourless laugh.

"Hell if I know, I didn't even know I was over three centuries old." Merida pressed her lips together, yet Niah couldn't find it in herself to feel guilty for the hurt that flashed across her ocean blue eyes. She had kept something so important from her. Whether it was because Merida was still searching for answers or not, she should have said something.

"Did she say how she knew you?"

Niah gave her a withering look, "No. She called me Ember. I've never heard that name." Merida was quiet as she considered that.

"Neither have I, then again, I didn't know what your name was. Marina hadn't decided before..." the unspoken words hung between them.

"What can you tell me about my mother?" Niah asked quietly. Merida smiled and got to her feet; she crossed the room to the mantle above the fireplace where a small clock sat. She reached behind it, pulling a small piece of paper out and handed it to Niah.

She gazed down at the crumpled, old picture. The woman in the photograph was holding a baby wrapped in a light blanket, gazing down at her with all the love and adoration in the world. She had long dark hair and matching onyx eyes. She was beautiful. A flicker of familiarity lashed through Niah's mind. That woman, the dark hair. She had seen it before. In the picture of her false parents, Nolan, and Karliah, there was a woman in the background. It was her, the same woman that Merida claimed to be her mother. Niah caught Merida's questioning gaze.

"If this was taken centuries ago, how is *that* even possible? I'm pretty sure cameras weren't invented then," Niah questioned, hoping it was enough to stop Merida from searching her face.

"Magic is a wonderful thing, there are rumours that it was a spell weaver who invented the first camera that humans know of," she shrugged.

Niah turned back to the picture, hoping it would give her more of an emotional connection to it, to her disappointment; she felt nothing. Only a deep confusion as to why her mother would be standing behind people she knew to be working for the Shadows, maybe even with them. Maybe she should tell Merida about the picture, but despite understanding why her Guardian had kept the truth from her, the trust between them had cracked.

"She was a hard woman. Very stern and had a bad temper, but she was smart, beautiful, and fierce. She was kind above all else. You're very much like her," Merida said fondly, "she was so big when she was pregnant with you, I was sure you would either be a massive baby or she was carrying twins." she laughed lightly, "But a demon has never produced multiple offspring at one go."

Her mother was half demon, half spell weaver, Niah's father was an angel. So her mother wouldn't be able to birth multiple children due to her demonic blood. But then...

"Why not?"

Merida shrugged, "It's not possible for them to do so."

Niah's head snapped up then. Twins weren't possible, so how was there a set of them sitting in the Chambers at that very moment?

"Nyx and Cole are twins."

Merida's brow furrowed, "That can't be true."

"They look almost identical, Nyx said they were twins," she said quickly. It wasn't exactly related to herself; her mother was only carrying one. But it meant that what they thought they knew about demons not being able to sire twins could be wrong, "Who said it wasn't possible for demons to produce more than one child at a time?"

"It's common knowledge, written in the book I gave you when you arrived." Niah vaguely remembered reading something like that.

"Surely having a set of twins in the Chambers proves that it's wrong?" Niah said. It wasn't that the fact that twins were real among hybrids, but if the Elders were the ones who wrote that book, if they were the ones who said twins weren't possible, then why? Why would they want to keep it a secret? And if they were willing to lie about something like that, what else were they lying about?

Perhaps it was her cynical mind looking for any hole in which she could save herself from trusting the Alliance. Perhaps they really didn't think multiple children in one go was possible. Either way, Niah couldn't bring herself to ignore it.

"Who would know more about this?"

"The Elders, I suppose," Merida murmured, still staring wide-eyed into the fire.

"We need a meeting with them."

"Niah, slow down. It's late, get some sleep. I'll try to arrange an audience tomorrow," Merida groaned tiredly.

Niah clicked her tongue and strode for the door, "Okay, tomorrow."

"Niah," Merida said gently, Niah turned back, her hand on the handle. Merida gazed at her with wide, ocean blue eyes, and crossed the room to her in a few steps. She wrapped her arms around her. Niah tensed all over, taken off guard by the gesture, but hugged her Guardian back.

"You know, I always wanted a daughter," Merida whispered, Niah felt her arms grow tighter around her, "but it's not possible for hybrids. When your mother asked me to be your Guardian, I was over the moon. It meant I had a child to love and protect as my own. I thought I failed you, failed your mother. When I felt you die...I didn't stop crying for weeks, it felt as though something inside of me just withered away. When I found you again, I wanted to tell you everything. But I didn't want to overwhelm you, I didn't want to scare you or try to force you into trusting me. I was wrong, I know that now. But I need you to know I love you, as much as hybrids can love. You're the daughter I could never have. I'll do anything I can to help you, Niah." Merida pulled away from her with glistening eyes as tears rolled down her pale cheeks. Despite herself, Niah's chest swelled with warmth. For the first time in weeks, the abyss grew a little smaller.

"I'm glad you're my Guardian," Niah muttered, and meant it. Merida smiled, and Niah stepped out into the street.

She might be the only one awake. The windows were all dark, the streets quiet. The only light was the glow of flickering flames from the torches lining the streets. Her hand went to her throat where her locket would usually rest, her fingers only brushed bare skin. A pang sliced through her chest, and she sighed, kicking herself that she still let it bother her. Some wounds took longer to heal than others, finding out her parents weren't who they said they were, was taking far longer than she cared to admit.

Her hand fell limply to her side as she walked the quiet street, it had been such a long day, and an even longer night. Tiredness gripped her, but her mind was swirling with a mass of information and theories. No matter how much she chased a ribbon of thought, it always slipped away.

Niah could have stayed angry at Merida. Thought it would only be fair if she did, but the truth was, she wasn't. Maybe it was the bond between them, maybe she had just accepted that there was more about herself that she didn't know. Either way, Merida was her Guardian. She was still coming to terms with what that meant, but it felt right. Like home. It wasn't forgiveness, not yet, but she wasn't angry. Whatever trust was between them had cracked. The same for Fin. It didn't matter whether she understood their reasons or not, they should have told her.

She would always prefer to be hurt by the truth, than protected by a lie.

Her room was dark, lonely. She unlaced her boots and kicked them off, sending them clattering across the floor. She stripped down to her underwear and climbed under the covers. The bed was soft, the covers cool against her skin momentarily. Her muscles were tired, she should have slept hours ago, but her mind was humming now, unable to rest. Closing her eyes, she willed sleep to take her. It didn't.

With a groan, she swung her legs out of the bed, pulling on the t-shirt that Fin had left there the night before. It smelt like him, spices, and sandalwood. She left her room, creeping along the hall, and cracked the door open before slipping inside and closing it gently behind her.

Heavy breathing of sleep filled the room. She crept around to the free side of the bed and slid under the covers. He stirred, instinctively wrapping an arm around her, pulling her close. She lay on her side, gazing at him as he slept. He looked so peaceful. All humour gone, all Commander like presence vanished. His lids fluttered open, and he blinked a few times, clearing the fog of sleep from his vision.

"I wasn't expecting you," he mumbled in his gravelly, sleepy voice.

"Should I leave?" she whispered, he shook his head quickly, tightening his arm around her.

"How are you feeling?" he asked, struggling to keep his eyes open.

"I'm fine," she murmured; he mouthed the words as she said them.

"You're always fine."

With a sigh, she raked her hand through her hair, "It's not every day you find out you're three hundred years old."

"I guess that means I have a thing for older women," he smirked with closed eyes, she smacked him playfully in the chest, he chuckled. Her hand lingered on his bare skin. Slowly, she trailed her fingers down his torso, over the ridges of his stomach, and down to his hip. She stilled. He smirked slightly. He was naked. She couldn't feel the waistband of pyjama bottoms or boxers. Quickly, she moved her hand back up to his chest.

"As I said, I wasn't expecting you," he said softly.

"Well, you did say I could come by."

"When you say you need space, that usually means all night," he smiled as he sat up, and tossed a pillow at her face.

"Don't look," he said as his weight moved from the bed, she peeked above the pillow. He was already mostly into a pair of boxers, only the top of his buttocks visible. Her cheeks burned, and her pulse quickened as she sucked in a breath. He turned and grinned when he spotted her peeking at him.

"I could always leave them off," he shrugged.

"No, it's fine," she said quickly, he chuckled slightly as he climbed back into bed.

"Does it bother you?" she asked, he gazed at her blankly.

He flopped onto his back, snaking his arm around her, cradling his head on his free arm, "Need you to be a little more specific than that."

"Does it bother you that we haven't...you know, had sex?" he exhaled slowly, rolling onto his side, propping his head on his elbow to look down at her, stroking her cheek with his thumb.

"No. It doesn't bother me. This is new to you. Despite how our lifestyle is, the whole polyamorous thing, the first time is still a big deal. It's up to you when you want to take that step, and I do hope it's me you decide to do it with," he said with an easy, lopsided smile.

Niah cocked her head to the side, "Why wouldn't it be you?"

"We're not monogamous beings, our wants and desires change all the time. I know I want you and only you, but I've been around longer, well, actually living for longer anyway, you are an old woman now," he joked, she rolled her eyes, "you could change your mind quicker than I'm likely to. Or I could change my mind." he shrugged, "I don't think I will, I'm happy being loyal to you." His silvery eyes darkened slightly as he watched for her reaction.

She knew what he meant, had read all about their romances, their way of life. She knew things changed all the time, knew there may be a day when she didn't want Fin in that way, or he might not want her. Regardless of when that day might come, if ever; she wanted to enjoy the time they had when it was just them. At that moment they both only wanted each other, and it was enough for her.

"I understand, Fin. And I'm sure, if I could love the way humans love, I would love you," she said, a small smirk dancing at the corners of her mouth. His expression lightened, he chuckled at the realisation that she had repeated his own words back to him from their first kiss in Australia.

"You'll be the death of me," he sighed.

"What?" she questioned; his eyes widened slightly as if he had let something slip.

"It's something I've been saying, usually you're unconscious, don't ask me why. I don't know," he shrugged. She smiled and rested her cheek on his chest.

After a long moment he asked, "Are you mad at me?"

"No."

"Do you forgive me?"

"No."

"What can I do to earn your forgiveness?" he asked. Her eyes were closed, sleep suddenly making them unbearably heavy.

"You can let me sleep."

He chuckled and kissed the top of her head, "I *will* make it up to you and earn your forgiveness, and your trust again." She wanted to say something, but the darkness of sleep was already dragging her under.

"Hmm." Was all she could manage.

"I'll do anything to make it right," his whisper echoed through her mind until she was pulled under the surface and fell asleep in his arms.

She woke feeling like she needed more sleep. Her lids were heavy, her muscles ached, and her bones cracked as she stretched her arms over her head. Fin was already gone, she groaned as she remembered he had early patrol; guilt washed through her for waking him.

Her stomach rumbled, she hadn't eaten the night before and was famished. Pausing at the door before leaving, she glanced over her shoulder at the unmade bed. She never bothered making her bed, it was pointless only to get back in it the following night, but Fin was neat and always made her bed.

She lifted the duvet and dropped it down, fluffed the pillows and tucked in the edges of the quilt. It still didn't look right, but at least she tried. With a shrug, she pulled on a pair of his jogger bottoms which were so big on her that she had to hold them up as she jogged down the hall to her room to shower. The water cascaded over her, chasing away the remnants of sleep. Feeling fresher and awake, she dressed in training clothes. Black leggings and a loose tank top. Braiding her wet hair down her back, she made her way to the kitchen where pots and pans were banging, and chatter echoed through the building.

Other people were sitting around the ridiculously huge table eating eggs and bacon. She grabbed an apple from the fruit bowl and sat next to Misha as they all exchanged greetings. One of the things she was still getting used to was how friendly everyone was. Whenever she passed someone or walked into a room, they would greet her like they'd known her forever. Some people were suspicious of her, those in Benjamin's circle, but the majority were accepting enough. Dark circles lined Misha's lidded eyes as she held a mug of steaming coffee between her hands, gazing at it as if it were some miracle.

"You good?" Niah asked as she took a bite of her apple. Misha jumped as if she hadn't even noticed Niah sitting next to her. She was wearing training clothes too, loose-fitting jogger bottoms with a long-sleeved thermal top.

"Can't talk...too early," Misha grumbled, Niah huffed a snort, she often felt the same way when Fin woke up in one of his bouncy moods.

"Anyone else wants bacon and eggs?" the boy standing over one of the stoves called, he was average height with shoulder-length auburn hair and dark brown eyes, Nate, another warrior who had been in Perth with them, a very adept fighter who moved like a shadow through the night. A few hands went up, including Niah's. To her surprise, he didn't moan. He turned back to the stove with a grin, plating up scrambled eggs and crispy bacon. The smell alone was delicious.

"So, you caught two hybrids yesterday?" the girl sat opposite her asked, Nina; her eyes large and deep blue. She had carroty red hair, pale skin, and a smattering of freckles across her cheeks and arms. She wore a black tank top and jeans as if ready to go patrolling. Some of the people at the table who had been chattering suddenly went quiet, waiting for her answer.

"Uh...yeah," Niah said hesitantly before stuffing her mouth with eggs.

"Slow down, nobody's going to take it from you," Sai scoffed as he strode into the kitchen, running a hand through his dishevelled jet hair.

"So, who were these prisoners?" Nina pressed, Niah took her time swallowing.

"Just two people who were in the wrong place at the wrong time," she shrugged, better to act uninterested herself; then they might stop asking questions. She caught Sai's gaze, the ghost of a smile on his lips as he turned to pour himself a mug of coffee. Nina looked dissatisfied with her answer but didn't press the matter further. Niah finished her breakfast quickly and washed hers and a few other plates, thanking Nate for cooking before rushing out of the barracks.

She jogged to Merida's house, getting in some exercise since she wasn't sure if she would have time to train. Merida was already standing in the street speaking to Gren. She smiled as she looked up to see Niah approaching, Gren gave a subtle dip of his chin.

"Did you manage to arrange a meeting?" Niah asked by way of greeting.

"Yes, I was just going to come to find you. Come on," Merida said. They all headed up the steps outside the Chambers and walked through the bustling halls toward the Council room where the Elders were already waiting with Morena, Nyx, and Cole, the two no longer bound. Nyx glared at the Guardians lining the walls with their spears poised.

"Counsellor Merida, Commander Grenville, and Niah. You requested a meeting with us today, why?" Ragnar greeted formally, his voice devoid of any unkindness, despite his scowling eyes. Merida nodded to Niah, she stepped forward and bowed her head before standing with her hands clasped behind her back.

"I wish to ask you what you know of multiple babies during one pregnancy. Nyx and Cole are twins, yet Merida tells me this is impossible. Why is that?" she questioned. Amarah and Ragnar exchanged a glance, a look Niah couldn't read. Amarah shifted in her seat.

"Demons are complicated creatures. They mate with humans or other species, creating half-bloods. As demons are only able to carry one baby, their half-blooded offspring do have the ability to carry more than one. It is possible but extremely rare. We have only witnessed one or two multiple births. Many pregnancies that include more than one baby usually end up with the weaker one being eaten by the other in the womb. I believe that is like human pregnancies, except theirs are absorbed. It is said that when more than one baby is produced their blood is split, one is more evil than the other, which leads to the stronger one eating the lesser," Amarah explained delicately, Nyx and Cole glanced at each other.

"But one of us isn't eviler." Nyx protested.

"You say that young one. Yet your brother spared you from having your memories projected yesterday and you let him, it could be said you are perhaps the darker twin," Ragnar countered. Nyx's face flushed red, Niah thought she might lunge for him. The Guardians must have thought so too, because they took a step forward, readying their spears.

"This is not meant to harm you. It is only the truth, as requested. Tell me, young Niah; why has this piqued your interest?" Ragnar asked, leaning forward in his seat, and resting his forearms on the desk in front of him.

"The connection didn't make sense to me. Nyx said they were twins, and when Merida told me it was impossible, I wanted to know why. But you're saying it's not impossible, only extremely rare. My next question is, why are hybrids led to believe it is impossible?" Ragnar stroked his sandy beard with silver beads running through it thoughtfully for a moment.

"An inquisitive one I see. Very well, it is because they are considered dangerous. If both children survive the pregnancy, it means that the one may be equally as light as the other is dark. They could potentially wield power we do not yet know about," he shrugged, Niah noticed Nyx and Cole glance at each other once again. Though when Cole turned back, his gaze fell on Niah. That same remembrance shining in his dark eyes. Niah averted her gaze to Ragnar.

"What power?" Nyx demanded; Ragnar regarded her coolly for a moment, a slow smirk spreading across his face.

"We simply do not know. As I said, we have witnessed only a couple of multiple births, they didn't find out about this power, we assume someone has because otherwise where would the whispers originate from? Though how they achieve that we don't know," he explained, Nyx looked almost deflated. Niah didn't feel any closer to the truth. Though she hoped maybe her questions had helped Nyx and Cole. She glanced at Amarah, who had been rather quiet throughout the conversation. Her golden eyes were emotionless as she gazed down at the twins, her expression unreadable.

"Does that conclude your questions, Niah?" Amarah asked, catching her gaze, and turning those gold eyes on her.

"No, Lady Overseer."

"Oh?"

"What are the circumstances in which twins or triplets would be born?" Niah questioned.

Ragnar rested his forearms on the desk, "Demons are unable to carry more than one child at a time, but they do mate with other species as you know, to create a half breed. That's how we end up with hybrids mixed with fey or lycanthrope." He didn't say spell weaver, "As long as the offspring is female and mates with an angel as they're known to do, a hybrid with mixed blood will be born yes, but the mother could also birth twins. As I said, it's extremely rare, but that's how it happens."

"I see."

"Does that satisfy your curious mind?" Ragnar asked.

Niah dipped her chin, "Yes, thank you."

His explanation made sense, but it didn't explain why they thought keeping it a secret would be best. If such children possessed power, wouldn't it be beneficial for them to find out what that power is? Niah slid her eyes to the Overseer, unnerved to find Amarah already watching her carefully, her golden eyes narrowed.

At the very least, she had confirmed her suspicions that the Elders had kept information from the public. Ragnar said twins could possess more power than they could imagine, were the Elders worried that if such beings discovered that power, that they may rise up against the Elders?

"Now, the matter of whether you two will stay or leave. What will you decide?" Amarah demanded, turning her gaze to the twin hybrids standing before her. Nyx and Cole stared at each other for a moment, Cole stepped forward, and Nyx grabbed for his arm, though he didn't seem to notice.

"We would like to stay," he declared. Morena stepped forward, producing the truth stone from her pocket.

"Hold out your hand," she ordered, he did as he was told, bracing himself for what was about to happen. As soon as the stone touched the palm of his hand, it blazed with a bright light before dimming back to the dull stone.

"That's it?" he asked incredulously.

"That's it," Morena said as she took the stone from his hand. She turned to Nyx, who shifted uncomfortably. She held out her hand hesitantly. Morena placed the stone in her palm. The light blazed brightly, Nyx pressed her lips into a hard line, her hand trembling. She cried out, dropping the stone. Morena snatched it out of the air, glowering at the girl.

"What was that?" Nyx glared, holding her hand to reveal an ugly red burn at the centre of her palm. Niah's gut clenched.

"The truth stone shows your true intentions. It appears you do have a dark heart." Ragnar drawled, bored by the whole ordeal.

"You know nothing of my heart," Nyx hissed, Cole went to his sister, taking her into his arms.

"What happens now?" he asked, his eyes wide and urgent.

"You have a choice to make," Amarah said gently, "you must choose whether to stay, or leave with your sister."

"That's ridiculous, you really won't let me stay?" Nyx demanded, shoving free of her brother's grip.

"Nyx..." he said warningly, she ignored him.

"The truth stone shows your true intentions. We cannot house anyone who bears us ill will," Amarah said, venom thick in her voice, enough to make Nyx flinch.

"Can we discuss it in private before I give you my answer?" Cole asked, Nyx turned her gaze on her brother, betrayal spread over her features.

"Yes." Amarah sighed impatiently. They were escorted from the room. Niah's stomach twisted, Cole would go with his sister. He wouldn't stay here. If she had any siblings, she would choose them over anything. She turned to Merida who was staring after them, her lips pulled down at the corners, and she knew her Guardian felt the same.

"Young Niah, you look disappointed," Ragnar noted, she turned back to him and bowed her head before answering.

"No, Lord Ambassador. I am grateful you told me, it just didn't help as much as I thought it might."

"The truth doesn't always help us."

"Surely it is always better to hear the truth though?" she questioned; Ragnar leaned forward in his chair once again.

"Do you think that's the same for every situation?" he asked quizzically, his eyes dancing with curiosity.

"I think I would prefer the truth, even if it hurt, Lord Ambassador." Niah felt Merida stiffen beside her.

"Tell me, young one. Do you think it helped the twins to hear that one of them is dark of heart? Do you think it helped them to hear they may or may not have power but would never be able to find out?" he asked, a smirk at the edges of his mouth.

"The truth hurts." Niah shrugged, almost forgetting herself.

"Indeed. Would a lie not be more beneficial in some cases? A dying man told that he was forgiven, even though he wasn't, just so he could be allowed to die peacefully, would that not be fair?" he inquired, Niah's brow pulled together slightly.

"That speaks more of mercy to me, Lord," she replied, Ragnar chuckled.

"Mercy, yes, is that not what lies are? Mercy? In some cases at least," he said, grinning.

"In some cases, Lord. Though all lies have an expiration date," she said quietly, her eyes flicking to Amarah who was watching them both intently. His mouth fell into a grimace, his eyes hardened.

"And that, my child, is the bitter truth."

Niah stood and stared for a moment, frozen in place. Something clicked inside her. All lies had an expiration date. They never lasted. How many more lies would be told before she finally found the truth? How many lies were from their own Elders?

Amarah shifted in her seat as the silence draped around them. Niah kept her eyes low. A good, obedient warrior around her superiors.

Yes. All lies did indeed have an expiration date.

Cole

"You can't actually be suggesting this?" she screamed when the door closed behind them, sealing them inside the windowless room they slept in the night before. Cole stared at Nyx, red-faced and furious.

"I could find out more here, these guys are fighting the Shadows, the same ones we've been hunting for decades. I could stay, learn what they know and come to find you. We could go after them together." he tried to reason with her, she paced with her hands on her slim hips, those sharp canines snapping down.

"What about me in the meantime, huh? What will I do?"

"You're not exactly weak, Nyx. Come on, you could more than take care of yourself," he sighed as he slumped down on one of the beds. It would be hard to be away from her, they had never been away apart since they had been born. But they needed revenge, they needed justice for what they and every other hybrid had been through in those labs. They had been chasing their tails for decades, and now they may finally have a chance to get some real leads.

"That's not the point, Cole! How are you so okay with this? Don't you care about me at all?" she accused, he got to his feet then and took her in his arms.

"Don't say that, you're my sister, my *twin*. I will know if anything happens to you, we still have the necklaces, right? If you're in trouble, activate it and I'll come. You know I will come," he pleaded with her; she was silent for a moment.

"I don't want to lose you," she said in a quiet voice.

"You will *never* lose me," his chest ached at the thought of saying goodbye to her, but they needed this chance. These people hadn't been horrid to them in any way, they had treated them well. Given them food and shelter, somewhere to rest. And were now offering to let him stay. Apart from the whole memory thing, they had been treated far better than they had at the Shadows.

He understood that their laws were laws, it was the same in every country. Still, he hated the idea of saying goodbye to her. Bringing the Shadows down was all they had been focusing on since they escaped, they always said if there was a way to get information, they would take the opportunity, no matter the cost. Though he never imagined the cost would be saying goodbye – even temporarily – to his sister.

"You'd better come to find me before you do anything," she grumbled.

"Of course," he said, he kissed the top of her head and pulled back to look at her. He gave her a reassuring smile which she didn't return. It was easier to convince her to go without him than he thought it would be. Though that didn't mean it would be easy to say goodbye to her. Another thought flashed through his mind.

"I know the dark-haired girl from somewhere," he frowned, Nyx's eyes turned hard.

"Leave that well alone." she warned, he opened his mouth to protest, but she placed a finger firmly over his lips, "Whatever is going on, it's none of our concern. I mean it, Cole, not a word." she glared at him, he rolled his eyes, and she removed her hand. He agreed and hugged her tight once more.

He went to the door and opened it; they were led back to the room they were in previously. The black-haired girl, Niah, looked as if she were going to throw up. They stood before the two figures on the platform.

"What have you decided?" the bronze-skinned woman with way too much eyeliner asked, her gaze icy with those strange gold and silver eyes with no pupils.

"I will stay, my sister will go. Though our weapons were confiscated when we were brought here, I would ask that she be given her weapon," he said clearly, yet not without respect. The guy that had been in the room, the moody blonde stepped forward holding a belt with a sword through it and a bag. Nyx took it from him and rummaged through it to find food and smaller weapons inside. She nodded gratefully, if not stiffly.

There were no more words after that, the guards ushered them from the room, the raven-haired girl followed with the grumpy guy. They stood in a room with a shimmering moss coloured portal that rippled like water. He hugged his sister fiercely. She tapped her shirt where her necklace would be underneath it as she stepped toward the portal. His heart was racing, how had he possibly chosen this over her? His sister.

Perhaps he was the one with the dark heart. He watched her step through the portal, leaving him alone in an alien world, with nobody but strangers. But at least he wasn't alone like she would be. He cursed himself, he could go after her, but she wouldn't forgive him if he put her through this only to return empty-handed. He had to stick it out now, no matter how much his chest ached. He turned to see the guy standing with his hands shoved into his pockets, the girl with her arms folded across her chest, disappointment in her eyes.

"What now?" Cole asked, suddenly feeling very alone and naked in the middle of a lion's den. Which had only happened once or twice.

"Come, we'll take you to your room," the sandy-haired man said, turning on his heel and striding from the room with Niah behind him. He knew her. Recognised her. But his mind was blurry, the image foggy. Where had he seen her? Nyx had called her Ember, the name sounded familiar. He shook the thoughts from his head, they wouldn't do him any good even if he did remember because she didn't know him.

Outside the round building was a whole town, they walked down the steps onto a cobbled stone street bustling with people. Some wearing athletic clothes and some in jeans, normal clothes. He heard the banging of a hammer against an anvil and turned to see an old-fashioned armoury with an outdoor forge as people forged blades. The buildings were all the same, stone with slate rooves and single-paned windows. It almost looked like the whole thing was built decades ago, though there was a pristineness to it that made it seem far newer as if it hadn't long been built.

A little way away from the steps of the Chambers, sat a large fountain with various creatures, hybrids, angels, demons, wolves, fairies, vampires, and spell weavers. He had heard the name used before, though he had always just referred to them as witches, which only seemed to piss them off. He followed the two through the town, getting odd stares as he went.

They came to a large building. The inside was all wood and stone, a large stone fireplace with people sitting in the couches surrounding it, reading. The two climbed the stairs to the next floor and stopped outside a room. The man pushed the door open for him and he stepped inside. A large double bed dominated the space but left more than enough room for drawers, a wardrobe, a desk, and another door on one side, a bathroom perhaps?

His heart swelled before it plummeted, this was the nicest room he had ever seen, and yet his sister would be sleeping in abandoned houses or apartments. Some of them were nice, most of them not. A guilty pang twisted in his gut. The girl strode into the room and opened the wardrobe that wasn't a wardrobe at all. It had hooks in place for weapons, but it was bare, apart from a wooden trunk at the bottom of it.

"You won't need to arm yourself just yet. You need training first," she said, her expression unreadable. She had dark eyes with the same silver ring as his own, except her eyes seemed to be able to see through into your soul; it made him uncomfortable.

"I can already fight," he mumbled, a flash of amusement danced in her eyes as she glanced at the man and back at him, smirking.

"Not very well it seems, I disarmed you in less than a minute," he didn't have an answer to that. He had forgotten about that, and suddenly felt rather emasculated. Another figure appeared in the doorway, a tall, broad guy with muscular arms. He had silver eyes that shimmered and dark brown hair sticking out in all directions as if he had never heard of a brush. His eyes fell on Niah first before sliding to Cole.

"Commander Fin," Niah greeted, "this is the new guy, Cole. This is Commander Fin, and Commander Grenville," she pointed to each of the men as she said their names.

"I should get you to call me that more often," Fin murmured to Niah. Subtle. "It's good to see you when you're not, 'ya know, all unconscious," he grinned and chuckled when Cole's brow furrowed.

"Fin arrived after you passed out yesterday," Niah clarified. Why did it feel like they were mocking him? He shrugged.

"So, you are really lucky because you get to be my new trainee," Fin beamed, was he always like this?

"Think I'd rather train with the girl," Cole muttered, Fin's eyes danced with amusement, Grenville chuckled.

"Do you have a death wish?" Fin asked, Niah smacked him playfully in the chest, he gave her a soft glance before turning back to Cole, looking him up and down.

"Your clothes are weird," he observed. Cole looked down at himself, he wore dark jeans with holes in, black boots which were unlaced, a baggy black, long-sleeved top which also happened to have holes in it, and a long black coat with a large hood. They didn't have many opportunities to get decent clothes.

"Are you just going to make fun of me the whole time?" he demanded; Fin pondered that for a moment.

"More than likely. Now, change into training clothes, I need to assess you," he said as he turned on his heel and strode from the room with Grenville behind him. Niah hesitated in the doorway.

"Your sister, she called me Ember, Why?" she asked, Cole's heart thudded loudly in his ears. He honestly didn't know what her name was, she just seemed vaguely familiar.

He shrugged, "Beats me."

"Can I ask you something?" she asked, her arms folded across her chest. He shrugged again. "Why did you choose to stay here rather than go with your sister?" he gazed at her for a moment as she stood in the doorway. He said nothing, only kicked the door shut, not too gently. Already regretting his decision to stay.

4
Fin

The three of them sat in the kitchen to wait for Cole, Fin had skipped breakfast and made sandwiches for them, mostly because Niah complained of being hungry and he didn't trust her in the kitchen yet.

"So, what did you find out?" Fin asked before taking a bite of his cheese sandwich. Merida had caught him when he returned from patrol and told him about Cole staying and Niah wanting to ask questions, about how it was impossible for there to be hybrid twins.

"Not much, less than I would have liked," she sighed, attacking her sandwich, he chuckled.

"So, what's the plan now? Not only do we need to figure out how the hell you're three hundred years old, and still pretty hot for your age I might add," he winked, she rolled her eyes, her cheeks turning rosy, "we also need to figure out what the Shadows plan is and how to find them."

Gren frowned, "Sounds easy enough."

"I suppose we could go through the archives, see if there's any records of previous Shadow attacks, maybe we can piece together an image of what they have planned, and maybe find a clue as to where they are?" Niah suggested, Gren nodded in agreement.

"Sure, you and I will do that today then, neither of us have patrol," Gren said as he leant against the thick wooden table; Niah hummed in agreement with a mouthful of sandwich.

"You have no manners," Fin said teasingly, she held up her middle finger with a sweet smile. He grinned at her, his chest growing warm. He knew he had a lot to make up for, knew he had to work to earn her trust again. But it was a start.

Cole appeared in the doorway, his dark hair hanging across his forehead, hands shoved in the pockets of his baggy jogger bottoms.

"Right, we'll be off then. See you guys later," Fin said, stroking his hand down Niah's arm as he got up to leave, she offered him a warm, yet somewhat uncomfortable smile as she stood to clear away the plates, Gren moving to help her. He wondered whether she would ever be comfortable with public affection.

Cole walked beside him in silence. His face dark and brooding, he reminded Fin of Gren. Maybe he had been a bit too hard on him. He supposed he could try being nicer, Cole did just say goodbye to his sister after all and was now on a strange island with people he didn't know.

They walked through the town toward the training grounds. Clouds had set in, causing the colour to drain out of the world. The once luscious green fields now looked almost pale and dead. Still, despite the darkened weather, quite a few people were training outside. Hybrids training with swords, some sparring with fists, spell weavers and casters practising magic, lycanthropes in wolf form wrestling with other wolves or hybrids. Fin caught Cole's gaze as he stared in wonder.

"It's like Hogwarts," he muttered, Fin knew what he meant, had watched the movies, Niah read the books. Fin nodded in agreement, if he weren't from this world, he doubted he would have believed it existed.

"So, what's your other half?" Fin asked as he came to a stop and turned toward Cole.

His brow scrunched, "My what?"

Merida had told him what was said during the meeting, how twins were only possible if a demon mated with a fey, lycanthrope, or spell weaver, and the female offspring mated with an angel. It was a lot to process.

"You heard what the Elders said. In order to be a twin, your mother would have been a demon crossed with either a fey or lycanthrope. Morena would have picked up on any magic if you were part spell weaver." Cole didn't look any clearer on the subject.

"Uh...I have no idea," he shrugged. He was too thin, muscled yes, but too thin. He had the build of someone who would have broad shoulders but didn't have the muscle to fill himself out.

"We'll have to find out, your other half could work out to be a gift to use to your advantage." Fin dragged a hand through his hair, "Niah, for example, is part spell weaver; a very rare combination."

"What's the deal with Niah?" he asked, Fin smiled lightly. He knew why he was asking, he liked her, or at the very least found her attractive. "Like, where did she come from?" at that, Fin paused.

"Why do you ask?"

Cole shrugged, "Just curious." Fin narrowed his eyes at the boy, but Cole was looking at the ground. It seemed a weird thing to ask about another person, why wouldn't he ask her himself?

"So, you two are together?" he went on, meeting Fin's gaze once more.

"As much as hybrids can be," he answered guardedly, trying not to give it away that he felt uncomfortable with the topic being Niah's past. His skin prickled, a slight rumble built in his chest, almost as if he was about to growl.

He cleared his throat.

"So, do you not know where she came from?" Cole pressed, "Just I noticed something between you two," Fin tensed and took a deep breath before plastering a fake smirk on his face.

"You'd have to ask her, it's not my business to tell," he shrugged, pretending like he didn't care, despite his stomach twisting at the thought.

Cole nodded and turned away. Why was he asking so many questions about her? He'd seen the way he and Nyx looked at Niah, like they both knew her from somewhere but couldn't quite figure out where from. But there wasn't a hint of recognition in her eyes when she looked at either of them.

He pushed the thoughts from his mind, not being overly keen on the unfamiliar feeling in his chest. He frowned. The guy was new, he didn't understand. Maybe he liked Niah, and Fin couldn't blame him for that. Or maybe it was something else, he had seen the way Cole had looked at her, it wasn't attraction. Fin couldn't put his finger on what it was, either way, he wouldn't let it interfere with training. He was there to help Cole.

They began running. Despite his wiry frame, Cole had great speed and stamina. Even Fin struggled to keep up with him at one point. They stood on the training grounds panting, sweat covering their skin. While Cole was distracted, Fin took advantage and threw a punch at his jaw. Cole saw it at the last second but was too late to dodge or block, Fin's fist connected with Cole's chin, and he sprawled on the ground.

"What the *hell*?" Cole yelled, scrambling to his feet, and squared up to Fin, who tilted his chin up, crossing his arms over his chest.

"Testing your reflexes," he shrugged, Cole was glaring at him with narrowed eyes. His hands balled into fists at his side.

"You don't like me, I get it; you don't have to be a prick though." Cole snapped, clearly annoyed as he backed away a couple of steps.

"You think I did that because I don't like you?" Fin asked, cocking a brow. He had never been accused of that before; most people just accepted the blow for what it was and tried to hit back harder.

"Why else would you do it?"

"As I said, I was testing your reflexes. You need to be alert at all times. If that had been an enemy with a sword, you'd be dead. Don't confuse my training with anything other than what it is, if I didn't like you; you would know." he explained as firmly as he could, authority leaking into his voice. Cole didn't seem to notice, only rolled his eyes, and said 'fine' like a sulky youngster.

"You've not seen much of other species," Fin observed as Cole gazed around the open field at the others training.

He shrugged, "Not really," great; he was acting like a child. Fin whistled. Two lycanthropes looked up in the distance, one of them waved as they started toward them. When they got closer, Fin started patting his knees, whistling, and saying, 'come on boy, come here'. Nick laughed but launched himself at Fin, he stepped aside, the boy righted himself and turned on him.

"You can't just summon us with a whistle every time, 'ya know. We're not dogs," Nick said with a lazy grin. Fin patted him on the head.

"I'll bring you a treat next time."

"I resent that," Rae retorted as she stood with her hands on her hips, glaring at him with narrowed, dark brown eyes. Cole stood staring at Rae, she fixed him with a glower that made him look away.

"What do you want anyway?" Nick asked, stretching out his arms and cracking his neck.

"New recruit, Cole here has never seen a lycanthrope, much less fought with one. I thought it might be beneficial for him to spar with you," Fin smirked, a glint flashed in Nick's eyes as he removed his shirt, showing off the decorative cross tattoo on his back, spanning the width of his shoulders and running down his spine. Rae stepped back, she wasn't the biggest fan of sparring, despite being quite good at it. Nick lowered himself into a crouch, Cole blinked but raised his fists.

"Go." Fin said. Cole stepped first and swung his arm with a closed fist, Nick bent lower under the swing and jabbed him quickly in the ribs. Cole cursed. He was too slow.

This continued for a while, Cole throwing punches or kicks, Nick dodging or blocking and giving him a quick jab here and there. Cole was quickly getting frustrated, so Fin gave Nick a subtle nod, the wolf grinned in response.

His eyes burned bright amber, almost gold, as his teeth lengthened. Cole stared wide-eyed as a growl burned through Nick's throat. Cole crouched low defensively and planted his feet wide. That was good at least.

Nick launched himself at him, Cole's arms went around him and squeezed tightly. Nick struggled to get free of his grip. His skin turned to dark fur, his teeth lengthened further, and his face morphed into that of a wolf. A huge, deep brown wolf, easily fifteen feet tall. Cole staggered back, gazing in shock as the wolf snarled, snapping his powerful jaws. Fin smiled lightly before stepping between the two of them.

"Thanks, Nick," he said over his shoulder, the wolf made an indignant noise before he straightened up into his human form. Naked.

"It was just getting interesting," he grumbled, snatching up his shirt from the ground and wrapping it around his lower half. Rae sighed and shrugged out of her jacket, tossing it to him.

"What did you think of that?" Fin asked, turning his attention to Cole who was still gaping.

"That was weird...really weird," he muttered, Fin chuckled, closing the space between them, and draping an arm around his shoulders.

"It only gets weirder," he said as the two walked back to the town. In hindsight, he hadn't done too badly, very inexperienced considering his time with the Shadows; though it seemed he was used more as an experiment rather than a soldier. He could do well though.

Nyx

It was raining heavily. Her clothes were soaked through, and her hair dangled in front of her eyes as she walked through the busy streets. If her body didn't regulate itself to the temperature, she'd be shivering. People passed with umbrellas, or their hoods pulled up. A group of young women giggled, holding their bags above their heads as they dove into a diner wearing short dresses and strappy heels.

The sky was dark with dense clouds rolling overhead, blocking out the stars. She found the building she was looking for. An old apartment building that had long since been abandoned, boarded up windows with graffiti over the front of it. A painted black doorway with an emblem of a shadowy figure with wings at the top of it. Nyx pushed on the door; it gave easily under her touch. The first floor was how you'd expect to find it. Bare wooden floors, leaking and mouldy ceilings, peeling walls with holes in them. Bottles and cigarette butts scattered around, an old mattress, and a thick stench of smoke and stale alcohol in the air.

In the centre of the space was an old, almost completely collapsed set of stairs, the railings were missing on one side along with a few steps. She picked her way up, finding a door at the top. The same shadowy figure with wings at the top of the door. Twisting the knob, the door opened into a bright white room. It was all white tiles and painted walls with fluorescent lights lining the ceiling. It brought back bitter memories of her childhood. Shoving the thoughts down, she closed the door behind her.

Throughout the room were tables with computers, tablets, scientific and medical equipment. People were sitting behind the desks, their fingers tapping away on keyboards. Nobody looked up at her, almost as if they couldn't see her. They all wore long white lab coats, the women's hair tied back into neat buns at the backs of their heads, the men's combed and slicked back with gel.

She made her way through the room to another door at the far end. Beyond it, was a long corridor with doors leading off either side, at the end was a set of black double doors. Without pausing, she headed straight for it. The doors clattered open. Inside the room was bare and completely black.

Her heart thundered, though she managed to keep her breathing steady. Images blurred into focus before her, images of people sat at desks. Men and women all sat around a large table. They were as clear as if they were actually in front of her. There was a single figure at the head of the table. She was shrouded in a cloud of darkness swirling around her. She had narrow eyes that seemed to bore into you, her mouth curled up in a cruel smile. Nyx walked to the centre of the room, her palms growing slick.

"Nyx, how nice to see you," the woman smiled, she was beautiful and terrible at the same time. The darkness swirled around her as if trying to keep her hidden.

"And you, your Grace," Nyx said with a bow of her head, lowering her eyes out of respect as she clasped her hands behind her back.

"Tell me, where is your brother?" she asked as she gazed around the room. Nyx straightened her spine but kept her eyes low. Her clammy hands trembling behind her back as she struggled to calm her erratic heart.

"He is with the Fury Alliance," Nyx answered quietly, the woman's mouth curled upward. It dawned on her where she was, who she was speaking with. Nyx didn't remember deciding to come here, but she had. Fear gripped her in the same way it did when she was a child and she heard that soft voice. A voice laced with a serpent's venom. Her whole body began trembling.

"You have been with them too, I assume?" the woman asked, tilting her chin upward, her hair cascading over her shoulders like a curtain.

"I have, your Grace," Nyx answered, the woman's lips spread into a grin. Nyx swallowed hard, her heart was unyielding. It didn't make sense, there was no reason why she should be there, yet at the same time, it was the *only* thing that made sense. As if something was stroking her mind, telling her it was all okay and not to be afraid. She was terrified. She should be running, screaming at the woman before her, but the words would not form. Her feet refused to move. Panic rose quickly.

"Can you tell us where they are?" the woman asked, Nyx stiffened. A tendril of darkness caressed her mind, coaxing the truth out of her, making her *want* to give up the information she had found.

"They took us through a portal, we stepped out somewhere I've never seen before. A building with no windows," Nyx explained, her voice trembling slightly. Inside her mind, she was crying. Inside her mind, she pleaded with herself to say nothing more. Only sweet laughter echoed through the darkness that threatened to consume her.

"I see, your brother still has his necklace?" the woman asked with narrowed eyes, Nyx nodded; unable to form the words in her throat. This woman shouldn't know about the necklaces. The woman leaned down and pulled a tablet from a drawer in her desk – she assumed – she tapped the screen a few times, her brow furrowing in confusion.

"He is nowhere to be found," the Queen breathed, "It appears they have created an extremely powerful barrier. I assume the Code of Thamere has been performed, excellent," she said to herself as she dropped the tablet on the desk and

75

placed her elbows on the surface, clasping her hands together as she rested her chin on them, leaning forward in her seat. Nyx expected her to be angry, but the woman's eyes were bright with delight, that cruel mouth pulled up at the corners.

"You told your brother to call on you, didn't you?" she inquired, a light voice radiating through the room. Nyx's stomach churned, she had said that to Cole, but how did this woman know that? Come to think of it, why had Nyx left him there at all? Why didn't she drag him with her? Her stomach roiled.

"Yes, he said to activate my necklace if I'm ever in trouble," she replied shakily, glancing around the room at the other faces scrutinising her. She felt naked. Vulnerable. Violated.

"You have done well, Nyx. I am impressed, there may be a spot as Captain if you keep this up," the woman grinned; Nyx's breath caught in her throat. She only wanted her brother. "Do you know why we picked you above your brother?" the woman went on; Nyx shook her head.

"Speak when asked to!" a terse male voice snapped from the side, the woman silenced him with an icy glare.

"N_No, your Grace." Nyx's hands were balled into fists behind her back. She was speaking without intending to. No longer in control of her own body, barely holding onto her consciousness.

"Your brother is too soft. You are brave and bold. You get things done. That is why we chose you and that is why you will rise through the ranks quickly. I am impressed, Nyx." the woman smiled, a warm, yet untrustworthy smile.

"Thank you." Nyx breathed.

"Be sure to stay close, we will let you know when the time comes, and when it does; activate your necklace. Now that we know your brother is with the Furies, we may have a use for him after all." the woman smiled a devilish smile. Nyx bowed her head, and the images disappeared into the blackness. Her heart began to slow as she lowered herself to the floor, pulling her knees into her chest as she struggled to collect her thoughts and regain control over herself.

Searing pain tore at the back of her neck where the seal once was. She gripped her neck, biting her lip to keep from crying out. It lasted only a moment, but she knew the mark had been reinforced. Her pulse slowed to a steady beat, her palms dried, her mind suddenly clear and focused. She couldn't remember why she had been so nervous, so frightened. Slowly, she left and stood on the steps of the apartment building under the rain, tilting her head back, feeling the water splash onto her skin. She took a deep inhale, feeling stronger somehow. She would obey her Queen. She loved her. And she would prove herself to her.

5

Niah

They sat around one of the tables in the library. The fire crackling to the side as she held her mug of coffee in one hand, the book open on the table in front of her, flicking between pages with her free hand. Stacks of books filled the table. They had been at it for hours. Even Sai and Dea had come to help. Dea, none too happy about being dragged into archive studying, sat on top of the table with crossed legs, skimming through books, only to be scolded by Gren for not taking it seriously.

"What are we going to find in these things anyway?" she scowled as she closed another book and placed it on the 'read' pile.

"There may be some clues as to who we're dealing with," Sai muttered as he gazed down at the pages before him, leaning his head on his hand propped up on his elbow.

"Wouldn't we have found it by now?" she grumbled, nobody answered, she sighed heavily and picked up another book from the 'to be read' pile.

"Hey, what's this?" Niah asked, pushing the book toward Gren. She had been reading about hybrid abilities, speed, strength, and something she hadn't heard of before, demonic possession.

"It's a state we can transform into, it's something we only do in dire situations. There are three different states altogether," he said as he pushed the book back.

"The first state is our human form as we are now, the second state is a partial demonic transformation. We look human, with some demonic traits like a tail, horns, that kind of thing. The third state is when we completely transform into our demonic state," Sai explained, now sitting up and leaning forward eagerly.

"I never knew," Niah muttered, gazing at the picture of a woman with long horns and talons instead of fingers.

"It's not something we introduce straight away, it's not easy to control, stage two isn't too bad, but stage three is dangerous; we can lose ourselves to the demonic power and be stuck like it permanently. As I said, it's only used in dire circumstances," Sai said as he leaned over further to look at the book, Niah pushed it toward him so he could see better.

"Have you guys changed?" she asked, Gren shifted uncomfortably.

"I've been to stage two," Dea said with a small smile, "I have long fingernails like claws and a tail with like a bone blade at the end, like *Tachra* demons," she shrugged, almost looking disappointed.

"Has anyone been to stage three?" she asked, Sai looked at Gren.

"No one has for decades, most don't want to because of the risk. Though the last person who did was able to control himself fully," a smile tugged at the corners of his lips.

Niah cocked her head to one side, "Who was it?"

"Fin," he said, she stared for a moment. Something so powerful and risky, something that could consume you entirely and turn you into a demon. Yet Fin was able to control it, warmth spread through her chest.

Many of the books were the history of their races, not just hybrids. Things called Sages popped up a lot, though there was no explanation as to what or who they were.

"What's a sage?" she asked, feeling suddenly stupid for having so little knowledge on her species. She knew they were supposed to be searching for any mentions of the Shadows, but they could be written into any of the books before them.

"They're just myth, apparently there's like eight of them, but there's only ever seven mentioned in any of these books," Dea sighed as she closed yet another book and threw it on the 'read' pile. The books mentioned Sages, though not what they were, they were only ever mentioned in sentences like: 'this was discovered by a Sage', or 'a Sage found this was the answer', it was very vague. She felt like there was more to it, wanted to know more; though if people thought they were just myths, how could she possibly find any more answers?

It wouldn't be the first time that the people were wrong about what they believed, it wouldn't be the first time that the Elders kept something so important away from their followers.

There wouldn't be anyone in Thamere who would know anything about it, and she didn't trust the Elders not to lie, but there might be those who live outside the protection of the Furies who might be willing to talk. Though she had no idea where to start looking.

It was frustrating that the Elders felt the need to keep such information secret. What would be the incentive behind it? From what was written in the books, the Sages were key figures in some war centuries ago and came up frequently throughout history, then all of a sudden at the end of the last war, they disappeared. Why would such important figures be remembered as nothing more than a myth? It was almost as if they had been erased from memory. Once again, the darkness Niah had been feeling crept into the back of her mind.

The rogue clans and packs would be a good place to start. Even if they didn't know anything about Sages, which may or may not even be real, they may have information on the Shadows. At this point, Niah was willing to settle for any information she could get her hands on.

Her adoptive parents worked with or for the Shadows, along with Karliah and Nolan. The woman Merida claimed was Niah's mother was in a picture with the four of them, and she certainly didn't look like she was being held captive. She supposed it could have been taken before Niah was born, but how was it possible that Merida didn't know about it? If she and her mother were as close as Merida claimed, how did she not know she was working for the Shadows?

It wasn't that she thought Merida was lying, but she didn't necessarily trust her either. Not in the way she once had. The way Merida spoke about her mother, the look in her eyes when she saw the picture, or just in the way she looked at Niah, no, her Guardian didn't know her mother was involved with the Shadows.

Niah doubted herself when she thought about it too hard, was she remembering the picture properly? Did she just want to see something that wasn't there? There could be a perfectly logical explanation, maybe her mother *was* working with them and left when she found she was pregnant? Many theories floated around in her head. Questions she wouldn't get the answers to from books. If anything, they only left her with more questions. It was beginning to get tedious, forever searching for answers, only to be left with nothing.

"Gren, how can we go about finding rogues who may have information on Shadows?" she asked, Gren eyed her curiously.

"It's not a bad idea, though I wouldn't expect them to be much use. Vampires might be the easiest place to start, they have their ear to the ground at all times, listening for any juicy bits of information that might serve them. But you're not going alone, we'll come with you," Gren said, glancing to Sai and Dea, who nodded in agreement.

"When can we go?" she asked as she closed the book, her fingers lingering on the cover. In the top right was a symbol stamped into the leather, a snake in an infinity sign with thorns wrapped around it, piercing the skin. She had seen that symbol on some of the other pages throughout other books.

"I have a meeting to go to now, but after," he said as he got up from the table and strode from the room. She glanced down at the symbol, there was an odd fluttering feeling in her stomach when she looked at it, a feeling she hadn't felt before. She frowned at the book and shoved it into her bag before grabbing another and opening it in front of her.

This one contained some history on hybrids. Centuries ago they were free and wild, territorial, and hostile; their demonic blood turning them into feral beings. They were given a purpose, to fight in the armies that were fighting the demons. Though the name of the organisation under which they fought wasn't mentioned. It was then that they were captured and used by the demons. Nayli freed them. Niah had already heard the story, why they celebrated that day. It was amazing really, how one woman was able to free so many and lead an army to beat back the demons. How powerful must she have been? Where was she now? She frowned at the pages, that niggling feeling at the back of her mind growing darker and more insistent.

Fin

He changed quickly after training, putting on a pair of dark jeans, boots, and a button-down grey shirt. Though formal wear wasn't expected during Council meetings, he still felt like he should at least make an effort. The Council room was already full when he arrived, and Gren had moved to sit next to him.

"How were the archives?" Fin asked quietly as he took his seat. Gren shook his head, 'I'll tell you later'. This probably meant either something important, they found nothing, or they were going to do something a little crazy.

One of the Guardians standing to the side of the door banged his spear on the ground, everyone got to their feet as the Oracle Conclave entered the room, taking their seats at the top of the platform. He seemed to spend more of his time in meetings than anything else, and it was beginning to grind on him not having an outlet for his energy.

Fin glanced around, Benjamin was not in his usual seat, or even in the room. He glanced at Merida, who looked completely unphased, though he knew she would be pleased.

The doors closed, standing just inside them was a tall, slender man with a lean layer of muscle over his frame. He had tanned skin, with dark brown iris' ringed in silver, and dark brown, almost black hair that curled around his ears. He gazed out over the room with an expression Fin couldn't read, it made him uneasy.

"Thank you all for gathering so quickly. This is an urgent meeting," Amarah announced as she gazed out over the faces before her with narrowed eyes surrounded by black liner which made them look impossibly gold.

"As you may know, one of our squads brought back two hybrids as prisoners from patrol. Counsellor Benjamin reacted poorly to the situation and attacked one of the warriors on the squad. As a result, he has been stripped of his title and has been exiled from the Fury Alliance, and therefore, Thamere. He has been sent back to the human world," she explained, waiting for a response. A low murmur ran through the room, some in annoyance, others glad. It appeared Benjamin's number of supporters had grown since the first meeting.

Fin's chest tightened. Merida glanced over her shoulder at him, her lips pulled down at the corners, but there was no mistaking the triumph glittering in her eyes. Merida wasn't one to gloat, but even Fin couldn't deny the satisfaction he felt upon hearing the news. What troubled him, was the growing number of accusatory glances in their direction, and the sudden blanket of tension that draped around the room.

"As much as it pains us that we have had to turn away one of our own, we will not tolerate such behaviour toward another of our warriors. Due to us now being a Counsellor short, we have named Matias, a seasoned warrior of the Santander facility, Counsellor, in his place," she went on, gesturing to the dark-haired man standing by the door, he bowed his head out of respect.

The room was silent. One of the Guardians stepped forward and handed Matias the usual white robes of the Counsellors. He moved to take his seat where Benjamin's had once been. Fin glanced at Merida, her expression now completely unreadable. Nothing else was said about Matias, Fin could have sworn he recognised him from somewhere, though he drew a blank when trying to think of where. A new Counsellor. He glanced around the faces in the room, some of them looked pleased, others sceptical.

Once the meeting was over, he left the Chambers with Gren who was as quiet. He gestured for Fin to follow him, and the two made their way to the edge of the training grounds near the forests. Gren turned to him with a grimace.

"Niah wants to go to see a rogue vampire clan," Fin's stomach clenched tightly at the thought. Niah hadn't had much experience with vampires that weren't in the Alliance, if any. Rogue clans, packs, or fey, were not to be taken lightly. They had survived centuries without the protection of an alliance. They were ruthless.

"Who gave her that idea?" he asked, letting no trace of emotion seep into his voice.

"I did," Gren shrugged, Fin gazed at him blankly. "Don't look at me like that, Fin. She's not stupid, she would have found out sooner or later and she would have gone. I told her we would all go with her."

"Why?"

"The rogue clans may have information on the Shadows that we don't, many of the leaders have been around longer than the Alliance has so it's only logical." When Fin didn't answer, he added, "It's a good idea."

It was. He couldn't deny that.

Fin raked a hand through his hair, "I don't like this."

"Neither do I. But it could give us answers," he answered, gazing at the sky.

"Or end up in disaster." Fin sighed again, he couldn't disagree though. He said nothing more, and they began walking back toward the barracks to change into their patrolling clothes.

"She doesn't need wrapping in bubble wrap," Gren murmured as they passed through the winding streets of the town.

"I know," Fin answered darkly. He didn't need Gren or anyone else to tell him he shouldn't be so protective of her, she was more than capable of looking after herself; she didn't need anyone else. But she was too reckless, she didn't think things through entirely and acted on impulse. He'd seen how she was at the compound, saw the bloodlust and anger in her eyes as she cut down soldier after soldier. The way she didn't hesitate to hand herself over, or step in front of the other, growling at them as if she barely knew them.

All a ploy, he knew, to let Nolan and Karliah think they were nothing to her. So that they wouldn't be used against her.

"What is she hoping to find out from the rogues?" he questioned. Gren had already mentioned the Shadows, but he wondered if she were looking for information about herself too.

Gren exhaled slowly and dragged a hand through his sandy hair, "The Shadows mostly. She read about the Sages and wants to know whether they know anything about them too. I get the feeling she's keeping something from us though."

"Yeah, I can't exactly blame her for that though." Fin chewed out through gritted teeth.

Gren eyed him curiously, "What did you do?"

"Niah is over three hundred years old. Don't ask me how it's possible, we don't know."

"We?"

"Merida and I. She's Niah's Guardian." Gren sucked in a sharp breath.

"How long have you known?"

"Since before we found her."

"Damnit," Gren hissed, "this doesn't work without trust, Fin. If she's keeping things from us because she doesn't trust us, it could get us all into a serious mess."

"It's not her fault. It's mine and Merida's. We have to be there for her right now, show her she can trust us."

"Of course. *She's* not the one I'm annoyed with." That was all Gren said.

"Trust me, no one's more annoyed at me than I am."

Gren eyed him, "Is there anything else I should know?"

Fin paused, "It's not my business to tell." Merida was the one who should tell them, all of them. But he knew she wouldn't until she was ready.

"Well, let's just hope Queen Leandra isn't in the mood for one of her petty games." Gren murmured. Fin was inclined to agree. The vampire Queen was cold and cruel, she had a nasty tendency to play games with the Alliance because she despised everything they were.

Niah was playing a dangerous game, with rogues she knew nothing about. He only hoped she would trust him enough to listen when things got bad. Because it was inevitable that they would.

He decided to leave Cole in Thamere, he wasn't trained enough and would have been more of a liability. Fin met up with the others outside the Chambers, giving Niah a quick kiss on the cheek as always. She smiled, her cheeks turning rosy as she glanced around to see if anyone was watching.

Dea looked like she was going to a party, wearing blood-red lipstick and thick dark eye makeup as well as thigh-high heeled boots; her snowy hair falling down her back in curls. Her spear was strapped to her thigh, and he knew an assortment of daggers was hidden on her person. He didn't question her attire, he'd seen her take on a pack of demons in higher heels than that before.

They stepped through the rippling portal to find themselves in a wet alley between two tall buildings. It was night, rain poured down around them as people with umbrellas hurried by just outside the opening to the alley. They each pulled their hoods up, Dea sulking as her hair got wet and the curls fell out; he couldn't help but laugh.

The streets were alight with street lamps, billboards, shops, and restaurant lights. People hurried past, taking shelter in shops or diners, people laughing, people frowning, people arguing. They made their way through the busy streets until they came across a large dark doorway with a minimalistic sign hanging above it saying, 'Underworld'. A queue of people lined the wall, a large dark-eyed man stood outside the door, holding the rope aside for people to come through as another equally muscular man with blonde hair checked their id's.

Fin stepped in front of the first man. His dark eyes raked over him as if to say, 'who the hell does he think he is?', Fin cocked his head to the side, giving him a lopsided smile. The man straightened his spine, tilting his chin up in response.

"I guess you're not going to fall for my charms?" Fin smirked, the man's nostrils flared, he opened his mouth to speak, but quickly shut it when Dea sashayed toward him. She grazed the back of her fingers down his cheek, his lids fluttered, and she gave him a dazzling smile. The man was completely at her mercy. Fin glanced over his shoulder at the others, Sai stifling a laugh while Gren shifted from one foot to the other, Niah was staring up at the building, likely looking for escape routes.

"What about *my* charms?" Dea whispered in his ear, he cleared his throat and stepped aside. Loud groans and curses echoed from the line of people as Fin and the others hurried inside the club.

The music thumped through the ground, up through his boots and into his bones. It reminded him of that night on Niah's birthday in Perth. The lighting was mostly dark, blues and greens streaked across the room like lasers dancing along with the music. At the far end of the room was a platform with a huge screen behind it, colours danced across the screen to match the lasers, below was a DJ booth with a man bobbing his head to the music with headphones over his ears.

The dancefloor was just below them, steps leading down onto the almost glass looking floor as bodies swayed and bounced to the beat. Booths lined one wall with people sitting in them, shouting over the music. Humans. Smoke floated along the floor, engulfing the legs of the dancers.

There was a spiral staircase near the bar which looked as if it had been moulded from ice. Standing at the bottom of the staircase stood a large man with a shining hairless head, his hands clasped together in front of him.

He eyed them approaching, his eyes danced with amusement and something darker as his gaze slid over Dea, then Niah. He glanced at her, if she noticed how she was being ogled, she didn't show it, and scowled at everyone the same way she did when he saw her in the compound.

"Private." the man said sharply as they stepped closer to the staircase. Fin grinned wickedly.

"We're here to see the Queen," he announced, the man eyed them suspiciously. He muttered something into the radio on his shoulder before nodding and stepped aside to let them through. The top of the stairs opened up to a long balcony overlooking the club. It was full of tables and booths with people sitting around them, each holding a glass of something thick and scarlet. Blood.

At the far end of the balcony was a set of black double doors with gold decoration engraved into them. Two muscled men stood on either side with the same look as the guard at the bottom of the stairs. The men pushed the doors open without meeting their gaze.

Inside was a dark room with slate floors and black walls with gold lining the ceilings. Either side of the room was lined with black leather booths with tables at the centre. They were all full of attractive people with more glasses full of blood.

At the head of the room was a dark stone platform with a huge black throne sat upon it with thick animal furs around the base, draping down the steps. The throne looked to have been made, or at least decorated to look like it was made of painted bones. The crown of it was skulls with gold rings around the eye sockets. Sat upon the throne was a dainty woman, wearing a tight, ebony dress that fell over her legs and brushed the floor, a slit running to her hip on one side, baring her slim legs. Her arms rested on those of the throne, her long fingers dangling over the edge with sharp nails painted black with gold tips.

She had narrow, crimson eyes, impossibly bright within all the black in the room. Her hair, matching the colour of her eyes, piled high on top of her head in thick braids. She wore a golden crown, which looked to be made of painted gold skeletal hands, and thick makeup with bright red lipstick. Her skin was pale and poreless, smooth as glass. Her mouth narrow in her oval-shaped face as she sat with amusement glinting in her eyes as they raked over the five of them, blazing wickedly. She made a small, indignant noise. And smiled.

Niah

The woman before them was as beautiful as she was deadly. She had the grace of a dancer as she gestured for the man to her left to bear his wrist. He wore a single bow tie around his neck, and a pair of faded blue jeans, his chest bare. He offered his wrist to her without hesitation, and she took hold of his arm firmly as she opened her mouth. Her incisors lengthened into sharp fangs as she bit down on his wrist, non-too gently. The man winced. Niah's blood spiked in annoyance, her hands balling into fists as her mouth pressed into a firm line.

It was all she could do to stop herself from launching at the so-called Queen and ripping the crown from her head. The vampire woman released the man, he stepped back cradling his arm as blood dripped onto the floor. He was smiling, a pink flush covering his cheeks.

The woman turned back to them, not bothering to wipe away the blood trickling down her chin. She was challenging them, showing them they had no control or power here.

"Hybrids, what do you want?" the vampire drawled, her eyes narrowing into scarlet slits as she crossed one leg over the other.

"Queen Leandra, how nice to see you," Fin smiled with a respectful bow of his head, the Queen smirked.

"Manners of gold as always. It's been a while, Fin," she said with a grin as she rose to her feet, the black of her dress pooling around her feet.

Fin straightened his spine, "I have come to ask you for some information," her gaze darkened slightly, and she slid her eyes over their faces before they rested on Niah. She held her gaze, unyielding; despite the elbow to her ribs from Dea.

"This one doesn't have the same respect as you do," Leandra murmured as she tore her gaze away, turning back to Fin with a scolding glare. Fin stood completely still. Niah glanced at him, hoping he would let her rip Leandra's smug head off, but no such luck.

"Forgive her, she is young," he said, his voice flat and toneless. The woman tilted her chin upward and descended the dais. She wore a metallic bracelet on her right hand, the chains ran along the back of her fingers, reaching caps on her fingertips, long and decorative, as black as night and as sharp as a blade. *Ruclite*.

"What information is it you desire?" the woman asked, glancing over her sharp nails absentmindedly, feigning disinterest.

"We wish to know any information you have on the Shadows," Fin answered firmly, yet still with respect. At this, the woman's eyes flashed up to meet his and narrowed.

"Such information will not be cheap," she said, a wicked grin dancing at the corners of her mouth as she took her seat on the throne once more.

"What is it you require?" Fin asked, she looked thoughtful for a moment.

"I want to drink the blood of a hybrid, I hear it's divine," she dragged her tongue along her top lip for emphasis, Niah felt her friends stiffen around her, the tension suddenly palpable.

"You know we cannot do that," Fin murmured through gritted teeth.

"I know the Fury Alliance does not allow you to, but how about for personal reasons?" she inquired, quirking up a delicately arched brow.

"You know full well the reasons why the Alliance does not allow us to be drunk from," Fin said tersely, respect vanishing from his voice.

"Because you would be bound to me for eternity? Come now, Fin, don't tell me you believe in such myths," she said with a slow, easy smile. An image formed behind Niah's eyes, a feeling, a colour. Her magic stirred in response.

"If only it *were* a myth. Queen Leandra, you know full well if you drink from a hybrid, your venom will cause that being to be loyal to you, bound to you in all matters." Dea retorted, the woman's eyes shifted to the snowy-haired warrior as if she were seeing her for the first time.

"If you do not agree to payment, you will not have your answers," she said with a shrug of her narrow shoulders as she leaned back in her throne. Niah stepped forward.

"Drink mine," she said firmly, the woman's eyes widened with delight as she got to her feet.

"No." Fin protested, "Niah, you don't understand, if she drinks your blood, her venom will cause you to obey her, your freewill will be stripped from you." her magic swirled in her veins, pushing against her skin. She had no idea what it was, but she trusted her magic. Trusted the feeling flooding her veins.

She gave him a hard look, hoping he would see what she was trying to tell him, "We need answers." He held her gaze for a long moment, realisation finally shone through them, and Niah turned back to the Queen. Leandra's eyes danced excitedly, wickedly. Niah held her wrist out, the woman almost leapt from her throne and took hold of her firmly. Her teeth lengthened, and she bit down hard.

Searing pain spread through Niah's wrist and up her arm as the vampire's fangs plunged deep into her skin. A burning sensation ran through her veins, quickly chased by an icy embrace as her blood drained from her. She gazed at the woman drinking her blood curiously. An unfamiliar feeling, though after the first few seconds, it dulled to an almost pleasurable ache. Niah remembered the feeling and colour that had shown itself to her and concentrated on imagining it spreading down her shoulder and arm to her wrist, and being sucked up by the vampire Queen.

The woman quickly jerked away clutching at her throat. The vampires in the room were on their feet in an instant, advancing on them with bared fangs, hissing like snakes. One of them pressed a pistol to Niah's temple. The others struggled against the vampires, she heard Fin shout her name, but Niah remained perfectly still, expressionless as she watched the woman gasping for breath in front of her. She lowered her arm to her side, the puncture holes already healed, her skin smeared with black blood.

"Stop!" the Queen shouted as she struggled to straighten herself up, she was panting, her wide eyes locked with Niah's, "Let them go, lower your weapons. Now!" the vampires reluctantly did as they were ordered, retreating to a safe distance, though still poised if needed.

"What did you do?" Leandra hissed, she spat, black tinted saliva spattered on the floor.

"Nothing at all," Niah smirked. The woman was outraged. She launched herself at Niah with her metal-clad fingers outstretched. Before the claws could touch her, Leandra cried out in pain and dropped her hand to her side, breathing hard.

Niah wasn't smiling anymore.

"What have you done to me?" Leandra screamed. Niah said nothing. She didn't know what she had done.

"Regardless. You agreed to give us information on the Shadows if you fed on hybrid blood. Honour the bargain." Gren warned.

The Queen glared at Niah, "Fine. Follow me." she turned toward the back corner of the room where a dark door hid in the shadows. Niah didn't turn back as she followed the vampire

Queen through the door into a large room filled with shelves upon shelves of books.

"This is all the information I have on them." Leandra sneered, gesturing to a shelf of books, and striding to the large desk to wipe her mouth on a handkerchief.

"Thank you," Fin said graciously.

"Just take them and get out." Leandra hissed, turning on her heel and stalking from the room, the door slamming behind her. Niah didn't turn to face the others, she didn't want to see the looks on their faces.

"What *was* that?" Dea asked, though not specifically at Niah.

"Is it possible we were wrong?" Sai asked.

"No, it's been known for centuries." Fin answered. She could feel his gaze burning into her, though he made no move toward her. She turned to Gren, he dipped his chin and handed her his rucksack, the two started silently filling it.

How could she explain to them what had just happened when she wasn't even sure she understood it herself?

She had no idea what she had done, only that a thought or feeling had manifested. Perhaps Cassia or Vinaxx would have some answers. She turned then, Gren and Fin exchanging an odd look, Sai and Dea muttering about some of the vampires.

She turned away from them, her heart pounding relentlessly. Leaning her hands on the desk, her head lowered as she closed her eyes and took a few deep breaths, willing her heart to calm.

She had never felt more undeserving of her power until that moment. She didn't even know what she had done. She clenched her hands into tight fists to stop them from trembling and stared down at the wood of the desk. Someone pressed into her side, but she didn't look up.

"What was that?" Fin murmured close to her ear, a shiver crawled up her spine. She shook her head.

"I don't know," she looked up, his silver eyes shimmered slightly, worried. He nodded once and turned away to shove more books into Gren's bag.

Niah was pleased to be in the cool night air. The building had suddenly felt too small as if the walls were closing in, the air too thick to breathe. The rain had stopped, the air was fresh and clean as they made their way through the streets until they found a dark alley where they could activate the orb.

Fin ran his thumb over the glass surface and threw it at the wall, it shattered into a shimmering green portal. Despite the orbs shattering, they would automatically become whole again on the shelf in its assigned space.

They stepped inside the portal room, each signed the book in blood to show they were who they appeared to be. Outside the Chambers, the streets were bustling. People were hurrying, hanging white sashes from the lampposts, from buildings, vines of bright green leaves and white flowers. Candles were set up throughout the streets leading toward the training grounds where a huge pyre was being built. Archways with more white cloth, vines, and flowers curled around them, leading the way to the main event. Tables and chairs and benches lay scattered about on the grass. Trees stood where they hadn't before with jars dangling from the branches with candles inside. During the daylight, it didn't look particularly amazing, though at night; it would be magical.

"What is all this?" Niah breathed as she gazed around at the beauty that was Thamere.

"We're getting ready for the Day Of New Life celebration. It's the one event we hold annually," Dea said with an excited grin as two fey women hung more jars in the tree branches, another wrapping the trunk in glistening white silk.

"I heard about it, but I never imagined anything like this," Niah muttered, Dea caught her hand.

"You will learn."

"I'm going to put these in my room, we can study them later. We should help get things set up," Fin said as he slipped the strap of the backpack from Niah's shoulder. He gave her a small smile before hurrying through the crowded streets. Niah frowned after him but turned to follow Dea into the flow of people.

As well as white flowers, silks, and luscious green vines, people also carried baskets of pink and pale blue flowers, baskets of food like bread and cheese, fruits, and vegetables.

"The feast is very traditional, tomorrow will be spectacular, you'll see," Dea enthused as she picked up a basket of flowers from one of the long tables on the training grounds, Niah picked up another.

Her mind was still reeling from what happened at the club. In her confused state, she had forgotten to ask about the Sages, had forgotten to ask for more information on the Shadows rather than just books. It wasn't likely that Leandra would have answered any of her questions anyway. Not after what she had done to her.

Still, it did nothing to ease her growing suspicion that she was missing something.

They walked toward a group of girls sitting on the grass, making chains out of the flowers. Cherry blossoms, azaleas, begonias, calla lilies, hydrangeas, and blue stars. The girls chained them together in a pattern of blue, pink, and white.

"Do they have a meaning?" Niah asked as she attempted to chain two flowers together, but they ended up crumpling between her fingers. Dea's fingers, however, were swift and delicate as she chained the pattern together quickly.

"The white is for purity and cleansing. After the hybrids were freed, they wanted something pure to relate to. The pink and blue are just pretty," she smiled, keeping her eyes on the task at hand. "Which reminds me, we need to find you a dress for tomorrow."

Niah didn't have dresses, the only dress she had ever worn was the entirely too short black dress Dea had insisted she keep on her birthday.

"Do we *have* to wear dresses?" Niah groaned, hoping it wouldn't be mandatory.

Dea looked up and smiled, "No, not if you'd be comfier in something else. It just has to be white."

Niah had never been girly, not really by choice. Between her usual style or being girly, she would rather wear jeans because it was all she knew before she met Dea. She grew up in the compound where she didn't exactly get to choose her clothes, they were all given to her by Karliah. She had no friends, especially female friends to teach her femininity. She had grown up beating them instead, which never seemed to go down too well.

The thought of having her own style had never occurred to her. She never thought about dresses or makeup. Though Dea seemed to pull off being both feminine and fierce better than anyone else. As she glanced around the group of girls; they were the same. Some had more of a boyish look, some wore makeup and prettier clothes. Niah shrugged, she was comfortable with what she wore. But maybe it wouldn't hurt to try it. After all, she hadn't hated wearing the dress on her birthday.

In the time it had taken for Dea and the other girls to finish chaining together the rest of the flowers from the basket, Niah had managed to form a half-decent single chain. Dea had squeaked and clapped when Niah sheepishly presented it to her. The two got to their feet, it was nearly sunset as they walked into the centre of town toward the clothes shop next to the armoury.

Though shop was the wrong term for it. The Alliance had no currency, they didn't exchange items or money, they simply made things and whoever wanted it could have as their own. It was a very simple way of life.

Money wasn't needed in Thamere. They grew their own food, the farmers being those who were looking for a quiet life rather than being a warrior; though they were expected to fight if the need arose. The same for anyone who chose to make clothes or armour or weapons, the bakers, the restaurant, and bar owners. If anything was needed, the spell weavers found a way to acquire it.

Dea was skimming through the racks of dresses, there were plenty of them, all white and floaty for tomorrows celebration. Niah's fingers grazed over the soft fabric. Many of the dresses were light and floaty, almost transparent.

Dea pulled out a long white dress with narrow straps and a sweetheart neckline. The material was thin, with two pieces of material on either side of the waist to tie together around the back. The skirt hung almost to the floor, a small slit running to just above the knee on one side.

"This is it," Dea breathed as she held the dress out for Niah, she took it hesitantly, it was so delicate that she was afraid she may tear it. It was beautiful.

"Thank you," Niah smiled lightly, she didn't know what else to say. She forced a smile, wanting to please Dea and show her gratitude, but her mind was on Leandra, on Fin and the look he had given her. It felt as though a rift was forming between them. She wanted to trust him and told herself time and time again that she could. After what he'd kept from her, she was sceptical as to whether he was hiding anything else. At the very least, he had trusted her when dealing with Leandra.

She sighed, running a hand through her hair, she needed to speak to him.

"Can I ask you something?" Dea asked, her tone suddenly serious, Niah's heart skipped a beat, "What happened with the Queen?"

Niah's brow furrowed slightly as she turned for the door, "My magic, I imagined it going into her as she drank my blood. I don't exactly know what it did, but it stopped her having control over me." Dea nodded and didn't press the matter further.

"I'm going to go shower," Niah said quickly, not bothering to wait for a reply before running down the street toward her building, the dress gripped tightly in her hand.

She closed herself in her room and dropped the dress on the bed, numbly removing the weapons from her person to hang them up in the cupboard. Her head throbbed as she stripped and stepped into the shower, not bothering to wait for the water to heat.

Sometimes it was all too much. With so much going on inside her head, constant thoughts and theories swirling around, it became almost impossible to focus on just one thing. She had tried spending time alone to try and sort through the jumble in her head, trying to come to terms with everything that had happened in England and Perth.

Katarina and Jeremiah were alive. She may have destroyed the locket and thrown away the book, but that was only a small piece of what they had left behind. Whether she liked it or not, they had left their mark on her, and there was no way to rid herself of it. The same could be said of Nolan and Karliah.

Her real mother was out there somewhere, likely held captive by the Shadows. Merida was her Guardian. It all felt like it was moving too fast. Like there was a constant hum in the back of her mind that was growing more insistent as the days dragged by. Whenever she tried to think things through, all the noise in her head would fall silent, and there would be nothing but numbness in her body, her heart.

Keeping herself busy seemed to keep the thoughts at bay, but how long could she go on like that for before she boiled over? Even now, the embers in the pit of her stomach flickered in response to the demanding thoughts. She tried to hide it, tried to ignore it, but it was always there. Smouldering away, demanding blood, demanding revenge.

Oh how she wanted to obey. If only so the thoughts would go away. If only so that she wouldn't feel so *angry* all the time.

She could have just cut her palm and squeezed her blood into a glass for Leandra to drink, but no, she wanted to see what her magic could do. She wanted to see the vicious Queen choke. Something within her purred in response when it all happened. Not her magic, usually so innocent and playful, but something beneath that. Something dark and insistent that stoked the fire of anger in her stomach.

A shiver crawled up her spine.

It wasn't until Leandra lunged for her and cried out that Niah sobered from the bitterness flooding her veins and realised what she had done.

She glanced down at her trembling hands and wondered what lurked beneath her skin.

6
Fin

He didn't go to his room as he had said, and wasn't sure why he lied. Or maybe he had fully intended to go to his room, but his legs automatically took him somewhere else. He wasn't sure which. His mind was racing with solutions, explanations as to what had happened with the vampires. He found himself heading for Merida's house. She didn't answer when he knocked on the door, and it opened when he tried the handle. The house was in darkness, the curtains pulled shut, the fire unlit. A sudden twist formed in his gut as he closed the door behind him.

"Merida?" he called, no answer. Not even a whisper of movement in the house, perhaps she wasn't in. That's what a normal person would think. But Fin had seen this before. He dropped the bag at his feet and crept through the house. He took the stairs one at a time soundlessly. Her bedroom door was open, though there were deep claw marks embedded in the wood, the same on the railings, walls, and floors. He pushed the door open. There, huddled in the corner was a figure. She was quivering, her knees pulled tight into her chest, her head buried behind them as she hugged them to herself like a protective barrier. Her lank hair fell free over her shoulders, and her skin was greyer than he had seen it in a long time. Dark veins appeared under her skin and worked their way up her arms, down her thin legs.

He crouched in front of her; his hands up so she could see he wasn't a threat.

"Merida," he whispered gently; she didn't move. She was trembling, muttering something to herself that Fin couldn't make out. He edged closer.

"Merida," he said again, louder. She froze. He involuntarily stopped breathing as he watched her head begin to slowly rise. Her eyes narrowed as she looked at him, the whites of them had turned black, the iris still the same dark blue with the familiar silver ring around them.

Her nails were long and blackened. Her fingers twitched as though they had a mind of their own. Her head cocked to one side with an audible crack, a growl forming in her throat: low and guttural. She launched herself at him, claws and canines bared. He caught her and they fell backwards, his back colliding with the wall.

"Damnit," he cursed under his breath as he struggled with the squirming ball of rage perched on his chest, slashing down at him with her claws. "Merida! Merida, stop!"

She raised her hand, bringing it down hard, slicing through his jacket made to protect him against this sort of attack. Blood bloomed on his skin, staining his shirt.

Pain seared through his chest, then his cheek as she slashed at him over and over with those sharp claws. He knocked her away from him, but she kept coming. Fin scrambled to his feet as she lowered herself into a crouch. She lunged. He stepped around her, catching her in his arms, and pressing her back into his chest. She squealed and struggled to get free, his grip held.

"Merida?" a familiar voice called from downstairs.

"Vinaxx, hurry up," by some miracle, the very person he needed turned up. Boots thundered on the stairs, and the white-haired man barged into the room. His eyes were wide as he gazed at Merida. His hands glowed white and he pressed them to the sides of her head.

Merida went limp against him, no longer fighting. Her breathing deepened as she fell into unconsciousness. The veins receded on her skin as it turned a lighter grey.

He scooped her up and lay her on the bed. Opening one of her eyes to find the whites of them had returned to normal. Vinaxx slumped on the stool at the desk in the corner of the room. He was breathing hard, suppressing Merida's demonic state drained him. And it was only getting worse as the days went on.

"We must go to the Oracle Conclave with this," Vinaxx muttered, clear and stern.

Fin was already shaking his head, "You know what they will do."

"My regular administrations are no longer enough, I cannot keep this up, and neither can she," Vinaxx said angrily, glowering at Fin. He held his gaze.

"We can't, not yet." he protested, turning back to Merida. Vinaxx sighed, raking a hand through his hair.

"The next time this happens, we will have to." Fin nodded. Vinaxx left without another word or even a second glance at Merida. Fin frowned after him, he usually stayed for a while after to catch his breath and keep an eye on her.

Fin retrieved the bag from downstairs before sitting at the desk in her room and flicking through them while she slept. No matter what she said, she would need him there when she woke up.

The books were mainly records of events from history. Any mention of the Shadows was brief and nothing they hadn't already known.

One interesting thing was that the books said the Shadows were ruled by a Queen, which is where Queen Leandra got the idea to call herself Queen of the Nights Legion. She was the main leader of the rogue vampires, though there were other clans throughout the world, most of them reported to Leandra.

Another thing he noticed was that throughout the books was the same symbol of a silhouette with wings. He hadn't seen it before; it could be the Shadows emblem perhaps. There was mention of an assassin they had in their army. An assassin so lethal that no one ever saw them coming. An assassin so deadly they were known as the Angel of Death.

The account of the assassin was brief. There was an order to flee on sight. There was nothing that described who the assassin was, if anyone knew their identity, they hadn't lived to tell the tale. The assassin was responsible for thousands of hybrid deaths. They killed many rogues too and destroyed an entire illegal market within a matter of minutes.

Other than that, there was nothing useful. He sighed heavily as he gazed down at the pages, his head began to throb. How much more of this could they endure?

The sun had set outside, the room darker now. Merida shifted, sitting bolt upright on the bed, panting hard as she gazed around the room; her eyes resting on Fin.

"Fin_I_W_What happened?" she rasped, the fear in her eyes showed she already knew.

"You lost control," he said flatly. She flinched. He felt no sympathy, she should be telling him when she feels as though she's about to snap. He wanted to comfort her, to go to her; but he kept his place at the desk. Her eyes widened, her hands fluttered to her mouth, he realised she was staring at his chest.

"I did that to you? And your cheek?" she asked, he rubbed his thumb over the skin where the cut had healed, and the blood had dried. He nodded. She began shaking her head, tears spilling down her cheeks.

"I don't want to be like this anymore." she sobbed, Fin got to his feet and crossed the room to sit on the edge of the bed. He took her hand in his, smoothing the skin of her knuckles with his thumb.

"You must, only for a short time," he muttered.

"But...I want to go," she whimpered, he gazed at her for a long moment. He wanted to do as she asked, to take her to the Overseer; but she had made him swear a long time ago that he wouldn't let her go until she had found both Niah and Marina.

"We must find Marina first," he murmured. Her teary eyes widened; her face crumpling as she started to cry harder. He folded her into his arms, her body racked with sobs against his chest.

They had run out of time.

Niah

She knocked on the door to Cassia's room in one of the spell weaver buildings. The woman opened it with a grin, wearing a bright pink coat belted together at the waist with a thick black leather strap, her hips flared out to the sides with a dark blue skirt floating down to her ankles. Gold bracelets jangled around her wrists as she stepped aside to let Niah through the door.

The room was much larger than it appeared from the outside. A large four-poster bed sat against one wall, along with a set of drawers, nightstands, and a wardrobe that looked as if it were an actual wardrobe rather than a weapons cupboard. In front of the bed sat a long pink upholstered sofa with black claw-like legs sticking out the bottom, a dark coffee table, and a fireplace holding a pink flame.

On the other side of the sofa in a small alcove was a table with two chairs facing each other. The small room was filled with shelves of books and jars of various ingredients; it was more like a studio apartment rather than a bedroom. Niah slumped down on the pink sofa, the leather groaning as it adjusted to her weight.

"What is it, child?" Cassia asked as she leant forward and poured two mugs of tea from a pot that hadn't been there a moment ago.

"I did something today, something I've not been shown how to do," she said carefully, watching for Cassia's reaction, the weaver only smiled, her eyes regarding her thoughtfully.

"How wonderful."

Niah's brow furrowed as she reached to take the mug of tea that Cassia held out to her, "Wonderful?"

"Yes, you are learning things on your own, it's a good thing." Cassia smiled warmly.

"What do you know of vampire bites?" Niah asked, trying a different approach.

"Well, they turn humans into vampires. If a human gets bit, the venom acts as a drug, causing the human to crave being bitten. To turn a human into a vampire, the victim must die with vampire venom in their system. It doesn't have much effect on us magic types as we use it in potions, it can make lycanthropes mad and cause them to stay in their wolf states in severe cases. Hybrids would be bound to them, their free will stripped away, made to do the vampires bidding." she explained almost absentmindedly as if checking off a list in her head.

"Leandra bit me."

Cassia stilled, her tea halfway to her lips, "Then how are you here?"

Niah shrugged, "That magic I told you about, I'm not sure what I did, but I was hoping you could tell me." she watched for Cassia's reaction, the weaver pressed her lips into a firm line, gently placing her mug on the table between them.

"Explain what happened," Cassia murmured. Niah told her the story, the colour or feeling forming in her mind and going into Leandra.

Cassia was quiet for a long time before saying, "You nullified the venom."

"I'm not sure, she acted as if she had swallowed poison." Niah frowned, a shudder crawling up her spine at the memory.

"Interesting."

Niah sighed irritably, "How so?"

"I've just never heard of such a thing. I must ask you not to tell anyone else about this. I would like some time to try and find anything that may help you." she said as she got to her feet and hurried into the alcove, sifting through various books. Niah sighed and scratched at the back of her neck, her throat closing up as she turned for the door.

"Sure." she mumbled.

Niah was opening the door when a pulse hammered through her veins. Her eyes widened as pain lanced through her chest, the air hitching in her throat. A name formed in her mind, *Merida*.

A strangled whimper escaped her clenched teeth and she stumbled back, falling back into the room. Cassia was there immediately, her eyes wide and burning bright pink, the door slammed shut on a phantom wind. Niah couldn't get enough air into her lungs, her chest heaving with the effort as that voice whispered Merida's name into her mind once again.

"What's going on?" Cassia demanded; her hand glowing as she pressed it to Niah's chest. Her heart instantly calmed, her mind settling as she regained control of her breathing.

"I think something's wrong with Merida," she rasped, Cassia's hand dimmed, but her eyes were still wide.

"Go to her," she said firmly. Niah was instantly running despite the burning ache in her chest.

She slammed into Merida's door; freezing when she reached the bottom of the stairs. The house was in darkness. The sun had gone down, and thin streams of light streaked across the floors through the gaps in the curtains.

Up the railings were deep claw marks gouged into the wood, on the walls, on the floors. Niah palmed her dagger and crept up the stairs. The faint sound of sobbing rippled through the house. The voice whispered once again and she took the stairs two at a time, darting across the hall to find Merida crying in Fin's arms.

He pressed his lips together, his silver eyes wary and guarded. Merida didn't look up. She looked so small and fragile in Fin's arms. Niah's chest cleaved open. Merida was always so strong and doing so much for everyone else, seeing her reduced to such a state was almost unbearable. Niah knew she wasn't well but had no idea it was so bad.

Fin gestured for her to come into the room. Her feet moved on their own and she dropped to her knees in front of the two. Dread curled in her gut as she watched her Guardian. Merida jerked away when Niah reached for her hand, her eyes impossibly wide as she trembled with fear.

Her skin was sickly pale, her hair plastered to her forehead. The backs of Niah's eyes burned, and her hand fell limply to her side. Her stomach roiled as she tried to swallow the tightness in her throat.

Merida looked at her then, the fear vanishing from her eyes, leaving only tearful joy, "Marina," Merida gasped, throwing her arms around Niah's neck.

It took a second to drag herself out of shock before she hugged Merida to her chest. Niah didn't know what to do. She cradled her Guardian against her chest, rocking them both side to side slightly as she hummed a gentle tune.

She was aware of Fin watching them. His eyes were shimmering silver pools when she met his gaze. He said nothing, only laid his hand atop hers, his thumb stroking across her knuckles.

"Marina, how did you get here?" Merida croaked, pulling away slightly to meet Niah's gaze. Her chest ached. She had no idea Merida was so ill. She'd known there was something she was keeping from her, but she didn't imagine something like this.

"I'm Niah," she whispered; her brow pulled together as she gazed at their interlocked hands on the bed. Merida's hands stilled in hers, Niah looked up to see hurt and bewilderment on her features. She whimpered, fresh tears rolling down her cheeks as a small smile tugged at her lips.

"Of course, you are. My Niah," she smiled weakly and cupped Niah's face with a shaky hand. Niah rested her hand over Merida's where it remained on her cheek. Something warm tugged at her chest, something she had felt during her first meeting with Merida. A confirmation of the bond they shared. Niah pressed her forehead to Merida's, closing her eyes briefly.

"I'm here."

Merida quivered and broke down into sobs once again. Niah only held her, smoothing her lank hair as she wept, and wept, and wept.

Niah understood why they wanted, no, *needed* to keep this a secret. It did little to ease the guilt gripping her chest, did little to ease the pain of seeing her Guardian in such a way. For the first time, she understood the bond between them. She had felt it when Merida was in pain. In that instant, everything else melted away, and she only wanted to be there for her Guardian. It didn't matter whether she forgave her or not, some things were more important.

Once Merida had stopped crying, and had dried her eyes, Niah asked, "Please, tell me what's going on with you."

Merida took a deep, shuddering breath, "Sometimes, when hybrids get as old as I am, we begin to turn into our demonic selves. Depending on our parents, there usually isn't enough angelic blood in us to counter the demonic half. It doesn't happen to everyone; some have stronger angelic blood and some balance out perfectly. My demonic self is taking over. I fear it won't be long before I will completely turn." Her voice trembled, her eyes growing wet with tears as she kept focused on Niah's hands on the bed. A spark of annoyance ignited in the pit of Niah's stomach, she'd been so preoccupied with searching for answers that she'd missed what was important.

"You could have told me," she whispered; the annoyance faded as Merida looked at her with round blue eyes.

"I know, but it is not your burden to bear. You have much to do without worrying over an old woman." a weak smile pulled at the edges of her mouth as she tried to stay light-hearted.

Niah's heart felt like a tonne of bricks.

How had she been so blind? So wrapped up in herself that she hadn't noticed how much her Guardian was suffering? Her stomach churned.

It didn't matter that she'd only known her a matter of months. Merida was the only mother she would likely have, who defended her at every turn, and she was slowly dying. Niah had to be there for her now. If Merida didn't have much time left, then she would spend as much of it with her as possible.

Her throat tightened.

One day, maybe too soon, Merida wouldn't be with them anymore. It wouldn't only be Niah who would feel that pain.

"You're my guardian. Let me be there for you," she squeezed Merida's hands gently. Merida smiled, tears rolling down her face as she leaned forward, hugging Niah once more. Afraid she might hurt her, Niah delicately wrapped her arms around her, feeling how frail and bony she was in her grasp. After a few moments, Niah realised that Merida had fallen asleep; Fin helped ease her back against the pillows. She straightened and gazed down at the sleeping woman.

Merida was the strongest person she knew. To be going through something so difficult, keeping it a secret, and still being there for all of them, still doing her duty. Pride and pain flickered in her chest.

Unable to stand the burning at the backs of her eyes, she turned away.

"I'll stay with her," she murmured into the darkness as Fin got to his feet and took her hand in his to lead her downstairs into the living room.

"I'll stay with you," he said quietly, pulling her into his lap as he sat on the sofa.

She shook her head, "You don't have to."

"This is as much for Merida as it is for you, or myself," he smiled, stroking his thumb across her cheekbone. She smiled as much as she could, though not even Fin could coax a real smile from her.

"I'll go and get some of our things, you stay here," he said as he moved her out of his lap and got to his feet. She nodded; he stroked her face once more before heading for the door, though he paused with his hand resting on the handle.

"I'm sorry," he murmured, and then he was gone. She stared after him for a moment. Sorry. What a funny word. A meaningless word. She wasn't angry with Fin, she knew Merida would have sworn him to secrecy. She was angry at herself. She was angry because of all the people walking this damned Earth; Merida didn't deserve this.

She was kind, brave, strong, and loyal. She deserved the world, she deserved every good thing. And yet, she was suffering. Niah was powerless to do anything to help her. Which only frustrated her further.

She leaned forward, resting her elbows on her knees, and let her head fall into her hands. She didn't let herself cry. Only allowed herself a quiet moment of weakness. And once that moment was over, she locked everything away in that box at the back of her mind. The box that allowed her to do what needed to be done. She would be Merida's strength, and she would never be alone again.

Fin

The streets were quieter now. People still moving about, some going on patrol, others walking around with baskets of fruit heading toward the training grounds. The candles and torches were lit throughout the town, casting a warm glow along the streets and buildings.

He felt exhausted down to his bones. Worrying didn't do anyone any good, yet he felt as if that was the only emotion he knew lately. Worrying for Merida, worrying whether he could keep her secret, worrying about the Shadows and whether they would be able to find anything useful about them, let alone stop them.

The trip to the vampire Queen in London hadn't served much use. One of them could have ended up her slave; if Niah hadn't done what she did – not that he knew what that was – things could have turned out very differently. He groaned loudly, raking a hand through his hair.

He wished he could make it all better, like waving a wand or saying a few silly words to stop all of this. It was never that easy though, was it? Nothing ever had been. He thought about his life then, the things he had done when he was only a youngster. The damage he had caused, the way Merida looked at him when she found him. The way he looked at Gren when they found him half-naked and covered in mud, wrestling with a werewolf on a full moon. He wasn't proud of the things he had done, but they were all a part of him, like his demonic and angel blood were a part of him.

"Fin!" he heard a familiar cry, he glanced up to see Dea bounding toward him, her snowy hair flying free behind her, a bright smile on her lips. Her eyes bright and alive as she jumped up, wrapping her arms around his neck. He gave her a quick kiss on the cheek before she released him and fell into step beside him.

"You know, the whole brooding thing doesn't suit you," she grinned, Fin raised a brow.

"I can't be my usual hilarious self all the time, 'ya know?" he retorted with a smile that he didn't feel committed to. He hated deceiving with smiles. Dea narrowed her eyes.

"What's going on?"

"Those books didn't have much information in them," he frowned; it would be a logical thing to be frustrated about because of the trouble they went through to get them, and it wasn't entirely a lie, only a half-truth.

Dea sighed and twirled a lock of her hair between her fingers, "What *did* you find out?"

"They're ruled by a Queen, no name though. It also had an emblem throughout the books, a shadow with wings," he told her, waving his hand dismissively; though he couldn't shake the nagging feeling in his mind that it meant something. He had never seen it before, so ruled out there being any information on it in the archives.

"The Shadows emblem perhaps?" she suggested.

"I think so. It seems like something they would have, a shadow with angelic wings," he shrugged, his head had begun hurting a lot more lately with all this new information and trying to figure everything out. Before the last few months, it had always just been 'there's demonic activity' and they were off fighting demons. Now it seemed they were playing detective with no clues as to what they were doing.

"Anyway, are you looking forward to the celebrations tomorrow?" she asked.

"Food and partying? Hell yeah," he grinned, she clapped her hands together and began telling him about the dress she had helped Niah choose and how she was useless at making flower chains; not that it surprised him.

He still remembered the time when she punched Logan and sent him flying into the wall of the training room. A stab of pain shot through his chest at the memory of Logan pleading with them because he didn't want to die, then the quick snap of his neck. Her fingers were made to do what needed to be done, not chaining flowers together. He feared before long they would once again be coated in blood.

They reached the barracks, Dea carried on along the hall to her room as he pushed the door open to his. He stripped out of his patrolling gear and pulled on a pair of normal jeans and a dark t-shirt.

He shoved some more clothes into a bag before heading toward Niah's room, she had left it unlocked which was unlike her, though he guessed she must have been in a hurry. Her bed was unmade as usual, he rolled his eyes as he picked up a shirt hanging over the back of her desk chair and tossed it in the wash basket by the bathroom door.

Grabbing her messenger bag from the top of the desk, he started gently putting in clothes. Jeans, tops, underwear, and socks; the essentials. He also grabbed a couple of books from her overflowing shelf. Fantasy books. Stories on angels and demons, vampires, werewolves, and such. It suddenly dawned on him why she liked these books, they were written by humans because they wanted to believe in magic; it was another world within her world which she could escape to.

He flicked through one of them to find she had highlighted certain words or phrases and had shoved a separate piece of paper in the back with explanations of what they meant. A sudden pang of sadness stabbed him in the chest. This was one of the books she had brought with her from England, he remembered picking it up when he bumped into her outside the library. This is what she did to learn how to interact with people, to learn humour or the way people should behave. She had never learnt any of that from anyone because she didn't have anyone else.

He closed the book gently and put it in the bag with a few others. Something white caught his eye, a dress strewn across the bed. He picked it up and smiled, imagining her wearing it, her dark hair contrasting against it. He placed that in the bag as well.

He closed the door to Merida's house and heard pots and pans clanging, and Niah swearing. It wasn't something he heard very often, despite her sometimes foul temper, she cursed very little.

He dropped the bags on the sofa and stood in the archway to the kitchen. Folding his arms across his chest, he leaned against the wall, silently watching her with a growing grin as she stabbed something in a pan on the hob with a wooden spoon. A pot in the sink was smoking, and various foods and mess was spattered over the sides and up the walls.

"You are a truly *evil* turnip," she hissed at whatever was in the pot, apparently a turnip. He chuckled.

"Evil turnip?"

She whirled on him with blazing eyes, "Yes. It's not doing what I want it to do." he strode toward her and peered over her shoulder to see what was, indeed, a burnt black turnip.

"Well if you meant to cremate it then I'd say you're doing it right," he smirked, she turned and whacked him with the wooden spoon.

"Would you like to join it?" she demanded as she pointed the spoon at him. He took it from her.

"What were you trying to make?" he asked as he glanced over the other pots and pans. Cheese stuck to the bottom of one. Pasta burnt in another, it looked like she hadn't realised it had to be cooked in water.

She clicked her tongue, "I don't know."

"I should teach you how to cook," he grinned as he turned the hob off and emptied the pan into the bin.

She snorted, "You mean like you taught me humour?"

"Exactly, you're hilarious now. Evil turnip?" he acted out a chefs kiss, "gold." she struggled to conceal a grin and turned back to the pots in the sink.

"You tackle those, I'll cook," he said, rolling up his sleeves and went to the icebox to grab cheese and bread. After a few minutes, the kitchen began to smell like toast and cheese rather than a burnt turnip. She finished the pots and turned back to him as he plated up cheese on toast. She raised a brow.

"Try it," he encouraged as he took a bite of his own. She picked up a piece and popped it into her mouth, he had the satisfaction of watching her eyes close momentarily as she chewed. It reminded him of that first meal they had at the rest stop in England, her first taste of pastry and coffee.

She smiled lightly as they stood in the kitchen eating their cheese on toast. He washed the plates after, and they slumped down on the sofa.

"There's a spare room upstairs for you, I'll sleep here," he said, patting the back of the couch. She raised a brow at him.

"You can sleep with me," he had thought of that, but didn't know whether she would want to be alone with everything that had happened.

"You sure?"

"We've slept in the same bed many times," she pointed out, he bobbed his head in agreement. They sat together, gazing into the crackling blue fire. His fingers absentmindedly working through her raven hair. He wanted to ask her about earlier with the vampire Queen. It didn't seem like the right time, but he supposed if she didn't want to talk about it, she would say so.

"About earlier, with Leandra," she stilled, "what happened?"

She ran a hand through her hair and exhaled slowly, "When she was asking about drinking one of our blood, my magic stirred, I felt...sure, that nothing would happen if she drank mine. I wasn't expecting what happened though. I've asked Cassia already, she told me not to tell anyone else," but she told him.

Warmth flooded his chest, she trusted him enough to tell him that at least. It made sense, she had given him that look in the club, one that begged him to trust her. And he had. Trust went both ways, and if he wanted her to trust him, he had to trust her.

"Thank you for telling me." He whispered, kissing her temple gently, "Why did you want to speak to the rogues?" he knew she wanted to ask about the Shadows, but Gren said she'd been interested in the Sages too.

She looked up at him, sighed, and moved so that she was facing him cross-legged, "Merida thinks Marina is being held captive by the Shadows, but I'm worried she might be working *with* them. I found a picture at the compound, my adoptive parents, Karliah, and Nolan were all in it, and in the background was a woman that resembled my mother. It might not be her, could be someone completely different," she shrugged, "but it looks like her. I have a few different theories, but I'm not sure about any of them. While we were going through the archives, I kept seeing mentions of Sages_"

"They're a myth," he cut in, unable to stop the words.

"So I've heard. But if that was the case, why would they be mentioned so much? Don't you think it's a little odd that nobody believes in them, yet they're referenced in our history so often? It wouldn't be the first time the Elders have tried to keep something out of public knowledge. They did the same with multiple births because of the power they may be able to wield. I can't say I completely trust the Elders."

"Why didn't you tell me this?" he murmured, but he already knew the answer.

She pressed her lips together before sighing, "I didn't know if I could trust you, or Merida. I'm tired of being lied to, Fin."

"I know," he breathed, "I'm_"

"Don't say you're sorry again, I understand why. That doesn't mean I particularly like it, but I get it." she gripped his hands between them, "I trust you, you proved you trust me in the club, and I trust you. All of you, but I don't trust the Conclave."

He dragged a hand through his hair, "I'm not sure there's much we can do about that other than trying to uncover the secrets they're keeping."

"Then I guess we have a lot of work to do." she sighed.

"As always." He smiled, leaning forward to brush his lips against hers. He wondered if he would ever get used to the softness of her lips, or the way she leaned in further, deepening the kiss despite her shyness in public.

When they pulled away, he curled a lock of her hair around his finger, "I thought you'd want to ask about yourself, how you could be three hundred years old and only remember eighteen years." She gazed into the flames, her eyes turning soft and contemplative.

"I doubt they'd know anything about that. The only ones who would are the Shadows. What does it change anyway?" she murmured, "They stopped my aging when I was a baby and restarted it later," a shrug, "I don't feel any different." He wrapped an arm around her shoulders and pulled her close.

"It changes nothing, but if you want to find out the truth, then I'll help you."

"I don't think I want to know."

At that, he pulled back to gaze at her, "Why not?"

"I don't know how I feel about there being more to my past that I don't know. What if I didn't stop aging when I was an infant?"

"But you remember growing up?"

She sighed and pinched the bridge of her nose, "I know, I don't understand it. Maybe it's better if I leave well enough alone."

"If that's what you want."

"Right now it is. We have so much to do, and now with Merida," her voice wavered, she swallowed hard but continued, "It's not right to be worrying about it now."

"You're so strong, Niah." He whispered, and meant it. She met his gaze then, her brows knitted together.

"I don't feel it."

He chuckled, "We never do. What you did for Merida earlier meant the world to her, being here now will mean everything to her. It means everything to *me*. I didn't know who you were to Merida before we found you, but she never stopped trying. Having you here is all she's ever wanted." Niah's dark eyes shone, lined with silver as she turned away, blinking the unshed tears form her eyes. She took a trembling breath before meeting his gaze.

"Where are the books?" she asked. He chuckled, surprised, and impressed she had gone so long without mentioning them.

"They're upstairs," she moved and dashed upstairs, he smiled after her. He'd never stop enjoying the flush of colour that spread over her cheeks whenever he said something that meant a lot to her.

A moment later, she reappeared carrying the pile of books.

"I've already been through them," he mentioned, she didn't seem to hear him as she sat cross-legged on the couch with a book open in her lap. He watched her lashes flutter as her eyes scanned the words, her fingers grazing the pages as she thought she found something useful before frowning and flicking to the next page.

"That's weird," she muttered, "these say the Shadows were formed recently, though there's no dates or indications of how recently. There's also no telling how old this book is."

"I found that as well, I figured it wasn't worth mentioning," he shrugged, his lids were beginning to grow heavy, tiredness seeping into his muscles. She glanced at him, he forced a half-smile; his lids growing heavier.

"Come on," she said, setting the book aside and held her hand out for him to take as she stood up. He let her lead him upstairs to the spare bedroom after checking in on Merida; she was still asleep.

He stripped down to his boxers and climbed under the covers as she rummaged through her bag to find a tank top and shorts. She pulled them on, the curve of her back was almost mesmerizing as she moved. She swiftly slid under the covers and curled into his side. She felt so slight and dainty against him; yet strong and coiled as if ready to pounce at any moment. The green jewel of her dagger glinted as she rested it on the nightstand.

Since they'd been together, she'd been having less nightmares. Sometimes she woke in a cold sweat and had to rush to the bathroom to throw up, sometimes she'd toss and turn, getting tangled in the sheets. Other times, she'd wake with the dagger poised at her throat. It was those nights that had his heart pounding, afraid she would drive it the rest of the way. He didn't dare say a word, only listened to the relentless pounding of her heart, and waited for it to calm before gently taking the dagger from her and holding her until she drifted back into sleep.

Sometimes it took minutes, others, hours. He didn't mind. He'd stayed up with her all night on multiple occasions because she couldn't get back to sleep. He always asked her what the nightmare was about, sometimes she told him, sometimes she didn't. Never did she tell him about the one where she aimed a dagger at her throat.

His lids were heavy, his breathing deepening as his lids fluttered closed. He thought he heard her mutter something, but sleep had already taken him.

Dea

The barracks were quiet. The fire crackled gently as she gazed at the sketch pad open in her lap, the set of pencils next to her, balancing on the arm of the sofa. Sai was lounging in one of the armchairs, staring at the ceiling, occasionally huffing and puffing. Gren sat next to Dea, writing in a large notebook. She had asked him what he was writing many times, he had just shrugged the way he always did.

She hadn't thought about what she had been drawing, but now that it was beginning to take shape she could see it was a warrior, dressed in black armour with a great sword, though the face was still blank. Drawing was relaxing, it calmed her forever racing mind. Sai huffed again, Dea glanced at him and smirked.

"When are we going to get electricity?" he demanded as he leant forward, resting his forearms on his knees.

"Why?" Gren asked, not looking up from his notepad. He knew exactly why; he was just trying to wind Sai up. Dea shook her head.

"I miss my games, man." He groaned, "You guys have your...whatever you have, and I have video games, I'm bored...okay?" Dea glanced at Gren, who was now smirking to himself.

"Well, why don't you find a new hobby?" Dea suggested.

He turned to her, his eyes pleading, "Like what?"

"Like reading, or drawing, learn an instrument or something, there's plenty you could do," she said with a smile, Sai rolled his eyes.

"Sounds pretty boring," he grumbled, "I just need something to keep me occupied." he flopped his hands down over the arms of the chair as he leaned back into it.

"You could train me?" a voice suggested from the stairs, they all turned to see Cole standing with his hands in his pockets, his dark hair dishevelled as if he had been asleep.

"I thought Fin was training you?" Sai asked as Cole descended the rest of the stairs and came into the living space, slumping down on one of the sofas.

"You're bored and so am I, I figured it might be more entertaining," he shrugged. Sai bobbed his head from side to side as he pondered it and slapped his hands against his knees.

"Well, we are both already in training clothes."

"I'll come watch," Dea grinned. She liked watching people train, she learned a lot by watching. Gren huffed but closed his notebook and followed them out of the house and down the street toward the training grounds.

They weren't entirely alone, some people had just come back off patrol, some just going out; some people were training, and some were admiring the decorations for the celebration.

She lost herself in the beauty of it for a moment. Strings of candles in jars hung from archways and the branches of trees. Long tables and benches were being set up. Bright and sweet-smelling flowers woven through the archways with shimmering white silks.

She loved the celebration. She had experienced Christmas with her human parents. It was so magical. Completely ridiculous, but she never cared. She loved the stories. The decorations. The food, the festive cheer. And every year they would donate whatever they could to those less fortunate.

Her parents were Christian, and it wasn't just a once-a-year thing that they gave to those in need. Every weekend they would volunteer, host charity events, do marathons to raise money. They weren't saints, her parents. But they were kind, loving people. They made mistakes like any other, they fought, they scolded her when she was bad and praised her when she was good. They encouraged her in any way they could. She missed them fiercely.

She glanced up at the lights in the trees, her chest contracted tightly at the memories of her parents. Of the blissfully happy years she spent with them. A wistful smile brushed her lips as she gazed up at the stars twinkling overhead and allowed herself to wonder where they were and what they were doing. They'd be old and wrinkled now. She hated leaving them. It broke her heart a thousand times over. No matter how much she missed them, leaving was the right thing to do. She only hoped they had found something to fill that hole she would have left behind.

Sai and Cole took a defensive stance when they reached a quiet area on the training grounds. Dea and Gren sat down on the grass, and she rolled onto her stomach, her feet in the air as she rested her chin on her hands propped up by her elbows.

Cole was tall and had the bone structure to rival Fin's broadness. His eyes were so dark green they were almost black. His hair had a blue hue which seemed to stand out more in the pale moonlight. He was nimble on his feet, watching for Sai's movements, but he made clumsy mistakes. Dea frowned. They all knew he still had the mark on his neck, though it was faded and had no control over him, but what if it affected other things like Niah's mark had?

She watched for a few more moments, Sai was faster, though that could just be because he was trained. Cole struggled to keep up with him, struggled to keep his balance, and just struggled with everything.

"Cole?" Dea called, the two stopped sparring and walked toward her as she pushed herself into a sitting position. "Did the Shadows ever tell you what that mark does?" she gestured to the back of her neck. He was thoughtful for a moment.

"No, I never had my own thoughts though, I was made to do things I didn't want to do."

"Do you know whether it suppressed your strength at all?" she questioned. Gren picked his notebook up again and started scribbling information in it.

Cole shrugged, "I guess? When it faded I felt stronger, why?"

"Maybe we should get it completely removed?" she suggested. It wasn't something they hadn't thought about, they just hadn't wanted to act on it because of how severe the procedure was, and it seemed like the mark wasn't active. She got to her feet and started toward the town; aware the others were automatically following.

"Wait, we're doing this *now*?" Cole gaped.

"Duh," Dea snorted, sauntering through the streets toward one of the spell weaver buildings. They made their way quietly through the corridors on the first floor until they came to a door. She knocked and Velig pulled the door open, his silvery hair stuck out in all directions, and he wore a scarlet, satin robe with matching pyjama bottoms.

She'd thought about going to Cassia first, but after what had happened with Char and Logan, she didn't want to bother her friend with anymore mark business.

"Do hybrids ever sleep?" Velig asked grumpily while trying to stifle a yawn.

"Can you do a spell?" Dea asked, he gazed at her in disbelief.

"You mean *now?*" he demanded, though the tiredness of his voice softened the sharpness. A pang of guilt struck her, but it was important.

"I'll get you something pretty," Dea fluttered her eyelashes with a dazzling smile, he narrowed his eyes.

"It better be freaking beautiful," he grumbled, stepping aside to let them into his room. It was exactly as she had imagined. A dark wooden bed with scarlet satin sheets, a wardrobe big enough to be a second bedroom, a seating area around a fireplace, and a few shelves of various ingredients and books.

Velig waved his hands as they glowed crimson, his eyes like red fire. Four walls went up around them, swirling the colour of blood. Cole glanced around worriedly.

"Relax, it's only a barrier so we don't wake the entire house. Some of us like to sleep, you know?" Velig rolled his eyes, pushing Cole back to sit in a red armchair.

"We like sleeping too, we just prefer sleeping *with* each other," Sai winked, Velig's cheeks flushed rosy as he waved his hands over Cole; trying to ignore Sai. Dea shot him a warning look, but he just winked. Gren shook his head as he stood with folded arms, leaning against the door.

Cole's fingers began digging into the arms of the chair, his teeth gritting together. The air in the room grew thick, the scent of sulphur heavy. The glow radiating from Velig's hands blazed into a bright crimson light. Cole cried out once in agony before clamping his eyes and mouth closed, he immediately slumped in the chair as the light in Velig's hands burned brighter. After a short while, his hands dimmed and he stepped away, panting hard as he removed the swirling walls from around them.

"Here," Dea said, helping to lower him onto one of the plush sofas.

"Was that a bad one?" Sai asked as he checked on Cole who was still unconscious.

"No, it was already mostly faded, there wasn't much magic left in it. That reminds me, I meant to come to you earlier. One of my contacts within the Lunar Coven said they heard of a place where Shadows usually go," he told them, still breathing hard.

"A place where Shadows go? I didn't know they were allowed such a long rain," Sai muttered.

"They all bare the mark, they have no real free will, they can't run or turn against the Shadows, so some of them are allowed out." Velig shrugged.

"How do you know that?" Dea asked as she sat on the sofa next to Cole, reaching to brush his hair from his forehead, he was quite attractive, and sleep certainly became him. He looked calm, peaceful, no longer scowling at everyone. He reminded her of Niah in that way.

"I told you, contacts," Velig said with a dismissive wave of his hand.

Gren sighed, "I'm guessing you're not going to tell us who this contact is?"

"No, of course not, they barely trust me as it is since I'm aligned with the Alliance, I'm not going to risk that trust," he said firmly. Fair enough.

"I'm surprised someone from the Lunar Coven has agreed to help you at all," Sai scoffed, Velig gave him a long glare.

"I had a life before I joined the Alliance. You don't know what it was like centuries ago, the older hybrids do, but you youngsters could never know," he explained with a mournful gleam in his eyes.

"Tell us?" Dea pleaded. He gazed at her for a moment.

"Fine," he sighed, "the world has always been a dark place, though the last few hundred years or so it has considerably improved. There were a lot fewer hybrids when I was born, and a lot more demons. I There were four main species, the spell weavers and casters, lycanthropes and werewolves, vampires, and fey. We each had our main coven, clan, or pack, with branches that spread across the world. There were hybrids, though not many, all of them possessed half-blood. We were on the verge of losing the world to demons. And then Nayli freed the hybrids locked away in the demon realms, formed an army, and the Alliance was born. Although she disappeared a couple of centuries ago, Amarah was quickly elected Overseer.

Many of us felt safer with the Alliance after the war, so we stayed. Others felt like the Alliance was a way for the Furies to keep tabs on them and prevent them from living how they always had, free. As you can imagine, that sparked more hatred between the races, and a deep mistrust embedded amongst what we now call rogues. Many of them call those of us who agreed to join the Alliance traitors to our race. They live outside of our laws because they want to be free, but that means they also live outside of our protection." he explained with pain clear in his eyes as he spoke gently.

Dea knew the history between the species was painful, though she never knew how bad it was. To them, it must have seemed like the hybrids came and took over everything. She hadn't thought about it before, she was born only fifty years ago and was still a youngster.

Velig had told her when they first met that he was still young when the Demonic War started, only thirty years old, the war ended four hundred years ago.

"Why did you decide to join us?" Grenville asked as he stood with his hands shoved into his pockets.

"A few reasons. During the Demonic War, many of my friends were killed. The Lunar Coven seemed more interested in regaining their freedom than honouring our fallen. Whereas the hybrids mourned their dead so passionately, it moved me; I began to see that the Coven was cold and bitter. I also liked the protection aspect. As well as actually being able to do some good in the world, helping the hybrids has been humbling.

The Coven has brilliant minds and very powerful weavers, but they lack humility. I've always found it strange that the race which has no human blood, has the most humanity." he told them with a small, wistful smile.

"Do you ever miss it?" Dea asked. At that, Velig shook his head, he said nothing more on the matter, and Dea didn't ask. It was clear the subject pained him, and she didn't want to cause anyone unnecessary pain. Cole stirred, Gren lifted him easily and slung him over his shoulder. Dea gave Velig a swift kiss on the cheek before they left.

Dea couldn't help but wonder whether yet another war would soon be upon them.

7
Niah

Sun streamed in through the curtains. She scrunched her face against the light, pulling the cover over her head with a grumble. The scent of something warm and sweet wafted into the room. Groggily, she pushed herself onto her elbows. Fin wasn't there, and she could hear the faint murmur of voices downstairs. Her stomach rumbled, despite her large feast of cheese on toast the night before, she was famished. One of the downsides to being so active with training and patrolling was an enormous appetite.

She swung her legs over the side of the bed and went downstairs without changing. Fin was sitting at the small table with a mug of steaming coffee in his hands, Merida at the stove flipping pancakes in a pan. She glanced over with a smile. The colour had returned to her skin, she didn't look as painfully thin, and she had showered, which illuminated the chestnut in her hair. Her eyes were free of dark circles, the silver ring around them shimmering once more. Fin's hair stuck out in every direction as he raked a hand through it quickly. His eyes were still slightly puffy from sleep, she guessed he hadn't long woken up.

"You've heard of a hairbrush, right?" he asked, her hand instinctively went to her hair, it felt dry and messy.

She arched a brow at him, "Have you?" he grinned, "Merida, how are you feeling?" she asked as she sat opposite Fin at the small table. Merida was plating up the pancakes and hurrying about fetching syrup and sugar. A pang of guilt clenched at her stomach, Merida should be resting. Though she knew if she brought it up, she may well end up being swatted with a spatula.

"Much better," Merida beamed as she placed a plate in front of each of them before sitting down with her own. The pancakes were delicious, fluffy, and sweet.

"Are you two looking forward to today?" Merida asked as she held a mug of coffee between her fingers. Niah gazed at her blankly. "The celebrations?"

"Oh, yeah," she answered as she popped another chunk of pancake into her mouth. She had seen the decorations, heard people talking about it, but it was hard to get excited about something if you had never experienced it before; not when you weren't entirely sure what it was about.

She knew it symbolised the day when hybrids were freed from the demons, but she had never celebrated anything before, the first time she ever celebrated her birthday was only because Dea took them all out. Her chest warmed at the memory of that night, her stomach churned at the memory of the morning after.

"So, what happens about patrols?"

"The weavers and lycanthropes will take the day shifts, the fey and vampires will take the night. They understand this is a special day for us and want to help us celebrate as best we can, while also joining in," Merida smiled. It was almost as if new life had been breathed into her during the night.

She wore a long, floaty white dress with long sleeves which hung loosely around her arms and trailed down her sides, Niah couldn't help but think she looked rather angelic. Even Fin was wearing a white shirt that was almost transparent. He wore a pair of dark blue jeans, but no shoes, Merida's feet were also bare.

After a quick shower, she rummaged through her bag to find the white dress Dea had picked out. She lay it flat on the bed and gazed down at it with a small smile. The material was soft, it grazed over her skin delicately, as if she were wearing nothing at all.

She tied the two pieces at the sides behind her back, showing off the curve of her waist, something she wasn't used to seeing. Her hair hung down her back, slightly curling into long, loose curls as it dried naturally. Without putting shoes on, -nobody else was – she went downstairs and found that she didn't feel uncomfortable or as awkward as she thought she would be wearing a dress.

Merida and Fin were talking in the kitchen when she strode into the room. Fin froze mid-sentence, his eyes raking over her, lingering for a moment on her face. He smiled a bright smile that reached every inch of his face and brightened his silver eyes.

Merida turned to see what he was looking at; her eyes widened. She made a slight squeak as her hands cupped her mouth. Her eyes began to well. *Now* Niah felt awkward. She waved her hand dismissively, but Merida got to her feet and placed her hands at the tops of Niah's shoulders, holding her at arm's length.

"You look beautiful," she breathed, a single tear slipping down her cheek. Niah said nothing, her cheeks burning as she shifted on her feet and offered a smile.

"Turn around," Fin said when Merida released her, Niah stood with her back to him. He untied the knot at her back and re-tied it.

"It should be a bow," he murmured into her ear, his breath tickling her neck. He ran his hands down her arms and kissed her shoulder before taking her hand in his and offered his elbow to Merida – who took it with a great smile – and the three of them left the house.

The streets were busy. Music echoed through the buildings, cheerful harmonies which sounded like flutes and harps. Everyone was smiling, joyous and laughing as they made their way through the streets carrying flowers and white silks. They were all making their way to the training grounds.

They found Dea with Sai and Gren along the way. Dea looked like an angel in her knee-length, figure-hugging, white dress. Sai and Gren both wore floaty white shirts like Fin, except Gren wore matching linen trousers. His sandy hair loose and hung down by his ears rather than slicked back. He looked boyish, though he still had his hands in his pockets. Thankfully, he no longer wore his usual grumpy expression.

"Are you ill?" Niah had asked him, to which, much to her surprise, he laughed and shook his head as he walked ahead with Fin, leaving her staring after him open-mouthed.

"This is the one day a year he actually enjoys," Sai grinned, gazing after the two men in front. Misha had joined them as they reached the training grounds, wearing a loose, plain dress that came down to the middle of her calves. The pink and green scales shimmering with added glitter across her shoulders. Dea had glitter across her cheekbones, making them sparkle in the sunlight, Velig had the same idea except for added glitter across his forehead and lips as well.

Dea started grabbing flowers from baskets and was expertly placing them in Misha's, Merida's, and Niah's hair as well as her own. The air was thick with the scent of hundreds of flowers. She gazed around the grounds, it reminded her of a poster she had seen in the human world. A poster that spoke of love and peace. She felt it as she stood there, the peacefulness of it all.

She never hoped she was wrong about her suspicions more than she did as she watched the festivities unfold around her.

Games were taking place throughout the fields, ball games and games like leaning under a stick, even a maypole. Children ran around laughing. A lycanthrope in wolf form offered some of them rides on their back, the children shrieked with laughter when they tumbled off.

Nick and Adora joined them as they all sat on the thick grass, talking, and laughing amongst themselves. Nick had no top on, revealing the decorative cross tattooed on his back, Adora was trying not to stare; whereas Dea made no attempt to hide her appreciative gaze.

An uneasy feeling washed over her. A pang of guilt attacking her gut as she watched the people around her looking so carefree and enjoying themselves. How could they all act as though nothing was going on outside of this island? As if there wasn't a threat looming over them? She bit her lip and frowned down at the grass between her toes, trying to push the thoughts from her mind.

"What is it?" Fin murmured into her ear. She was sat between his legs, leaning back into his chest as he leant back on his hands. Only now his chest was pressed against her back, his face close to her ear. His breath on her neck sent a shiver running up her spine.

"I feel like I can't enjoy this, not properly," she answered quietly as to not draw the attention of the others and ruin their time.

"I thought the same thing," he sighed, she turned her head to glance at him over her shoulder. His hair shining with hints of bronze and gold in the sunlight, flopping over his forehead. It made him look younger. The silver of his eyes shimmered, almost luminous in the morning sun.

"We're no closer to finding out anything about them," she muttered as she turned back to face the others, still engaged in their conversations.

They had no additional information other than a Queen and an emblem. Whoever the Shadows were, they were keeping it well hidden. At that moment, Velig, who had been sitting with Dea turned to them with a look of alert remembrance on his pointed features.

"I cannot *believe* I forgot to mention this," he started with mock horror, "I know someone who told me the location of where a lot of Shadow warriors go, a bar it seems." pride spread across his face as Niah stiffened all over. She leaned closer to him.

"What place?" she demanded under her breath; a shadow passed over his face as he glanced at Fin over her shoulder.

"It's a bar in New York called The Steel Queen," he said slowly, yet oddly deliberately. Her heart began thrumming. A lead, a real lead. Something they could use, finally.

"We will go tomorrow," Fin murmured into her ear delicately.

"We need to go now," she chewed out through gritted teeth, she could feel herself trembling with anticipation as her fingers dug into the grass beside her.

"Perhaps I should have waited..." Velig trailed off and turned back to the others, who didn't seem to notice Niah almost vibrating with anger.

"Niah, even if we wanted to; we wouldn't be allowed through the portal. Today is a sacred day for us, there is no fighting on this day, it's supposed to be peaceful," he warned, his gaze was careful as he watched her.

She turned on him then, her jaw set stubbornly, "There is no peace. It's delusional to think that there is." he tilted his chin up, narrowing his eyes slightly.

"You're right," he said, to her surprise, "but there are times to act and times to be patient. And right now, I need you to be patient. Just for today." His voice was low and stern, which made her want to argue.

Merida leaned in toward them, "First thing tomorrow, Niah," she smiled warmly. Niah opened her mouth to argue, but Merida gave her a hard look. She felt as though she were being treated like a child. Sitting in her white dress with flowers in her hair, suddenly feeling as if a hole had been punched through her chest.

She bit her lip to stop herself from yelling and going through the portal anyway. She felt powerless. Her body ached with longing to go to The Steel Queen.

One more night. Just one more and she would get some answers. She'd go on her own if she had to. Some part of her wanted to leave and not come back until the Shadows were nothing more than a distant memory. But if something happened to Merida while she was gone, she would never forgive herself. It did little to ease her rising hatred for the organisation responsible for so much suffering.

For the first time in her life, she felt torn two ways.

Before arriving in Australia she had nothing but a bitter desire for revenge. And now she had people she cared about, people she wanted to protect. She had a Guardian who didn't have long left to live, and she wanted to spend as much time with her as possible.

But that hatred hummed beneath her skin. A disease eating away at her sanity the longer the days dragged by. The longer she had to wait, the longer she had to go without answers dragged her down. It made her impatient. It made her want to risk everything, just so that her mind would finally be quiet.

But for now, she had to play along. Had to at least try to engage in the celebrations, and deep down, she did want to enjoy it. She forced a smile and said nothing more on the matter, it would have been useless anyway.

As the day went on, no amount of laughing or dancing could thaw the ice in her veins. No amount of love or smiles could quench the unbearable thirst for revenge. What scared her most wasn't how much she craved revenge, it was that she had been so willing to give up everything to get it.

That thought destroyed her above all others.

Fin

The sun was beginning to set, casting golds and oranges and pinks across the sky. Soon the fires would be lit to symbolise the new day. Rather than the celebrations winding down, they were just getting started. People feasted on bread, cheese, fruit, and meat, drinking from horns of ale and wine.

Fin was thoroughly enjoying himself. Most of the stress and anxiety had left his body. Their troubles were far from over, but for one day, they could let themselves relax and unwind. They could forget about everything else for a little while, even if sometimes the bitter ice of guilt gripped his chest that they were having fun while others suffered at the hands of the Shadows.

The music picked up into an energetic rhythm rather than the soothing melody it had been all day. He looked around for the band but only found musical instruments sat on a stage, moving of their own accord with sparks flying off of them.

Niah had been distant since Velig told them about The Steel Queen. She had smiled and laughed, but still held a thick tension in the set of her shoulders. Her words echoed through his mind, *There is no peace. It's delusional to think that there is.* As much as he may want to disagree, she was right. There wasn't peace. There was no guarantee there would ever be peace

He hoped there would be, sometimes that's all anyone had, hope. He'd fight for that hope. He'd fight for the day when there might be peace.

Niah was fighting for something very different. He understood why she wanted revenge so desperately, but it was a disease. There was a difference between wanting to stop them because of what they were, what they did, to wanting to destroy them. It was hard to say she was wrong for wanting revenge. He'd seen the book her captors kept on her, saw the hateful words they wrote about her.

In truth, he had wanted to rip Karliah's throat out the second he saw the woman. They had conditioned Niah from such a young age to hide her emotions, to not show or feel them, and in doing so, she had only anger and revenge. It was by design. So he couldn't exactly blame her, because she knew nothing else.

Maybe he could show her a better way. He tried and tried to talk her down from that devastating goal, but she wouldn't budge.

He watched Niah as she sat talking with the others. She was animated enough, smiling, and laughing, though her eyes told a different story. They were distant, as hard, and black as onyx, the silver shimmering brightly in the setting sun.

He felt himself being torn two ways. As much as he wanted to help her, he was a Commander. His duty, and his hope of a better future, of peace, made him question whether he should be helping her at all. She was walking a dangerous path, and he wasn't sure how far she was willing to go to get revenge.

The thought terrified him.

Of course, he would never tell her that. If she knew, she would stop coming to him about it, stop telling him what was going on, and he still needed to know. Not just as a part of his responsibilities, but for her. For his sanity, he had to know.

He was better at hiding his emotions than she was. Niah had only known loss, anger, and loneliness. He learned to put his personal feelings aside when he was given the title of advisor. Once he realised Merida valued his opinion and relied on his council, he learned to concentrate on what was best for the

Alliance. Now all that seemed to be crumbling around him, the wall he had built slowly cracking.

Night had completely fallen, candles hanging in the jars from tree branches were alight with a warm yellow glow. Colourful pixies danced through the air, illuminating the skies with soft light. The huge pyre at the centre of the festivities remained unlit.

Lady Overseer and Lord Ambassador climbed the platform in front of the tables. Amarah wearing a long white dress with intricate beading and gold stitching, Ragnar wore a white tunic with silver embroidery down the front and around the collar.

"Our friends, today is a joyous occasion for our hybrids, and we're so incredibly happy that our comrades from the Alliance could join us," Amarah announced, her voice carrying musically across the vast fields, "Today, we celebrate when hybrids were freed from the tyranny of demons. We light this fire to symbolise our will, that we'll never be used for someone else's gain." she held her arms out to the side as she spoke.

People with torches stepped around the pyre and lit the branches at the bottom. The flames licked upward, engulfing the wood quickly. The fire raised into the sky behind the Elders, both looking brilliant and terrifying. Cries and whoops sounded across the field; the music turned into drumming as the hybrids began swaying to the rhythmic beat.

He glanced at Niah, who was gazing in awe at her surroundings. He took her hand, spinning her so she was pressed against his chest, moving gently to the beat. The music drummed through his feet, into his veins, his bones, his chest. His heart raced as he held her, moving with the music, a sheen of sweat covering their skin. He traced his fingertips over her shoulder blades and had the satisfaction of feeling her shudder slightly beneath his touch. She gazed up at him with wide eyes, her cheeks flushed.

Just as he was reaching down to kiss her, she snaked her arms around his neck and reached up on her tiptoes to press her lips to his. He pulled her into him tightly, feeling her heart hammering through the layers of their clothes, suddenly very aware of how thin their clothing was.

It was an effort to push the thoughts away to save himself getting excited around all these other hybrids, not that he imagined anyone would care or even notice, many of them would be doing the same thing, or worse.

Her lips parted with the smallest of coaxing from his own, tracing her bottom lip with his tongue, tasting the sweetness of her. She moaned gently as she mimicked his movements. His hands moved into her hair, stroking the silky raven strands between his fingers, the flowers falling out one by one.

She traced her hands over his back, his shoulders, and down his chest. He groaned deep in his throat and felt her smile against his lips. She nipped at his bottom lip, causing electricity to shoot through his body. He chuckled against her mouth, and she pulled back slightly, giving him a quizzical look.

"Where did you learn that?" he asked, his voice thick and gravelly.

"A book," she grinned mischievously. Even though it seemed like she was perfectly relaxed, he knew better. He knew she wasn't feeling quite herself, could feel the tension radiating from her. She was wound like a coil ready to spring. It wouldn't be right to take things to the next step, he stopped his presumptuous thoughts. Instead, he spun her around, she laughed, a bright, musical laugh that warmed his heart brilliantly.

Dea caught hold of her, spinning her around. That hadn't been his intention, he wanted her to himself for a bit longer. Though seeing the look on her face, despite whatever anxiety she may be feeling, he couldn't take this moment away from her. She was truly laughing, dancing with her friends.

He watched them all from a near distance. Merida making a fuss over Niah and Dea, saying how beautiful they both were. Niah kept a protective eye on Merida at all times. Sai and Gren were both laughing and spinning the girls around with Misha swaying to her own beat, waving white silk through the air. Nick, Rae, and Adora joined in, Niah twirling between the lycanthropes like a butterfly.

Velig and Cassia both shot sparks from their fingertips into the sky; other spell weavers and casters were doing the same thing. Lighting up the sky in bright fireworks as everyone watched in appreciation at the beauty of it.

Niah sauntered toward him, her eyes slightly unfocused from the dizzying high of dancing and music. He snaked an arm around her waist and gazed up at the colourful sky. When he looked down at her, she was watching the display; the colours reflected in her dark eyes.

He observed the field. So many people, everyone mingling with other species. People kissing, dancing, gazing at the fireworks. The world was beautiful. He found he didn't feel quite so guilty about not working. For that one moment, everything was perfect.

Cole

He'd been watching the celebrations from the side-lines. Not understanding what they were celebrating, and no one had told him. He supposed that was because he hadn't bothered asking. Still, he watched as women twirled and danced, wearing white dresses, and the men dancing with them or drinking, or playing some sort of game, all wearing white shirts, some with matching trousers.

He had seen baskets of flowers and food being carried around, trees - which weren't there before - on the training ground covered in white silks and jars of candles.

The day was full of games and laughter. He wondered what Nyx would make of it all. If she had been there she would have made fun of them, called them stupid. Though as he sat on the grass watching the people go about the day, it didn't feel stupid. It felt oddly familiar in a way he didn't understand. He had seen Fin and the others, had thought about going over to them but felt like he would just be an outsider.

What shocked him was how inclusive and welcoming people were. A group of lycanthropes and fey had come over, they smiled and said he should join them rather than sitting on his own. He had for a short while as the sun began to set. Keira was a lycanthrope with tanned skin and honey-coloured hair, her eyes were a brilliant bright green. She told him about the celebrations, that it was the first time the other species were invited to join.

There was a speech, and a huge bonfire was lit. After that, the music picked up and everyone whooped as they danced, many people making out with each other or skulking off into the shadows of the trees at the edge of the field, or even just laying down in the grass for all to see.

The candles in the jars were lit, strange glowing winged creatures fluttered around casting a slight glow as they went. Pixies. He gazed around the field, for the first time since he had arrived; he felt like he was where he was supposed to be. Which only made the guilt of leaving Nyx that much worse.

He spotted Fin and the others dancing near the bonfire, he was dancing with Niah, kissing her. Cole looked away, feeling oddly uncomfortable. Dea spotted him and waved him over. She wore a tight, knee-length dress that showed off every curve of her lithe body. He swallowed hard as he took her in and averted his gaze.

"You made an effort," she beamed as she sauntered toward him, brushing up against him with a dazzling smile. He glanced down at himself, he hadn't even noticed he'd put a white t-shirt on this morning. He shrugged.

"How are you feeling?" Sai asked, clapping him on the shoulder in a familiar greeting.

"Fine now, thanks," he answered, glancing around at the festivities. He didn't remember much from having the mark removed, only the searing pain that lasted only a minute before he descended into darkness. When he woke, his head was thick and foggy, but after having some food, he found his mind was clearer than it ever was before. A weight had been lifted from his chest, like the mark had still held some power, and no longer did.

"We can go over training tomorrow, but right now, have some of this," Sai said, thrusting a horn full of yellowish liquid into his hand. Cole shrugged and tipped it back, draining it. It wasn't bitter like he thought it would be, but rather sweet and refreshing. Though his head swam when he lowered the horn from his lips, it was an effort to stop himself from swaying on his feet. Sai was gazing at him with wide eyes and burst into laughter.

"You're not supposed to down it that fast," he took the horn away from him and tossed it onto the table.

Cole cocked his head to the side, "Why?"

"Because it's a sipping drink, one sip goes a *very* long way," Dea giggled, her eyes were slightly unfocused as her gaze passed over him from his feet to his eyes. He shifted. Dea was beautiful, her flowing white hair mesmerising as well as her large blue eyes. She reached up and kissed him, catching him off guard. He was vaguely aware Sai and Gren were around them. She detached herself with a smile, twirling away in shrieking laughter. He stared after her, bewildered, his mouth hanging open.

"You'll get used to it," Gren grinned as he took a sip from his own horn of yellowish liquid before striding for Dea.

"I don't think I ever could," Cole muttered, "Is it always like this? Everyone makes out with everyone?"

Sai arched a brow, "Pretty much, we're not monogamous, and genders don't matter so much to us, we don't get jealous, and we just do what we want with who we want." Cole gazed at Sai, he had short dark hair, the lower half shaved in an undercut. His eyes were brown, almost caramel with bronze flecks running through them. He had sharp features, but a boyish quality to his face. Cole couldn't deny he was handsome, the thought made him flush and clear his throat, quickly tearing his eyes away.

He had never looked at men that way before, had never really looked at anyone that way before. He had always been with his sister, and they never really met anyone else.

Sai smiled and took a step closer to Cole, whose heart hammered in response. He was so close that Cole could feel the warmth radiating off of the other boy, even if just for a second.

"Are you curious?" Sai murmured, his breath thick and sweet from the yellowish drink. His gaze flicked to Cole's lips, and it was a surprise, but Cole found himself leaning into him. Sai's answering grin sent sparks rippling through his body. It was a gentle brush of lips against lips.

Sai pulled back slightly, watching for Cole's reaction. Cole surprised himself again, closing the gap between them and kissed Sai again. The other boy grinned into his mouth, an arm wrapping around Cole's waist as he held his drink in his other hand. Cole reached up and stroked Sai's face as he kissed him, the other boy moaned slightly in appreciation before they both broke apart, Cole breathing hard, Sai's eyes sparkling brightly.

"It's an easy way of life, we have fun, we enjoy ourselves. You can relax here," Sai said, his voice gentle as he stepped away a fraction.

Cole's heart was still pounding when Dea bounded back over with Gren in tow a few seconds later. He had never thought about romance. Had no idea what it was. The kiss with Sai had been passionate, and entirely as comfortable as the kiss with Dea. There was no embarrassment, no awkwardness, it was all so comfortable and easy.

He let himself relax.

The people had started disappearing, the training grounds emptying. He watched as Fin and Merida strode away with a white-haired man and a woman that appeared to glow with pink light. He spotted Niah standing under one of the trees with candles in jars hanging from its branches, she was gazing up at the night sky, her arms gently wrapped around herself.

"Do you want to come back with us?" Dea asked with a coy smile.

"Later," he grinned, she didn't look hurt or upset, none of them did, they simply strode away, Dea bouncing along before hopping up on Sai's back.

Cole walked with his hands in his pockets toward Niah. It was an effort to walk in a straight line, the world was spinning in weird directions, or maybe it was just his eyes playing tricks on him.

She wore a long white dress with a small slit up one side to her knee. The wind blew her hair over one shoulder, a single white flower was tucked behind her ear. Her gaze was distant, despite the slight smile on her lips.

She turned to him as he approached, she was beautiful, her nose slightly too long for her face, but beautiful, nonetheless. And vaguely familiar. It was the eyes, he remembered those eyes. But whenever he did, a chill gripped his insides, as if warning him to stay away.

"Have you enjoyed today?" she asked in a breezy voice, turning back to gaze at the stars.

"More than I expected."

"It's a lot to take in, isn't it?" she sighed wistfully, still not meeting his gaze.

"You can say that again." After a moment, he asked, "How long have you been here?"

"A couple of months," she answered, almost coldly as if the memory of something awful had struck her. He was quiet for a long moment, guessing she didn't want to talk about where she had been before. He understood that, he didn't want to be reminded of where he had come from either.

"Revenge," he blurted, she turned to him then with guarded eyes, her brow furrowed, "you asked me before why I chose to stay and let my sister go. It's for revenge." That drink really was powerful, his words were slurring together, and there were now two Niah's. He should stop talking before he said something stupid.

Her eyes hardened, "Revenge on the Shadows, I assume?"

"Yes, for the years they experimented on us, tortured us. We had been going around in circles for years trying to find out how to get to them. When you guys offered for me to stay, I thought it was an opportunity to find out information, and then go back to Nyx to take our revenge." he explained, not entirely sure why he was telling her any of this. Her shoulders were tense, her whole stance was tense as she stood with her arms folded, a severe expression on her sharp features. He wasn't sure how someone could look so delicate one moment, yet so fierce the next.

Her voice was empty when she said, "They seem rather skilled at that."

"Do you guys know anything?"

She exhaled sharply, dragging her hand through her hair, "Not as much as I would like," he didn't answer, they stood for a long moment under the dying lights of the candles. Eventually, she took a deep inhale of breath.

"So, Sai, huh?" she said with a wicked arch of a brow. His cheeks burned and she chuckled. "Don't panic, everyone is like that here," she started walking back toward the town, and he followed.

"So I've been told," he mumbled, "are you like that?"

She shook her head, "No, I'm loyal to Fin," a gentle smile brushed her lips. She looked younger all of a sudden.

"I didn't think hybrids were monogamous," he wondered aloud, she sighed wistfully.

"We're not. And it may not last, but we're both happy like this and see no reason not to enjoy it while it does last."

"It seems we get to make up our own rules when it comes to that kind of stuff," he said as they walked through the thick grass.

"I've never known anything like it," she said with fondness in her voice. But he could have sworn he heard the ghost of something dark as she spoke, a flicker of something haunted in her eyes.

"What else have you known?" he asked, with that, it was like a wall went down. Her expression hardened, her eyes grew distant, and her body turned rigid with tension.

"Many things." was all she said before falling into silence as they walked toward the barracks. He stopped outside to say goodnight, but she had already gone ahead toward the centre of town. He frowned, and went inside to his room, wondering what it was that had happened to her.

8

Fin

Fin, Merida, Vinaxx, and Cassia had all been called before the Oracle Conclave. They sat on their platform in the council room, still wearing their celebration clothes. It must be incredibly important if they were pulled away from their most sacred day. Fin gazed at the serious faces before him, even the Guardians weren't wearing their usual immaculate grey attire. Though they still carried their shining shields and spears.

"We're sorry to have pulled you from the festivities," Amarah said in a low, careful voice.

"Of course, Lady Overseer," Merida bowed, forever respectful, this pleased Amarah, and a ghost of a smile passed over her lips.

"The sword you brought back, Commander Fin, what can you tell me about it?" Amarah asked. The purple dragon sword. It was a short sword, a bright ultraviolet purple in its entirety, a flame licking across the blade as it stuck in the ground; dimming to a swirling pattern when he touched it.

"Nothing I haven't already told you, Lady Overseer. It was carried by a rider wearing purple armour. He was huge and had another purple sword with him, he used the dragon sword to stick into the ground and open a rift for demons to escape through. When I touched it, the flames stopped and turned to a moving pattern over the blade." he explained again, at that, the doors opened and in strode a tall man with bright, flaming blue hair and matching eyes. He carried the dragon sword across a plush red velvet pillow with gold lining. He bowed to the Oracle Conclave before turning to face Fin and the others.

"Akius here has found something very interesting about the sword," Amarah said, gesturing for Akius to take over.

"Thank you, Lady Overseer. The sword opens rifts into one of the demon realms," he began, "in your report, you said the rider told you he was one of the Five, is that right?"

Fin nodded, "Yes."

"So, that would reason that there are four more swords like this one with magical abilities," Akius went on.

"We're aware of this, what have you found that we don't already know?" Ragnar demanded, making Akius jump slightly.

"This kind of sword cannot simply be crafted by a normal bladesmith. It would need to be someone with extraordinary talent in making weapons, or magic, or both," he said quickly, not wanting to annoy the Ambassador further.

"So, what are you saying?" Ragnar asked impatiently when Akius didn't immediately continue.

"I believe this sword was made by more than one person, I believe they were made by two of the legendary Sages," he said, at that, the room fell silent. Fin remembered reading about Sages in the books, though there was never much information about them, many of the books still referred to them as myths.

And Niah hadn't been convinced that's what they were, she believed the Elders were keeping information about the Sages secret. Amarah and Ragnar exchanged a look with the other Elders on the platform. Was she right? Were their government keeping things from them?

"You believe the Sages are the rulers of the Shadows?" Ragnar asked with a furrowed brow as he leant forward in his chair.

Akius shook his head, "I cannot say for sure, but I think it was Sages who made this sword."

"Sages are real?" Fin blurted.

"They are, Commander, though we keep it away from common knowledge, I would ask you to do the same," Amarah spoke gently yet firmly.

"Of course, Lady Overseer. May I ask why we're not informed of them?" he asked, feeling slightly irritated that this kind of information could have come in handy a lot sooner had it been common knowledge.

"The Sages are very powerful beings, they were the first of their kinds. Centuries ago, they made a treaty with us. We were no longer allowed to contact them for help, they wanted to be left in peace." Ragnar explained. Fin tried to imagine them, for some reason he pictured ancient-looking beings with grey hair and a million wrinkles.

"Is it possible that two Sages would make such a sword?" Merida asked, Amarah looked thoughtful for a long moment.

"I don't know, we haven't had contact with them in so long, many of their abilities are unknown to us. Akius, which two Sages are you suggesting could have made this weapon? And how is it *you* know of Sages?" Ragnar demanded as an afterthought, Akius jumped at the sound of his name.

"I knew of them when they were around centuries ago, though over the years many have forgotten them and the people who knew of them are a very small group, I remembered when my former master spoke of them fondly. However, it appears no one within the Alliance knew the Sages personally, and as I said, those who knew of them is a very small number. I will keep the secret, have no fear, Lord Ambassador. As for which two, I believe the Sage of Blades and the Sage of Spells would be the most logical," he explained with tension thick in his trembling voice, his hands shaking as he held the pillow with the sword balancing on top.

Fin narrowed his eyes, why would no one know about the Sages? If they fought in the last war, why was there no one within the Alliance who knew them? And why would the Elders want people to think they were a myth? Ragnar's explanation didn't sit right, just because there was a treaty, didn't mean people shouldn't know of them.

He glanced at Merida, she pressed her lips into a thin line, but smoothed her features quickly as she stepped forward, "Elders, I request that we put together a small team who will need to know about the Sages, that team will find any information about the Sages and will try to locate the rider in which this sword belongs, as well as finding the truth of the Shadows," the Elders turned to each other to mutter amongst themselves.

"Who were you planning on putting on the team?" Ragnar asked, Merida glanced at Fin before turning back to Ragnar.

"Commander Fin, Commander Grenville, Niah, Dea, Sai, spell weaver Velig, and lycanthrope Nick," Merida told them. The Elders turned back to each other for a long moment, deliberating once again.

"Why these particular warriors?" Lyra of the lycanthropes asked, her light brown eyes gazing at Merida, clearly surprised at the mention of one of her lycanthropes.

"They're all incredibly skilled, they're well respected, and they usually patrol together anyway, so they shouldn't be missed from other squads," Merida explained.

"Very well, though in the absence of two Commanders, I would ask you to elect two in their place, even if only temporarily," Amarah spoke softly, Merida bowed her head in thanks.

"I would elect Misha and Nate from my sector," she answered.

"Fine," Ragnar said, waving a dismissive hand.

"I would also like to request one more to be a part of our team," Fin said, Ragnar sighed but nodded for him to continue, "I would like to bring the newcomer, Cole."

Ragnar's brow furrowed, "Explain your reasoning."

"Cole has spent more time in the human world than any of us, he was also held captive by the Shadows and may be of use," Fin explained, Ragnar nodded once in agreement.

"Very well. But only those in this group will know about the mission, this is secret to the highest degree. Cassia, I would ask you to build a house for the team. They will be discussing things that others cannot hear, so please put a muffling barrier around it as well." Amarah said, Cassia nodded and bowed her head.

"You will also need any documentation on Sages. We will send these to the house once it has been built. I will also send a pack explaining in full detail the objectives of the task. Merida, you will remain a Council member, but I expect the team to report to you and you to keep us filled in on any progress. Cassia and Vinaxx, you are also to be a part of the team," Amarah instructed, everyone nodded, bowing their heads. "Very well, dismissed."

They quickly filed out of the room and down the steps of the Chambers. Dawn had set in, pale blue lined the sky and cast everything in a pale light. The dawn of a new day, and possibly the turning point in their investigations. Niah had been right, the Elders were hiding things from them. At the very least, they were now in a position to freely look into things without being blocked. He only hoped they found what they were searching for.

His eyes flicked to Merida. She had done a good job of hiding her intentions in the meeting, but he knew that gleam in her eye. She had found something, and had jumped on the opportunity to have a team looking into it. He took her hand and held her back while the others went ahead.

"What's going on?"

"I believe this may be the turning point we all needed." Merida said, her voice edged and sharp, despite the smile tugging at the corners of her lips.

"By finding the Sages?"

She nodded, "If we can find them, it may mean the difference between winning this war, or losing."

"Would the Sages be able to stop the Shadows?" he asked. Merida turned to meet his gaze, her ocean blue eyes glistening.

"They'll stop all of our enemies."

Niah

Someone was gently shaking her awake, startled, she reached for her dagger and a hand closed around her wrist. Her eyes met silver, and her heart settled quickly. Fin chuckled as he lowered himself onto the edge of the bed.

Pale blue light trickled in through the open curtains. Fin was wearing the same clothes as the night before. There was an emergency meeting during the celebration, he must just be getting back. She moved across the bed, making room for him to join her, but he shook his head.

"As much as I would love to climb into bed with you, we have to go," he muttered, at that, she pushed herself into a sitting position.

"What is it?"

"I'll tell you all when we get there," he said. His tone had her out of bed in an instant and pulling on a pair of jeans. She glanced by the door to see his trunk and a large bag. He followed her gaze.

"You should pack too," was all he said as he rose from the bed and left the room. Her heart was racing, her fingers twitching as she yanked on her boots and shoved what little clothing she had at Merida's into a bag.

Her mind raced, why hadn't Fin told her anything? Perhaps there wasn't time? With a sigh, she glanced around the room, making sure she hadn't forgotten anything. Fin came back into the room a few minutes later and grabbed his things as they met Dea, Gren, Sai, and Cole downstairs. They all wore the same wary expressions with various bags at their feet. Fin said nothing, only walked out of Merida's house.

The early morning sun cast a golden glow over the town, illuminating the water in the fountain like tiny diamonds. They came to a stop in front of a large house that hadn't been there the day before. It was similar to a Counsellors house, grand from the outside, made of stone and wood with a tiled roof.

Fin opened the door and stepped inside to find they weren't alone. Inside stood Merida, Cassia, Velig, Vinaxx, and Nick. Only Merida wore a light smile. To Niah's relief, her Guardian looked healthy. More so than she had done in days.

"Your rooms are upstairs, go and put your things in them and come back down," Merida instructed in her authoritative tone that yielded no argument. Niah blinked and closed the distance between them as the others disappeared upstairs.

"I'm staying with you," she murmured, Merida smiled lightly and placed a hand on her cheek.

"I'm staying here too, don't worry," she told her gently. Niah pressed her lips into a firm line, she'd promised to be there for her, to look after her. Satisfied that she wouldn't be far from Merida if she were needed, Niah nodded and climbed the stairs to find her room.

She dumped her things inside the door of the only room left, not stopping to take it in before turning and hurrying back down the stairs.

Merida, Cassia, and Vinaxx were no longer in the main living area, muted voices echoed from a room down the corridor. The hallway was surprisingly long, with doors leading off on each side. She came to a set of double doors on the left where the voices were coming from and pushed them open.

Inside was a large round table with a wooden chandelier hanging over it, books piled high on the surface with chairs surrounding it. Underneath the piles of books, was a world map that had been painted on the table with the added island of Thamere. On the far wall stood a large corkboard with pins pushed into it. The other walls were lined with shelves of more books.

"What's going on?" Niah asked, her arms folded across her chest.

"Take a seat," Merida said gently, though still with that authoritative tone. Reluctantly, she did as instructed as the others filed into the room and sat down. Fin moved around the table to stand next to Merida; his expression just as serious as hers. Niah sometimes forgot that Fin was a Commander, that he was Merida's advisor above all else.

"What you're about to be told is extremely secretive. You must all swear an oath that you will not tell anyone else about anything that goes on inside this house," Merida said calmly, her eyes fierce as she gazed over the faces before her.

She took a gleaming black, *Ruclite* dagger from Vinaxx, a ruby winking in the hilt, and passed it to Nick who was closest on her right. He cut an X into the skin on the back of his hand between his thumb and index finger.

From what Niah knew of blood oaths, they were rare and taken seriously. If one was to break a blood oath, they could forfeit their life. Which meant that whatever they were going to do, meant risking their lives to keep hidden from everyone else on the island. Fin met her gaze across the table, his silver eyes gave nothing away.

"I vow never to tell anyone of what we are about to be told or what actions we are about to take that relate to this meeting," Nick muttered, loudly enough for everyone to hear clearly. The X cut into his skin glowed with a faint white light before burning away, leaving the skin smooth and untouched. The others did the same as the dagger was passed around the table until it eventually reached Niah. It was heavy in her hand; uncomfortably so. The tip pierced her skin and she sliced the same spot everyone else had, murmuring the same words, the X glowed white and burned slightly before dying into nothing. The room fell silent, all eyes gazing at Merida, waiting for an explanation.

"Good," Merida said as Niah handed the dagger back to her. Her Guardian clasped her hands in front of her, shoulders rigid with tension, her lips pressed into a firm line.

"In these books, you will find a great deal of information, on a subject that has long been forgotten and forbidden. Sages," she said guardedly, watching for the other's reaction. Niah was still, she met Fin's gaze once again, he gave a slight nod. She was right.

Sai shifted in his seat, "Sages are a myth."

"That appears not to be the case. Sages are extremely old and powerful beings, they are said to have been the first of their kind. Centuries ago, we made a treaty with them, we would not contact them so they may live in peace. Unfortunately, it may be that we now have to break that treaty," she explained with a flat tone, "I cannot say they will be happy about it, nor can I tell you where to find them or how to contact them, because nobody knows. Akius believes that two Sages created the purple dragon sword, the one used to open a rift into the demon realm during the raid at the compound."

Niah fought to keep her expression neutral, Merida kept saying 'we', but she knew it was the Elders behind everything. The Elders would have been the ones to agree to the treaty, the Elders kept the Sages a secret. And for what reason? It didn't make sense. If the Sages were such a huge part of their history, why not tell people about them?

"But that sword belonged to a rider, he called himself one of the Five, whatever that means," Dea frowned, her snowy hair falling over her shoulders as she leaned her elbows on the wooden surface of the table.

"That's correct, but the rider was also able to open a rift into a demon realm using this sword. Akius believes only the power of a Sage could create such a thing, though their reasons for doing so aren't clear, seeing as part of the treaty was that they would never work against us." Merida answered. Convenient. The only reason such a clause would exist is if the Alliance and the Sages parted on bad terms.

"Maybe they weren't intentionally working against us?" Gren suggested.

"Perhaps, in any case; it's your job to find out." Merida pinched the bridge of her nose, everyone fell silent. "The purpose of this team is to find the Sages. Do that, and we may have a chance of finding out who rules the Shadows. If we can find the Sages and convince them to help us, it may well be an end to all wars."

Niah didn't miss the way Merida had said *all wars*. Something dark lurked beneath the surface of her Guardians eyes. Something she didn't think was related to her illness. Merida was hiding something.

"Fin will be your initial Commander, he will be reporting to me, and I will be reporting to the Oracle Conclave, it will look less suspicious if I have meetings alone rather than all of us. While the investigation is underway, Misha and Nate have been temporarily promoted to Commanders since Fin and Grenville will be focusing on this task," Merida watched for their reactions, no one protested, only nodded.

"I will leave you all to it. Fin, I expect a report tonight," she said, Fin nodded, and Merida left the room.

"We have somewhere to be," Fin said after a long, agonising moment. He was gazing at them now, his shoulders squared, eyes narrowed and oddly distant.

"Never thought I would be under the command of a hybrid before," Nick scoffed with a playful grin.

"Better get used to it," Sai winked.

"Are we all going?" Dea asked, twirling a piece of her hair around her fingers.

"Yes, I don't know what to expect at The Steel Queen, I'd rather be overprepared," Fin sighed, raking a hand through his hair, Niah caught his eye as he gestured for them all to leave. The room cleared, leaving the two of them alone as the doors closed. The air was thick was tension, as was Fin. She got to her feet and strode around the edge of the table until she was stood in front of him.

"What is it?" she asked, maintaining a small distance between them, even with the gap, she could feel the electricity between them.

"I should have known," he murmured, shaking his head slightly.

"About what? The Sages? Fin, nobody knew."

"You knew."

She sucked in a sharp breath, "I didn't."

"No, but you suspected the Elders were hiding something, and they were."

"Stop this." he met her gaze then. "You can't keep blaming yourself for not knowing something, you're not an oracle," a small smile danced at the edges of his lips, his silvery eyes sweeping over her face.

"I think I'd make a rather dashing oracle," he mused, his shoulders sagging as the tension ebbed away.

"There's something else you're not telling me," she whispered, the smile vanished.

"This is going to be dangerous. Possibly more so than anything we've ever faced," he muttered as he reached to tuck a lock of hair behind her ear and let his hand rest on her cheek.

"We're warriors, it's what we do. Besides, how much trouble could we face at a bar?" she smirked, he sighed.

"I didn't mean the bar," he murmured, "the Sages, if they did create this sword, imagine what else they could do. Breaking a treaty may lead to a war," his eyes were haunted, and for the first time, she saw a flicker of fear. Reaching down, she took one of his hands in hers, waiting until his eyes met her own.

"Whatever happens, we'll face it together," she whispered, her voice edged with such fierceness that he just stared at her. Finally, he sucked in a sharp, trembling breath and pulled her into his arms.

"Thank you."

She frowned, her next words were careful, "What is Merida planning?" he stiffened slightly and sighed.

"I have no idea."

The town was heaving with people. Many of them tidying away the decorations from the previous day's celebrations.

The group wore their patrolling gear, tougher jeans and leather jackets or t-shirts and hoodies with various weapons strapped about their persons. They marched through the town toward the Chambers, Niah found it a chore not to race ahead. Fin was calmer, though he still carried the usual tension in his shoulders, the way he always did when they left on patrol.

Velig was completely unphased by any of this, wearing a bright emerald suit jacket with sparkling black, skin-tight pants with dark purple cowboy boots, a slash of green running through his silver hair. Nick wore a black leather jacket with a hoodie underneath and a white t-shirt with dark jeans and boots, he seemed less enthusiastic about the arrangement than the others.

They signed their blood in the book, Fin grabbed an orb from the shelf and shoved it into his jacket pocket. The

Guardians surrounding the room said nothing, barely even looked in their direction as they positioned themselves in front of the portal.

"We may be bringing a prisoner back," Fin informed them, the Guardians exchanged a glance but nodded once in approval. They strode through the shimmering surface and out into a dark alley.

Niah guessed it was nearly midnight where they were, maybe a bit later. Clouds overhead blocked out the moon and stars. The air was muggy and thick as they treaded through the alley. Rubbish piled high on either side, sending a gut-wrenching stench into the air.

"Damnit, my boots," Dea groaned, jumping back from a puddle with rubbish floating in it. She scowled at the water before falling into step next to Niah, who couldn't help but smile.

"It's not funny," Dea mumbled, elbowing Niah in the ribs.

She shrugged, "Kind of is."

The mouth of the alley came into view. Beyond it was a quiet street. The ground wet from an earlier downpour. They stepped out under the light of a yellow streetlamp and glanced around. Streets lined with shops and bars, some with bright signs; some were dim and grungy. Humans walked past, not paying them any attention, apart from Velig, who received multiple strange looks.

"Humans have so little taste," he sighed, waving a dismissive hand.

"I don't think *they're* the ones with no taste," Nick muttered, Dea giggled and offered Velig an apologetic shrug when he turned to her.

They followed the street until the open shops turned to boarded-up shells, and brightly lit bars turned to sketchy dives. The people they passed grew fewer, and after a while, the people were no longer human. Rogues. She noticed the points of ears, wings, tails, hooves in some cases, she saw the luminous glowing eyes of spell weavers, the pale skin of vampires, even the glowing amber eyes of lycanthropes, no halflings though, and luckily, no demons.

Her blood was practically humming with excitement, more so when a group of vampires bared their fangs and hissed at them from across the street.

Eventually, they found a bar with a chipped sign of a silver crown. The Steel Queen. The windows were blacked out, the faint sound of music radiating from within, along with a stale stench. Fin pushed the loudly protesting door open. The air grew thick and bitter as they strode into the bar, though that could have been the tension that washed over the place as soon as they stepped foot inside.

The floors were wood, covered in a thin layer of sawdust. One wall lined with red leather booths, many of which were torn, and the stuffing was spilling out. The rest of the space comprised of tables and chairs that looked to be on their last legs. The tables all had knife marks or carvings etched into the surface.

The bar sat to the left of the room, long and lining the entire wall until a doorway opened up at the end leading to what Niah assumed was the toilets. The bar was sticky, water rings stained the dark surface, nutshells lay scattered across it, and behind the bar was a large grimy mirror along with shelves of liquor.

Despite its unpleasant appearance and aroma, the bar was full. Groups of men and women sat at the booths and tables, at the far end was a pool table with a small group around it. Others were focusing on the TV hanging on the wall showing a football game. Slowly, the customers looked up, the already thick tension now almost suffocating. Niah almost wished they had concealed their weapons better, humans couldn't see them, but supernatural creatures could.

She quickly shoved the thought aside, let them see them. Let them know exactly why they came.

They made their way over to the bar where two young women were talking at the far end. One of them looked up and froze. Niah's hand curled around the hilt of the dagger at her hip. The woman muttered something to the other girl before making her way over, the other girl disappearing through the door at the back.

The girl walking toward them was short and had bright green hair, her eyes the same shade, showing no whites; her nails were sharpened into long claws and painted black. No wings. Not all fey had them. The girl had pointed ears with multiple rings through them.

"Well well, we don't get many hybrids in here," she sneered, raking her green eyes over the group, her eyes lingering on Niah.

"What about halflings?" Fin asked with his most dazzling smile. The girl paused, her eyes narrowing.

"I think you should leave," she hissed, Niah took the opportunity to glance around the room. Twenty-three in total, none of them appeared to be carrying weapons or looked to be fighters. She was confident they would be able to beat them if it came to a fight.

In the far corner, in a booth underneath the TV, was a group of four, one girl and three boys. The girl was sat on the side facing them, she was staring at them. One by one, her companions turned to see what she was looking at, all of them shifted when they found Niah staring at them.

Only, Niah realised they weren't shifting because they were uncomfortable, they suddenly had weapons in their hands.

Swords, familiar swords. She had fought against those swords, trained with those swords. They were halflings.

"It seems we have some friends here, I think we'll stay," Niah said, tilting her head to the side as she looked at the fey bartender. Fin saw them before the others, a smirk at the edges of his mouth. The fey glowered at her, Niah only offered a silencing glare before turning to the booth.

Apart from their weapons, the four Shadows were dressed normally. The girl wore black denim shorts and a loose-fitting t-shirt with ankle boots, the boys wore jeans and short-sleeved t-shirts. They all had the same black iris.

They strode toward the table, more eyes focusing on them now, murmurs running through the bar. They came to a stop in front of the group of halflings, they stared up at them with cold contempt. It was only when they were standing in front of them that Niah realised how young they were. They couldn't be more than fifteen, and yet they sat in a grungy bar. If it weren't for the weapons they carried, she might have doubted they were with the Shadows at all. If it weren't for that hateful look in their eyes, she might have thought they were just ordinary teenagers. A part of her wished they were. So young, and ready to fight, maybe even kill.

"Get out." Niah barked over her shoulder at the other patrons. None of them moved, and a man even laughed. She reached and gripped the hilt of one sword over her shoulder, turning her head slightly to glare at the man that had laughed.

"*Now.*" she growled, her eyes blazing with blue fire. They stilled, decided it was better to leave than engage in a fight, and slowly got to their feet to leave. The bartender watched with annoyance, moving to the far end of the bar. Niah turned back to the four youngsters, anger flooding her veins. The Shadows were stripping them of their free will, turning them into killers when they were so young.

"Hi there," Fin grinned devilishly, "you must be with the Shadows."

The girl glanced at the boys around her before letting her gaze fall on Fin. They were children. Did they even know what the Shadows were doing to them? Did they realise they had no will of their own?

"And you must be Furies," she hissed through her gritted teeth. Niah cocked her head to one side, she couldn't help wondering how much of that fierceness was her, or the mark affecting her.

"We are. We have some questions for you," Fin said steadily, carefully. The group was silent as they glanced at each other. The boy sitting closest to them laughed and met Fin's gaze, who was still smiling.

"As if we would answer to you?" the boy sneered, his eyes glancing to Niah briefly before flicking back to Fin. His smile widened, Niah felt Dea stiffen next to her as her fingers inched toward the spear strapped to her thigh.

"You're outnumbered, I don't think you have much of a choice," Fin grinned, the boy glowered at him. A loud bang hammered through the room as the front door blew open. The fey bartender screeched and fled through the back door where the other girl had disappeared through earlier.

Niah glanced over her shoulder, Shadows stood dressed in black, not the shining armour they wore at the compound. *Shiasium* suits with matte black plates over their chests, shoulders, and legs. They wore black motorcycle helmets, with glowing red lights where their eyes would be.

"Now who's outnumbered?" the boy sneered; Fin turned calmly to him, a huge grin spread across his face.

"Come now, this is a party," he quickly reached out, grabbing the boy by the back of his jacket, and hauled him from the booth. The girl's eyes went wide, the other two boys looked as though they may try to attack, but one glare from Gren had them sitting back in the booth.

"Furies. Step away from our younglings," one of the black-clad figures bellowed near the doorway. Fin turned slowly, as did Niah. Sai and Gren kept facing the three behind them. More Shadows poured in through the back entrance, they were greatly outnumbered now. Electricity surged through Niah, her veins burning with adrenaline.

"We only want to ask some questions," Fin shrugged, still wearing the same smirk.

"As I said, they are younglings. They don't know anything." the figure said darkly, taking a step forward. The Shadows drew their weapons, swords, daggers, spears, and the odd gun. Thankfully, not the strange white ones they'd used in England.

Velig turned and waved his hands, crimson swirling walls went up around the booth, trapping the three halflings inside. They banged against the barrier in outrage, but the walls wouldn't give.

"You dare to imprison them?" the male figure boomed, taking another step forward, his great sword in hand.

"Nothing personal," Fin grinned. The man roared and charged straight for him, "I think this one has anger issues." Fin mused, shoving the boy through an open door that Velig had opened in the barrier, and quickly closed it.

Niah drew her blades as the other Shadows surged toward them. A masculine figure brought his sword down in a vicious overhead swing. He grunted as she shoved him back. It was just like at the compound. The Shadows looked like they were attacking with everything they had, but when they fought *her*, they used the flat of their blades.

With a flick of her fingers, she launched a figure aiming for Dea over the bar. The mirror and bottles of liquor shattered on impact. Another went flying through the front window. Her power danced in answer, and flowed through her veins at every command she gave it.

"Velig! Get us out of here," Fin shouted over the clanging of swords and shouts. Velig's hands glowed red as he raised them, he slapped them together and a pulsing shockwave rushed outward, pushing the Shadows back. He took the opportunity to raise another barrier around them. The Shadows were slamming against it angrily as the wall holding back the four younglings dissipated. Niah quickly snatched their weapons from them, the four of them too stunned to resist as they were hauled to their feet.

Fin smashed the orb against the wall, the portal opened, and Gren, Sai, Dea, and Cole went through, each holding onto one of the four youngsters, Nick followed. Velig held the barrier in place. Fin was shouting at Niah to hurry up and go through the portal.

She knew she should go back, they had people they could potentially get answers from. Things had changed. But her blood demanded a fight. She wanted to obey, to give in to the urges coursing through her body. She gritted her teeth. Fin still shouting her name. A hiss escaped her lips as she turned on her heel and stalked back through the portal.

9
Niah

They marched the four younglings through the lower levels of the Chambers. They were shouting so much that Velig had to silence their voices to save attention being drawn to them. Since they had brought back prisoners before, the Oracle Conclave thought it best to have cells made beneath the Chambers. They were made of stone, underground tunnels with small rooms cut into the walls. The front of the cells looked as though nothing was stopping the prisoners from escaping, though when dealing with supernatural creatures, magic was the best form of holding them.

Ruclite could have held them, but it was too precious to use on such things. They placed the three boys in individual cells but escorted the girl to a room far down the hall. Inside was a single chair with restraints over the arms. Merida, Cassia, and Vinaxx were already waiting there for them when they arrived. They sat the girl in the chair but left the restraints off.

She had a round face with thin lips and mahogany hair that hung to her shoulders. She gripped the edge of the chair, glowering at each of them. Niah noticed Cole staring at the girl, his hands balled into fists. Fin must have noticed as well because he asked Velig, Nick, and Cole to go back to the house to read through the books. They left without a word, Cole pausing in the doorway before leaving. Niah understood how he felt. This girl was nothing more than a puppet used by the Shadows to do their bidding. The way he once was. The way Niah was too.

"What is your name?" Merida asked when the door closed. The girl said nothing, just chewed her lip. Vinaxx stood behind the girl and moved her hair to look at the back of her neck. She jerked away from his touch, but he had already seen what he needed to see.

"We're not going to hurt you," Merida said soothingly as Vinaxx moved closer to Fin and Niah.

"The mark has faded, but it is still there," he murmured into Fin's ear, his brow furrowed. Why would the mark have faded?

"Liars!" the girl screeched, she was breathing hard between gritted teeth. Her fingers curled around the arms of the chair, her knuckles turning white.

"I know you don't trust us. We only need to ask you some questions," Merida said calmly.

"And then what? You just send us back to the Shadows? You think they would take us back after this?" she screamed, leaning forward in the chair, her eyes wild and furious. Now and then the girl's eyes would flick to Niah.

"That is true, I suppose." Merida said thoughtfully, "It would be your choice. We will let you go should you wish it." The girl stared at Merida for a long moment. She slumped back into the chair, still glowering.

"I won't tell you anything," she growled and folded her arms over her narrow chest. She was a dainty little thing, her limbs were spindly, despite the thin layer of muscle, her eyes too big for her face.

"We can get the information another way," Merida said, warning now creeping into her voice as she squared her shoulders and narrowed her eyes slightly.

The girl watched her as she gestured to Vinaxx. He took a step forward, his hand glowing white as he approached her. The girl stared, her eyes large and round, pressing herself against the chair, trying to get away; Niah could hear her heart pounding from where she stood.

"No." Niah snapped. Everyone turned to gaze at her in surprise, including the young girl. "Let me speak with her, alone." the others were silent for a long moment. Merida crossed the room, taking hold of Niah's arm and steering her to face the wall.

"What are you doing?" she muttered.

"Look at her, she's terrified. If we do this, we are no better than the Shadows." Niah murmured in a low tone. Fin had come to stand with them.

Merida held her gaze, hurt flashing across her eyes, "What makes you think you could get answers?"

"I was in the Shadows," she said, "I need everyone to leave." Merida was already shaking her head.

"It's not a bad idea, but I want to stay," Fin answered. Niah didn't meet his gaze, she was watching Merida. Her Guardian couldn't be comfortable with allowing Vinaxx into the girl's mind either. She had seen what happened to Cole, had seen the agony on his face when Morena looked through his memories. No, she couldn't allow that to happen to a young girl. Shadow or not.

"We will be outside if anything happens," Merida answered, her voice gentle. She gestured to the others, and they filed out of the room, the heavy metal door clanging shut behind them. Niah and Fin turned back toward the girl, she was staring blankly at the closed door; almost as if she didn't notice them at all.

Niah took a step closer to the girl, snapping her out of her daydream. The girl flinched as Niah held her hand out toward her.

"May I?" she asked, gesturing to the back of the girl's neck. The girl watched her hand for a moment before nodding and leaning forward. Niah brushed the girl's hair away from her neck, Fin hovered over her shoulder. The mark was indeed faded, but it was not a mark she had seen before. This was a shadowy figure with outstretched wings, the same symbol that had been in the books from Leandra.

"What does this mean?" Niah asked softly, surprising herself; she never knew her voice could sound so delicate.

"I can't tell you," the girl whispered; her body slumped forward. Niah caught hold of her and gently pushed her back against the back of the chair. Her eyes rolled back into her head, Niah stared at her, panic rising in her chest.

"Is she dying?" the marks could kill, the Shadows would know the youngsters had been taken, would they kill children to keep their secrets? Fin was at her side in an instant, lifting his hand to press his fingers to the girl's throat. He exhaled and shook his head.

"She's just unconscious."

"The Shadows can kill with those marks. If they know they've been taken, why haven't they done it already?" she asked as Fin scooped the young girl up into his arms, cradling her head against his chest as they headed for the door.

Guilt roiled in her stomach, they hadn't been thinking when they dragged the youngsters through the portal. For all they knew, the Shadows could indeed kill them. Just because they hadn't, didn't mean they wouldn't. The thought that four young halflings could lose their lives because of what Niah and the others had done sickened her.

"I don't know," he answered. They stepped out into the corridor. Gren, Sai, and Dea were no longer there, only Merida with Vinaxx and Cassia. They stared as Niah and Fin walked toward them.

"What did you do?" Merida breathed, rushing to them, and brushing the girl's hair back away from her face to get a better look at her.

"Nothing, she passed out," Niah replied as she marched through the corridors back to the cells. The hall was lined with Guardians.

They passed by the other cells holding the boys, they were asleep as well. Fin lay the girl down on the small bed in the cell. She didn't so much as stir as he left. Niah stood beside him as Vinaxx waved his hand, and the swirling, translucent wall blocked off the entrance to the cell.

"What did you find out?" Merida asked as they turned to leave the cells. Niah glanced over her shoulder, catching a glimpse of each of the youngsters sleeping soundly. Her hands balled into fists at her side.

"The mark she has isn't like the other marks we've seen," Fin said, though Niah wasn't entirely sure why Vinaxx had only told them the mark had faded, and not that it was different. She slid her eyes to him now, but he was looking straight ahead.

"Yes, yes indeed...it is very different, not one I've seen before, I don't have much experience with this mark...no, not at all," he rambled, still not looking at any of them.

"How is it different?" Merida asked as they stepped through the doorway and out into the airy corridor of the Chambers.

"We should discuss this at the house," Fin warned, Merida nodded. They walked through the Chambers, murmured voices emanated from one of the rooms. A door was cracked open, and she paused outside, but couldn't hear what they were saying. There was a small group of people standing inside with a dark-haired man speaking before them. The man cut off mid-sentence, the door was pushed closed from the inside and locked. She considered breaking the door down and demand to know what they were discussing, but she had no such authority, and she had her own problems to deal with.

The house was buzzing with tension as they walked through the front door. Voices radiated from the meeting room. With a sigh, Niah unstrapped her weapons and dropped them on the table along with her jacket.

"There's an armoury down the hall for those," Merida said with a small smile as they made their way down the corridor.

"I'll sort it later."

Dea and Sai were huddled over the same book where they sat next to each other, Gren was making notes while reading another. Velig and Nick looked bored as they flicked through pages. Cole was standing next to the sideboard, gazing blankly at the open book in his hands.

"This looks like it's going well," Cassia smiled, she had been uncharacteristically quiet for some time. She still seemed her usual vibrant self, wearing her usual bright clothes with many bracelets and a charming smile, but like everyone else, she carried thick tension in her shoulders.

"There's so much in these, it's a shame we weren't allowed to know about any of this sooner," Gren muttered, gazing intently at the pages and scribbling notes furiously. There was a spark in him she hadn't seen before.

"It seems only the Oracle Conclave and a few others knew of this," Merida frowned as she pulled out a chair and sat down, resting her head on her hand.

"So, about this mark," Cassia started, waving a hand over the table, a pot of tea and various cups appeared, "you said it wasn't normal," Niah slumped in one of the chairs, and pulled a leather-bound book toward her. It had the same emblem she had seen before; the snake in an infinity symbol with thorns wrapped around them.

"It was a shadow with wings, it was faded though." Fin said as he took a seat beside her.

"Isn't that like Cole's mark?" Dea asked glancing up at Cole who seemed completely disinterested with everything going on.

"Cole's was faded yes, but it was a completely different shape. Cole, are you sure you don't know what the difference is between these marks other than their appearance?" Fin asked, Cole froze in place. He turned to the expectant and hopeful faces before him.

"Why would I possibly know that? I was a test subject, remember?" he snapped, slamming the book he was reading closed and tossed it onto the table before stalking out of the room.

Fin sighed, "Everyone's in such a bad mood today."

"Fuck you," Cole shouted from the corridor as he stalked away. Dea got to her feet and dashed after him, Nick suddenly jerked upright, blinking, leaving a small puddle of drool on the table, apparently he had fallen asleep.

"Attractive," Velig murmured, handing him a red handkerchief from his blazer pocket, Nick gave him a thankful dip of his chin and wiped his mouth.

"For heaven's sake," Merida snapped, "this is important, Nick," she pinched the bridge of her nose between her thumb and finger.

"In all fairness, I don't even know why I'm here," Nick sighed, handing the handkerchief back to Velig, who quickly declined.

"You're here because you're a very skilled warrior of the lycanthropes, your sensory prowess alone will be of great use, and I suspect that our young Cole is part lycanthrope," Merida gave him a withering look.

"I guessed the same thing," Fin agreed.

"Hold up, why do you think he has lycanthrope blood?" Nick asked, scrunching his eyebrows together in frustration. Niah continued to read, half-listening to the conversation around her. Cassia pushed a cup of tea toward her, which she took with a smile. The tea was sweet and aromatic, the headache that had been forming quickly receded, and she found she had more energy.

"He's a twin, demons can't carry more than one child. Only demons crossed with another species can do that. Any spell weaver would have picked up any magic in him, vampires can't produce children since they're technically dead, he has no fey signs that I know of, so I assume he must be part lycanthrope." Merida explained, picking up her cup of tea.

Nick lounged back in his chair, "He could still be part fey, they don't all have a fey mark."

"That's true, though I believe there is more chance of him being a lycanthrope, that temper of his is very much like a wolf. Just, see if you can help him in some way," Merida sighed, closing her eyes briefly as she sipped at her tea. Niah thought she saw Merida's nails sharpen slightly before receding to their usual length, she frowned, how much longer did she have?

Nick sighed, "What a drag."

Niah didn't meet Fin's gaze while they sat studying the books. She knew he would bring up what happened at the bar, and she didn't feel like talking about it. She would have stayed. Almost did stay. She had never felt such a bloodlust before. Even now, the darkness of it lingered in her veins. What's worse is that she had wanted to surrender herself to it.

The thought scared her enough that she had gone through the portal. Things *were* different, they had a way to get information, even if the very thought of it sickened her. They'd kidnapped four young halflings. She wasn't sure how to feel about it. In one way, they had gotten them away from the Shadows, in another, they had taken them away from the only thing they had known. Were they better than the Shadows? As much as she hated to think it, there were undeniable similarities between the Shadows and the Furies.

It wasn't just the information or fear that brought her back, it was Merida. She didn't want to leave her Guardian, no matter how healthy she appeared, there was no telling when the next attack would hit, and Niah wanted to be there for it, regardless of whether she could do anything for her or not.

She buried her rotten feelings and lost herself in the pages of the books.

Dea

Cole was already out the front door by the time she caught up with him. He didn't seem to realise she was behind him, and she decided to take advantage and follow him. He marched through the streets toward the Chambers, standing at the bottom of the steps and looked up at the round building. His hands balled into fists at his side. He sighed and turned, finally spotting her.

"Oh...hi," he said, a thick line of tension running through him. His dark eyes were distant, haunted even. Her fingers itched to stroke his face, to take him in her arms and tell him it would all be okay.

Her parents had done that whenever she felt lost as a child, whenever she felt like she didn't belong. She saw that same loneliness in Cole. She saw it in Niah too, but whereas Niah was all cold rage and revenge, Cole wore it all on his sleeve. He couldn't hide his emotions.

"What's wrong?" Dea asked, falling into step beside him as they walked toward the fountain. She watched his features while he gazed at the various creatures carved out of stone.

"What will happen to those kids?" he asked in a low voice. Dea stared, she had no answer. It wasn't her place to say, she wasn't in command.

"I don't know."

He glanced at her then, his eyes wary, worried, "I was like them you know...well, kind of," he turned back to the fountain. She said nothing, giving him time to let it all out, to decide how much he wanted to share without probing him.

"I know it's not entirely the same, I was an experiment in the lab, they look as if they were being trained, but still," he shrugged, she wanted to reach out and touch his arm or face. It comforted her to be hugged or touched affectionately when she felt down. She always imagined others liked the same thing, until she met Niah. Dea tried to hug her once without warning, and she had nearly jumped through a wall.

"Still, it must be hard seeing them like that. Not to mention you're still fitting in here. It hasn't exactly been quiet," she said, trying to make her voice light.

A smile tugged at his lips, "It's very different," she took a step closer and gripped his hand in hers. His eyes widened slightly as he searched her face.

"It will get easier," she whispered, he sighed and pulled his hand free, taking a step toward the fountain and sitting down so he was facing her.

"That's what I'm afraid of," he frowned, she cocked her head to one side and sat next to him on the edge of the fountain.

"Why?"

"I feel like the longer I'm here, the less I want to leave," he said grimly, gazing down at the ground.

"Why is that a bad thing?" she inquired, twirling a lock of her white hair between her fingers.

"Because at some point I will have to leave, I will have to go to my sister," he said, pain clear on his features. She abandoned all thoughts and wrapped her arms around him, holding him tightly. He stilled for a second before relaxing into her embrace, letting his head rest on her shoulder.

"I'm sorry," Dea whispered, she wasn't entirely sure what she was apologising for. It was a habit, her adoptive parents had always told her she should apologise when people were sad. Not necessarily because she was the person who caused that pain, but sorry that that person was feeling that way. Cole raised a brow, questioning why she had said it.

"Human thing," she said with a roll of her eyes and a dazzling smile.

His brow scrunched, "You're part human?"

"No, I was raised by humans," she laughed, though her chest ached with the memory of her parents.

"How did that work?"

"My demon parent dropped me at an orphanage, I got adopted and they raised me," she said with a small shrug, still trying to keep her voice as light-hearted as possible.

"Are they still alive?" he asked, her heart throbbed again.

"I don't know," she murmured, her voice breaking, "I left years ago, I let them think I was dead. I stayed away because I know if I see them, I will want to go to them," she was surprised at the honesty of her own words. She hadn't wanted to say anything about her parents, had barely told anyone about them. Yet she found herself wanting to tell Cole.

"Do we always have to make such sacrifices?" he asked, Dea was quiet for a moment as she thought about that. She had never really considered herself to have sacrificed anything. If she had stayed with her parents, she may have ended up killing them by accident. Hybrids needed something to draw their focus, so when she was found, she thought of it as a blessing rather than a sacrifice. But that didn't stop the bitter ache in her chest, knowing what she had put her parents through. Knowing they would have mourned her.

"I think that depends on how you look at it," she replied, blinking away the tears that threatened to spill.

He sighed, "I don't think Niah likes me very much."

"Niah doesn't like a lot of people. But trust me, you would know if she didn't," Dea laughed musically, relieved for the change of conversation.

"How come?" he inquired, Dea shifted uncomfortably. It wasn't her place to talk about other people, especially her friends.

"Cole, trust me. If she didn't like you, you would know," she said with a friendly, yet firm tone to let him know she was done talking about it. He gazed at her blankly for a long moment.

"You're so...bright," he muttered, she gave him a quizzical smile, cocking her head to one side, "I mean, you're so happy and lively; it's like you're this bright light."

She shrugged, "I try to find the good and beauty in things."

"What do you see in me?" he asked, his cheeks turning slightly pink. She smiled.

"I see a lost boy. Someone who's trying to do what's right by his sister, someone who's strong and brave," she spoke softly, he said nothing; only stared at her. He wrapped an arm around her shoulders, pulling her in close to him.

"Thank you."

Fin

He was still awake when the sun rose the next morning. Niah had fallen asleep with her head literally in a book on the table, thankfully, she wasn't a drooler like Nick. Gren was still awake, two full notebooks in front of him. Velig had long since gone to bed, Dea was still out with Cole, or they had got back and just hadn't come in. Sai was lounging in his chair, his head tipped back, snoring loudly. Vinaxx had disappeared too, and Cassia was in the kitchen making tea. Her bracelets rattled together as she came back into the room, carrying a teapot. She could have prepared it with a wave of her hand without moving, but she said she liked doing things herself sometimes.

Gren and Fin both reached to take their cups after she poured the tea. The liquid warmed his body and sent sparks of energy through him.

"Is this one of your special remedies?" he asked, Cassia sat in one of the chairs, smoothing her skirts.

"It is," she beamed. Fin's muscles relax slightly with new energy, his lids no longer heavy. He'd never get tired of spell weaver brews.

The books had gone into detail about the Sages, there were eight in total; though one of them was said to be stronger than all of them put together. That one was referred to as the Sage of All. There were Sages for every species. The Sage of Wolves, The Sage of the Moon, the Sage of Spells, and the Sage of Wings were all said to have been the first of their kind and paved the way for the supernatural world. There was also the Sage of Wisdom, the Sage of Fists, and the Sage of Blades.

There was more information on the seven of them than the Sage of All. The books only said that the Sage was stronger and that the title 'Sage of All' was self-explanatory. Fin couldn't find a logical way in which a Sage could be all a lycanthrope, fey, spell weaver, and vampire, unless he was misinterpreting it.

Still, throughout the books, there was nothing to suggest where one might find a Sage. There was a whole book dedicated to the treaty they made with the hybrids once the last demon war was over.

As he read, he noticed that there was never a Sage of hybrids or halflings or Nephilim mentioned. Perhaps the Sage of All could have been one of them? He sighed as he ran his hands through his hair, his mind was swirling and his head throbbed, despite the rejuvenating tea.

Cassia had been going through the Code of Thamere all night, trying to find anything that may indicate why the Shadow marks may not be working through the barriers of the Island; not that it was a bad thing at this point.

His mind wandered, drifting to the day before when they were stood in that dingey bar, the portal open and the red swirling wall keeping the Shadows at bay. He had seen the look in Niah's eyes, as if she were being torn two ways. She was going to stay.

He didn't know why she decided to come back, nor had he asked. The important thing was that she was back. It would be her choice whether she returned or not. As much as the thought pained him, he would not force her to do something she didn't want to do.

Niah stirred and pushed herself up slowly from the table. Her eyes puffy from sleep and still half-closed. Cassia handed her a mug of tea, and she drank it gratefully, her eyes brightening after a few mouth fulls. She glanced at Fin, who smiled at her. Her eyes were still distant, they had been like that for a while; a pang shot through his chest.

"I'm going to go speak to our little Shadows in the cells," Fin said, not wanting to sit in an uncomfortable silence much longer. Niah drained her tea.

"I'll come too."

"No, you're not." Cassia said firmly, both he and Niah turned to her in surprise, "You haven't trained for a few days, you need to, come on." Cassia rose from her chair, smoothed her skirts, and hurried from the room. Niah rolled her eyes but reached up and kissed Fin gently on the cheek, his skin burning where her lips touched him. He caught her arm before she left the room, and she turned to give him a quizzical look.

"Is everything okay?" he asked, she gazed into his eyes, hers turning to liquid onyx. Her face softened.

"We'll talk later," she muttered with a reassuring smile. He kissed her forehead, and she hurried away. Gren was staring at him when he turned back.

"Well, that was awkward," he murmured, Fin sighed; he was right. It *was* awkward. He felt awkward for worrying about Niah when she was one of the most capable people he knew, yet there was something off about her. Something he couldn't put his finger on.

"Tell me about it," he groaned, "I'm going to the cells."

"I'll come too, would do me good to get away from these books and that damned noise," he flicked his eyes to Sai, who was snoring loudly. Fin grinned and grabbed the book that was open in front of Sai and closed it loudly over his face, causing him to jerk awake.

"What the hell, man?" he demanded, getting to his feet, his eyes too puffy to emphasize the glare he was trying to achieve.

"You were snoring," Fin shrugged, "we're going to the cells, are you coming?" he turned for the door, Gren followed and then eventually Sai, mumbling to himself.

"You could be a little nicer, you know?" he sulked as they climbed the steps to the Chambers.

Fin raised a brow, "What would be the fun in that?" Sai rolled his eyes and shoved his hands in his pockets.

"I'll get you back."

"Sure."

They walked the corridors of the Chambers to find Amarah strolling toward them, a book open in her hands. He had only ever seen her in her black robes and the white dress during the celebration, but now she wore light blue jeans with high heeled boots and a long-sleeved, black t-shirt, her braided hair swinging from side to side as she walked. She glanced up at them and came to a stop.

"Commander Fin, Commander Grenville, and Sai. Lovely morning, isn't it?"

"It is, Lady Overseer." Fin agreed, they bowed their heads briefly, instinctively standing with their shoulders squared and their hands clasped behind their backs.

"Respectful as always. Commander Grenville, I hope you are not too put out about your position being put on hold while you attend to this highly important matter?" she asked, gazing at Gren.

"No, Lady Overseer, Counsellor Merida assured me this is only temporary," he answered with a bright voice he only used when addressing his superiors.

"That is true. Young Sai, do you have ambitions of becoming a Commander?"

"I'm not sure yet, Lady Overseer," he replied, Fin always assumed Sai would be a Commander one day, he seemed the type for it. But Sai enjoyed his freedom, he didn't like meetings or responsibilities, not in the same way Gren did.

"Very well, I trust everything is going well?" she asked, her voice musical as she turned back to Fin.

"Yes, Lady Overseer," he answered while lowering his eyes. She said nothing in return, only smiled and continued down the hall. They made their way through the maze of corridors until they reached the door to the cells, the Guardians standing guard said nothing, they barely seemed to notice their presence. Their stillness was eery, unnatural.

"You don't know if you want to be Commander?" Fin asked as they descended the stone stairs to the cells.

He shrugged, "I thought I did once, but I don't know, man, seems like a lot of responsibility." Fin regarded him thoughtfully for a moment but decided not to press the matter further.

They came to a stop in front of the four cells. The girl was sitting on the edge of the narrow bed, the boys either pacing or lying on their backs. The girl looked up, her eyes widening as she took them in.

Sai and Gren stood a little way back, he thought it might be less intimidating for them. One of the boys looked up, he had short blonde hair with dark eyes. They were all so slight. How was it possible they were being trained as warriors?

"What do *you* want?" the boy barked venomously, glaring at Fin. The other boys heard and stepped close to the swirling wall in front of them. One of the boys had hair as black as coal, the other had carroty red hair with freckles across his nose and cheeks.

"Have you eaten?" Fin asked.

"Yes." the girl answered sheepishly, he gave her a quick smile before turning back to Sai and Gren.
"Would you guys mind grabbing some food? I've not had breakfast myself yet," both of them nodded and turned for the stairs. Fin walked forward a few paces and pressed his hand to the black panel on the wall, the swirling barrier disappeared, leaving nothing between the younglings and him. They were

hesitant, but stepped out, glancing around, noting the Guardians lining the walls.

"Come on," Fin said and turned to walk the other way down the line of cells. The corridor narrowed into a set of double doors at the end, through the doors was a large canteen with tables and chairs set out. To the far side were sofas and shelves of books. It wasn't much, but it was better than the cells.

He sat down at one of the round tables and gestured for them to sit with him. The girl and two of the boys quickly took a seat, the blonde boy remained standing and crossed his arms. Fin just smiled and turned to the girl.

"How are you feeling?" he asked gently, she was quiet for a moment, keeping her head low as her eyes darted about the room.

"Fine," she muttered, the blonde boy glared at her before turning his icy gaze on Fin, who cocked his head to one side as he regarded the boy.

"You have an attitude."

The boy scowled, "You don't know me."

"I don't need to know you to know that you have an attitude problem." he mused and turned away from the boy to look at the others sat before him.

"My name is Fin, Commander Fin if you want to be formal."

"Fin?" the red-haired boy asked incredulously, "What kind of name is that?" he glanced at the blonde boy, the two of them sniggered.

"I've never really thought about it, there are weirder names," Fin shrugged, keeping his expression unreadable; not that the rudeness of teenagers bothered him anyway. The red-haired boy's smirk faded.

"What are *your* names?" Fin questioned, gazing mainly at the girl, she appeared to be wavering the most and hesitated before answering, glancing at the boys, who were giving her stern looks.

"Klara," she murmured, Fin felt triumphant as he watched the betrayal etched on the boys' faces.

"You idiot," the blonde-haired boy snapped, Fin turned and fixed the boy with an icy glare.

"She's the only smart one here, boy," he let every ounce of authority seep into his voice. The boy pouted and lowered his eyes.

The doors opened and Gren and Sai strode in, each carrying a bag of food. They placed the bags on the table and sat down on either side of Fin opposite the younglings. The blonde one glanced over his shoulder toward the slightly open doors. Without hesitation, he turned and darted for the exit, but Fin was faster. He was in front of the boy before he reached the door. The boy gasped and staggered back, Fin kicked the door closed behind him and advanced on the boy. The fear in his eyes sickened Fin to his stomach.

"What was your plan? Outside that door is nothing but Guardians, and they'll be far less lenient with you than I am," he said coldly, the boy's eyes darted from side to side.

"Isaac, come and sit down," Klara called to him, he pressed his lips together, his fists clenching at his sides, weighing his options. With a defeated sigh, he turned back to the table. Despite his obvious attitude problem, Fin liked his spirit.

"So, you're Isaac?" Sai said when they sat back down, Fin took hold of one of the bags, and shoved it toward the younglings. They dove into it like ravenous beasts. He frowned, his chest tightening as he watched them before pulling the other bag toward himself and his friends. Isaac nodded, chewing a piece of fresh, still warm bread.

"I'm Niklas, and that's Vincent," the black-haired boy said around a mouthful of meat, gesturing to the carroty haired boy next to him, also stuffing his face with meat and cheese. Klara picked delicately at an apple.

"Well, that took less time than I expected," Sai grinned, biting into a banana. Sai had been at the facility when Fin arrived, he had been the first to befriend him and helped him work through his anger issues. He had also been the first person Fin was ever intimate with. Sai was found when he was young, only five years old; Talon found him and brought him to the facility before he had a chance to know anything else, which Sai was always thankful for. He was also very adept at getting information from people, interrogations, and such. Isaac scowled at him but quickly went back to eating.

Gren shifted in his seat, "Did the Guardians not feed you well?"

"They did, we're just so hungry. We don't get fed much," Klara said in a small voice.

"Is that a part of the training?" Sai asked, Fin saw Sai watching every detail in each one of their faces, looking for any subtle changes that may indicate what they were thinking or feeling. They all nodded slightly.

"Why is that?" Gren asked, Isaac looked up briefly.

"It takes away our impulses for our needs," he shrugged.

Sai cocked his head to one side, "It's strange for warriors in training, especially ones so young, to be allowed out publicly." at that, they all glanced at each other.

"The mark prevents us from running. We don't want to go anywhere other than to the Shadows," Niklas answered, gazing directly at Sai.

"Do you not feel that anymore?" Sai pressed, the boy shrugged and went back to eating.

"Do you know where we can find the Shadows?" Fin inquired; Klara glanced at Isaac, who shook his head quickly; she turned and also shook her head.

"There are doorways dotted everywhere, as far as I can tell they all lead to the same place," Vincent sighed, Isaac leaned around Klara to glare at him, Vincent shrugged, "It's not like we can go back to them now anyway." A pang shot through Fin's chest, they couldn't go back to their home, the Shadows were all they knew.

"Are you all halflings?" Sai asked.

"Yes." Klara answered, she held Fin's gaze, "Where is she? The woman you were with yesterday," Isaac glowered at her, driving his elbow into her ribs, hard enough to coax a wince from her. Fin couldn't stop the growl escaping his clenched teeth, Isaac's shoulders curved in as if he could shrink out of sight and lowered his eyes.

"Niah? Why?" Gren questioned, his green eyes narrowing. Klara was silent for a moment.

"No reason," she mumbled. Fin narrowed his own eyes at them, none of them looked him in the eye, they were all looking down at the table. They knew something about Niah. He frowned and got to his feet.

"We'll have a physician check you over, wait here, I'll be back." he gave a knowing look to both Gren and Sai, they gave him a subtle nod before he hurried from the room, jogging through the corridors.

"Vinaxx," he called, when he arrived at the weavers office, Vinaxx was sitting on the sofa, reading a book. He glanced up at the urgency in Fin's voice.

"Whatever is it?"

"I need you to check the kids over, make sure they're healthy," he said. While Vinaxx wasn't working in the house with them, he served as the head healer and worked in an office within the Chambers. The weaver wasted no time in following Fin from the room.

"I was curious, is there a way to see through someone's memories without hurting them?" Fin asked, walking with Vinaxx back toward the cells.

"No...not really, the spell is...brutal, but effective in certain circumstances," he answered, his high-pitched voice wavering as it usually did.

"I see."

"Is there something you need?" Vinaxx asked, his voice sharp and focused. Fin glanced at him and sighed, raking a hand through his hair.

"A magic ball would be nice."

"Oh no! You do not want to mess with a magic ball...trust me...very bad...very bad voodoo," Vinaxx rambled, Fin sighed again; he should have gotten Cassia. They walked back into the small canteen in the cells.

"This is Vinaxx, he's a physician of sorts," Fin introduced.

"Yes, yes indeed...a physician, very well put, Commander. Now, where are_ah, there they are, yes...indeed. Come here, dear." he gestured for Klara to go to him. She hesitated but did as she was told. He pressed a hand to her forehead and closed his eyes, his fingers glowing with white light. He muttered something to himself as Klara shifted uncomfortably beneath his touch. After a few minutes, Vinaxx pulled away and shrugged.

"This one is perfectly healthy," he said with a lopsided smile, Klara gazed at him, blinking in confusion. Fin's brow furrowed as she walked away in a daze. Isaac was next to be examined. Fin placed a hand on Klara's shoulder, she looked up at him blankly, almost through him.

"You asked about Niah, why?" he asked, her brow scrunched, "the woman from yesterday, long black hair?"

"Oh...I thought I recognised her, but I was mistaken," she answered, her voice flat, void of emotion. What changed? Had the boys said something to her while he was away? He met Sai's gaze, he shook his head.

He glanced at Vinaxx as he was finishing with Vincent, the last one to be checked. Fin narrowed his eyes, Vinaxx's hands were trembling, his eyes darting around wildly.

Had he done something to them?

"Well, indeed, the children are all perfectly healthy...a little on the thin side...no matter! Some food, yes definitely food is the treatment." he rambled, quickly making his way for the door. He could go after him, but Vinaxx was powerful. If he had done something to the children, then the question was why. The boys had the same dazed look in their eyes as they wandered over to the table and sat down.

"What's going on?" Gren murmured, Fin hadn't even noticed him come to stand at his side. He was too preoccupied watching the youngsters absentmindedly dig into their food as if stuck in some kind of haze. Perhaps it was just a side effect from the check-up, but Fin couldn't shake the niggling feeling in the back of his mind.

"Honestly? I have no idea."

10

Niah

Niah was breathing hard as she sat on the grass opposite Cassia cross-legged, her palms pointing toward the sky where they rested on her knees. A layer of sweat covered her skin, glistening in the sunlight. A stone sat between them, Niah was trying to bend it. Over the weeks, she had been through rigorous training with Cassia. Learning how to move objects, including people. She had learned how to summon fire and water and had mastered bending wood, stone was a lot harder.

"It's only the same as bending wood," Cassia sighed for the millionth time.

"It isn't though, is it?" Niah snapped as she glared at the rock.

"You're right, you need more power." Cassia shrugged.

Niah narrowed her eyes, "What? You mean you knew, and you didn't tell me?" Cassia laughed musically; her bright eyes dancing mischievously.

"Well, you didn't ask," she beamed.

Niah rolled her eyes and groaned in frustration, "How do I get more power then?"

"You can draw power from anything around you, the most popular one is nature, you can also draw from the sun, the moon, or a special lunar event; you can draw from other beings too. Ironically, humans give off the most energy." she explained. Despite her frustrations with her shortcomings, Niah liked hearing Cassia speak about magic.

"How do I draw from those things?" she asked, dragging a hand through her hair.

"Just imagine the flow of energy being absorbed by your skin, the magic within you will devour that energy. Your magic is even stronger than most spell weavers because your magic is drawn from your demonic and angelic blood. But because you've not done this before, you won't know how to harness that strength," Cassia said softly.

Niah nodded and closed her eyes, imagining the nature around her seeping to her skin and mixing with the electric blue of her magic. It started as slight pin pricks, thousands of tiny needles piercing her skin. It wasn't painful, not even uncomfortable, nothing more than a tingling sensation all over her body.

The colour expanded in her mind and even pulled flecks of greens and browns within the blue. She imagined the mass of colour spreading down her neck, over her shoulders, down her arms and chest, all the way to the tips of her toes.

"Whoa," she murmured, her muscles felt stronger, bones felt harder. She could feel the magic coursing through her veins, alighting her nerve endings brilliantly.

"Good, now focus on the rock, and bend it," Cassia encouraged. Niah gazed at the rock, imagined every surface of it, every detail. She imagined stripping away the structure of the rock from the inside out. To her surprise, the surface began to ripple slightly.

"Good." Cassia breathed, Niah continued, pressing further. She harnessed the power surging through her, the rock didn't quite bend, but a small dip formed in the surface.

"It's still not good enough," she ground out through her teeth, releasing the spell, the rock hardened once again.

"No, but it will come," Cassia smiled as she rose to her feet, Niah stood with her.

"It's so frustrating," she grumbled as they began walking back to the town.

Cassia snorted, "It's magic, what did you expect?"

"I don't know, I didn't even know it was something I could use until I came to Perth. I've never struggled with learning anything," she frowned, not meaning to brag, but whenever it had come to fighting or weapons, she had picked it up like a fish learning to swim, it came naturally.

"We all have difficulties with some things. Your magic will grow and become stronger the more you use it. You'll be able to use a lot more for a lot longer. Think of it like a muscle being exercised," Cassia smiled lightly. As they made their way through the town, they noticed another house had popped up next to the house they had moved into. Except this one had Guardians stood outside the door, and all around the building.

Merida emerged from the door to the new house, spotted Niah and Cassia and made her way toward them. Her hair was in disarray as she ran her hands through it, her shoulders thick with tension. Worry gripped Niah's chest.

"What's wrong?"

"Those kids are a nightmare," Merida sighed, pinching the bridge of her nose between her fingers. Niah glanced over Merida's shoulder toward the house and raised a brow.

"Do all kids make your face look like that?" she inquired with a slight grin, Merida looked up with a scowl.

"Fin was one of the worst, but these are pretty close," she sighed, turning to their own house.

"Why have they been moved?" Cassia asked as they made their way into the kitchen, Merida fumbled with a pot of water and placed it on the hob to boil.

"Because apparently, Fin has a huge soft spot for lost children," she sighed, slumping down in a chair at the table. Cassia placed a comforting hand on her shoulder and moved to take over making tea. Niah sat down at the table with Merida.

"Is that such a bad thing?" Niah asked, gazing at the woman as she dropped her head into her hands.

"It is when we don't know anything about them," she groaned, Niah frowned and looked to Cassia for help.

"It is odd, that such kids seem to be so brazen. I would have expected the Shadows to have hammered that out of them," she said absentmindedly, readying three cups.

"Not necessarily, look at Niah," Merida sighed.

"I resent that." Her Guardian shot her a withering look.

"They also had the mark on them, it has faded now, they have their own will and thoughts, the mark is put on them to take that away." Merida frowned. Niah thought back to her time with the Shadows, they weren't particularly strict, they were brutal sometimes in their teachings and punishments; but she was never told she had to act a certain way.

The marks on the kids may well be very different to the one that was on her. She always retained her free will, for what reason she didn't know, it made more sense to place a controlling mark on her if they wanted to use her as a weapon. But the kids had a different mark, it was possible that they were controlled with them and were made to act the way that they had at the bar.

"I went through the books; it seems the barrier is far stronger than I realised. The barrier may be stripping the marks of their power," Cassia told them as the water came to a boil, she spooned in a powder and a golden liquid and poured it into mugs.

"Well, that's something at least," Merida sighed as Cassia set a mug down in front of her.

"Did you manage to find anything out about the Sages?" Cassia asked as she took a seat in between the two hybrids.

"Nothing exactly clear. There's information on what they are, nothing on who or where they are though," Niah grimaced, she took a sip of her tea, already feeling the energy coursing through her body.

Merida sipped at her tea and set the mug down, "Finding them will be the key to everything."

"How so?" Cassia questioned.

"I don't believe the Sages vanished simply because of a treaty. I don't believe the reason a treaty was formed in the first place." deafening silence draped around the room. Niah's heart stuttered.

"You don't think they wanted to be left in peace?" she asked. Merida sighed and took another swallow of tea.

"The Sages have been around for over two thousand years, they're the first of their kinds, the strongest of us all. Do you believe they would even *need* a treaty if they wanted to be left alone?" Merida's words hung between them. Cassia shifted in her seat, but said nothing. Niah regarded her Guardian thoughtfully.

"How do you know so much about the Sages?"

Merida shook her head, "That's just what was written in the books. The rest is just a theory."

Niah wanted to ask her what she really thought. But not while Cassia was there. As much as she thought of the weaver as her friend, if Merida thought the same as Niah in regards to the Elders, then it was better as few people heard it as possible.

"I'm going next door to speak to the kids, are you coming?" Niah asked, getting to her feet and glancing at Merida, she shook her head.

"I don't think I'm their favourite person right now. Sai is with them," she answered before taking a swig of tea. Niah frowned but turned and headed for the door.

The Guardians outside the house nodded as she approached. She pushed the door open and found Sai lounging on the sofa opposite the unlit fireplace. He looked up as she closed the door and grinned.

"You're on babysitting duty?" she smirked, lowering herself next to him, tucking one leg underneath herself. He chuckled lightly and gazed at her; his brown eyes seemed almost bronze with the light streaming in from the window reflected in them.

"Something like that, Fin said they trust me," he shrugged.

She glanced around, "Where are they?"

"In their rooms, they do *not* like Merida."

"She sent them to their rooms?" Niah raised a brow, Sai nodded with a grin.

"As soon as she came in the blonde one started shouting at her, the other boys joined in pretty much straight away and she sent them all to their rooms."

"They actually did as they were told?"

"Merida can be quite scary when she wants to be."

"I can't imagine that." Niah shook her head, the ghost of a smile brushing her lips.

"You should have seen her when she was trying to tame Fin," he laughed.

"Was he that bad?" she asked, remembering Merida's earlier comment about Fin being one of the worst kids she had ever known. She would never guess he would have been like that, but she remembered when he told her what he was like before Merida had found him.

"I was already at the facility when Merida brought Fin back. He's older than I am, but I was found before he was, I was only a kid myself. Fin must have been around twenty or so, something like that. He was just a burning ball of rage, angry at the world, at himself." Sadness lurked beneath the surface of his eyes.

"You think these kids are going through the same thing?"

He sighed, "Well, whatever they went through in that place, I can't imagine it was pretty."

She stared into the unlit fireplace; anger spiked in her veins. The Shadows were expert deceivers, but all lies had an expiration date. That wasn't the real problem, lies may not last forever, but the effects of those lies could last a lifetime. How would the lies affect those four? She knew how they affected her, drove her to an unbearable thirst for revenge.

Whether the four youngsters chose to stay with them or not, they would suffer from what happened with the Shadows for quite some time. She couldn't help wonder how long she would be hellbent on revenge, would she be able to stop when she achieved it? Would it fill the void inside her? There was only one way to find out, she supposed.

A footfall sounded on the wood floor behind them, she turned to see the young girl standing at the bottom of the stairs. Her eyes were large and dark, her face softened when she saw the two of them.

"I thought you were that other woman," she said weakly.

"No, my name is Niah," she answered with a smile, the girl walked to them, stopping a safe distance away.

"Go on, I haven't told her your name," Sai encouraged, the girl glanced between the two. Niah couldn't believe how shy she was, was she even the same girl as the one she had witnessed yesterday? With the venomous glare and stern voice. The marks must have more of an impact than they thought.

"I'm Klara," the girl muttered, Niah smiled and held out her hand for the girl. Sai had done the same thing when they had met, later he had told her it was a human way of greeting. The girl stared at Niah's hand, and hesitantly reached out, her skin was cool to the touch. Niah frowned, hybrids could regulate their body temperature to match the weather, but halflings couldn't, they were still half-human.

"Are you cold?" Niah asked, the girl nodded. Niah's eyes awoke into blue flames, the girl jumped back but Niah turned away and waved her fingers at the fireplace, sending sparks into the pit. Electric blue flames leapt and danced. Niah turned back to the girl who was gazing in awe.

Klara moved to sit in front of the fire by the coffee table, she held her hands over the flames, rubbing them together to warm them. Niah hadn't expected it to be cold in Thamere, though as she looked out the window, night was beginning to draw in.

"So, what are you?" Klara asked in a small voice as she twisted around to look at Sai and Niah.

"We're both hybrids, half demon and half angel," Sai answered gently. She would never have guessed that Sai had a soft spot for children, would never have imagined he was good with them.

Klara tilted her head, "Can you do that too? With the fire?"

"No, just Niah. She has spell weaver blood," he replied, Klara's brow furrowed.

"What's a spell weaver?" she asked, Niah sighed. She half expected as much, she had to learn so much about the other species when she arrived with the Furies. Her chest ached slightly, she felt for these kids. It made her angry at the thought of how many more were with the Shadows, deceived and not informed about the real world.

"Why don't you go and get the others? We'll tell you everything," Sai suggested, Klara got to her feet and disappeared up the stairs without hesitation.

"I know it's frustrating," he murmured, sensing Niah's mood darken.

She raised a brow, "It's not just frustrating, it's barbaric," he nodded in agreement. She took a deep, steadying breath and gazed into the blue flames.

"You would make a good Commander," she said gently, not meeting his gaze.

"Oh yeah? Why's that?"

"You care."

He snorted, "We all care."

She met his gaze, "Not like you do, Fin does, Gren does; and you do."

He was quiet for a moment, his eyes resting on the fire, "I can't be responsible for lives."

"Why not?"

"Because if someone died on my watch, I couldn't live with myself," he said, his expression unreadable. She frowned, that thought had never occurred to her before. Then again, she had never thought about becoming a leader. She only ever had one goal, one purpose. And she was willing to do anything to get it.

They were interrupted by the sound of feet coming down the stairs. The boys introduced themselves, the blonde one not looking all too impressed to be in her company.

They took a seat while Sai and Niah explained about what they were, what the kids were, what Thamere was and the other species that lived there. They explained what they knew about the Shadows. The kids listened, surprisingly intently, except for Isaac, who seemed mostly bored.

"You guys said there were doorways that would lead to where the Shadows were, where can we find one?" Sai asked once they stopped asking questions. Niah thought they might clam up at the question, but they didn't. Sai met her gaze, dipping his chin slightly. He'd earned their trust. It wasn't surprising, he had earned her trust quickly enough. Had the youngsters ever had someone to speak to like this? To take the time to explain things to them?

"I don't know, they always move around, they're never in the same place twice," Klara shrugged, Isaac glared at her; annoyance flashed through Niah as she watched the boy. He looked up at her, surprised to find her already watching him.

"What?" he snapped.

"What's wrong?" she asked coldly.

"Do you honestly think we'll help you get to the Shadows?" he glowered, Niah held his gaze, narrowing her eyes.

"Why protect them? What have they done for you?" she asked quietly, carefully. They were just kids, she couldn't lose her temper with them.

Isaac straightened his spine, "They gave me a roof over my head, training."

"And barely any food by the looks of you, they lied to you. Placed a mark on you to strip you of your free will, trained you to be in their army. So again, why are you protecting them?" she demanded, Sai stiffened next to her.

"What would *you* know about it? You've all been living a pretty cushy life by the looks of this place," the boy snapped, Sai chuckled humourlessly at that.

"I was raised by the Shadows too." Niah growled, the boy's eyes widened, "They lied to me too. They trained me to be a weapon, used my hatred and anger and conditioned me to crave revenge more than air.

I was found by the Furies and they told me the truth. The Shadows put a mark on me to suppress my power because I have angelic and magic blood as well as demonic. They destroyed a whole facility with our kind inside as well as other species, they killed children, *experimented* on children, and when their experiments failed; they dumped the bodies on our doorsteps.

They have magic strong enough to turn us against each other and kill our own. *That* is who you are protecting." The faces before her paled, their eyes widened.

Isaac's mouth closed, his lips pressing into a firm line as his cheeks burned pink. Sai placed a hand on her shoulder, though she barely felt it. Anger was all there was, remembering everything that had been done made her relive the memories over and over again. She got to her feet and stormed from the house into the cool night air without looking back.

It was impossible. They could list off every terrible thing the Shadows had done and were still doing, and it wouldn't make a blind bit of difference. The youngsters finally had a taste of their thoughts, free will, and they were finding it difficult to adjust. Finding it difficult to accept who and what the Shadows were. Something she understood all too well. She wasn't angry at the younglings, only angry at what they were going through.

11

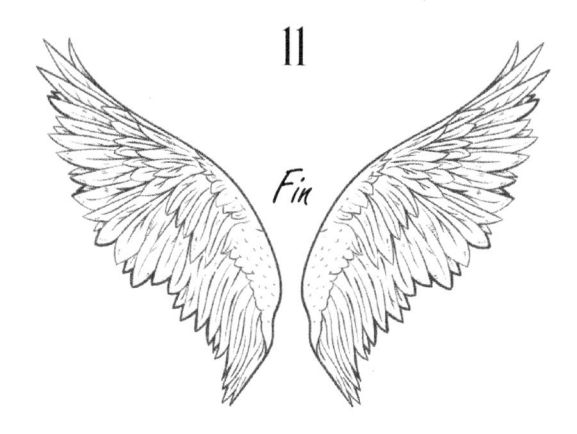

Fin

He was walking with Gren back through the town. After the morning he had, he needed to blow off some steam and saw no better opportunity than training Cole. He sparred with Nick while Cole went through drills with Gren and Dea. By the time he was finished, sweat trickled down his back and he fought to get air into his lungs. It wasn't enough, he was still restless. He had gone to the Oracle Conclave after they spoke to the youngsters and explained the situation, his request to move them into their own house under guard was approved, and the materials were arranged ready for a weaver to put them all into place. Amarah had been sceptical and initially refused, to Fin's surprise, it was Ragnar that talked her round.

Night had fallen and they were walking back to the house when a door slammed, and he spotted Niah standing outside the kids' house, her face tilted up to the sky with closed eyes, her chest rising and falling quickly. Gren clapped him on the shoulder and gave him a 'good luck' nod before going into their own house with Dea, Nick, and Cole. He walked cautiously toward her. She heard him approaching and rushed toward him, crashing into him, and wrapping her arms around his neck. Startled, he wrapped his arms around her, stroking her hair soothingly. People in the streets stared, but a glare from Fin had them quickly averting their gaze.

"What happened?" he asked softly, she shook her head, pulled away and took his hand as she led him down the street toward the training grounds, only stopping when she was sure they were out of earshot from anyone, she let go and began pacing.

"Niah, what's wrong?" he asked worriedly, she was biting her nails, she never did that. His chest fluttered uneasily.

"We need to do something, quickly," she said, her voice wild and unsteady, her eyes unfocused and distant.

"What happened?"

"Those kids, they're so brainwashed, well...Isaac more than the others, he wants to *protect* them." he stayed completely still. Having never seen her so unsettled, so frantic.

"It's the only life they've ever known," he said softly.

"But it's *wrong!*" she yelled, her voice high and wavering. She whirled on him, her hands balled into fists at her sides, her eyes blazing bright and blue.

"I know, we'll stop them; we can help whoever is there. We *will* find them," he told her firmly.

"We need to go now, we need to go and not come back until we find them," she growled, he knew it wasn't directed at him, none of this anger was. It had been building up for years, all that rage finally bubbling to the surface.

"We can't, Niah," he said pleadingly, he wanted to ask her to calm down, but that would be like throwing petrol on a fire.

Her voice was cold and hard, "Why not?"

"Because we have leads, we have things we need to do here. We can't just go off on our own, we'll be killed," he said, trying to reason with her, but she was already shaking her head, "That's why you hesitated before coming through the portal, you were going to stay and do this on your own," anger sparked in his chest. Why did she have to be so damned reckless? He knew she was battling with herself, knew it wasn't them she would be leaving, that she would only be chasing revenge. But to go on her own? It was insane. No matter how strong she may be, she couldn't take on the entire army of Shadows.

"Yes. And I wish I had stayed." she hissed, he pressed his lips into a thin line, her eyes widened, and her mouth fell open as she realised what she said.

"Do you trust me?" he asked calmly.

"What?"

"Do you trust me?"

There was a long pause, "Yes."

"Then why don't you trust that I know what we're doing? Why don't you trust that I want to find these bastards as much as you do?" he demanded; she was silent. She raised her fists and clamped them to the sides of her head.

"I just want it all to be over," she murmured, her voice low and cracking as she pulled her fists away. The blue of her eyes turned to hard onyx, glistening in the moonlight. Fin realised she was crying. He wanted to go to her, to fold her into his arms, but willed himself to stay still.

"Niah, we can do this, okay? But we need to do it properly," he said gently, a sob racked through her body, and she fell to her knees.

"Damnit," she cursed, wiping the tears away from her face. He went to her then, kneeling in front of her, and gently pulled her hands away from her face, she looked up at him with watery eyes, tears shining as they rolled down her cheeks.

"Listen, this isn't something we can just go in all guns blazing. For a start, we don't even know how to find them," he whispered, brushing away a tear.

"I know," she sighed, "I just...I don't want to feel this way anymore," fresh tears streamed down her cheeks. He stroked them away with his thumbs as he cupped her face in his hands and gazed down at her.

"What do you feel?"

"I just feel...rage, all I can focus on is revenge, I'm scared I'll lose myself if I feel anything else," she muttered, her voice breaking.

"You don't have to hold onto it, you can let it all go." She was already shaking her head.

"I can't."

"Why not?"

A sob escaped between her gritted teeth, "Because it's all I've ever known."

His heart shattered. It didn't matter that he already knew that small fact, but hearing it from her lips, hearing the pain in her voice as she said the words. It tore at him from the inside.

"Come with me," she whispered, he stared at her.

"I can't, I have a duty here. You know that you're better off here, we can work together," he said pleadingly. Her eyes searched his. The tears stopped falling and she sighed.

"I understand," she murmured, leaning forward and resting her forehead against his shoulder, he held her for a long time. His chest throbbed, torn two different ways.

"I'm sorry," he whispered.

"Don't be, it was wrong of me to ask." she said. Her understanding only made the pain worse, he knew he had to turn her down, he had a responsibility, not only that, but they would get further if they worked together in Thamere.

"I won't leave Merida," she breathed, pain flashed across her features along with guilt. She gazed down at the ground, her shoulders trembling.

"I will do *everything* in my power to help you, Niah. But we need you here, we're stronger as a team, all of us," he murmured gently, she took a shaky breath and nodded once, looking him in the eye.

"Okay." he kissed her forehead and held her tight, feeling as though he had been left empty and raw. A hole punched through his stomach. He wanted nothing more than to help her, to be there for Merida and still do his duty. For now, he was able to keep her with him, though he feared the day when he would be forced to choose.

"I'm scared, Fin." Her words were little more than a strangled whisper. His heart stilled at that. Never did he think he would hear those words from her mouth. Now that he had, his heart broke for her.

"Of what?"

"I'm scared we'll fail, and I'm scared we'll succeed." She pulled away to look him in the eye, for the first time in what felt like months, her eyes were wide open. No longer guarded and distant.

"Isn't that what you want? Revenge?"

"It's not just revenge, not anymore. If we're successful, what do I do after? Who will I be?"

He folded her in his arms and cradled her to his chest. For years she had dreamed of nothing but revenge. It's the only thing that kept her going all those lonely years in the compound. It's what drove her. All that anger condensed from those torturous years was beginning to burn too brightly, and she was scared. Terrified that hatred had consumed her so entirely that once she finally got revenge, there wouldn't be enough of her to continue.

"You'll be whoever you want to be. You can start over. Hell, you could start over now if you wanted. Maybe you'll heal over time, maybe you won't. Maybe you'll be haunted with what could have been no matter what you choose, but it's *your* choice to make. And no matter what that choice is, I'll be by your side. You mean everything to me, and I don't want to lose you."

She buried her face into the crook of his neck, "I'm sorry I asked you to choose, it wasn't fair."

It must have been so hard for her to struggle with those feelings and have no idea what to do with them. He kissed her gently, and they walked back to the house hand in hand.

They readied for bed in comfortable silence. It was a huge step forward for her to talk to him the way she did, and he was thankful for it. Now he just had to deserve her honesty and be there for her.

She curled into his side, resting her head on his chest. He stared up at the ceiling with his arm under his head, his free hand tracing circles absentmindedly onto her back. After a while, her breathing deepened until he was certain she had fallen asleep.

"You'll be the death of me," he whispered into the darkness. He looked down at her sleeping form. Even asleep, she didn't look entirely peaceful. Her eyes flickered beneath her lids, her hands trembling. He would choose her. He would always choose her.

Cole

After his and Dea's conversation at the fountain, Cole felt more relaxed. He had been worrying about his sister, questioning his decision to stay in Thamere. She hadn't activated her necklace, which reassured him that she was okay, but there was still a nagging feeling in the back of his mind. Something dark that made him think there was something wrong.

He sat on the edge of his bed in the new house, alone, feeling as if he hadn't truly had a moment to himself since he had been in Thamere.

So much had happened already and it seemed like it was only the beginning. He had arrived while they were on the brink of war, or already in a war; he wasn't quite sure which. There had been a battle, but that was all he knew.

He traced his thumb over the skin where there should be an X scar between his thumb and index finger, but the skin was smooth as if it had never been touched. He had seen magic before, but never to this scale.

He thought back to his conversation with Dea. He'd been on his way to the Chambers, the portal room specifically, so close to leaving, until he turned and found her standing there. He wanted to be angry that she had followed him, but how could you be angry at someone who only ever had good intentions?

More than anything, Dea was a friend. She was trying to be there for him, and if he were being honest, he needed someone to tell him it would all be okay. Up until Thamere, that person had always been Nyx. Without her, it felt like a piece of himself was missing. They'd been together through everything, and he'd chosen to stay.

He frowned, his head beginning to throb, he was overthinking the way he always did. Usually, Nyx would knock him out of it, but she wasn't there to do that anymore. Because of a decision he made, and wasn't entirely sure he regretted it. Not anymore. Not now that he was beginning to feel like he belonged, not now that he was starting to understand the way of life on the island. Not now that he was finally getting the answers they wanted, the answers they *all* wanted.

He kicked off his boots and threw himself against the pillows. The bed was soft, he was lost in it instantly. Falling into a deep sleep.

<hr>

The next morning, he woke to a knock at the door. His muscles were stiff and aching, and he was in dire need of more sleep. The knock came again, louder this time. With a groan, he swung his legs over the side of the bed and answered the door. Nick stood on the other side, his dark hair pulled back.

"Get dressed," he yawned, stretching his arms above his head. Cole glanced down at himself, already in the training clothes he'd been in the night before.

Nick sighed, "Clean clothes, you stink. I'll be downstairs." With that, he stalked off down the hall. Cole ran a hand through his hair as he shut the door and rummaged through his drawers to find clean clothes.

In his hurry, he bumped into Dea in the corridor on his way out. She wore bright red athletic clothing, her snowy hair hanging in a braid down her back.

"Hey," she grinned as Cole fell into step beside her.

His cheeks burned, "Hi."

"Are you going to train?" she asked, he nodded as they descended the stairs.

"About time," Nick groaned, hauling himself from the sofa.

"I was barely five minutes," Cole argued, Nick rolled his eyes and yanked the door open before striding into the early morning light.

As always, the sun was shining brightly. It was one of the things he loved about Thamere, the almost constant sun. They strolled down the street toward the training grounds.

More and more buildings had been popping up as of late, even more fey were living in the town. When he first arrived, he was told they mainly kept to themselves in the forests as they had in the human world. It seemed that because they no longer had to hide, they wanted to be closer to everything else, the same with the lycanthropes and werewolves, which he still didn't entirely understand the difference between.

Cole wasn't looking forward to training with Nick. The last time he had no idea what to do when Nick changed into a wolf. He remembered the jaws snapping, the claws digging into the ground. How could you possibly fight a wolf? Especially one that *big*.

They came to a stop at the centre of the training grounds, it wasn't quite as busy as Cole remembered it. Which he was thankful for. If he was going to get his arse handed to him again, he wanted as few witnesses as possible.

Just as Nick was about to speak, a man wandered over toward them. Cole didn't think he had seen him before. The man had sandy hair with a matching beard. He wore jeans and a grey shirt which was buttoned up to the top with a narrow black tie hanging around his neck.

"Who's this?" the man asked with a warm, yet uncomfortable smile.

"Hi Talon, this is Cole," Dea chimed. The man, Talon, glanced at her with a fond smile before turning to Cole, despite his smile, his eyes were wary. Cole merely dipped his chin in greeting.

"Nice to meet you, we haven't had many newcomers since we came to Thamere," he said, Nick began pacing to the side, clearly uninterested by the blonde man.

"Oh..." Cole muttered, not sure what else to say.

"Cole, Talon has been here for decades, nearly a century isn't it?" Dea asked.

Talon grinned, "It will be a century next year."

"That's it. He was at the Perth facility for all that time, helping Merida with the running of it," she told him, Cole glanced at Talon, a strange look flashed across his eyes, but it was gone before he had a chance to read it.

"Important man then," Cole noted, Talon was hesitant before answering.

"Not as important as some. If you'll excuse me," he said with a brilliant smile before sauntering toward the town, Cole frowned as he watched the man leave.

"He's weird," Cole murmured. At that, Nick came back over to them, grimacing as he watched Talon leave.

"Yeah, too right."

"What do you mean?" Dea asked, her brow furrowed slightly.

"Nothing. Anyway, Fin and Merida think you are part lycanthrope, that's why we're here," Nick answered, quickly changing the subject. Cole stared at him blankly for a moment, Fin had told him he must have the blood of another species to even be alive considering demons can't birth more than one child at a time. Though in all honesty, he wasn't sure he believed it. Surely he would know if he had the blood of another species?

"I still don't understand this whole blood thing," Cole said, shaking his head.

"Well, you know demons can't have twins. A demon would have had to mate with another species, in this case, a lycanthrope. The offspring from that combination would be a demon crossed with a lycanthrope and would have to have been a female. The daughter would then mate with an angel, creating a half-blooded hybrid." Dea explained, his head began to throb.

"So, my mother is a lycanthrope-demon hybrid, and my father is an angel?" he asked.

Dea nodded, "Yeah, that would be about right."

"Are there any demon crossed with other creatures here?" he asked.

"There are some, not many. Unfortunately, demon-lycanthrope hybrids don't live very long, they're usually sickly because their mortal blood doesn't agree with the demonic half of themselves." she frowned.

"So, lycanthropes aren't immortal like us?"

"No, they originated from humans. Werewolves are turned, lycanthropes are born, but the lycanthropy gene can lay dormant for generations, it depends on the child's blood whether it manifests into lycanthropy. But they are mortal and age like humans do, vampires are undead so they're immortal, spell weavers and casters can choose whether to be mortal or immortal, and we don't have human blood so we just age until we reach our full growth and stop," she shrugged. Was this ever going to start getting easier to understand? He sighed and raked a hand through his hair. She took a step closer and placed a calming hand on his arm.

"It'll get easier," she smiled warmly. He didn't feel any better.

"So, now that you've had a biology lesson, can we get on with it?" Nick asked impatiently, Cole rolled his eyes and stepped away from Dea as she retreated to a safe distance.

"How are you going to know if I'm part lycanthrope or not?" he questioned, but Nick had already lunged for him with long claws extended from his fingers. Cole only had enough time to duck under the wolf's hand.

"What the hell?" he demanded angrily, straightening his spine. Nick's eyes glowed bright amber, almost gold, his canines lengthened into wolf-like fangs. He didn't answer, only lunged again and again, getting faster and faster. Cole found that unlike the last time they fought, he could read Nick's movements easier, and wasn't struggling so much to keep up.

Despite his faster reflexes and heightened speed and strength, going up against an angry lycanthrope was no easy task.

Nick let out a growl from deep in his throat and darted one way, turning swiftly on the balls of his feet, and lashed out, his claws slicing deep across Cole's stomach. The fabric of his shirt tore apart, black blood spilt down his stomach, soaking the waistband of his joggers.

The wound stung, but it was bearable. His heart began to race, and his breathing became erratic. Cole didn't understand. If Nick was angry at him, why wouldn't he have just said something?

Cole's eyes began to burn, his head throbbing. He clenched his fists on either side of his head as pain shot through his gums, like something trying to pierce through. He jerked away as blood welled in his hands, and sharp nails sliced into his palms.

He looked at Dea helplessly, who was staring with her hands cupped around her face. He turned to Nick, now with his features returned to normal, a triumphant smile on his lips.

"What the hell is this?" Cole demanded with a lisp as he tried to speak around his long canines. Nick chuckled. It only irritated Cole further as panic rose through his gut.

"Well, Merida was right; you are part lycanthrope."

"You did this on purpose?" Cole spat, gesturing to his stomach, except when he looked down, the gash had already healed and only blood was left smeared against his skin.

"Lycanthropes are very quick to anger, our first change is usually because we're overwhelmed with rage. That was actually very easy to get you to change into the first state. It takes others much longer," Nick explained, taking a cautious step closer. As Cole's heart rate slowed and his breathing steadied, his nails and teeth shortened to their usual length, and his eyes stopped burning.

"So, does this mean I can turn into a huge wolf?" Cole questioned, gazing down at his hands.

Nick chuckled, "More than likely. Some lycanthrope hybrids can't, they have too much hybrid blood to get a full change. But like I said, you seem like you may have more lycanthrope blood, so a full change should be doable. We have some work to do first though," the tension and anger had vanished, he now stood with his hands in his pockets and a lazy smile.

"Like what?" Cole asked, sitting down in the grass, the others followed suit, Dea picking daisy's and chaining them together.

"Well, right now you can only change when you're angry. You need to learn to control that, learn that your power doesn't come from anger. It will be easier to change after that and you'll be in control. If I had pushed you any further, you may have gone on a rampage," Nick frowned.

"How do you manage it?"

"I found that meditation helps," he shrugged, leaning back against his hands.

"Seriously?"

Nick sighed, "Look, it's up to you if you want to learn what being part lycanthrope means. I just think it will benefit you to learn more about it so that if you do get angry, you're not likely to run amok and hurt someone."

Cole gazed at his hands dangling over his lap, only a few moments ago he hadn't even recognised them as his own. He tried to think of a time when he was so incredibly angry and drew a blank. He had been angry at the Shadows when he got his will back, but he was more focused on getting himself and Nyx out as fast as possible. He didn't have time to focus on anger. The last time he trained with Fin and Nick, he felt himself beginning to get angry, but Nick changed into a wolf and surprised him. It was like having a monster inside of you, never knowing it's there; only to have it jump out and latch on. He sighed heavily and collapsed into the grass, gazing at the sky overhead.

"Don't get too comfy, we still have a lot of training to do. You're still way too slow." Nick teased, he got to his feet and held his hand out for Cole. He reached up and took it, getting to his feet to begin his training. With his eyes newly opened to the possibilities of what he may be able to do one day.

12

Niah

"I hate you." she snapped as she flung the frying pan with a blackened circle burnt to the bottom into the sink. Smoke quickly filled the kitchen. Gren sat at the table with a mug of coffee in his hand, grinning with amusement.

"You talking to me or the pan?" he asked with a cocked brow, she turned and threw the spatula with burnt bits of pancake stuck to it at him. He caught it out of the air and turned it over between his fingers.

"Don't mock me, I *will* end you," she growled, snatching a banana from the bowl, and wolfed it down quickly.

"*End* me?" he inquired, glancing around the room at the mess spattered over the sides and up the walls, "I really don't know how you manage to make such a mess." weirdly, he seemed to be in a better mood lately. He was sat at the table with his notebook in front of him, the one he seemed to carry with him most places.

"I don't know why I bother trying to cook," she sighed as she took another banana from the bowl and slumped down in the chair opposite him, he eyed her quizzically.

"Why don't you just...you know," he wiggled his fingers, "Use magic to do it?"

"Cassia hasn't taught me how yet; she says I need to learn to do it on my own first, and apparently it doesn't work that way." she sighed. She had slept deeply for a while before waking up to find Fin gone. It wasn't as if he was going on patrol, those duties had been suspended. He hadn't been in the house either, which made her think maybe he had gone to check on the kids. Gren nodded absentmindedly as he took a swig of coffee.

"What's that?" she asked, eyeing the notebook, he glanced down at it, the smile fading from his lips.

"I like to write. And I've been making notes on those Sage books," he shrugged, his sandy hair wasn't gelled back as it usually was, it made him look younger with it falling around his face, and his jawline look softer.

"What do you write about?" she asked before taking another bite from her banana.

"All sorts. My past, our missions and patrols, anything that seems important, I guess," he said quietly as he gazed down at his book. She wanted to ask more, wanted to ask if he would show her. But in this world where there wasn't much privacy, she couldn't ask him to give that up.

The front door opened and closed, Merida strode into the kitchen and froze, staring at the mess in the kitchen.

"What happened?"

"Niah tried to cook," Gren mused, Merida turned her gaze to Niah, who just shrugged with a sheepish smile, her cheeks warming.

"Niah, as talented as you are in most things, maybe you should quit trying to cook," she muttered tightly, turning back to the kitchen, and sighing once more.

"I couldn't agree more," Niah muttered with a mouthful of banana.

"Apparently manners aren't one of the things she's good at either," Gren chuckled, she held her middle finger up with a sweet smile.

"Well, you better tidy this up," Merida sighed as she pulled out a chair. Niah got to her feet and began cleaning the pots and pans. It wasn't long before she got annoyed that the burnt pancake wasn't coming off and threw it out of the, luckily open, window. She turned back once the sides were clean, feeling oddly proud of herself, to find Merida shaking her head with a smile on her lips.

"You could have hit someone," Gren said, Niah shrugged and hoisted herself up to sit on the counter.

"Don't people usually know to look out for flying pans?" she smirked, Gren shook his head as Merida made an exasperated noise.

"Everything okay?" Gren asked before downing the rest of his coffee and gesturing as if to ask if anyone wanted a cup, both Niah and Merida accepted.

"There's a council meeting this morning." Merida frowned.

"Why is that a bad thing?" Niah asked as Gren handed her a steaming mug of dark coffee.

"It isn't usually, I don't know; I have a strange feeling." she answered dismissively as Gren handed her a mug before sitting back in his chair.

"Well, we'll find out later," Gren murmured, Niah had almost forgotten he was still a Commander and had to attend the meetings with Fin and Merida.

Niah felt relieved to see Merida looking so focused and clear-headed. She had filled out and looked healthier, her eyes were brighter, as was her hair. Warmth spread through her chest as she watched her Guardian drinking her coffee and talking like nothing had ever happened. She wondered how much longer it would last.

"What are you going to do this morning?" Merida asked, gazing at Niah.

"Go over the books, go see the kids," she shrugged, surprised at her own casualness over the situation. She had questions that needed answering and needed to do *something* other than sitting around twiddling her thumbs.

It felt like she had let something go the night before, something she had been holding onto for so long. She had cried. It felt good to let go. The idea of revenge still lingered in the back of her mind, it would for a while yet. But she could ignore it, focus on the bigger picture.

She needed to be there for Merida, needed to find the Shadows and the Sages, and if she were being honest with herself, she couldn't do it alone. It was hard to accept sometimes, that she needed other people. After spending so long with no one there, she now had people she could rely on. People she cared about. Sometimes she found herself drifting into those old ways, shutting everything out, reverting to running on anger. No matter how much she told herself that she wasn't that person anymore, that things were different, darkness lurked beneath the surface, something she couldn't explain or understand.

There was darkness hanging over Thamere too. Whether the others realised it or not, there was something not quite right. Like a picture that had been retouched a little too much. It was too perfect. Too bright and joyous. Perhaps it was just her cynical mind at work, but she had been in a place that promised safety before. She hoped she was wrong. Hoped for everyone's sake that she was wrong. Without proof, there was nothing she could do. Perhaps the only thing she could do was hope she found it before it was too late, hoped they could stop the Shadows, maybe find the Sages. It felt like a losing battle. A battle she was determined to win if it meant protecting those she loved.

Love.

It didn't seem to matter how many times she realised that she had people she cared about so dearly, it never stopped surprising her. Everything had changed so much in such a short time. *She* had changed so much in such a short time. It was those changes that made everything else seem a little more possible.

Merida eyed her quizzically but turned to Gren and asked if he was ready. Niah followed them outside and watched them disappear inside the Chambers before turning to the kids' house.

Fin emerged from the house, looking oddly relieved when he saw her and jogged the last few steps between them, he was dishevelled, his hair a mess, stubble covering his jaw, and he wore jogger bottoms with a loose-fitting grey t-shirt with no shoes on his feet.

She raised a brow at him, "Kids giving you a hard time?" he kissed her quickly on the lips, urgently even.

"Funny, but no. You must have broken through to them yesterday, they want to help us. They're going to help us find one of the doorways," he grinned from ear to ear, his eyes shining brightly, she blinked.

"You're kidding."

"Nope, come on, we've got to go," he said breathlessly, taking her by the hand and almost dragging her back to their house, she planted her feet.

"Fin, you have a council meeting," she smiled, he cursed, glancing down at himself, and darted inside. She stood on the cobbled street, calming her racing heart. It wasn't a sure thing that they would find the Shadows, but it was more than they had only moments ago.

Fin emerged from the house in less than a minute, wearing jeans and a button-up navy-blue shirt which brought out the colour in his eyes. He kissed her again before sprinting toward the Chambers. His steps appeared lighter, a slight spring in them.

Niah turned back to the house where the younglings were being housed. The Guardians nodded as she went through the door. Chatter radiated from the kitchen, with the sweet smell of syrup and pancakes wafting through the air, her stomach growled despite the bananas she'd eaten. Sai stood at the stove flipping over a pancake in a pan, the four younglings were sitting around the table eating and talking, even laughing.

"How do you get them to look like that?" Niah asked, peering over Sai's shoulder.

He grinned, "Did you burn another one?" she made a face at him and playfully smacked him in the arm, "Grab a plate, you can have this one." he gestured to the small stack of plates on the counter, she grabbed one and handed it to him.

The room had suddenly fallen deathly silent. She glanced over her shoulder to find the younglings staring at her. Slowly, she turned to Sai and mouthed 'why are they staring at me?', he glanced over her shoulder at the younglings and shrugged, turning back to the pan. She took a deep breath and sat at the table between Klara and Niklas, they continued to stare.

"What?" she demanded, Niklas jumped at the sharpness in her voice.

"Um...you were so angry yesterday, we thought you might still be annoyed with us," Klara answered in a small voice, Niah raised a brow. She didn't have much experience with kids, let alone ones that were afraid of her.

She sighed, dragging a hand through her hair, "I will be if you keep staring." she looked to Sai for help, but he was silently chuckling as he plated up pancakes for himself.

"What you said...it's true, isn't it?" Vincent asked with a frown, his shoulders hunched and his eyes low.

"Unfortunately."

"Well, I'm not apologising." Isaac snapped, she turned to face him.

"Well, I'm not either." His face softened and a smile danced at one corner of his mouth, he quickly looked away and continued eating. "Why did you decide to help?" Klara paused with her fork halfway to her mouth, and lowered it.

"You're like us."

Niah's heart skipped a beat.

"After you and Sai explained everything, after you told us what happened to you, we realised it was the same as us." Vincent said, sadness lingering in his black eyes, "But you're here, fighting to stop the Shadows, to free others like us."

Her gut wrenched. It wasn't the sole, or even the main reason why she had wanted to hunt the Shadows. It was purely for selfish reasons. Seeing the hope in the kids eyes warmed something deep in her chest. Everything else drifted away.

"We will do exactly that." Niah promised. Perhaps she shouldn't get their hopes up, but it was what she wanted. She wanted to find the Shadows, not for her own selfish reasons, but because there were countless others like Cole, like these kids, like her, held captive. They were suffering. That was reason enough.

Fin

The Council room was bustling. A thick tension hung in the air. There was something strange going on. The new Council member, Matias, was sitting oddly tall with his shoulders squared. Fin's heart was still racing along with his mind.

Unable to sleep the night before, he went next door to speak to Sai, but when he found them all sat around a blue fire in the living area, talking about Niah and what she had told them, he thought it may be a good opportunity to press them a little harder.

They weren't dazed anymore, but still had no memory of Niah other than their initial meeting and their conversation in the house. They *had* remembered her, and suddenly it was gone. Right after Vinaxx had touched them. Come to think of it, he hadn't been back to them since the house was built.

Klara was the one who suggested it first, said she would be happy to show them how to find one of the Shadows doorways. Isaac was hesitant, but after a little convincing, eventually agreed to help. If they were able to find a doorway, they would be able to get to the Shadows.

He hoped.

Guardians strode into the room, and everyone rose to their feet as the Oracle Conclave floated to their platform, sitting down gracefully as they took in the room.

"Thank you all for coming," Amarah started. The meeting was the same as any other, they spoke about the demonic activity in the world, which was still on the rise. Patrols had been doubled but there weren't enough warriors to deal with the activity. Search parties had been increased to find and recruit lost hybrids, lycanthropes, vampires, fey, and spell weavers. Anyone who wasn't within the rogue clans. Despite all the chaos, there was still no reports of Shadow activity.

"If that is all, then the meeting can be adjourned," Ragnar announced once the discussions had finished.

"There is one more matter," Matias said, rising to his feet, his voice carrying clearly across the large room.

"Oh? Do tell," Ragnar drawled, leaning his head on his fist.

"There is the matter of the young hybrid that recently came to us, I believe he was a twin. Where is his sibling?" Matias demanded confidently, Ragnar raised his brows, Amarah's eyes narrowed. The other members of the Conclave remained still, glancing at one another. The whole room seemed to hold its breath. No one took that kind of disrespectful tone with the Elders.

"Both he and his sibling were tried by the truth stone. He passed, the sister did not. She was sent back to the human world," Amarah told him coldly, those golden eyes burning with venom.

"How do we know he isn't here to get information?" Matias questioned, turning to face the rest of his room, and in doing so, turned his back on the Conclave. Everyone was silent. The elation Fin felt only an hour ago ebbed away quickly, leaving dread curling in the pit of his stomach.

"He passed the test, Counsellor Matias. What point are you trying to prove?" Ragnar demanded. A slow smirk spread across Matias' face.

"I believe he found a way to corrupt the stone," he spoke clearly, a gasp ran through the room, followed by murmurs. Both Amarah and Ragnar glowered at Matias as Morena White got to her feet abruptly, slamming her hands down on the desk.

"How dare you! The spell in that stone is too powerful to be corrupted by a hybrid with no magical abilities. You will do best to remember your place, Counsellor Matias," she snapped, her eyes blazing bright and silver. Matias tilted his chin up defiantly when he turned to her.

"Of course, Sorceress. But what about a hybrid with spell weaver blood?" his coy smile had Fin clenching his hands into fists under the desk. Morena blinked quickly, her mouth pressing into a firm line.

"That stone is beyond tampering, not even I could corrupt it," Morena hissed, her nails digging into the surface of the desk.

"Is it not true though, that you don't know for sure how powerful a hybrid with spell weaver blood could be? After all, there have only been a few that we know of, and no one here has ever encountered one before now." he addressed the rest of the council more than Morena, his eyes gleaming wickedly as he strode around the room proudly.

"Are you suggesting that a hybrid with spell weaver blood could be more powerful than the High Sorceress?" Shade Rainrock of the fey demanded, Morena's face drained of all colour.

"Would you not agree, Sorceress?" Matias asked sweetly, ignoring Shade. Morena glowered at him as the other Elders glanced from Morena to Matias.

"Counsellor Matias, what is the meaning of all this?" Lyra of the lycanthropes asked, her light brown eyes almost turning amber.

"Do you not think it strange; we have two former members of the Shadows on this island? That we know of," Matias grinned, casting a glance at Merida, then back to Amarah and Ragnar. He knew. He knew about the younglings. Fin glared at Matias across the hall, he knew exactly what the bastard was getting at.

"That we know of?" another Council member asked, a rumble of murmurs ran through the room. Amarah and Ragnar's expressions remained unreadable.

"It appears, there are even more than we imagined," Matias grinned, wide, and victorious.

"You still haven't told us what you are trying to say with all of this?" another Counsellor demanded, Matias turned to the rest of the room, turning his back on the Elders once again. Ragnar looked ready to launch himself at the Counsellor.

"I believe that the Shadows are getting hybrids to infiltrate, gain information, and launch an attack from within. Soon, they will be on our doorstep, I believe the hybrid Niah corrupted the stone and allowed more Shadows into Thamere," he told everyone, Merida stiffened, Fin's heart was pounding, Gren leaned forward in his chair, his eyes blazing with fury. Merida slammed her hands down on the desk and rose slowly to her feet with a death glare aimed at Matias.

"How *dare* you," she growled, "you are spouting the exact nonsense Benjamin did. Isn't that a bit coincidental? We have already discussed this at length, the Elders decided that there is no threat from the Shadows here. How dare you go behind their backs!" there was a mix of murmurs in agreement and some in anger. Matias, however, was delighted.

"You are biased though, are you not? You are Niah's Guardian after all," he smirked. Fin wondered what would happen if he launched himself across the room and ripped Matias's smug head from his shoulders. How did he know Merida was Niah's Guardian? How did he know about the youngsters?

"Counsellor Matias," Amarah bellowed, rising to her feet, "Be quiet." Matias looked mildly annoyed but simply smiled and bowed his head.

"As you wish."

"Dismissed." she muttered in a low, dangerous tone. Everyone scrambled for the exit, Amarah fixed Merida, Fin, and Gren with a stare that said, 'wait here'. The room emptied, apart from the Elders and the three of them.

"You realise this is an issue." Amarah sighed as she sank into her chair.

"Who asked for him to be made a Counsellor?" Fin asked.

"It was requested by a few people, though Talon pushed it the most. Vinaxx was also rather insistent," Ragnar muttered. Fin's blood turned to ice at the mention of the names. He'd known Talon since he first arrived in Perth, and Vinaxx had been with them longer than Talon had, almost as long as Merida.

"Talon? The same Talon from the Perth facility?" Merida asked, stunned.

"Yes." Ragnar answered. Merida was silent, a look of shock and betrayal clear on her features.

"The younglings, are they cooperating?" Amarah asked, sounding strained and tired.

"Yes, Lady Overseer. They are going to show us how to get to the Shadows." Fin answered, his hands balled into fists behind his back. Amarah shifted in her seat.

"Very good. They still have their marks, don't they?" Ragnar asked.

"They are faded but yes, they do," Merida answered sharply, everyone knew it wasn't directed at the Elders.

"Fine, have them removed from three of them. If they can only get to the Shadows by doorways, there's a chance the door will only open for someone with the mark." Amarah said firmly, the three of them nodded. At that, Fin narrowed his eyes. None of them had thought of that, perhaps it was because Amarah was older. Though even thinking it didn't make much sense. If Amarah truly thought the only way to get into the doorways was by someone possessing a mark, why would she not have ordered them to capture a Shadow earlier to test the theory?

None of them had the words for what they were feeling. Fin's hands were trembling with anger as he thought back on the words Matias had said. Not to mention that Talon had been the one to push for him to be elected Counsellor.

"I hope we don't need to tell you this," Lord Keir spoke softly, "that time is now of the essence. These rumours and conspiracy theories from Benjamin and Matias are growing into more than just a nuisance. Already people are beginning to agree with them." he'd seen it first hand, people were beginning to distrust the Elders and Fin wasn't sure how much longer they could keep on top of it.

"We understand_" Merida started.

"Do you?" Lyra asked sharply, "Do you understand? What progress have you made?"

Merida pressed her lips into a firm line, her fists trembling behind her back, "The youngsters have agreed to help us, we will be able to infiltrate the Shadows soon."

"Yes, the youngsters. You trust them to help? What if they lead you into a trap?" Morena asked.

"I believe them. Though I am concerned about the marks, they seem to have been rendered useless with the barriers around Thamere, but I worry that once they're back in the human world, that the marks will control them once again."

"I suppose that's a risk we're going to have to take." Amarah said gently.

"It's not all that surprising, the barriers were made strong enough to prevent portals opening directly on the island. The only way to bring them down is from the inside, and only I have the power to do that." Morena explained, "Take precautions when taking one of the children back to the human world, they may be willing to help now, but if the mark should return to normal outside of Thamere's barriers, they may not be willing to betray their captors."

"Understood, Sorceress." Merida bowed her head.

They were dismissed. Any excitement Fin felt previously had vanished, burned away by the anger building in his chest.

13

Niah

Niah and Cassia were sitting in the library. She had left Sai with the younglings when Cassia had come and told her it was time to train. The rock hovered at the centre of the table above the map painted into the surface of it. It was becoming easier to mould the rock to her own shape, it still didn't move like liquid as Cassia's had, but it was getting easier. The front door banged open. Cassia and Niah exchanged a look before jumping to their feet and rushing into the living area to find Merida, Fin, and Gren looking extremely agitated.

"What happened?" Cassia demanded as Vinaxx and Velig raced down the stairs to join them.

"Vinaxx, why did you put Matias forward for Counsellor?" Fin glowered, his silver eyes fierce.

Vinaxx blinked, "Oh dear...oh, you see, I thought he would be rather suitable...indeed, I have known Matias many years, very reasonable chap. Reasonable indeed," Niah eyed Fin quizzically as he crossed the room to the weaver.

Velig lodged himself between the two of them, blocking Fin's way.

"Enough!" Merida snapped.

"Someone tell us what the hell is going on?" Niah barked, folding her arms across her chest.

"Matias, he's trying to say you're in league with the Shadows still," Merida sighed, Niah cocked a brow. It wasn't as if she hadn't heard it before, though it was still a blow hearing it had come from someone other than Benjamin.

She shrugged, "The Elders know that isn't the case."

"The Elders aren't the problem, he made a spectacle of it, he made a speech. He said you had corrupted the truth stone, making Cole able to pass the test and stay, he also knew about the younglings somehow," Fin seethed, his voice tighter than she had ever heard it. His silver eyes flicked to Vinaxx once more.

"Again, the Elders_"

"This wasn't about convincing *them*," Fin interrupted, Niah narrowed her eyes, "he wanted everyone to hear it, he wanted to put that doubt in their minds. He wants others to speak up and stand with him." he raked both hands through his thick hair.

"For what possible purpose?" Cassia demanded, at that, they were silent.

"All we know, is Talon pushed him forward for the position," Gren muttered.

Niah baulked, *"Talon?"* her eyes widened. Fin caught her gaze and nodded once. Niah remembered the first time she had seen Talon at the compound in England. He had very much seemed like a professor, always so polite and wise. Though she had she thought it odd how he turned up so easily. His story never matched or felt right.

"Vinaxx, I need you to remove the mark from three of the younglings, we need one to keep it on," Merida said tiredly, Vinaxx nodded.

"No." Fin sneered, "Cassia, would you do it please?" Vinaxx stared at him with wide eyes but said nothing.

"Of course," Cassia breathed, glancing between the two, and hurried from the house with Velig.

"What does this Matias look like?" Niah asked, Fin raised a quizzical brow.

"Dark hair, tanned skin, almost Hispanic looking," he shrugged.

"I think I saw him in the Chambers, there was a meeting in one of the rooms, not a Council meeting. The door was shut before I could hear anything, but I saw someone like that at the front, talking to the others," she explained.

"So, that means there must be others that feel the same way as he does," Merida murmured, she sat down on the sofa, gazing into the unlit fireplace.

"We should speak to Talon, find out why he pushed Matias for the Counsellor position," Fin said, Niah nodded and the two of them left the house. Talon would be in one of the barracks buildings, he wasn't a Counsellor, so he wouldn't have his own house like Merida. They made their way through the busy streets until they came to the barracks they had lived in themselves previously.

Before they entered, Niah pulled him to one side.

"What's going on with Vinaxx?" she murmured under her breath.

"The girl, Klara, she asked about you when I went to see her, they all seemed like they recognised you in some way. I had Vinaxx look them over and suddenly they were dazed, they said they thought they recognised you but must have been mistaken. And now he's backing someone trying to pinpoint you as a traitor. It just seems like maybe he's involved in this too," he pinched his nose between his thumb and finger. She stared for a long moment. Vinaxx was involved? Not only that but someone else from the Shadows who seemed to recognise her. It was all too coincidental.

"We'll deal with that later, we need to find Talon," she murmured, he nodded, and they entered the barracks.

They jogged up the stairs and knocked on the door, when no one answered, Niah reached out and turned the handle, it was unlocked. The room was empty, the drawers were emptied, as was the weapons cupboard. The only thing remaining was the trunk full of armour.

"Hey guys, what are you doing in here?" a familiar voice asked, they turned to see Nate standing in the doorway with a half-eaten apple in one hand.

"Have you seen Talon anywhere?" Fin asked brightly, Nate shook his head.

"I think he went on patrol, I'll let him know you're looking for him if I see him," Nate said before turning to walk down the hallway.

"Let's have a look around, he may have left something behind," Fin suggested. They started searching the room, Fin checked through the bedding and under the mattress while Niah rummaged through the trunk. At the bottom was a small silver medallion. The back of the medallion had an inscription, one she was very familiar with.

In mortem, nos manere in fide.

In death, we remain in faith.

She turned it over, the front of the medallion had the Shadows mark on it, a shadow with wings stretched out from its back. Her stomach churned violently, the breath catching in her throat.

"He's working with the Shadows," she breathed, Fin stilled, his foot falling heavy on the floor mid-step. She straightened to stand beside him and placed it gently in his palm. He turned it over, his brow furrowing as he read the inscription.

"This looks familiar," he murmured, she told him what it meant, his eyes widened slightly as the memory of the photograph in Perth flooded back to him. The photo of the five of them fighting demons. The one that had been in Tyson's pocket when he was murdered by his lover because she was under the Shadows control.

"We have to go," he breathed, the two of them sprinted out of the building toward the Chambers. They ran to the Portal room, no one was there other than the Guardians.

"Did you see Talon come through here?" he asked the Guardian next to the book on the alter.

"I did," he confirmed in a monotone.

"How long ago?" Niah pressed.

"About an hour." the Guardian sighed.

"Did he say where he was going?" she demanded, the Guardian only shrugged.

"He could be anywhere." Fin hissed as they left the room.

"I don't understand why he would do this," Niah muttered, her brows knitting together. Fin shook his head, she glanced at him, but he was staring at the ground with his hands shoved in his pockets; Talon's betrayal cut him deep.

She inhaled deeply as a fresh gust of wind wrapped around them. They descended the steps in front of the Chambers, her mind racing with both logical and illogical reasons why Talon, someone well respected within the hybrid world; would betray them for the Shadows. Why he would push someone into the Council to insist that it was Niah and Cole who were with the Shadows. But of course, they would try to accuse someone else, it would shift everyone's attention from themselves. Niah would have done the same thing had she been in that situation.

Her heart stuttered when she realised she thought the same because that was how the Shadows taught her. They told her that manipulation was a proven method of seeding discord. She always preferred a more hands on approach, but the teachings remained the same.

They made their way back to the house. Dea, Cole, and Nick had arrived, and Merida was filling them in on what had happened. Dea's eyes watered, Cole was annoyed from being accused of working with the Shadows yet again, and Nick looked as bored as ever.

"I knew there was something off about that guy," Cole spat angrily as he paced around the room.

"Lycanthrope thing," Nick sighed, Cole gave him a quizzical glance, but Fin had already interrupted them.

"Talon has bolted, we found this in his room." he tossed the silver medallion to Merida, she caught it out of the air and examined it closely, her eyes narrowing as she read the inscription on the back.

"He left this behind? Seems very careless for Talon," she frowned, still gazing at the necklace.

"I found it at the bottom of his armour trunk, I think he left it on purpose," Niah said as she folded her arms over her chest. Merida's lips pressed into a firm line. He'd wanted them to find it, knowing full well it would hurt Merida and the others.

Cassia and Velig came through the door.

"Is it done?" Fin asked. His eyes had darkened, hardening to steel.

Cassia nodded, "Yes, the three boys had the mark removed."

Niah watched as Merida buried her face in her hands, the same pain in her eyes that had been in Fin's, Dea's, and Gren's. They all knew Talon, he had been with them for decades, he was an important figure in their lives, and he had betrayed them, all of them. Not only the ones she cared about but the whole Fury Alliance.

Hatred crashed over, destroying everything in its path. She'd kill him for what he'd done. What did that make her? Not to mention it would no doubt hurt everyone else to see him dead. Though if he were with the Shadows, sooner or later, he would have to die.

Betrayal was one thing, but mourning was another. Would they hate her if she ended his life for betraying them all? She wanted to protect them and would do anything to make that happen. What scared her wasn't the thought of revenge, it was that she wanted blood. She didn't just want him to die, she wanted him to suffer, and she wanted to be the one to see the light fade from his eyes.

14

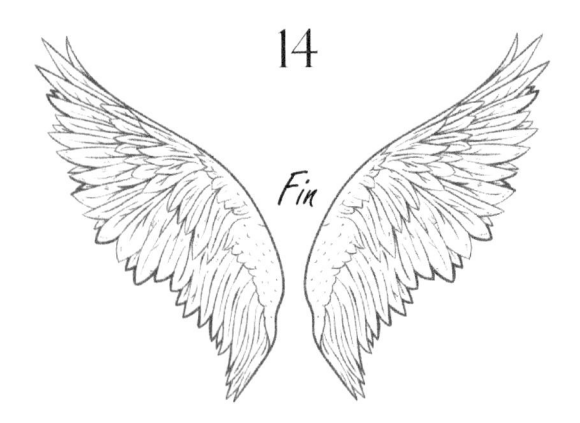

Fin

Numbness had set in. Like everything had slowed down and just stopped working. His insides had been carved out, his mind smashed to pieces. He hadn't believed it, not really, hadn't wanted to believe that someone he had known for decades could betray them like this. Yet when he saw the medallion in Niah's hand, his chest tightened, and his gut churned bitterly. Talon, the man that had helped him control his anger and funnel it all into logical thinking, had helped shaped Fin into the man he had become. The Commander he had become.

The same pain was etched on the faces around him, apart from Nick and Velig who hadn't been at the Perth facility with them. Who wasn't to know how kind and trusting he could be, how gentle and yet firm he was. He was a teacher, a confidante, a friend. Gren placed a comforting hand on his shoulder. A shiver crawled up his spine, he felt cold, empty. His thoughts seemed to fall into a deep void, never to be heard again. When

Merida lifted her head, he noticed the dark circles under her eyes. New and prominent, he glanced at Niah who's eyes were wide, she had noticed too.

"We need to think of a plan, now," Merida spoke darkly, the kind of voice that made everyone sit down and listen.

"Klara will take us to one of the Shadows doors, though I have no idea what we'll find inside," Gren said as he lowered himself carefully into an armchair. There was no time to process. No time to wallow in self-pity. They had a job to do, and they were quickly running out of time. If they didn't do something soon, Matias would only sink his claws in deeper into the rest of the council.

"I don't think we'll find the actual Shadows headquarters." Niah spoke almost softly.

"What makes you say that?" Cassia asked, Niah was silent for a moment as she ran a hand through her long, raven hair.

"They would already know by now that those kids were taken by us, the other Shadows would have told them. In all honesty, I don't think the kids would have access to enter the headquarters anyway. It would make more sense for the door to take us to barracks or training facilities," she explained as she began to pace around the room, taking slow, purposeful steps.

"So, you're saying it would be an ambush?" Gren asked.

She shook her head, "Not necessarily. There is a chance it could be, or they could have cleared everyone out and moved them to another facility. It could be a dead end. I suspect they will know we will try to find them; they will be ready."

"We need more warriors," Merida murmured, her voice strained and tired. He couldn't help but noticed her skin had paled, turning sickly and grey. She would need Vinaxx's administrations, but he didn't trust the weaver.

"I don't think we do," Fin protested gently, everyone shot him a quizzical look, all except Niah who was gazing at the ground, her brows pulled together.

"We have Velig and Cassia, they can create walls to keep us safe and get us out of there if needed. I don't see the point in taking a hundred or so warriors if there isn't anyone there. Not when there's this much demonic activity in the human world, they're needed for patrols," he explained, the room was silent for a long time. It wasn't the best idea, but he would rather have fewer people to organise and communicate with rather than taking a large force somewhere he didn't know.

"So, we're going in blind, without any idea what we're going to find in there?" Nick asked incredulously, Fin nodded. It was an insane idea, for an insane situation. He wished he had more time to form a proper strategy, but time was of the essence, and they had run out of it.

"Everyone should start preparing themselves, Fin and I have to speak with the Elders," Merida said as she got to her feet. The two of them left, and he glanced at the house next door, still with Guardians stood outside. Klara would go with them. There was no guarantee that the mark would come back to full strength once they were free from the barrier around Thamere. But he hoped that even if the mark remained faded, she would be able to open the doorway if that theory was correct.

He looked at Merida and placed a hand on her shoulder. She reached up and squeezed it tightly.

"How could I have missed this?" she muttered, releasing his hand.

"We both missed it," he said gently, he'd been thinking the same thing. If he was as close to Talon as he thought he was, shouldn't he have noticed when something was wrong? He sighed and raked a hand through his tousled hair.

She shook her head, "I wish I knew why he did it."

"If he is truly with the Shadows, we may be able to find out," he answered, even as he spoke the words, he knew it would be a long shot. They may never see him again; Fin wasn't sure what he would do if they did.

"It would explain how it was so easy for him to get into the compound, depending on how long he's been working with them," she shrugged.

Fin thought the same thing when Talon had told them how he had done it, but put it down to him just being smart. Which is why he found it so hard to believe that Talon would have left the medallion by accident. It was on purpose. It only made the pain that much worse. Talon was never cruel, but if the man was capable of betraying them, then maybe he didn't know him at all.

How could someone spend decades with those he was going to betray? Did he find it easy? Looking them in the eye, gaining their trust, laughing with them, suffering with them, fighting beside them? It was hard to fathom. Perhaps there was a logical reason, maybe he wasn't working with the Shadows and that medallion was planted there by someone else. Whatever the truth was, it wouldn't be any easier to deal with.

The Chambers were almost empty, other than people coming to and from the portal room. They made their way through the maze of corridors until they came to a small room with the stone table at the centre with the moving map of the world in real-time. After a few moments, a Guardian came into the room, holding his gleaming silver shield and spear.

"Counsellor Merida and Commander Fin," Merida announced, the Guardian nodded and turned on his heel, striding from the room. Fin gazed down at the map, clouds thicker in some parts than others, stormy seas, and ships in the ocean, even planes in the sky. It would be easier if the youngsters could simply point to a map and tell them where the Shadows were, but things were never that easy.

The doors opened and Amarah and Ragnar strode in, neither of them wearing their usual robes. Amarah wore a knee-length black dress that went high up her neck and left her arms bare, Ragnar wore black jeans with a blue checked shirt. It was odd seeing them both in regular clothes. Fin and Merida bowed their heads respectfully.

"There's no need for such formalities," Amarah said with a slight laugh, her golden eyes blazing.

"As you wish," Merida said with a tight smile, her shoulders stiff with tension.

"What do you want to tell us?" Ragnar asked, his icy blue eyes sliding over the two of them.

"Talon has fled. His room was empty, we found this in his room," Fin told them and handed the medallion to Ragnar. He took it with a furrowed brow and held it between him and Amarah who leant closer to examine it.

"The Shadows seal," she murmured, the smile turning into a grimace as she read the inscription on the back.

"With this news, it may also be possible that Matias is with them as well," Merida spoke carefully.

"Possibly, the other option is that Talon did not tell him of his involvement with the Shadows and simply wanted him to preach about us letting Shadow warriors into Thamere," Ragnar suggested as he handed the medallion back to Fin. The weight of it was almost unbearable.

"I believe Talon left this on purpose for us to find." Fin said in a gravelly voice, it even hurt to say, like an invisible hand was closing around his throat.

"I see. If that's the case, then he will know we will be on our way. Do you have a plan, Commander?" Amarah asked, Fin lowered his eyes as he told them the plan; they nodded in agreement.

"Very well, take this, activate it and you will get instant reinforcements wherever you are. We will assemble several warriors ready," Ragnar said as he handed Fin a small black object with a shining silver button at the centre. Fin pocketed it quickly.

"Thank you, Lady Overseer, Lord Ambassador." Fin said with a bow.

"Stay safe," Amarah and Ragnar spoke softly in unison.

"Until my last breath." Fin and Merida answered with lowered eyes. With that, they strode from the room, leaving the Elders standing over the large stone map.

Niah watched as they left. She could feel the anger pulsing through her, threatening to boil over. Dea was sobbing on the couch, Gren sitting beside her with his arm around her. So much pain blanketed them. She turned to Cassia, who had the same look of hurt and betrayal in her eyes.

"I need you to teach me something," Niah whispered as she moved to stand close to Cassia, her back to the others. Cassia glanced at her with quizzical eyes, but only nodded before the two of them turned and left the house.

Cole

Cole didn't know what to make of everything that was happening. He didn't know Talon. He'd only met him once and the guy had given him an odd feeling. It wasn't the first time he had felt it, though it was the first time since he had been in Thamere.

He glanced at Dea who was sitting on the couch beside Gren, leaning forward with her hands over her mouth, her eyes shining with unshed tears. He wanted to comfort her, to say something, anything that would bring the bright smile back to her face. What could he say? He couldn't tell her he understood how she felt because he didn't. He couldn't tell her everything would be okay because there was no guarantee it would be. Making false promises wasn't what you were supposed to do, not even when someone was inconsolable.

He couldn't bear to lie to her, not when she had been so honest and kind to him. Instead, he placed a comforting hand on her shoulder. She turned to him, lowering her hands, and offered him the smallest of smiles. She probably didn't mean it, but it was something. He turned to Nick, who was still staring at the ceiling.

"You said it was a lycanthrope thing, what did you mean?" he questioned, Nick lowered his head then and gazed at Cole incredulously.

"Damn, you know nothing, do you?" Cole sighed and shook his head, he wasn't in the mood to argue, or to be mocked.

Nick sighed, "We can sense certain energies, if something seems off, it's usually because it is."

"Oh." was all Cole could muster, what else could he say? He had only just learned what he was and hadn't even thought about what it meant or what kind of abilities he would have. He sighed and ran a hand through his dark hair, wondering what Nyx would make of the news that they were part wolf.

He remembered they were running through a forest one day, night fell, and the full moon rose into the sky. The howls tore through the night like a knife. It wasn't long before they were on them, a pack of around two dozen. They didn't look like wolves, not like the one Nick had shifted into. They stood on their hind legs, humanoid in form, with a huge wolf's head and fur covering their bodies with a long tail and claws. He remembered their eyes more than anything, the bright amber of them.

They had cornered them; Cole had been sure they would be killed. But they sniffed the air, catching their scent and howled before fleeing quickly. Cole always thought it was because they were hybrids, but what if they smelt the wolf on them? He sighed, it didn't matter now.

The others were talking about going through the doorway to where the Shadows were. The thought of going back there made his heart race and his breath hitch in his throat. He could still smell the thick scent of bleach hanging in the air. Could still hear the screams. Still saw the blood and death when he closed his eyes at night. He wondered if he would ever be rid of it. Whether any of it would ever stop. He had been so scared for so long, and whenever he needed it; Nyx was his strength.

She was always telling him to man up, to focus on the sound of her voice. And now, when he needed her the most, she wasn't there. Because of a choice he'd made. He chose to stay and let her go. His stomach hurt. His chest hurt. He stood abruptly and stormed from the house, needing fresh air.

He gulped lungful's down greedily. Tilting his head to the sky and closing his eyes.

One day it wouldn't hurt so much.

"What's going on?" a familiar voice asked, he jerked to the side, and stared at Sai. His hands shoved into his pockets and his hair sticking out in all directions, his eyes bright with worry.

"Nothing." Cole rasped, not realising he was panting.

Sai frowned, "Doesn't look like nothing."

"Shouldn't you be with the kids?" Cole asked, steadying his breathing.

He ran a hand through his hair, "They're all asleep, thought I would come over and see what was going on."

"Some guy called Matias is trying to say Niah and I are still working for the Shadows. This other guy, a creepy dude called Talon pushed for Matias to be on the Council. Niah and Fin searched his room and found a medallion with the Shadows emblem on it," he explained, Sai's face fell, his mouth pressing into a firm line when he heard about Talon. Of course, how could he have been so careless? Sai would know Talon, just like the others. He had that same wounded expression Gren had worn.

"Shit." Sai muttered and brushed past Cole to stalk into the house, Cole followed.

"Is it true?" Sai demanded as he stood before the others. Gren's eyes glanced between Sai and Cole, he felt like he was about to turn to ice. Gren sighed and took a step closer to Sai.

"Unfortunately," he muttered. Sai was silent for the longest time. His hands, now free of his pockets, clenched and unclenched repeatedly at his sides. Dea watched him, her eyes wary. She wanted to go to him just like Cole had wanted to comfort her. Yet she stayed where she was. Gren filled Sai in on the plan to enter the Shadows realm or whatever they called it.

A few minutes later, Merida and Fin strode through the door, closing it gently behind them. Fin leaned back against it, his head tipped back, eyes closed. He looked defeated. Cole wondered how someone so strong could look so utterly deflated. Strength didn't mean that things didn't get too much sometimes. Strength didn't mean you had to appear strong all the time. Sometimes, that strength needed to crumble away. To leave things raw and out in the open, only then could it be built back up.

Fin opened his eyes and sat in one of the armchairs. "In a day or two, we will go. In the meantime, we should train. Prepare ourselves as much as possible." he said in a voice so low he was sure he would have missed it if he were any further away. Fin turned to him, his silver eyes hard and unyielding.

"Cole, Nick, with me," he said and got to his feet.

They didn't go to the training grounds. Instead, they turned down a narrow street lined with shops on either side.

They came to a large shop and stepped inside. The walls were lined with swords, spears, daggers, crossbows, guns, and other weaponry. Cole gazed at the gleaming weapons, polished and shining brightly, even in the dim light. Some of them had decorative engravings on them, others were plain but just as beautiful, just as deadly.

"Pick a weapon or two that you feel comfortable with," Fin said as he perched himself on the counter at the back of the shop. A short, stocky man emerged from the back room. He had dark brown eyes with silver rings around the iris and pointed ears.

"Commander," he nodded when he noticed Fin.

"Jackson, how are things?" he asked, the two fell into an easy conversation as Cole turned his back to them.

He had never seen such weapons. It was overwhelming to be faced with such tools designed for killing. Nick was turning over a shining black dagger with a wolf's head moulded into the pommel in his hands. Cole picked up a crossbow from one of the tables. It was a particularly hard kind of wood, not something he recognised, with detailing of gold leaves swirling over it.

"Can you aim with that?" Fin asked from the back of the shop with a wicked grin that didn't meet his troubled eyes. It wasn't the first crossbow he had held, it was his weapon of choice for many years, up until his last one broke and he couldn't find another.

He loaded it with a bolt, turned his head away from Fin, raised the crossbow, and fired. When he turned back, Fin was holding the bolt in his hand, less than an inch from his forehead. To Cole's surprise, he was grinning. Fin cocked a brow and twirled the bolt between his fingers.

"You know that wouldn't have killed me, right?" Fin asked as he pushed off from the counter and sauntered toward him. The bolt was a training bolt, plain wood.

"I wasn't trying to kill you," Cole shrugged as he raised the crossbow to rest it against his shoulder. Fin handed the bolt back to him.

"Good shot," he murmured, turning on his heel back toward the counter. Cole picked out a dagger and some throwing knives as well as a long sword with a green jewelled hilt and a shotgun from the wall. Nick picked the wolf dagger and another dagger with leaves imprinted into the blade, along with a shotgun.

"Jackson, would you mind getting these packed up and bringing them to the house next to Counsellor Merida's please?" Fin asked politely, the man, who looked no older than anyone else, smiled and nodded.

"Of course, Commander," he said and held out his hands for Cole to give him the crossbow, which he did, almost reluctantly. They left and walked across the street into what was an armour shop.

A tall woman was standing behind the counter with a black garment in one hand, a large sewing needle in the other. Beside her was a lanky man with thick blonde curls sprouting from his head. He looked up and smiled, the woman barely seemed to notice anyone had entered.

"Need armour?" the man asked with a huge smile spread across his face.

"Indeed." Fin said, a look of remembrance crossed his face and he turned to Cole and Nick, "Was what we thought true? You're lycanthrope?" Nick nodded. "Excellent, full change?"

"Not yet, but very likely in time," Nick answered with his hands in his pockets. Fin looked pleased with the news and turned back to the two behind the counter.

"How has the new armour been coming along?" he asked as he leaned against the counter. The woman looked up at that and leaned back in her chair.

"We've just finished it, but we only have a handful of suits available at the moment," she said with a gloating smile.

"More than enough. How do they work?" Fin asked, eyeing the garment in the woman's hands.

"They're still *Shiasium*. The spell weavers developed a new material, they call it *Dragonsilk*. It's woven into the *Shiasium*, a unique blend. The *Dragonsilk* changes to the wearer, it would shift to a wolf as much as it would to a fey with wings or if a hybrid changed to the next states. It's been tested, and it works." the woman explained.

"Sounds complex, and the *Ruclite* plates?" he asked, the woman glanced to the man beside her and smiled.

"We don't need to do a thing with them, you already know they mould themselves to fit each individual, they do the same when the form is changed," she smirked, her eyes dancing playfully.

"Perfect, can I have two suits delivered to the house next door to Counsellor Merida's please?" he asked, the woman nodded with a small grin.

"Don't say I never buy you anything pretty," Fin mused as they left the shop.

"Dinner and a movie next, is it?" Cole smirked, Fin glanced at him sideways.

"You sound almost eager." he grinned, Cole rolled his eyes as they continued down the street toward a large building. Inside was a huge space with athletic equipment and people training. He guessed this was the real reason they came out. Fin was trying to act as though he wasn't bothered by Talon's betrayal. He was a Commander and had to act like one, not putting his personal feelings before his duty.

"Why are we waiting a day or two? Why not go now?" Cole questioned, striding into the centre of a ring painted on the floor.

Fin regarded him thoughtfully, "One, the kids are still unconscious from having the marks removed. Two, I need to make sure you're fully outfitted and can handle yourself. I considered leaving you behind, but you may recognise something if we make it inside. Three, I need time to formulate a plan that won't end in our instant deaths."

He wouldn't have been offended if he had been told he had to stay behind, he may have even been pleased about it. In all honesty, he didn't want to go back there. He didn't care how much of a coward it made him. The thought of that place sickened him, even now, he could feel panic building in the pit of his stomach.

Fin caught his gaze and gripped Cole's shoulder, "The choice is yours. You don't have to come with us."

"Is Niah going?" he asked, unable to stop the question. Niah had been held by the Shadows too, it may have been different, but she was still a prisoner. When he looked at her, there was no fear in her eyes, no hesitation.

Fin searched Cole's eyes as if reading those very thoughts, "She is. I don't think any of us could stop her even if we wanted to." maybe it wasn't the same, but if she was willing to go back, if she was willing to fight against them, then maybe he could too. It still terrified him, but he wasn't alone, he could do it as long as they were all by his side. Fin smiled lightly when Cole nodded.

"You'll be coming back with us, don't worry. We won't leave you behind." It was exactly what he needed to hear.

15
Niah

The moonlight streamed in through the curtains along with a soft breeze from the open window. She stared at the ceiling, willing sleep to take her; but it wouldn't come. With a heavy sigh, she swung her legs over the side of the bed and padded downstairs, not surprised to find she wasn't the only one who couldn't sleep. Merida sat on the sofa in front of the fireplace, the fire crackling softly and bathing the room in a warm glow. Merida barely seemed to notice her presence, she was gazing into the flames with haunted eyes. Niah sat down, snapping Merida out of her reverie.

"Sorry," she murmured, Merida forced a smile. She was wearing the same clothes she had been all day, jeans, and a black t-shirt. Only now she had a white robe over the top.

"Don't be. Can't sleep?" she asked gently, Niah shook her head, "I imagine that this will be pretty scary for you, going back into the Shadows lair I guess?"

"I'm not scared," she replied, a little firmer than she had intended. Merida's smile grew wider.

"Of course, you're never scared. You're so brave," she said as she reached over and took Niah's hand in hers. It was an effort to stop herself from flinching, Merida was so cold, even if Niah could only feel it for a few seconds. Her hands were bonier, the circles beneath her eyes darker.

"I don't feel brave," she murmured, Merida's eyes widened slightly, her thumb circled the back of Niah's hand.

"Why?"

"I'm worried about you, I worry about what will happen to you," she muttered, lowering her eyes to their entwined hands. Merida's thumb stilled.

"My dear, it happens. I have lived a very long life, my only regret is that I couldn't find you and your mother sooner," she whispered, Niah looked up at her, her eyes large and wet, threatening to spill over at any moment.

"We'll find her," Niah breathed, though she wasn't sure she felt the truth in her own words.

The memory of the picture burned in the back of her mind. She wanted to ask about it, wanted to tell Merida what she had found out. Merida believed her mother was a good person, but what if she wasn't? What if she too was working with the Shadows? After being betrayed by Talon, Niah wasn't sure she wanted to pile it on. Not in Merida's current state.

"I hope so," Merida smiled weakly, Niah squeezed her hand. She didn't know what else she could say or do. Nothing would make any of this better. Merida had been betrayed by a close friend; someone she had known for decades. Not to mention she was turning more demonic by the day. She hoped she would have more time with her Guardian. The grey of her skin, the dullness of her eyes only told Niah they were on borrowed time, and that there was little of it left.

"You're so good," Merida whispered, Niah looked up with wide eyes, her mouth falling open.

"How?"

Merida chuckled, "You want to protect people."

"I don't think I'm good," Niah shook her head, lowering her eyes, "when we found out about Talon, seeing the pain on all of your faces. My first thought was that I want to kill him," she raised her eyes once more, expecting to see disgust in her Guardians eyes, and found only love and understanding.

"And your second thought?"

Niah's breath hitched in her throat, "I thought about what that death may do to you all, whether that would cause more pain than the betrayal," Merida smiled lightly and raised her hand, placing it gently against Niah's cheek, her thumb stroking her cheekbone.

"That is why you are good. That is why you are a protector," her smile widened. Niah shook her head.

"I'm too murderous for that."

Merida laughed softly, her hand still on Niah's cheek, "You care about those around you, and as far as I can tell, you're only murderous toward your enemies, or frying pans," Niah couldn't help but smile at that. "We all make mistakes, you'll be fine," Merida said soothingly, they were quiet for a long time. The fire crackling gently.

"I envy humans," Merida muttered after a long while, her hand dropping from Niah's cheek to their clasped hands in the middle of them.

"Why?"

"They can live, truly live. They grow old, they find the one they're supposed to be with, have children," she said, keeping her eyes low.

"Is that something you would want?" Niah inquired, Merida raised her eyes at that, the ghost of a smile on her lips.

"I think sometimes I would, but the rest of the time, I am thankful that I got a chance to meet you. To be a part of your life, you are the daughter I could never have, despite how short our time together may be." Tears rolled down Merida's cheeks.

Even her fake parents had never called her daughter. She leaned forward and wrapped her arms around Merida. Her heart hammering in her chest as it swelled with warmth. It was then she realised how scared for Merida she was. She didn't know what her changing meant exactly, but she knew she wouldn't see her again when the time came. She would do whatever it took to delay the inevitable as long as possible. She would ask Vinaxx to teach her the spell and keep her going herself if she had to.

At that moment, the front door opened. Niah and Merida reluctantly pulled apart, though still clasping each other's hands. Fin, Cole, and Nick came into the room. Cole and Nick headed straight for the stairs. Fin stood with a fond smile on his face, his eyes turning to liquid silver in the dim glow of the dying fire.

"How did training go?" it was Merida who spoke first.

"Better than expected," he said quietly.

"The packages arrived earlier, they're in the armoury," Merida gestured to the corridor at the back of the room. Fin nodded.

"You both should be asleep," he said with a sly grin. Niah cocked a brow at him.

"Good point," Merida said and got up, she stroked Niah's shoulder and walked toward the stairs.

Fin sat next to Niah on the sofa. He looked tired, dark circles under his eyes, his skin pale. He pulled her into his lap, her legs resting on the seat next to him. He encircled her in his arms and pressed his forehead to hers, closing his eyes as he took a deep, steadying breath.

"What is it?" she whispered, he pulled away slightly and let his head fall back against the sofa. She reached up and ran her fingers through his thick locks. Touching him wasn't quite so scary anymore. She still didn't like to do it in public, but she learned to take comfort in his touch, relished in it even.

"We're finally getting somewhere, albeit we may be walking into a trap, but we're able to finally do something," he murmured, gazing up at her, the glow from the fire highlighting the sharpness of his jaw and cheekbones, the flat planes of his cheeks.

"Are you nervous?" she asked quietly, he pursed his lips, a slow smile spreading.

"Yes." his voice was thick and gravelly. She cocked her head to the side, half expecting him to say no. To tell her everything would be fine, that they had a plan. As if reading her mind, he said, "Not what you were expecting?"

"No." she shook her head, "I thought you would be fine."

"It's okay to be nervous or scared. In my case, I'm nervous because I'm leading us all into a trap_"

"We don't know it's a trap," she protested, but she couldn't deny she felt the same way. He regarded her thoughtfully for a moment.

"If it goes wrong, I will get us all out," he muttered firmly, she said nothing. There was nothing else to say. She knew he would protect them just as much as she would. She lowered her lips to his, catching him by surprise. He tightened his arms around her, deepening the kiss. A low groan erupting from his throat as she traced her tongue along his bottom lip and her fingers tangled in his hair, pulling him closer.

He hooked one arm under her knees and lifted her until he was standing, without breaking the kiss. He walked up the stairs and fumbled with the doorknob, she reached down and twisted it herself, they half fell through the door, laughing in hushed whispers as to not wake the others.

He set her on her feet, and she reached up to twine her arms around his neck, his own snaking around her waist, tightening so she was on her tip toes.

Electricity burned her skin wherever he touched, heat spread through her chest like a deep fire. The two of them pressed themselves together as if they could make themselves into one being.

Sometimes it still didn't feel real. That she could be with Fin in this way, and it feel like a constant, blessed dream. She'd never understood romance in her books, but being with Fin, running her hands over him, having his lips on hers, it was intoxicating.

And she craved every touch more than air.

More than revenge.

He lifted her and she wrapped her long legs around his waist, he groaned again as he let them fall onto the bed. He was on top of her, taking most of his weight on his elbows, but she wanted to feel every inch of him. His hand ran over her body, caressing carefully as she slid her nails down his back gently.

"Niah..." he panted into her lips, she pulled away reluctantly. His eyes were glassy and unfocused as he gazed down at her.

"Is this really what you want?" he whispered, he lowered his chin to trail kisses along her jaw. Her lids fluttered and a moan escaped her lips.

"It is, just maybe...not tonight," she breathed, almost unwillingly. She couldn't believe the words were falling out of her mouth. He finished the line of kisses at her collarbone and pulled back to look at her. To her surprise, he was smiling, his eyes kind yet wild.

"Of course, but can I ask why?" he asked gently as he rolled off of her to lay on his side propped up by his elbow and gazed down at her.

"I don't want to feel like I'm doing this because we're both worried about what's going to happen when we go through that door," she frowned, he nodded once but his smile didn't fade.

"You're worried?"

"I guess so," she shrugged, he chuckled softly and leaned down to kiss her once more. He pulled away reluctantly and pressed his forehead to hers, his eyes closed. Even with the slight distance between them, she could hear his heart hammering away.

"I never thought you were worried about anything," he murmured.

"Everyone worries at times." he opened his eyes, and reached up with his free hand to stroke her cheekbone.

"You never cease to amaze me," he whispered.

After that, it was gentle kisses and embraces, the heat still lingering under the surface, eager to get out. But he was respectful of what she wanted, not letting his hands wander too much.

At some point, she fell asleep in his arms. Dreams of them in the human world, as humans danced behind her eyes. Merida as well, all her closest friends. What it would be like if things were different. It was a beautiful dream, but she knew it would only ever be that, a dream.

16

Fin

For the first time in a long time, he slept straight through the night. Light poured in through the open curtains, they must have forgotten to shut them the night before. He blinked the sleep from his eyes and reached over to pull Niah close, but she wasn't there. He stared at her pillow and glanced around the room, nope, definitely not there. The smell of cooking wafting in through the slightly open door made his stomach rumble. His eyes widened, was she trying to cook again? He jumped out of bed and headed downstairs in only his boxers, coming to a stop under the archway leading into the kitchen to find Niah and Dea sitting at the table while Merida stood over the stove with a frying pan.

He placed a hand over his racing heart, "Thank *God.*" they turned to stare at him quizzically. "I thought Niah was trying to cook again," he threw a wink at Niah, who was now scowling at him while holding her middle finger up. Merida sighed and rolled her eyes with a smile. Despite her grey skin and dark circles around her eyes, Merida seemed like herself, smiling and cooking.

"I've given up with cooking," Niah announced as she lifted her mug of what he assumed was coffee to her mouth and took a large gulp.

"Oh, wow, I didn't realise it was *that* sort of breakfast attire," a voice sounded from behind him, he turned to see Velig wearing a black silk robe, which he was currently undoing. Before anyone had a chance to say anything, he dropped the robe, revealing all of his nakedness. Niah choked on her coffee, Merida almost dropped the pan and turned away telling him to put his clothes on, Dea blushed.

"Jesus," Fin grimaced, holding a hand out to block Velig's appendage from view.

"Am I that well-endowed?" Velig grinned as he glanced down at himself, his silver hair falling over his forehead.

"Oh, now it's a party," Sai laughed as he came into the house and closed the front door behind him. Fin sighed and threw his head back in exasperation.

"Velig, please put some clothes on. Sai, don't even think about it," he warned as he noticed Sai beginning to unbutton his shirt. He let his hands flop to his sides with a pout.

"Kill joy," he murmured as he wandered through the living room while Velig tied his robe back together.

"How are the kids?" Niah asked when Sai sat at the table.

"They're fine, a little weakened, but otherwise fine," he said, pouring himself a mug of coffee. Fin was relieved to hear it. It would mean they could begin their infiltration today. He turned and padded back up the stairs to pull on a baggy white t-shirt and a pair of jogging bottoms.

Back downstairs it was as if they weren't planning an almost suicidal raid. Everyone was talking, laughing as they would do usually. It was only Niah who sat with tension coiled through her body and a distant gaze that only he would notice. He thought it was good, that they were acting normally. Like nothing was wrong. Like they could potentially be going on a suicide mission.

"What happens with the kids now? Will they have to stay here, or can they go?" Dea asked, Merida – now sitting at the table after serving everyone bacon and eggs – regarded her thoughtfully for a moment.

"I don't know, I suppose that's for the Elders to decide," she said quietly, she looked thinner again, her eyes sunken in slightly more so than the day before. A gut-wrenching feeling punched through him, he would have to tell Vinaxx again soon. Though the thought of Vinaxx going anywhere near Merida turned his blood to ice.

"Does anyone even know much about halflings? All I know is that they're demon-human hybrids," Velig asked.

"They'll age as humans do. They're half-human after all. Although I'm not sure how true that is, it was what I heard from the Shadows. They said we needed a mark to stop our aging," Niah shrugged.

"It may well be the case, they managed to stop you aging completely when you were a baby. But you're right, halflings age, just more slowly than humans," Fin explained before popping a piece of bacon into his mouth.

"Isn't their lifespan more like two hundred years as opposed to eighty or ninety-odd?" Sai asked around a mouthful of eggs.

"Something like that," Gren muttered, he leaned against the kitchen counter with a plate of bacon in his hand. Fin hadn't even noticed he came in.

"We should all get ready," Merida murmured, suddenly serious. The room fell silent, all eyes locked on their Counsellor.

"We need to go now," she added, Fin gave her a hard look; she simply shook her head. Everyone started filing out of the room and toward the armoury to get geared up.

"Why now?" he asked quietly as she stood over the sink, staring out the window.

"I can feel myself slipping again, I don't have much time," she muttered.

"We can ask Vinaxx to_"

"No. I'm done asking Vinaxx to drain his energy on me. It's not fair," she said firmly as she turned to face him, "this is the only chance I'm going to get." Selfishly, he was relieved she didn't want to see Vinaxx, if only because he didn't trust him. He couldn't say anything to that, couldn't argue with what she wanted. He sighed and lowered his head, she came to stand in front of him. Putting her fingers under his chin to lift his face to look at her.

"I need you to promise me something," she whispered.

"Anything."

"Take care of yourself, take care of Niah and everyone. You're one of the only ones I can entrust everything to," she said softly, he rose to his feet and wrapped his arms around her. She held him tightly, his chest throbbed painfully. She had been like a mother to him.

"I'll be with you 'til the end," he murmured into her hair as he held her.

"Until my last breath," she whispered. They stood there for the longest of time, holding each other. When they finally broke apart, her eyes were wet and full of sorrow. He didn't know what to do, for the first time in a long time, he felt lost.

Merida had been his anchor for so long, she grounded him, made him see he had a bigger purpose than getting into fights. She had given him the confidence he needed to step up and take responsibility. Seeing her so frail, talking about promises for when she was no longer with them was too much.

It felt like his heart was clawing its way out of his chest just to stay with her a little while longer.

She smiled and raised her hand to his face, "You are so precious to me," his chest racked painfully, a stabbing pain ripped through his gut. He wrapped his arms around her once again, tears slipping down his face.

"You have grown into an amazing man, Fin. I only wish I had found you sooner," she said into his ear. He squeezed his eyes shut, willing the burn to subside. He pulled away to look at her.

"You're like a mother to me," he muttered, more tears rolled down her cheeks as a sob escaped her lips. Footsteps rounded the corner and stopped short. They both turned to see Niah standing in the archway. Her eyes wide as she gazed at them, full of worry. She was dressed in her armour, looking like she had been born to wear it. The blue tint of it standing out against the blackness of her hair.

"What's going on?" she asked, taking a step closer, her brows knitted together.

"I need to talk to you," Merida said, she took one last look at Fin, smiling. He turned to walk away, each step more painful than the last.

Dea

Dea was strapping a holster around her thigh when Fin came into the armoury. Even though he wore a faint smile, she could tell by the hardness of his eyes that something was wrong. He caught her gaze but shook his head. He would talk about it when he was ready. The tension in the room was almost suffocating. No one spoke as they strapped into their leathers.

They had marched into battle before. But this was different. They had no idea what they were walking into, they had no idea if it were a trap or simply a suicide mission. Still, her fingers were steady as she slid her shortened spear into her thigh holster.

Cole fumbled with the plate that strapped over his back. Gently, she moved his hands away and tightened the buckle. He nodded gratefully, though he didn't smile, his hands were shaking as he tried to strap his crossbow across his back. What must it be like for him? To not only be going back to the place where he was once held captive, but to be going without his sister.

She gripped his hand and he gazed at her, his skin pale. She gave him a reassuring smile, despite not feeling it herself. Everyone was nervous, scared. Velig hadn't even bothered with the coloured streak running through his hair. Instead, he had it slicked back. Despite being a spell weaver, he wore the same armour as the rest of them, a sword strapped to his hip. Cassia had exchanged her skirts and bracelets for leathers that showed off her curvaceous figure spectacularly.

Vinaxx had been advised to stay behind. Fin didn't trust him, after hearing his reasons, Dea wasn't sure she entirely understood. She thought Vinaxx was loyal, but then again, they had thought the same about Talon. A weight pressed on her chest at the betrayal. How long had he been working with the Shadows? Was he being controlled by a mark? As horrible as the thought was, at least if he were, it meant that he hadn't betrayed them. Not really.

They were nearly ready when Merida and Niah came into the room. Niah looking like a fallen angel dressed all in black with her hair hanging down her back in a thick braid, her swords poking out from behind her shoulders. She fastened her fingerless gloves with *Ruclite* plates across the backs and leaned against the doorframe. There was something oddly unsettling about her. Seeing her dressed like that with such emptiness in her eyes. It was haunting. Dea wanted to go to her, but one look from Merida had her freezing in place.

Merida was still wearing her pyjamas, her hair tied back in a high ponytail, her face set determinedly. She dressed in her armour quickly, the *Shiasium* suit moulded to her body flawlessly. She looked thinner somehow. As pale as Cole, her eyes sunken in. Dea helped her with the *Ruclite* plates as she struggled to clasp them together with her trembling fingers, Fin sucked in a sharp breath. Merida gripped Dea's hand, a tight smile on her lips.

"I have something I want to say," she announced, tilting her chin up proudly as she scanned the faces before her. Niah remained standing in the doorway, her face like stone.

"Today may likely be my last," she said, the room fell silent. Dea thought her heart had stopped. Her eyes widened as she gazed at the woman she had known for decades, the woman who had taught her so much. She tightened her grip on Merida's hand, she gave Dea a warm smile, though it didn't reach Dea's heart.

"Don't be daft," Sai scoffed, he looked to Fin desperately. Out of everyone, Sai had known her the longest. A lump formed in her throat, her heart racing as the words sank in, sending an icy chill slithering up her spine.

"I wish I were. I'm changing," Merida said firmly, yet with the gentlest edge to her voice. Sai gazed at her thoughtfully for a moment.

"You don't mean...?" he trailed off, the question hanging in the air like a blade. Sharp, and ready to strike. Merida said nothing, only frowned and nodded, watching for his expression. His mouth pressed into a firm line, his jaw flexing as he fought back tears. Gren and Fin stood side by side, Fin gripping Gren's shoulder. Nick didn't know what to do with himself, shifting uncomfortably from one foot to the other. Cassia rushed to Merida's side.

"We can postpone it, we can," she urged, her voice unsteady as she spoke. Merida smiled again, shaking her head.

"Vinaxx has been helping me more than I can say, I cannot let anyone else bear that burden," she muttered gently, casting a guilty glance over her shoulder at Niah, whose eyes were as hard as onyx, the silver shimmering brightly.

"Oh Merida," Dea whimpered, wrapping her arms around her. She was a lot thinner. Dea cursed herself for not noticing sooner. She looked at her now, saw the gaunt cheeks and the dark circles around her eyes. Her heart ached. How hadn't she noticed? How had none of them noticed? For the first time in a long time, she felt truly angry and disgusted. With herself more than anything.

"It's okay, I'm fine. I've come to terms with it. I need you all to do the same. We need to be focused on the mission. We can do this and get through it all together," she said as she pulled away and turned to the others. Sai came forward then and hugged her fiercely, she chuckled into his neck. The backs of Dea's eyes burned as tears rolled down her cheeks.

She turned to Niah and took her hand in hers; she was icy cold and barely seemed to notice Dea at all. How could she? Merida was her Guardian; she was the closest thing she had to family. Dea couldn't imagine how she must be feeling. As if waking up from a dream, Niah blinked and gazed at Dea. She thought she must be in shock and draped her arm around Niah's shoulders, pulling her close. They finished the hugs and almost goodbyes. Merida stood tall and proud; her chin tilted upward.

"I am so happy I got to meet each one of you, I'm so proud of the people you have all become," she said, her voice breaking at the end as a sob escaped her throat. She wiped away her tears.

"Now, let's go," she said firmly, her eyes darkening with determination. Everyone grabbed a long *Shiasium* trench coat with a large hood on it, they were going into the human world where their armour wasn't easily hidden, thankfully, their weapons were.

As they marched toward the Chambers, she noticed the streets were completely deserted. They walked in a circle formation with Niah and Dea at the back, Klara in the middle. She glanced at Niah, who was staring ahead with a set brow.

"Hey, are you okay?" Dea asked, realising it was a stupid question; hearing that your Guardian is going to change couldn't be the easiest thing in the world. Niah kept her eyes forward.

"I'm fine, you've known her longer, how are you?" she answered flatly, Dea frowned. Niah didn't show her emotions easily, but she had never been so cold about such a subject before.

"It's awful," Dea muttered, Niah only nodded. It also wasn't like her to take such a comment so casually and ignore it. Dea bit her lip to stop herself from saying anything further. Whatever Niah was feeling, she didn't want to talk about it.

Cole

His heart thundered as they ascended the steps of the Chambers. His hands had barely stopped shaking as he put the armour on. Even now, he trembled all over. He set his jaw and willed himself not to show it.

He couldn't help but think about his sister. Where would she be now? What would she be doing? He sighed heavily, what good would worrying do? He instinctively gripped the neckless around his throat. He promised her he would find her before they did anything, but he found himself wanting to keep her away from danger. Even if it meant she would hate him for it when they finally reunited, whenever that would be.

The Chambers seemed different somehow, the flowers on the vines that roped around the archways and ceiling beams were hidden, retreated into themselves as if hiding from danger. A coldness hung in the air, sending a shiver down to his bones. Not a physical coldness, his body wouldn't react to that. But a sickening feeling of impending danger.

Fin walked at the head of the group with Merida. He hadn't known what to say during the goodbyes. He had never known someone to *know* when they were going to die, or whatever was going to happen to her. He did know that Merida was Niah's Guardian, and yet Niah seemed completely indifferent.

He glanced over his shoulder at her and Dea walking at the back of the group, her eyes looking straight ahead, her entire body coiled. He frowned. No one could have someone that close to them and feel nothing when they found that person would soon no longer be with them.

A sudden flicker of annoyance sparked through him, how could she act like she felt nothing? His hands balled into fists at his side, he wanted to yell at her, tell her to go to Merida and spend as much time by her side as possible. But what good would it do? She wouldn't care what he had to say.

They found their way to the portal room. Fin took an orb off the shelf, Gren and Dea did the same. Cole glanced at Nick as the others signed their blood in the book. For the first time, he didn't look bored. He was alert, his eyes bright, even as he fidgeted in his skin-tight armour, his gaze never faltered.

Cole pricked his thumb on the needle by the book and pressed it onto the page. The blackness of his blood was stark against the crisp, white page before melting into it and disappearing. The portal swirled, the surface almost bubbling as a deep moss colour radiated throughout the room. Fin clapped a comforting hand on his shoulder, Cole turned to him, his eyes were as hard and cold as steel as he turned to face the portal before them.

They walked through the surface, colours exploded around them. He marvelled at their beauty as they rushed by in a single blur until he stepped again and out onto a damp, dark street. They hadn't come out into an alley like they had done last time. They were in the middle of a wide street with flickering yellow street lamps on either side, some broken. Shops lined the street, all lights were out, and the shutters were down. The air smelled fresh and damp, the way it did after a big downpour. There wasn't another soul in sight. The only noise was the wind whipping between the buildings and a train whizzing by on a bridge overhead somewhere in the distance.

A scream sliced through the air like a blade. They all turned to see Klara doubled over, clutching the back of her neck. Dea rushed to her side, placing a hand on the girls back. The scream was cut short when Klara started coughing, blood spilling over her lips, dripping down onto the ground and mixing with a puddle of water at her feet.

"Klara, what is it?" Dea asked frantically as she looked to the others for help. Cassia was there immediately, her fingers giving off bright pink sparks as she waved her hand over the back of the girl's neck. She moved her hair out of the way, the mark was ugly and black, redness surrounding it. Klara stopped coughing and screaming and took a deep breath before straightening herself. Her face perfectly calm, as if nothing had ever happened.

"Klara?" Dea said weakly, her voice wavering slightly. Klara turned to face her slowly, her eyes narrowed.

"Filth." she spat, glowering at the faces around her.

"She's under the Shadows influence once again. It won't last," Fin assured them, though he didn't sound entirely convinced.

"I can suppress it," Cassia murmured, her hand blazed pink at the back of the girl's neck. Klara gasped, her eyes flying wide as she choked. When she opened her eyes, she was panting hard, but at least she appeared to be more herself.

They started forward, knowing Cassia could only suppress the mark for so long. Klara had told them ahead of time that the doorways were to be found in abandoned buildings, places where human population was low on the outskirts of cities.

Klara winced as she pulled her coat further around herself. Cole glanced around; it was certainly a rundown area they had walked into. Old houses and apartment buildings with boarded-up windows, some with chain link fences around them with 'Danger' signs hanging on them. He started to see homeless people wrapped in sleeping bags on the sidewalk, leaning up against buildings that had long since been deserted.

Klara came to a stop in front of a locked chain fence. It was an old, small apartment building with ivy growing up the side, the higher windows had been smashed and the lower ones were boarded up with metal coverings. Fin reached and yanked the chain from the fence. Klara stared up at the building, her eyes wide, her chest rising and falling quickly.

"This is it," she murmured. Cole looked at the door at the top of a few steps. At the top of the door was a faded symbol, the Shadows symbol. His heart began to race, his palms slick with sweat.

Niah walked forward with Klara, holding tightly to the back of the girl's coat. She struggled as Cassia's hand fell away from her neck, her wrists were now bound where they hadn't been before. Klara resisted, but was being half-dragged by Niah, and didn't stand a chance of overpowering her.

They reached the door and rather than forcing Klara's hand forward until she was gripping the handle, Niah reached for it herself. The door swung open with a loud, protesting squeal. To Cole's surprised, Niah gave her an apologetic look before shoving Klara backwards down the stairs into Cassia's waiting arms.

Niah brandished a pistol from her thigh and glanced inside. Fin moved to the other side of the door, also holding a pistol and the two of them disappeared inside. It was only a few seconds before Fin appeared at the door and gestured for them to follow.

Cole grabbed his crossbow from his back and held it surprisingly steady as he stepped over the threshold. An eerie coldness washed over him, and a shiver crawled up his spine.

He raised the crossbow as they crept through the building. The ceiling had fallen through in some places, revealing the floor above. Floor tiles were missing, as were doors leading into the ground floor apartments. They were empty, except for the odd scrap of broken furniture and bottles and cans of stale alcohol.

They found a stairway at the end of the corridor, and at the top, another door with the same Shadows symbol above it.

Niah went to step up first, but Fin caught at her arm and stopped her. He made his way up and once safely at the top, tried the door handle. It didn't budge, so he gestured for Cassia to bring Klara forward. She had begun protesting louder, swearing at everyone. Her fingers grazed the handle and the door swung open, they were engulfed in bright white light.

17

Fin

Fin shielded his eyes from the brightness. When they adjusted, he saw that the corridor beyond was white tile from floor to ceiling. He picked up a piece of broken wood and flung it into the corridor. Nothing, no movement. He turned then to face the others. His heart pounding in his chest.

"We send her back now," he said, taking the orb from his coat pocket and throwing it at the wall opposite the bottom of the stairs. Klara was pushed through by Cassia who went through briefly, returning flustered, and shook her head as if to say nothing was wrong. She had portalled straight into the cells and put Klara in one, with her mark being reactivated, she was a risk to everyone, including herself.

He took a deep, steadying breath and stepped into the corridor. The others followed until the door banged shut behind them. He glanced at Merida who had appeared at his side. Her skin extremely grey under the harsh florescent lights. She nodded, her sword drawn, and started down the corridor. Multiple doors lined each side, the rooms beyond held numerous bunk beds and wardrobes. They were in what appeared to be barracks.

They crept down the hallway, branching off to check the rooms as they went. Nothing. It was too quiet. They could barely hear the sound of their own feet hitting the floor. Somehow, he managed to keep his breathing steady despite his erratic heartbeat.

The corridor ended in a set of double doors. He pushed them open gently to find a large room full of tables and chairs, and food bars. Trays of food lay scattered on the tables, they must have moved out quickly.

His heart sank in his chest, they were too late. He sighed as the others spread out in search of something but found nothing helpful. Fin glanced at the others, Cole suddenly froze. His hand flying to his throat, and yanked the necklace from around his neck, staring at it in horror.

"What is it?" Fin asked, closing the distance between them. He was holding a small pendant in the palm of his hand with a blue jewel at the front of it that was pulsing.

"It's my sister," he muttered, "she's close." he started for the door on the other side of the canteen before Fin could stop him. He cursed under his breath as they all raced after Cole, running through corridor after corridor, never once spotting another soul.

Every inch of his being screamed that something was wrong, that it must be a trap. Cole barged through another set of double doors and came to a halt on the other side, staring. Ahead of them stood a girl with long black hair with a slight blueish tint to it. She had her back to them.

"Nyx? Nyx it's me," Cole shouted to her; she didn't move. Cole started forward, but Fin caught at his arm firmly. He turned back to him with a furious, questioning glare. Fin shook his head with a warning gaze. Cole turned back to the girl. She turned slowly, almost robotic in her movements. Her hair falling over her face as her head hung slightly.

"Nyx," Cole said desperately, she raised her head slowly and opened her eyes. The silver ring surrounding her iris was dull, her eyes empty of emotion. A slow smirk curled on her lips. Vicious and cruel.

"My poor brother," she grinned, "you always were a fool," Cole looked wounded as he took a small step back. Fin kept a firm grip on his arm, more now for support rather than keeping him in place.

"What are you talking about?" Cole demanded, pain seeping into his voice. She tipped her head back, a shrill laugh erupting from her throat. When she lowered her face to them, she was smiling a terrible smile.

"Did you really think they would let us go?" she asked; Fin felt his stomach tighten as he pressed his lips into a firm line. The Shadows were always a step ahead of them, maybe more.

"You're still with them?" Cole asked in horror, the colour draining from his face. Dea moved through the others to stand next to Cole, her eyes narrowed and thunderous as she glowered at the girl. Nyx tore her gaze from her brother and let her eyes fall on Dea, she licked her lips quickly.

"I would be a fool if I had chosen your path, brother. Make no mistake, you're all going to die here," she smirked as she returned her gaze to her brother.

Cole yanked his arm free from Fin's grip and started toward Nyx. He shouted after him, but his voice was lost as the doors in the corridor swung open and Shadows surrounded them. Dea and Cole were cut off from the others. He couldn't leave them behind.

A low growl escaped his lips as he slashed at the Shadows with his sword, they fell before him one after the other. He could feel the weight of their deaths pressing heavily on his shoulders. He took no joy in killing. Shadows fell, the pristine white walls, and floors, even the ceilings, now sprayed with scarlet blood. There were too many.

Nyx stood with a stormy expression as she watched Cole stagger toward her, Dea at his side.

"Fool." she snapped, "You left me, brother. You chose *them* over me. Those filthy hybrids," she was trembling with unbridled anger.

"I thought we were going to get revenge on the Shadows for what they did to us," Cole protested, she laughed again.

"They made us what we are, without them we would be nothing," she hissed viciously. Cole conceded a step, almost stumbling over a body that lay at his feet.

"What do you mean?" Cole asked. Nyx smiled brilliantly, raising her hands and gave a single, loud clap. Long black spikes protruded from the walls and were launching themselves at Cole and Dea when two huge, glowing hands wrapped around them and pulled them free of the danger back to the rest of them.

Fin glanced over his shoulder to see Cassia and Velig breathing hard, Niah with her hand on their shoulders, giving them more power. Her eyes blazed bright blue as she stared past Fin at Nyx, who was glaring right back at her.

Niah started toward the girl, slipping through Fin's grasp as he reached for her. She was a whirlwind of silent death. Her blades sank into soldiers one by one. He guarded her back, not that she needed it. It was like she had eyes in the back of her head.

He grunted as he overbalanced, a Shadows sword aimed straight at his head. He parried at the last second, the soldier staggered back. Fin plunged his sword through his chest. The scrape of metal and bone sent a sickening twist to his gut. He yanked his blade free, and the soldier slid down the wall until he lay limp on the floor, a pool of scarlet spreading beneath him. His stomach churned bitterly. Killing never felt right. Not to him. And this, killing soldiers who were marked, seemed wrong.

The doors at the end of the corridor banged open. More Shadows strode in, though they were not there to attack. They were an escort party as two figures emerged from the bright light in between the two lines of Shadows, behind them, a hunched figure dressed in rags and long dark hair was being dragged along after them.

The prisoners head hung, hiding their face. A woman. Her hands were bound behind her back and chains around her waist and over her shoulders. As if she would be able to run. Niah froze, and Merida stilled beside Fin.

The two figures came into focus. Both wearing pristine white pantsuits, a man, and a woman. The woman had golden blonde hair pulled back into a severe bun just as Karliah's had been. Only her face wasn't as sharp, she had delicate features with a narrow mouth and long oval face. But her icy blue eyes were full of amusement. The man had dark hair, almost black, with large chocolaty eyes and a broad frame. They both stood in front of Nyx with their hands behind their backs.

Niah had frozen completely, the fire in her eyes burning brighter than he had ever seen. She gripped her swords viciously at her sides, so much so that he thought she may bend them. Her lips pressed into a thin line as she glared at the two.

"Thank you, Nyx. You did very well." the man said with a smile as he glanced over his shoulder at Nyx, who dipped her chin and backed up a pace. The woman in chains was forced to her knees in front of her, Nyx glanced down at the woman with disgust before raising her head to glower at the rest of them.

"Niah, how nice it is to see you again," the woman smiled warmly as she clasped her hands in front of her. Niah tilted her chin upward. Fin's heart was racing, it hadn't slowed since they had entered this place. He glanced at Merida, she was breathing hard, her skin looking greyer than ever, black veins spreading just beneath the surface of her skin.

They didn't have long.

"Katarina, I don't think she's happy to see us," the man mused as he turned to the woman for a second. She pouted slightly but didn't return his gaze, she was smirking at Niah.

Fin's heart stopped.

Katarina.

That would make the man Jeremiah. Niah's adoptive parents.

"We taught you better than to ignore your elders." the woman – Katarina – said with a warning tone, her smile turned icy as she narrowed her eyes. Niah, to Fin's surprise, smiled. Not a happy smile, but one that was full of excitement and bloodlust. Her canines long and sharp.

These were the people who raised her, the people who faked their deaths before her young eyes and kept notes on her like she was nothing more than a test subject. His stomach twisted in anger.

Her entire body was rigid with tension, he wondered if she was in pain. If she was, she didn't let it show. He glanced over his shoulder at the others, Cole looked as though he might be sick. Gren and Sai were both visibly furious, shifting in their places, itching to be thrown into action. Dea stayed near Cole, but her expression was colder than he'd ever seen it.

It was like Deja vu, two people Niah had known confronting them, Shadows aiming weapons at them. He used the time to try and think of a way out of this.

Niah

She stared at them. They hadn't changed a single bit. They were exactly as she remembered them, except maybe more put together. The air crackled around them, the tension rolling off the others in waves, and her chest tightened painfully.

It was going to happen one day, their paths would inevitably entwine once more. She thought she was ready for it, thought she had put those feelings to rest. As she stared at them, all those feelings of love, betrayal, grief, despair, all came flooding back, suffocating her as she tried to keep her head above water. She had spent years thinking they were dead, but the dead always found a way to haunt the living.

Niah flicked her eyes to her Guardian. Merida's skin was blackening around her fingers and eyes.

They were out of time.

"Katarina, Jeremiah; what do you want?" Niah asked sweetly, with a slow grin spreading across her face, giving them a flash of her sharp teeth. Jeremiah shifted; Katarina kept her sly smile.

"Why, we want our daughter back, of course," she grinned, Niah's insides clenched and churned, bile rising in her throat. Daughter. The thing they pretended she was for almost a decade. She swallowed the bitterness coating her tongue. Refusing to let them see how they affected her.

"I was never yours though, was I?" she answered calmly. They never taught her how to lie, so she let her hands tremble slightly, they needed to think she was vulnerable, that their presence made her reminiscent of days long since gone by.

"We so badly wished you were," Jeremiah crooned, his tone soft and gentle. She was a little girl again. Lying in her bed with the covers pulled up to her nose, cowering under the blankets from lightning. He was there, smiling down at her and stroking her hair, soothing her with that very voice. She pushed the thoughts away violently.

"Enough." Katarina snapped, she took a step forward, "Niah, come with us. Come with us and your friends will live, come with us and your mother, your *real* mother, will go with them." her mother? Niah's hands stopped trembling, she willed herself not to show surprise on her face.

"You're lying." she protested venomously. Katarina gave a bored sounding sigh and gestured with her hand. Nyx yanked the woman to her feet and dragged her in front of Katarina and Jeremiah, she pushed her down to her knees. Niah's heart was pounding. Nyx grabbed a handful of the woman's hair and pulled her head up. Merida gasped, Niah stood frozen in place. Hearing only a roaring in her head.

The woman's black hair fell free of her face. She had large black eyes, sharp cheekbones with a nose slightly too long for her face. She looked like Niah, or more; Niah looked like her. She felt Fin's grip on her arm but barely registered it.

This was her mother, her real mother. In chains, on her knees before Nephilim. Every emotion she had been keeping back bubbled to the surface. The woman – Marina – stared at Niah, half in confusion, half in remembrance. Chains. She was in chains. The picture flashed behind her eyes. Whether Marina worked with the Shadows before or not, it didn't matter. Not now.

"Ember," she whispered but was struck in the back of the head by Nyx, who looked up and smirked at Niah as if she couldn't do anything.

She would kill her first.

Ember. That name again. The same name that Nyx had called her.

"Niah, I won't ask again. Come with us and your friends and mother will go free." Katarina repeated sharply. Her icy eyes were narrow, her mouth pinched as she tilted her chin up in a superior manner.

"Let her go!" Merida screamed; she was panting hard. Marina looked at her friend, her eyes filling with tears as she gazed at her. Katarina turned her gaze to Merida as if noticing her for the first time.

"Hello, Merida. How nice it is that you managed to find her, I would suggest you keep quiet, this is her choice." Katarina hissed as she gestured to Niah with her finger.

"I have an offer for you, hand Marina over and *we* will let *you* live," Merida growled viciously. Her skin rippling. Katarina's gaze darkened, she started laughing.

"Look around you, we have the numbers," she shrieked, Jeremiah remained silent. From what Niah remembered, he was always the more reasonable of the two. Not that that counted for much.

"Let her go," Merida warned in a low, dangerous tone.

Katarina turned her gaze to Niah, "Last chance, will you come with us or not? If you don't, we will kill her." Nyx grinned and unsheathed a dagger at her hip, holding it close to Marina's throat, the blade kissing her skin, causing dark red blood to well on the metal. Niah's blood turned to ice, her sword threatening to bend beneath her iron grip.

Merida dropped to her knees, screaming. Fin was at her side in an instant as Niah knelt next to her. Merida looked up through the strands of hair that had fallen free of her ponytail, her eyes wide and wild.

"It's almost time." she rasped. Fear and panic gripped Niah's heart, her chest contracting painfully as if she had just been stabbed.

The others rushed around her, but Niah stood and told them to stay back, they all gave her protesting glares but stayed where they were. Niah turned and hauled Fin away from Merida who was jerking in various directions on the ground, her sword clattered to the floor as a scream ripped through her body. Her hair turned black from the root, most of it falling out. Her nails lengthened.

Katarina cocked her head to one side, Jeremiah looked as though he may be sick.

"Merida, no." Dea whimpered, Niah gave her a sympathetic wince and rubbed her shoulder as tears streamed down her cheeks. Her own heart was breaking, the promise screaming in the back of her mind. Merida's body jerked as she shrieked in agony, everyone stared in horror, not sure what to do.

The Shadow soldiers fidgeted nervously, gripping their weapons tight. Niah pinpointed each of them, knowing exactly which ones she would have to kill to keep them away from Merida. The guns were the same sleek, white ones that the Shadows had wielded in the compound.

Horns sprouted from her Guardian's forehead and stood straight up and sharp. Her skin had turned a deep grey and black veins decorated the surface. With one last howl, Merida stilled. Her body stopped jerking, she took a deep breath and straightened until she was standing. She was breathing hard, glowering at the Nephilim standing before her. Katarina curled her lip in disgust.

"Enough, Merida," a booming voice sounded through the corridor. Through the doors behind the Nephilim and Shadows, strode a man with sandy hair and a matching beard. Wearing a slate grey three-piece suit. Talon. Merida hissed, her eyes had turned completely black, even the whites of them were swallowed by darkness.

Niah gripped her swords. Rage rippled through her veins and her breathing came out ragged through her parted lips, a growl rumbling in her chest. Her power purred beneath her skin, letting her know it was ready.

"Talon, how nice it is to see you again, tell me, do you enjoy betraying your own kind?" Merida spat, venom seeping into her voice, that had changed, no longer soothing and melodic, it was coarse, deeper than it had been.

Talon regarded her coldly. Niah wondered if she could get to him before he had a chance to move.

"You should know about betrayal, Merida," he answered calmly, Merida tilted her head to one side. "For decades I served you, I was at your side, I helped you, did your bidding. And yet, when it came to choosing a new advisor, you chose *him*," he snarled at Fin. He snarled right back.

"*That's* what this is about? How petty. I thought better of you." Merida growled.

"That's not all. But it is what started it, now, hand over the girl," he demanded, his gaze drifting to Niah. The Shadows raised their weapons, they were the same strange guns they had during the last time they fought. If they were to get hit by them, they wouldn't get back up. She concentrated, seeing the colour in her mind, feeling the energy all around her seeping down into her bones.

"No," Merida said firmly, Talon smirked, along with Katarina, Jeremiah took a step backwards as he watched in horror. Nyx grinned, the blade kissing deeper against Marina's skin. Niah forced herself to stay still, not to take a step forward, as much as she may want to.

"Very well," Talon said with a smile, he snapped his fingers and the Shadows surged forward. At that moment, everything slowed down. Fin shouted orders, Merida let out a long scream-like howl. Nick began to sprout fur as his nose lengthened.

Cole's eyes turned bright amber. Cassia and Velig's hands glowed brightly with the colour of their magic. She could see the Shadows coming toward them, their fingers squeezing the triggers of their guns.

Niah sheathed her swords across her back, and held her arms out to the sides. She closed her eyes, and compressed the colour into a single ball, squeezing it tighter and tighter until it was almost cracking from the pressure.

Somewhere in the distance, someone was shouting her name. There was only a high-pitched whine in her ears as her power condensed smaller and smaller. It hammered through her veins, barrelling down her spine until the base of her skull began to throb and burn.

She slammed her hands together, releasing the power in a single burst. Magic exploded from her fingertips. An electric blue wave of groaning power rolled from her body, through the Shadows. But they remained standing. Talon and Katarina burst into laughter, Nyx smirking all the while.

"Looks like you still have a lot to learn," Talon smirked. Niah smiled, the smirk faded from his lips, "Shoot," he ordered. A swirling pink and red barrier went up around them, preparing for the blow.

But nothing came.

The Shadows looked at their guns, some checking or shaking them. These were the same Shadows they had seen at the Steel Queen, they wore the same matte black armour with full-face helmets. Not the ones in the shining silver armour they fought at the compound.

"I said *shoot!*" Talon yelled, his eyes full of fear and fury. Niah took a step forward. One of the Shadows slammed his gun to the ground and brandished a long katana from his hip, the others followed suit, discarding their useless weapons on the floor.

Niah glanced at Merida, her Guardian nodded once. She was still in control, though barely. Niah didn't know how long that would last.

"Kill them! But leave_" Talon's voice was swallowed by the sound of metal clanging against metal as the Shadows clashed with the Furies.

Cassia and Velig would struggle to help, as their attacks would likely injure the others as well. She felt an ache down to her bones as she twirled between Shadows with her swords raised, cutting them down one by one. They kept coming, pouring through the door like a rushing river. They wouldn't be able to keep this up for long.

A solid punch connected with her jaw, sending her sprawling to the floor as she slipped on a fallen sword. She tried to scramble to her feet, but a knee connected with her chin, sending her crashing back into the wall behind. The figure loomed up in front of her, dressed in matte black. He drove his blade downward, it scraped along the surface of the *Ruclite* plate protecting her chest and sank into her left shoulder.

Searing pain lanced through her arm and chest; she bit her lip to prevent herself from crying out.

As one hand went to the blade in her shoulder, the other closed around the hilt of her sword. She drove the blade up into the ribs of the Shadow, finding a gap between the plates of armour down his side.

He jerked back and cried out, dropping to his knees with a thud. She yanked the blade from her shoulder, it would heal soon. Scooping up her second sword, she sprang to her feet, black blood dribbling from the wound.

A huge dark brown wolf with armour down its back and legs sprang past her and knocked over a handful of Shadows, clawing and biting at them, ripping them to shreds. The

Shiasium suit contained his fur, making him look thin and odd, but it would protect him.

Niah spotted Nyx staring in fear at the scene before her, still holding the blade to Marina's throat. She couldn't see Katarina or Jeremiah in the chaos, but Talon remained, standing at the back of the corridor in front of the doors where more Shadows were pouring through.

Anger, unbridled and pulsing scorched through her veins. They had gotten away. Everything else ebbed away, leaving only the burning in the pit of her stomach, and a dull throb at the base of her skull. She ignored it. Using her rising anger as fuel. The Shadows barely had time to look up before she was upon them, a flurry of slashing blades and glinting canines.

The Shadows kept coming.

A never-ending wave of black clad soldiers.

She locked eyes with Cole for a brief moment, they went to lunge forward, but a shrill scream sliced through the corridor.

Everyone paused, silence enveloping them.

Merida.

She was clawing at her armour, the plates and *Shiasium* falling away as if it were made of rubber. She left herself bare as she crashed to her knees. She kept clawing and clawing and clawing, until her skin was torn open and raw. Bile rose in Niah's throat. She choked it down, unable to move, unable to breathe.

Black scales shone beneath the surface of Merida's skin. A long, serpent tongue fell from her mouth and licked her lips hungrily.

The Shadows staggered back as they watched her body elongate, bones cracking. Her arms lengthened, as did her legs, she dropped to all fours. Her face lengthened with horns sprouting from her head like a crown. Her teeth were long and sharp, and there were thicker, armour-like scales running down her chest, stomach, down her neck and over her back. A long tail had emerged with a large telson at the end like a scorpion. Her eyes were almost entirely black, leaving only a faint hue of ocean blue, and a fleck of silver.

Niah's arms fell limply to her sides, her heart aching as Merida hung her head, making small whimpering noises. One of the Shadows took a nervous step back and tripped over a gun on the floor. Merida's head snapped up, a low growl escaping through her teeth. She reared up on her hind legs and lunged for the Shadow, grasping him between her huge talons and tearing him in two.

He didn't even have a chance to scream.

The Shadows scattered, fleeing for their lives as Merida cut them down one by one. Nyx was frozen in place where she stood behind Marina. Niah swallowed the thickness in her throat and nodded to Cole, the two of them took off toward his sister. Someone shouted her name, but the voice was drowned out by screams and roars.

Before they could reach Nyx and Marina, Talon was there, brandishing a sword that hadn't been in his hand a moment ago. He started toward Niah, she shoved Cole out of the way as she met the blow with a deafening clang of blades. Vibrations shot up her arms, and she grit her teeth as she braced against her back foot.

He was so much stronger.

She didn't dare take her eyes off of him as she told Cole to go. Talon met her blow for blow, his reflexes, speed, and strength superior to her own. He could have killed her once or twice already, but he hadn't. Because he was ordered to take her alive, the same as back at the compound.

Niah had something he didn't. Her eyes glowed blue and she hoisted him into the air and sent him crashing into the wall.

Panting, she looked up to see Cole crossing blades with Nyx as the others dealt with the braver Shadows that refused to flee. Adrenaline coursed through her as she attacked, again and again. It made no difference, she wasn't strong enough to kill him.

"They will have you." he sneered as he swept her legs from under her. She landed on her back, but sprang up before he could grab her.

"Who is *they*?" Niah panted, jumping back, and slashing with one sword, he dodged it. Talon laughed, he wouldn't tell her anything.

Someone cried out, Niah risked a glance to see Cole standing over his sister, his blade aimed at her throat. He was wild-eyed and panting hard. He couldn't do this.

Niah crouched and swept Talon's legs from under him before racing across and pushing Cole out of the way. Nyx spat at her. Marina was still kneeling on the ground, her head hanging low.

"Cole, take her," she yelled, he nodded, already hauling Marina over his shoulder, and darted back through the throng of warriors clashing together, dodging blows.

"No!" Talon screamed, he rushed to his feet and started after them, Niah stepped into his path. Before he reached her, a long spike protruded from his chest. Black blood spurted over his lips as he coughed and spluttered.

Merida hoisted him into the air, skewered on the end of her tail. She flung him effortlessly at the wall with bone-cracking force, his body going limp as he slumped to the ground, black blood pooling around him.

Merida's eyes fixed on Niah and Nyx. She didn't know who they were, didn't even know who *she* was. Merida was no longer in control, and she would kill them both.

Niah hauled Nyx to her feet and the two began racing toward the others. The Shadows had either fled or been killed, it was only them left. Dea took the orb from her pocket and threw it at the wall. A large portal shimmered; Fin and Gren began pushing them all through desperately. Cassia and Velig had gone through, Cole and Marina, Dea, and Nick still in his wolf form, Sai followed.

Niah could feel the ground shaking as Merida stormed after them, she shoved Nyx through the portal and was about to go through herself when a voice rippled through her mind, the promise she made. It was a whisper at first, so faint she wasn't sure she had heard it properly.

Now...do it now. The voice said clearly, urgent, and desperate. She stopped in front of the portal, Fin and Gren both shouting at her to move, trying to drag her through.

She stood, her swords at the ready. Fin and Gren were yanking at her, but she remained in place by sheer will.

With a long roar, Merida launched herself at her and her teeth sank into Niah's shoulder. The world tilted, and they were thrown back through the portal.

Niah's sword had found its mark.

18

Fin

They landed in a tangled heap on the floor of the portal room. Fin scrambled to his feet and glanced around, Nyx was fighting with two Guardians as they hauled her away, Cole gazing after them with eyes full of despair and helplessness. Nick had turned back to his usual self and helped Gren to his feet, but Gren was staring at Niah. Fin followed his gaze; she was covered in black blood. For a second, he thought she was hurt, then he saw Merida. Lying half on top of her and half on the floor. She lay naked, her hair back to a dull brown, most of it missing, her skin grey and her eyes half-closed as she lay on her back, her head in Niah's lap as she cradled her, rocking back and forth soothingly.

Black blood was trickling from a wound in her ribs, the sword next to her, covered in blood. Her chest was still, with no rise and fall. She was dead. Niah held her tightly, her eyes low, and her face blank. A ring of several rows of teeth decorated her shoulder and neck, the *Shiasium* barely held together, her blackened blood dribbling from the wound.

She didn't seem to notice or even care. Fin dropped to his knees, his sword clattering to the floor. Gren, Sai, and Dea came to stand around them. Dea sobbing into her hands as she knelt beside Niah. Fin placed a comforting hand on Niah's shoulder, she didn't react.

The backs of his eyes burned, he knew this was coming. Or at least, he knew Merida didn't have much time. He didn't know she would be killed. He wanted to ask Niah why she did it. But now wasn't the right time, and deep down, he already knew.

He reached over and gently closed Merida's eyes, stroking her face slightly as he pulled away. Sai held Dea tightly, both sobbing silently as they gazed at Merida's lifeless body.

Cassia stood further back, tears leaving tracks in the grime on her face, Velig tried to comfort her. Nick had left with Cole. It was just them. The way it should have been. His head pounded, his throat growing thick as he tried to fight the burning at the backs of his eyes.

Something in his chest cracked, and he let go of it all. Tears rolled down his cheeks. He struggled to breath past the lump in his throat as he held Merida's hand. He wasn't ready to let go. Not yet.

He wished Niah would look at him. Her cheekbone and jaw were blue with bruises, the wound in her shoulder still bleeding. None of it pained him more than the hollowness in her eyes.

Footsteps raced down the hall, the Elders burst into the room. Amarah and Ragnar. Both staring in horror.

"What happened?" Ragnar demanded, his tone icy. His eyes fell on Merida, the colour drained from his face. Fin removed his long coat, draped it over her, and got to his feet. He bowed his head.

"She turned."

"Turned? I had no idea she was changing," Amarah muttered.

"She hid it very well, Lady Overseer," he answered flatly, none of them said anything for the longest time.

"How did she die?" Ragnar asked as he gazed at the faces before him. Fin hesitated before answering. Niah killed her, but what would they do to her if they knew that?

Niah moved Merida gently to the ground and rose to her feet. She stood with her hands balled into fists at her sides. Her shoulders squared and eyes empty.

"I killed her." the words were so blunt and sharp that he flinched. Amarah and Ragnar gazed at her, then at Merida and back again.

"I see. She had changed, she was lost to the darkness, I'm sure she would have thought of it as a mercy." Ragnar replied gently. There was a faint sniffle from the corner, they turned to see Marina sitting with her knees pulled into her chest, her hands still bound behind her back.

"Who is this?" Amarah asked, turning to the woman. Her golden eyes narrowing.

"Marina, Niah's mother." Fin answered, Niah was silent once again.

"I see. We must keep her for observation for a few days, she will be comfortable," Amarah said as she approached Marina slowly, holding her hands out as if she were approaching a wild animal. She helped her to her feet and escorted her from the room with Guardians following closely. Ragnar remained.

"We have suffered a great loss with Merida's death. We will begin the preparations for her farewell, in the meantime, go get cleaned up and rested." Ragnar ordered gently; his gaze soft as he looked over each of them.

"I will give you my report now, Lord Ambassador." Fin said as Gren steered Sai and Dea toward the door. Ragnar held up a dismissive hand.

"That can wait," he said in almost a whisper, moving aside for them to pass. Fin gazed down at Merida's body once more. He didn't want to leave her, but she wasn't there anymore. It was only a shell left. Niah strode from the room without so much as a backward glance. Ragnar gazed after her with concern in his eyes.

"Merida was her Guardian, yes?" he said, still watching her stride away.

"Yes."

"She dealt the killing blow." Ragnar frowned, "The Guardian bond is rare, but from what I know of it, she will be haunted by what she's done for quite some time."

"How so?"

Ragnar shook his head, "Another time, Commander. You did well. Go get some rest, I can wait for the report," Fin bowed his head. He didn't have the energy to ask further questions.

"Thank you, Lord Ambassador," he muttered.

He left the room, and walked through the corridors of the Chambers. His bones were thick and heavy. At least he had the chance to say goodbye.

Merida had known what was going to happen. She was always so gentle, so clever. Seeing her become that demon was like a punch to the gut. She had never been that person, had never been dark. How could someone who had more demonic blood be one of the kindest, most gentle people he knew?

He came to the top of the steps outside the Chambers. It was late afternoon, and the sun was beginning to set. He couldn't help feeling like it was oddly fitting. Merida loved sunsets.

His feet moved automatically, taking him to the house. He could hear voices as he approached the door, they all turned to gaze at him when he closed it behind him.

Dea ran to him, throwing her arms around him in a fierce hug. He held her tight, she was still sobbing. When she pulled away, her eyes were red and puffy, her cheeks stained with tears. She went to sit down between Sai and Gren. No Niah. Gren pointed a finger upward as if reading his mind.

"We should get cleaned up," Fin muttered as he started for the stairs, no one moved.

He knocked on Niah's door, no answer, only the sound of running water from the shower. He opened the door, pieces of her armour lay strewn across the floor, leaving a trail toward the bathroom.

He unbuckled his plates and set them gently in the corner of the room before stripping down to his underwear. He opened the bathroom door. She was standing in the shower, her hands pressed against the wall as the water cascaded over her. Her eyes were closed. The water ran black at her feet as the blood washed from her skin.

Above her right hand was a large dent where the stone had given way and cracked, her knuckles bruised, split, and bleeding. The bruises on her face hadn't healed yet, more of them covered her skin over her arms, ribs, her back. His gut wrenched as he watched her. She was battered, not just physically.

"Niah," he murmured as he took a step closer, her body went rigid. She didn't look up, "May I?" she hesitated but nodded, moving aside, not meeting his gaze as he stepped under the scolding hot water without removing his boxers. He gazed down at her and willed her to look at him. She didn't.

"Niah, please," he breathed, she looked up then. Her eyes half-lidded and dark, as hard as gems, they were wet, he couldn't tell if she were crying or if it was from the shower. The teeth marks around her neck and shoulder were still raw, though the bleeding had stopped. Demonic wounds took longer to heal.

He took the bar of soap from the small shelf inside the shower and began running it over her arms, her shoulders, down her torso and back and through her long hair. Once he was done, she held out her hand. He gave her a quizzical look, but she took the soap from him and began rubbing it into his skin. Even now, even with such a loss pressing down on him, her touch breathed warmth back into his icy bones.

It wasn't erotic in any way, just comforting.

"Turn around," she murmured, he did as instructed, and she washed his hair, his shoulders, and down his back.

"I'm sorry," she whispered, her hands stilled on his shoulders.

"Why?" he asked gently, wanting to turn to her, but felt like she may stop talking if he did.

"I killed her." she whimpered, her voice breaking, followed by a sniffle. He turned then, her face remained low, her shoulders shook gently. He folded her into his arms as she sobbed quietly. They stood under the water until she stopped. His heart ached, he often forgot that she could still be hurt. She was so brave and strong that he forgot it's not always keeping it together which is the strong thing to do.

He pulled away and turned the water off, wrapping a towel around her before himself. They sat on the bed facing each other, he gripped her hands between his and gazed at her.

"Why did you do it?" he asked gently, she stiffened then and looked up with large eyes.

"I had to," she said in barely more than a whisper. "I made a promise."

"She asked you to kill her?" he breathed, his chest aching.

Shed nodded, "She didn't want to be a demon."

His heart plummeted. Niah had been carrying the weight of it on her shoulders. She had known what needed to be done. His heart hurt not only for the loss of his dearest friend, but for the pain that Niah had to endure, that she will likely endure for years to come.

He wished there was something he could say or do to ease her suffering, but it wouldn't matter what he said. They were all hurting, all grieving. No words would fix it.

They dressed in jeans and t-shirts and headed downstairs to meet the others. Dea wore a long black dress down to the middle of her calves, her hair pulled back in a messy bun. Cole leaned against one of the walls with his hands in his pockets, his hair falling across his forehead as he watched the others. Vinaxx joined them and was comforting Cassia, Fin didn't have the energy to scold him for being there. Nick and Velig were nowhere to be seen.

There was a knock at the door, Fin opened it to find Amarah on the other side wearing her robes.

"It's time," she said weakly, her pupil-less eyes large and golden. The others followed him out, they walked with the Overseer through the streets. Ahead of them, Merida had been wrapped in white silk and was laying on a decorative wooden bier surrounded by sweet smelling flowers.

Niah took a picture from her pocket, and gently tucked it into the folds of the silk above Merida's heart. Merida had shown him the picture once before, it was of Marina and Niah when she was a baby. A chill crawled up his spine.

The Guardians stepped forward to carry her, but Fin shook his head and took up the front right corner, Niah took the left. Sai, Gren, Dea, and Cassia took the remaining points and lifted their friend.

The path was lined with floating candles. They walked through the streets, through the training grounds, through the forests and grasslands until they began their ascent up the mountain. A single peak that looked like the top had been sliced off, leaving a vast, flat plane at the top. The mountain stood at the most northern point of the island, looking out over miles and miles of ocean.

Along the way, people held candles, chanting prayers for her soul. It took hours to walk there. By the time they reached the top of the mountain, the moon was high in the sky. Casting a silvery glow upon the world.

Merida's bier was placed atop a huge pyre, decorated with silks and flowers and notes from people who had been in Perth with them. Those people were gathered before the others. The whole island had joined them to say goodbye.

"Today is the last day we will know you, but the first in which we will always remember you. Allow your soul to guide us when your body no longer can. We light these fires to honour your fighting spirit in the hopes the ashes will be carried upward. Your body will rest in the Heavens with our angelic ancestors. Your fight is over now. Until your last breath you fought bravely, now we will continue the fight as you watch over us. Until we meet again, fair one; until our last breath." Amarah and Ragnar chanted the words gently. The traditional speech for death.

Cassia and Niah waved their fingers and the pyre burst into pink and blue flames. The fire danced and licked higher, engulfing the pyre. The Elders began singing the song of farewell, and soon, the night was filled with voices, sending Merida on her way. The ashes danced into the sky, dark and shimmering like millions of tiny stars.

His breath caught in his throat as he said his final goodbye.

After the funeral, they sat around a large fire on the beach. It was a couple of hours walk to get to the small beach south-east of the mountain. Merida had always loved the beach; it was one of the reasons she loved the Perth facility so much.

Niah sat with her knees pulled to her chest, her arms dangling around them. Sai sat with Dea, Gren sat next to Fin, Cassia was passing around a bottle of liquor. Other warriors who had been at the Perth facility had joined them.

They talked about Merida, how she had been kind, how gentle she was, and what a great leader she was. They laughed at stories of her, cried at others. Niah remained silent throughout the whole thing, not looking up.

Fin wanted to go to her, wanted to comfort her. There was nothing he could do for her, and it broke his heart to admit that, but he had never known the burden of doing something so hard. He couldn't even begin to understand how she was feeling. More than that, he knew that if she was isolating herself, it was because she needed time to come to terms with what had happened. She needed to be alone right now, and he would give her that time. And be there if and when she needed to talk.

The sun started to rise, pale blues and greys drenched the world. He was gazing over the horizon when the sand shifted next to him, and Niah sat down. She said nothing, only followed his gaze over the ocean.

"What are you thinking?" he asked softly, she took a deep breath but didn't look at him.

"I was thinking that Merida got her revenge, but I'm not so sure," she frowned, he had seen Merida stab Talon through the back and throw him at a wall. He was dead, he certainly looked it.

"How so?"

"Just before we came through the portal, I looked over to where he fell, but his body wasn't there."

"Maybe you looked in the wrong place," Fin suggested, she shook her head and shrugged.

"Maybe," he draped an arm around her shoulders. She leaned into him as she gazed at the flames. They sat there in a comfortable silence until the fire burned to smouldering embers.

19

Dea

The town was unnaturally quiet as they walked back through. Not from the lack of people, the streets were bustling as usual. It was as if a blanket of silence had fallen over the island. They had the same sympathetic glances thrown at them as they had when they took the long walk up the mountain. Dea hadn't thought about it much before. She hadn't noticed. But now, in the early morning sun, she could see everything.

She couldn't pretend she didn't see them anymore. She wanted to run, to scream, but what good would it do? Her chest felt like her heart had been ripped out. It was true what the books said, hybrids feel loss much heavier than any other species. If this is what loss felt like, then she didn't want it. Only, the pain made her realise it was real. If she tried hard enough, she could still see Merida, standing by the fountain looking up at the sky, or waving from her bedroom window. Dea found herself outside her house, looking up at the window which would have been Merida's bedroom. She thought she saw a flicker of movement, but shook the thought from her head, she wasn't there anymore. She wanted to cry, but no tears would come. She feared she might have used them all. As she stood staring at Merida's house, Cole came to stand beside her. His hair a mess and his hands shoved into his pockets.

"I'm sorry," he murmured, he'd already said it enough times, and meant it every time. She stroked his arm and smiled, some of the tension ebbed away.

"How are you doing anyway? Have you been to see your sister?" she asked, remembering about Nyx being brought back with them and hauled off to the cells. He stiffened and looked down at the ground.

"Not yet."

"Do you want to?" he hesitated but gave a small nod. She took his hand in hers and led him toward the Chambers, he didn't protest. The mark should have faded from her neck now, and she should have her own thoughts back. They could ask her what had happened.

They made their way through the corridors until they came to the door leading to the cells. They were at the top of the stairs when they heard her shouting and screaming. They rounded the corner to find her throwing herself against the shimmering wall, her hair a mess and her clothes ripped where she had been struggling. She finally spotted them.

"Hello, dear brother," she sneered, standing close to the shimmering wall. Cole took a step forward, releasing Dea's hand. He didn't answer, that seemed to annoy her further as she banged her hand against the wall.

"Have you come to gloat?"

Dread curled in Dea's gut.

The mark hadn't faded.

"Gloat? What the *hell* do I have to gloat about?" he demanded, the venom in his voice made Nyx blink, but she smoothed her features as if the words meant nothing.

"Because I am in here, and you are out there. With your precious little hybrids," she spat, dragging her glare to Dea, she took a step forward and gave Nyx a level stare.

"We are both hybrids, Nyx. Why do you hate your own species?"

"Because I do not want to be a hybrid. I want to be Nephilim. They said I could be, you know. They said they could suck the demonic blood right out of me, and I would be a Nephilim," she said with a grin.

Cole turned to Dea questioningly, but she was just as confused as he was. That wasn't possible, it couldn't be. Demonic blood was a part of them as much as their angelic blood, you couldn't just remove one part of it and become a different species. Then again, with all the experiments the Shadows took part in, maybe they had found a way. The thought of how many suffered while doing those experiments churned her stomach.

"Is that what they told you?" he asked as he folded his arms across his chest.

"They're amazing, you know, they can do all sorts of things," Nyx sneered proudly, tilting her chin upward.

Cole sighed, "What about our lycanthrope blood? Did they mention that?" Nyx eyed him suspiciously for a moment.

"We don't have lycanthrope blood." she said steadily. Cole closed his eyes, when he opened them again; they were burning bright and amber. Nyx yelped and jumped back, staring in horror as if he were a stranger.

"You're a *monster*," she breathed, her voice trembling as she sank against the back wall. Cole's eyes turned back to normal as he gazed at his sister, his expression unreadable. Dea thought she would be shocked, but it wasn't like it was the first time the leaders of the Shadows had lied to their warriors or test subjects about what their race was.

"No, Nyx, we're just different. I guess they put that mark back on you, huh? It's okay, it will wear off."

"Fuck you, you're not my brother. You're just some disgusting *thing.*" she spat.

To his credit, Cole didn't flinch, only turned on his heel and strode from the cells. Dea hurried after him, Nyx's laughter echoed through the halls. He burst out of the Chambers. Dea felt her stomach churning, she shouldn't have suggested going to see her, not yet. She placed a hand on Cole's shoulder, he stood staring at the floor for the longest time.

"I'm sorry."

He turned his troubled gaze on her, "I needed to see her, I needed to see how far she had fallen."

"I can't imagine what that's like, seeing your sister like that," she grimaced, Cole shuddered slightly and carried on down the steps.

"Thank you." he said, "For coming with me." He offered her a small smile. She squeezed his hand, and the two of them stood and watched the water fall into the fountain for a while.

Fin

A few days had passed since the funeral. And now it was time for Fin to give his report to the Oracle Conclave. He took a deep, steadying breath as he readied himself before walking through the double doors to the council hall. It was empty apart from him and the Elders.

"Commander Fin," Amarah smiled, "how are you?" his stomach tightened. He couldn't tell her the truth. How none of them was doing all that well. Niah was more distant than ever, Dea was still crying herself to sleep, Gren had taken to training more often to burn off his frustration, so had Sai; except he drank far too much when night drew in.

"Better, thank you." he lied. The wound was still fresh, of course, it was, that kind of hurt wouldn't disappear in a few days.

"Good, please, your report," Amarah said, Fin told them of the events that unfolded during the raid. Finding the doorway in an abandoned building, being ambushed, finding Marina and Nyx, Niah's confrontation with the people who had raised her. Talon's confession of what started his hatred for his own kind. They listened intently.

"So, what have you found out?" Ragnar asked once he was finished.

"The Shadows doorways can only be opened by those who possess the Shadows mark. They want Niah, that much is for sure. Though for what reason we don't know." he told them, Ragnar stroked his chin thoughtfully.

"Niah is an interesting one, isn't she?" he said almost absentmindedly to no one in particular.

"Well, it may not be the answers we want. But it does give us a little insight. The girl in the cells, Nyx, still has the mark, it hasn't faded yet I assume?" Amarah asked.

"No, Lady Overseer, we checked yesterday, it's still very much there, it has changed as well. She has the full Shadows mark, not just the solid circle one she had before," he told her, they were quiet for a long moment.

"That will need to be monitored, and the woman in the room? Has she spoken yet?" Morena asked gently.

"I've been to see her, she is very frantic and confused. It will be some time before she can speak properly," he answered with a frown.

He had been to see Marina the day after they got back. She'd been given a few sets of clothes, her food remained untouched on the small table. She had changed into a long white nightdress, her hair still a mess. She was thin, but not as much as he would expect a prisoner to be.

When he walked into the room she jumped and ran to the corner, pressing herself against the wall with wide eyes. He could see the resemblance between her and Niah, the same shade of raven hair, the same slightly too long nose, the graceful curve of her upper lip, her dark eyes as they watched intently. He had asked her how she was doing, she said nothing, only shook her head. He tried to convince Niah to go and see her, but she said she wasn't ready. That Merida had been the closest thing to a mother, the way she had been for most others. He wondered if she was scared that her birth mother wouldn't be anything like Merida.

"Good work, Commander, please keep going with your task. There is one more thing," Amarah said. "With Counsellor Merida's death, we need to appoint a new Counsellor in her place, we would like to ask you," Fin paused and stared at the

Elders. He hadn't even said yes, and he could feel the weight pressing down on him.

"I'm afraid I would be no use as a Counsellor, Commander is more my thing, I must decline, please accept my apologies," he said with a bow of his head, Amarah smiled lightly.

"No apologies necessary, we would like your opinion on who it shall be though," she answered thoughtfully.

"I would suggest Commander Grenville, he has a very bright mind," he said with a small smile; he wondered how Gren would feel about being put forward for the job.

"Very well, thank you, Commander. that's all." Ragnar said, his expression unreadable. Fin bowed his head and hurried from the room.

Since the funeral, there had been one council meeting. It was strange being in the Council room without Merida in her usual spot, it was worse seeing the smug look on Matias' face. It appeared he was getting quite the following behind him, and more and more people were agreeing that Niah should be handed over to the Shadows. Not that she appeared to care when he told her. She had completely withdrawn. He raked his hand through his hair, knowing he needed to talk to her.

20

Niah

Niah lay on her back staring up at the ceiling. She didn't remember how she came to be lying on the armoury floor, much less whether she cared. She sighed, her head leaning against her arms. Since Merida's death, there had been a deep void in the pit of her stomach. She couldn't sleep because she saw Merida's lifeless body in her arms, the sword stained with her blood.

She glanced at her weapons hanging on the wall, the sword she used was among them. Washed clean and gleaming. She could have traded it in for a new one, she supposed. But something told her to hang onto it. She guessed it was one of few things which connected her to Merida, the promise she asked of no one else. Niah was honoured, if not mortified when Merida had asked her to promise. She didn't want to. But what choice did she have? She saw the fear in Merida's eyes when she said she was turning, heard the desperation in her voice, and known she couldn't say no.

Of course, it wasn't just her who was suffering. The others had known Merida a lot longer than she had, she wondered if they hated her for doing what she did. None of them would say it, they were too nice for that. Maybe it was just her thoughts of self-loathing getting the best of her. Not that she would blame them even if they did hate her.

She sighed again and got to her feet at the same time the front door opened and closed.

She wandered into the living room to see Fin standing in front of the fireplace, gazing down at the cold logs. She didn't know whether to disturb him or not, but just as she was about to walk up the stairs; he turned and smiled at her. The kind of smile that made her gut wrench and her heart flutter uneasily, she shouldn't be feeling this happy to see him. Shouldn't be feeling happy at all with what she had done.

She didn't want to forget the thing she had done, she deserved to feel the pain of it. And she did. She and Merida were connected. When she drove her blade through Merida's chest, Niah felt that same blade in her own. She thought she would die, *hoped* she would. But no. She continued to live, to breathe while Merida lay lifeless in her arms. And every night she felt that same pain stabbing in her chest over and over and over. She relished in the agony.

He took a step toward her, then another, until he crossed the distance between them. Bringing both his hands up to cup her face. His eyes searched hers, asking for permission, she tilted her chin, granting it. His lips came down on hers, his breath hot and sweet. She kept her hands firmly at her sides, her fingers itching to tangle in his hair. She wouldn't let herself. He pulled away slightly, a little breathless.

Whenever she was with him, she wanted to cave. To believe that maybe she did deserve to be happy once in a while, that he could be the person that eased her crippling guilt. She let herself melt into him for the first time in days. She didn't hold herself back, letting her arms wrap around his neck as he held her tightly. If she was going to damn herself to endless nights of agony, she would take this one thing for herself. Even for them, life was too short. With their line of work, she wasn't sure how long she would have with him. When she inevitably drew her last breath, she didn't want to die with regrets.

More than that, she loved Fin. She wasn't sure when it happened, maybe it was slowly, maybe it was all at once. But she loved him. There was no explanation for it, he'd told her many times that hybrids didn't feel love the same way as other species, and yet, there was no other word for what she felt.

She wanted to be with him in all ways, and she was tired of waiting. It didn't make sense that she loved him, she thought maybe she was mistaking the feeling of something else for love. But whenever she saw him, her thoughts became a little clearer.

"Come on," she muttered and led him up the stairs to her room. They sat on the edge of the bed, he gazed down at their clasped hands, his hair falling into his eyes. She wanted to know what he was thinking, though she couldn't form the words together to ask.

"I need you to talk to me, Niah, tell me what's going on. You're not the same, let me be there for you," he said finally, looking up at her with wide, worried eyes. Her heart ached savagely.

"I don't know how," she whispered after a long moment, barely able to even get those few words out. His brows pulled together, and he frowned.

"Close your eyes," he whispered, she gave him an incredulous look, "Please?" she sighed and did as he asked. She saw Merida's body, blood on the ground as if it were tattooed to her eyelids.

"You've not been sleeping, you barely eat, you're training harder than ever. What's going on inside your head?" he asked gently.

Her heart started beating faster as she thought about the last few days. She had woken in cold sweats in the middle of the night, without Fin there as she said she needed space. They had blurred together like one long nightmare. When she woke up after only an hour or so of sleep, she would go to the training hall and punch the hell out of the training dummy. Already, three of them were broken.

"I can feel her pain," she murmured, shocked by her honesty. As soon as her blade pierced Merida's skin, Niah had felt it. She had felt the agony washing through her body. She guessed the Guardian bond went both ways, Merida would know if anything happened to Niah, and vice versa. Ironic really, Niah caused Merida's death, and she would feel it every day. Some may even call it divine justice.

"You mean, literally? You felt the wound?" he asked. She met his gaze then, his eyes were liquid silver, warm and inviting.

"Yes, I could feel the rage going through her when she had changed, my blade stabbing her in the heart, the relief when she died and then...nothing. I feel the same pain every night when I dream about it." she sighed, defeated. There was no point in holding anything back from him. She found she even *wanted* to tell him.

She wanted to give everything to him. Everything she was and would ever be. The thought alone scared her. She was finally beginning to understand what it meant to love someone the way the characters did in her books.

It terrified her.

"Hell, Niah, why didn't you tell me?" he asked, hurt seeping into his voice. His grip tightened on her hands, she looked down at their interlocked fingers and frowned.

"Because I felt like I deserved it, I don't need you to tell me I did the right thing, that I only did what Merida asked me to do. I already know that, but I still killed her, Fin. I killed my Guardian, and I felt every second of it. I will continue to feel every second of it." she said, her voice cracking. He lifted his hand and pressed it gently against her cheek, she leaned into him for comfort, though she knew she shouldn't.

"I am here for you, always. Nothing I say can make any of this better for you, I know that. But I can *be* here for you in every way I can, you must know that," he said with urgency deep in his voice, his eyes wide and serious. It was the most perfect thing he could have said.

She leaned forward and kissed him. A soft brush of lips against lips, growing in heat and intensity quickly. She climbed into his lap, her legs on either side of his hips, her fingers tangling in his hair as he held her thighs. He pulled away to gaze at her thoughtfully.

"We don't have to_"

"I want to, Fin. I do." she insisted, he frowned and stroked her hair.

"I don't want to do this just because you're not in a good place, I don't want to take adv_"

"You're not taking advantage, I *want* to do this. Not because of all that's happened, but because it's *you*. The last few days have reminded me that we don't live forever, we're warriors, I could lose you or I could die any of these days. I want to do this because I want to have those memories, that experience before that happens. I just want *you*. But I understand if you don't want to," she explained.

More than anything, she hoped it would show him how much he meant to her. She didn't know how to tell him how she felt, and a part of her was scared to even try. But this, she could do this. Give herself to him.

He smiled lightly and pressed his lips to hers, gentle. Everything about him was gentle, the way he ran his hands over her hips and back, tangling his fingers in her long hair. He lay her down, hovering over her as he took most of his weight on his elbows. He kissed along her jawline, down her throat to her collarbone as she ran her hands over his shoulders and through his hair, hearing him groan in satisfaction.

With every piece of clothing removed, that wall she'd built around herself came tumbling down, brick by brick. With every kiss, the ice in her heart began to melt. With every touch, the darkness receded inch by inch. She lost herself in him. In the way he kissed her so tenderly, in the way his hands caressed her skin softly, forever asking for permission to go further.

When there was nothing left between them, no barriers of any kind, he looked her in the eye, trailing his fingers along her cheek. His eyes were shimmering silver pools, and she lost herself in them. Feeling safe and secure. And there was no fear, no nervousness. It felt right. She wanted Fin in every way. So she invited him in, and he obliged. She thought she might die with ecstasy.

For the first time, she truly understood what all those books meant about fireworks and butterflies. Her pain wouldn't go away overnight. But maybe with Fin by her side, they could be a little less unbearable.

They lay together afterwards, tangled up in sheets and each other. He lay on his back with his arm supporting his head, his other arm wrapped around her, drawing circles on her back as she rested her head on his chest.

"Thank you," he murmured, she propped herself up on her elbow to gaze down at him quizzically.

"Is that what's supposed to be said afterwards?" she asked, he chuckled slightly.

"No, well, you could, but that's not what this is. Thank you for telling me what's going on." the smile vanished as he spoke. She gazed at him, it felt like a weight had been lifted from her shoulders, like she was no longer drowning beneath the burden of her promise.

It would be with her for a long time yet, she would still feel the pain of it; that wouldn't just go away. She was glad the pain would remain for a while, it let her know that what she and Merida had was a bond that couldn't be easily severed. But she no longer felt alone. She had shut herself away, scared of what the others would think of her; but there was no need to be. She had a bond with them also, one that could not be severed so easily.

"Thank you for being there for me," she whispered, he grinned and pulled her in for a long, lingering kiss.

Fin

Night draped over the island. He and Niah had gotten up and he cooked cheese on toast, purposefully leaving most of his in the hopes that she would eat his too, which she did. He knew it would be a while before she was completely herself, but it was a start. Their bond had strengthened, not just because of what had happened between them physically. She had opened up to him, for the first time since Merida's death.

Of course, what had happened physically had made him feel things he had never felt with anyone else. There was something incredibly satisfying seeing her let go like that. Seeing her without her walls up, and more than that; he was the one who made her feel that way.

She had been confused afterwards because there was no blood like she was expecting, he realised the only experience she would have had with any of that was in the pages of those books, written by humans who would have very human reactions to sex for the first time. He explained that hybrids weren't born with a hymen, for the simple reason that it would just heal every time it was broken. She had blushed. He often forgot how naïve she was.

They sat at the kitchen table with mugs of coffee in their hands, talking about what had happened at the Shadows hideout. It had been a trap after all, not that it had gone as they were expecting it to.

"What was that thing you did? It stopped their weapons working," he asked before taking a large gulp of coffee. She cocked her head to one side for a moment, looking down slightly.

"Cassia showed me how, it dismantles the weapons from the inside. I noticed the guns didn't have bullets, only a chamber running along the top for storage. The guns work by absorbing energy," she lowered her mug to the table.

"How can something like that even exist?" he frowned. He didn't know much about energies, knew it was what spell weavers used to amplify and rejuvenate their power, but how could a weapon harness such a thing?

Niah shrugged, "Looks like their experiments aren't only on the living."

"At least we're finding out more information," he said, she didn't smile back at him, she was gazing off into the distance. He reached across the table and took her hand in his, stroking his thumb against her knuckles.

"What is it?" he inquired gently, she shook her head slightly and looked up.

"I think I should go see her, my mother." Fin nodded. She hadn't been to see her yet. He remembered how frantic Marina had been when he had gone to see her, perhaps seeing her daughter would ease her fright.

"Would you like to go now?" he asked, she said nothing, only nodded. He rose to his feet and held his hand out for her. She took it and stood up, the two of them walked hand in hand toward the Chambers. There was no moon that night, the stars all covered by dense clouds overhead. Despite the lateness, the streets were as packed as they ever were.

The town was turning into more of a city now, with bars and restaurants being built, more barracks for newcomers. The search for more and more hybrids and other races was turning out to be rather fruitful. They had found another sixty in the last week. Merida would be happy to see the development of Thamere, she would enjoy seeing the future of it being written. He smiled to himself, the pain of losing Merida would last for

320

years; though the memories only made him smile when he thought of her.

As they reached the top of the steps outside the Chambers, Niah stopped and turned to him.

"I think I should go in on my own," she said with large, nervous eyes.

"Of course," he said gently, she reached up and kissed him on the cheek before walking down the corridor toward her mother's room. He wondered what would happen, wondered whether she would come away upset or angry or happy. All he could do was be there for her.

Gren came up to him then, catching him off guard. His eyes glittered with amusement.

"You put me forward for Counsellor?" he asked incredulously, Fin chuckled.

"Yep."

"Why?"

Fin shrugged, "You'd be good at it," Gren gave him a thoughtful look.

"You know Dea wants to be a Counsellor, right?"

"I know, I would have put her forward for it, but she needs to be a Commander first." Fin answered. Dea had rambled about wanting to be a Counsellor since Thamere was born. She liked the political side of things more than Fin ever did.

"So, did you put her forward for Commander?" Gren questioned.

Fin ran a hand through his hair, "They didn't ask for my opinion on that, otherwise I would have. Though I think they may suggest I was being favourable toward my friends if they did," he frowned, the two started down one of the corridors.

"Well, that's true enough." Gren nodded. There was a commotion from down the corridor coming from the portal room. A woman shouting and what sounded like Nate trying to calm her down. Fin glanced to Gren who shrugged and followed the noise.

He rounded the corner of the door to find Nate, Nina, and the lycanthrope Keira standing around a small group, two men and a woman.

The woman was of average height with a shapely, yet strong figure with wide hips. She had shoulder-length scarlet hair cut choppily, a delicate heart-shaped face with full lips and a sharp nose. The most striking thing about her was her eyes, violet, with the same shimmering silver ring around the iris. It wasn't uncommon for hybrids to have unusual eyes, but he had never seen violet ones before.

His chest contracted pleasantly. No, it was his heart. His stomach dropped and his eyes burned. It was as if the sun had suddenly appeared in the room. His whole body came alive with electricity. His nerve endings singing. A name formed in his mind and danced on the tip of his tongue. His skin tingled all over. Every cloud of darkness that had formed in his mind was chased away by the brightness of the woman. The breath left his lungs. Comfort washed over him, a sense of home and rightness he had never felt before. His heart had been racing, now perfectly calm and tranquil.

"Ren," he whispered, the woman stopped shouting and turned, her violet eyes narrowed, but when her gaze fell on him, they widened.

"Fin." she breathed. The sound of his name on her lips did things to him he didn't know was possible. The eyes in the room had all turned on them curiously, but they were only staring at each other. He was unable to move, every nerve in his body screamed at him to go to her, he craved her to no end.

"Fin? Is this...?" Gren trailed off as he glanced between the two, Fin said nothing, only nodded with his mouth hanging open.

"Is this what?" one of the men standing with Ren snapped.

"She's the second half of his heart," Gren informed them firmly.

The two men looked at each other, blinking. Fin barely heard them, his heart was aching for her, he could *feel* her heart beating as well. The words Gren spoke hadn't scared him like he thought they might, instead, he welcomed them as if they were home. He had found her, the second half of his heart. It was as if there had been nothing before her, and he knew instantly, there would be nothing after her.

EPILOGUE

Talon walked the long, white corridor in dreaded silence, Katarina and Jeremiah on either side of him. The personal guards lined the walls, wearing shining gold armour, their hands resting on the hilt of their swords at their hips. Only their eyes were visible through the narrow slits in their helmets, entirely black eyes, devoid of any white.

Talon felt his breath catch in his throat as he walked. The wound in his chest had healed, though he barely managed to survive it. If Merida had aimed slightly to the left, she would have pierced his heart and he wouldn't have been able to heal. He cursed himself inwardly that he managed to get distracted enough to be injured so badly. The whole thing was a blur, it would have been over quickly if that damned brat hadn't ruined their weapons, which still hadn't managed to be fixed. They would have killed them quickly and had it over with. He scowled ahead of him as the double doors came into view.

The guards stood outside the doors stepped back to let them through. The doors were heavy and made of stone, grinding as they opened. The room beyond was large, the floors grey slate, the walls were bare concrete with pillars holding up the stone ceiling. There were a couple of steps leading up to a higher point in the room where two dark wooden desks sat. The entire back wall behind them was glass, overlooking dark red mountains and stormy skies. At the bottom of the steps, was a thick fur rug on the ground with black leather sofas around it and a fire pit sunk into the floor. Another wall was completely lined with glass bookshelves. Everything was dark, open, and airy.

An ominous feeling washed over him; a thick tension of rage clung to him as the doors closed behind them. There were two large chairs behind the desks, one was facing away from them toward the window. On the left of the raised floor was another door, which opened now, and the sound of heels clattered on the slate floor. His heart began to race.

In she walked, her shoulders back and head held high. Her raven hair falling in waves down her back. She wore black jeans with a long-sleeved black t-shirt. She stopped beside the desk closest to her, the one with the chair facing away from them. It turned then, and a young man was revealed. The same black hair and dark eyes, only his eyes were more a dark green-black, whereas hers were jet, both with the silver ring around the iris.

The woman turned to face them then. The man's expression furious, whereas hers was one of amusement; there was something dangerous about the way her gaze slid over them. The three of them bowed before the two on the raised platform. When they straightened, the woman was gazing at Talon. He felt his insides turn to ice.

"Tell us what happened," she said firmly, her voice seeping with authority as she lowered herself into the chair behind her desk. Talon glanced to the others who had gone unnaturally quiet. He took a step forward.

"They got away." he kept his eyes low.

"Oh? And how did that happen?" she asked, her voice low and almost melodic.

"The girl, she used some kind of magic to disable our weapons. The Guardian changed, almost killed me," he explained, he looked up then. Her eyes were dancing with wicked amusement. The man's eyes were narrow, dark slits.

"What a pity that would have been. Where is Marina? I went to see her earlier, she wasn't there." she said venomously, the smile fading from her lips.

"We used her as bait, we thought the girl might come willingly if we bribed her with the freedom of her mother," Talon told them, a loud bang echoed through the room. The man was standing now, his fist on the surface of his desk, his eyes wild with rage. The woman didn't seem to notice his outburst.

"Morons! They took her, didn't they?" he demanded scornfully. Talon nodded; all words failed him. His palms grew slick.

"If we didn't need you for the next phase, I would kill you myself." the man growled, lowering back into his chair. Talon felt his chest contract painfully.

"No matter, we will get her back. Tell me, Talon; were you able to fulfil your duty while you were in Thamere?" the woman asked.

"The doubts have been planted; Matias is proving himself very useful. Unfortunately, we underestimated how strong the barriers around Thamere are, they were able to render the marks useless," he explained, the woman nodded along as he spoke.

"Very well. We may have to use the other riders. Do they have Nex's sword?" she asked, Talon hadn't seen it while he had been there, though he had noticed Niah and the others going in and out of a new house next to Merida's.

"If it's there, I didn't see it."

"You two, you've been very quiet in all of this. What do you have to say?" the man demanded, Katarina and Jeremiah stepped forward.

"We apologise for our failure. We're afraid they captured our other bait." Katarina said in a bleak, shameful voice.

"What does she know?" the woman asked, her tone suddenly icy.

"More than I would like her to," Katarina grimaced. The raven-haired woman stared daggers at her.

"You have failed us once before, do not let it happen again. All of you, work with Karliah and Nolan. I want Ember and Marina back here, now. Do you understand?" she said in a low, dangerous voice.

"How are we supposed to do that? We cannot get into Thamere." Jeremiah asked.

"You have riders, use them. Draw them out."

"Of course," Jeremiah said with a bow of his head.

"Now go, I believe it's time we spoke with Silver." the woman glowered at them. The three of them scurried from the room, breathing hard, his hair pasted to his forehead. He hadn't realised how much he was sweating.

The three of them hurried down the hall until they reached the intelligence room. The room was huge, bright, and white with three of the four walls covered in surveillance screens, showing images from various parts of the world. The heart of the room were rows of desks with holographic screens and keyboards with people sat behind them typing furiously. The desks were arranged in a circle, at the centre was a large holographic glob which turned. The small spot where Thamere would be highlighted in red.

Sitting at a round table in the far corner of the room were Karliah, Nolan, and Samara Quel; she was essentially the

Queen's right-hand woman. She had copper hair tied in a tight bun at the back of her head and bright blue eyes, her features delicate and soft, though her gaze was forever icy. She looked up at them as they approached, her mouth twisted into almost a snarl.

"What have you three done?" she demanded, the three of them sat around the table and explained the events that had taken place. Once they had finished, she shook her head.

"Idiots," she spat, "well, the two have been kind enough to tell you what to do. I wouldn't suggest failing again." Talon glanced at the others, despite him being stronger than them, they all looked down on him because he had demon blood and they were Nephilim.

He said nothing, only nodded. His hands clenching into fists under the table. Raising a rider seemed dangerous, they were unpredictable and extremely powerful, especially with those swords of theirs. He didn't know why the Queen was so determined to get Ember back, she had never been bothered before. She was willing to raise hell to get her back. The thought terrified him.

DELETED SCENE
THE PROMISE

She had never seen him look so defeated before, not even when Talon betrayed them. She grabbed his hand as he passed her, he offered a weak smile before giving her a quick kiss on the forehead and heading out of the room. She watched him go, his shoulders hunched slightly. Merida was still shedding fresh tears. Niah rushed to her, taking her hands in hers.

"What is it? Do you need Vinaxx?" she asked urgently, her Guardians hands felt so bony and frail in hers.

Merida shook her head, "No, I need you to promise me something," she gestured to the table and they both sat down, still with Merida's hands in Niah's.

"I'm turning, I don't have the energy to keep fighting anymore," she said, Niah's blood ran cold, "when I turn, I don't want to be sent away. I will stay that creature and I will never be myself again. You understand what I'm saying, don't you?" Merida asked, her gaze steady, her voice firm. Of course Niah understood what she meant. Her heart was racing, how could Merida be asking this of her? How could she possibly go through with it? She was already shaking her head, unable to form the words in her throat.

"Niah, you're the only one I can ask this of," Merida said firmly.

"Why?"

"Because you are the reason I've kept going for so long. Please do this for me?" Merida pleaded, her eyes wide and urgent. She could say no. She could say she couldn't do it. Yet, Merida had never asked her for anything, other than her trust.

She hung her head, defeated as she felt the weight press down on her shoulders.

"I know it's a lot to ask. But you are the only one who could carry such a burden. I am sorry I must place it on you, I truly am." she said sadly, Niah raised her eyes to hers. She felt as if she had been forced underwater. Waves crashing over her, the weight and blackness swallowing her whole. If she were to do this, she needed to completely detach herself.

She felt like clawing her heart from her chest and stamping on it. Everything hurt, every inch of her body screamed at her that it was wrong, that she couldn't do this. She pushed the voices down as far as they would go, locking them into a tight box. She raised her eyes to Merida's once more, they were wide and pleading; it broke her heart.

"I will, when the time comes, I will kill you," she said, her voice completely devoid of emotion. Merida exhaled, relieved. It was at that moment Niah realised how much Merida needed this. She was suffering, so thin and pale, her skin grey. She shouldn't have to live in that condition. Merida reached for her, pulling her into a tight hug. She felt numb. Her whole body felt as if it were suspended in mid-air. She held her back, not too tightly, too afraid she may break her.

"Thank you." Merida whispered into her ear, "One more thing, if ever you find yourself without a home. Look in my desk drawer." Niah wanted to ask what she meant. But her throat was thick and burning as she clung to her Guardian and allowed herself to cry. Niah felt her heart tear in two.

THE STORY CONTINUES
IN
THE DARKEST HOUR
COMING 1ST OCTOBER
NOW AVAILABLE FOR PRE-ORDER

If you enjoyed this book I'd be eternally grateful if you would leave an honest review on Amazon and/or social media. You can find me @thatauthorsue

Coming Soon:

THE DEMONIC CONVERGENCE - BOOK 3 – THE DARKEST HOUR

THE FORGOTTEN CHRONICLES - BOOK 1 – THE CRUCIBLE

THE SONG OF RUIN – BOOK 1 – CROWN OF BLOOD

Printed in Great Britain
by Amazon